I0612963

The Culpeper Deception

By

Ian M. Ferguson

ISBN   Paperback 978-0-9917589-6-8

e-book 978-0-9917589-7-5

1st edition/printing June 2016

Other published works by Ian M. Ferguson

<u>Novels</u>

Unintended – e-book

The Elephant Theory – e-book

Operation Counterpunch – e-book

Cristal's Revenge – e-book & Paperback

<u>Short stories</u>

Culpeper – e-book

Author page http://www.amazon.com/-/e/B00A8XSOGQ

(E-books on Amazon - Paperbacks at Createspace)

Dedication

In memory of Harold Marshall Turcot (1924-2014), a great man and a great friend who fought for his country in WW II, seeing action on D-Day, raised a wonderful family, had a great career, lead many of our community's activities, kept us all together through the years and always did it with a smile.

Hal never said a bad word about anyone … except for Jihadies and most politicians.

You will be sorely missed by all of us.

Acknowledgments

I'd like to thank all of those I borrowed names from especially Harold, Evelyne and Ann Turcot. Harold unfortunately passed away part way through the writing of this book but he was kind enough to agree to the use of his name much earlier. Other folks who allowed me to use their names as characters were Bob Glass, Natalie Lelievre-Ferguson, Eric Lawrence, a lady named Violeta, Kylie, Carmen, and a Great Dane named Samson.

Of course none of the characters in this novel resemble their namesakes in any way – except Samson.

As always, I deeply appreciate the work of Dan Ferguson on cover art.

A special thank you to my reviewers and editors Bob Glass and Humphrey Pickering for their painstaking and endless proofreading and edits and finally Graeme Woodley who apart from editing and proofreading offered sage advice on plot development, style and structure.

Foreword

For those of you who read the previously published short story CULPEPER this novel is a more complete treatment of the same fictional premise.

Readers had asked me to expand on the short story and this novel stays true to most of the short story with a few significant changes to support the full yarn.

Both stories stand on their own.

In addition, readers of the previously published 'Cristal's Revenge' might notice the reappearance of a couple of familiar government characters shared between the two novels.

I hope you enjoy it.

The Untimely Death of a President

From his window seat the view was breathtaking and suddenly he realized it was a perfect day to die.

On the ground, the silence of the crisp dawn on the cliffs overlooking the Grand Canyon was broken only by the screams of the bald eagles heading out for a feast of trout in the angry Colorado River far below.

The normally boisterous gaggle of press were almost completely silent, listening to the eagles and huddling together against the cold breeze until the first of them glanced towards the horizon hearing the incoming helicopters.

Excitement grew as the two big Sea Kings, which often carried the call sign Marine 1, approached. This would be the first time since his surprise resignation three days ago, that President Harold Turcot would face the press.

They had been told that there was no guarantee he would take questions but they'd all picked up on the subtle hints and knew better.

The event had been billed as a long-planned trip for the former first family to see the canyon, but having been organized with press in attendance by the new Administration, they were expecting to get much more than a photo-op out of it.

The official 'rumor' was that President Turcot's ailing nineteen-year-old daughter Ann had been promised a trip to the canyon as the single item on her bucket list, and now her dad had the time to deliver. Ann was known to have Lou Gehrig's disease or ALS, which was quite rare in a young female, and given she had not been seen in public for many months, there was morbid interest to see how far the disease had progressed. After all, her illness was his cover story for why he had resigned.

A makeshift boardwalk over the sandy soil and a viewing stage extending over the edge of the canyon had been hastily constructed by the military and the National Park Service, replete with flowers as a backdrop and lining the walkway for the best photos.

As the big helicopters swooped in low, one of them set down close enough to the walkway that it threw up an enormous cloud of desert dust, causing all the cameramen to hurriedly cover their gear.

The press had been held back about twenty yards on the other side of the boardwalk with a rope line, but not far enough to escape the massive dusty wash from the big Marine helicopters. Within seconds of the landing and as the dust settled, they got their first glimpse of the former first family.

Ann was a horrendous shock to everyone, as two Marines in full dress uniform lifted her in her wheelchair down from the helicopter and carried it to the walkway. The former most eligible bachelorette was crumpled up in her wheelchair and looking nothing like her most recent photos. When Turcot won his second term about two years before, there had been hopes of a White House wedding for his very photogenic teenage daughter before he left office. Now it was clear to everyone that Ann was near the end of her fight with the wicked disease.

All the way down to the tabloid photographers who wanted to get the first photos, there was instant sympathy for her and her famous parents. They suddenly realized the President had been dealing with all of this privately, on top of everything else in the last year. It made one wonder how the man had survived in office as long as he had, and certainly added some credibility to his resignation address, where he claimed he needed to spend more time with his family.

Still many suspected there had to be much more to it. After all, he had become public enemy number one with the Washington establishment in the last few months.

As Turcot glanced at the insatiable press he smiled knowing their collective narrative on his supposed predicament. None of them could know how wrong they were.

All watched in silence as the stately former Commander-in-Chief pushed his daughter's wheelchair over the uneven boardwalk accompanied by his wife Evelyne towards the temporary viewing stage. Mostly the women in the Press Gallery had deep empathy for 'Ev', also a recluse for most of the last year. She too was clearly showing the signs of how her daughter's illness had worn her down.

There'd be time for questions after, but the photojournalists couldn't sacrifice this opportunity and were clicking away getting photos of the tragedy of it all.

Shocking those gathered, the last person out of the helicopter was none other than President Turcot's political nemesis Fraser Carmichael, the right-wing billionaire entrepreneur who many thought was possibly the real genesis for the President's demise.

Turcot picked up on their reaction out of the corner of his eye. 'Another red herring', he thought to himself. In some ways, now that the pressure of the office was gone, he found this teasing of the press delicious.

A vicious political foe, Carmichael was thought by many to have conned the President into a path of self-destruction that had cost him his presidency. Yet here he was, the lone invited guest at a family outing as if he was their closest personal friend. How he had come to be included in this family event was a juicy mystery to be investigated and provided more pointed questions for the President when he paused to take questions.

The official schedule called for only a few photos at the canyon but the tip-off was the proximity of the rope line to the walkway. It was an unwritten rule and signaled that the President would be within earshot of the reporters and would likely take questions after the photos.

For a few moments the family, along with Carmichael, stood facing the canyon taking in the early morning sunrise and the awe-inspiring views. The press briefing had said they had specifically picked this early morning winter viewing spot on the recommendation of a local Havasupai tribal chief.

As the President, his family and Carmichael turned and started to arrange themselves for photos there was a loud crack from their viewing stand and to the horror and screams of everyone assembled, all four of them disappeared over the side of the cliff, falling over a thousand feet to their certain deaths.

Exactly as it had been planned.

The Funeral

'History is a set of lies agreed upon.'

Napoleon Bonaparte

The funeral was spectacular, somber, and heartbreaking for Mary. Everything she had hoped for her fallen President and long-term boss. Even with the raging controversy, they had put on the full pomp and ceremony accorded a fallen American president.

There was no risk in celebrating him now. He was permanently out of their way and they could take their time undoing all the good he had done.

There was no outward sign of the much-reported animosity from the Washington elite. A Democratic President who was revered by Joe Six-pack of both parties, yet loathed by Washington including many in his own party. A man who started out as the 'establishment' choice, yet in recent months had ended up betraying them all. At least that was the way 'they' all saw it.

It was a typical Washington winter morning, cooler than normal yet with blinding sunshine and a promise of spring in the air. The pageantry was spectacular, still she couldn't stop weeping from her comfortable heated chair in the exclusive presidential viewing stand.

She was under no illusions about her future, as ex-presidential secretaries had a hard time finding employment, especially coming from an Administration so recently hated by most of Washington. The few press who had gotten to her all wanted to know if she planned to write a book. The thought of disclosing any confidences, which would certainly be demanded by any publisher, was repugnant to her.

In his final days, he had been one of America's boldest presidents, having been strong for the people in a time of crisis and disaster.

His recent resignation, under pressure, from office was highly unpopular, as the average voter really didn't care what toes he had stepped on and generally had wanted him to stay and fight for them.

His story of wanting to spend more time with Ann had been dismissed by many who thought he had just finally caved to the pressure from the Hill. The recent grotesque pictures of Ann all over the media, curled up in a wheelchair on the day of the tragedy had tempered that feeling somewhat. Clearly Ann must have been on his mind all the time and must have contributed tremendous stress.

But to die with his entire family and that untrustworthy interloper three days after leaving office, well that was fodder for any number of conspiracy theories and she was sure there would be many.

So much in the last few months had been just too weird even for her, and in her position as his personal secretary, she felt she should've had a better handle on what was really going on. But for whatever reason he had become much more secretive in his final months.

There were rumors, as she left the White House, that certain recordings from the Oval Office were missing or blank. She put that down to the typical talk that happens at a leadership change. Idle minds looking for some way to diminish the guy they were replacing. Those rumors hadn't hit the press yet but that was only a matter of time. Alleged missing recordings could be part of the overall campaign to discredit him too. They were going to need a whole host of complaints to justify undoing all his recent Executive Orders.

The world loved him too. Finally there was a politician on the scene who spoke in a straightforward manner and had a plan for the future. Developed countries, and even their hard-working citizens, all knew the manufacturing jobs would never return from the third world or the persistent move to robotics. Here was a man who was willing to admit that and plan for an optimistic economic recovery for the developed world.

His few remaining supporters in the press were reporting that he had been treated monstrously by the establishment in Washington, yet because of all the secrecy, much of that was informed speculation or uncorroborated rumor. There was no proof of insidious backroom deals but that didn't make it untrue. And now he had been taken at much too early an age and was unable to defend himself against whatever narrative Washington wanted to put forth. She suddenly remembered the old Napoleon Bonaparte quote that Hal Turcot was about to fall prey to, 'History is the set of lies agreed upon'.

Many had thought he might dedicate his life to clearing his name, but now the much-promoted congressional hearings into what had really happened were at a dead end. Their chief witness was about to be buried today at Arlington and his sole accomplice was already in the ground.

Rumor was, the new gang in the White House, backed up by the Hill, realized it was going to be a herculean task to undo what the insiders and the establishment considered was the immense damage he had left behind. It was most fortuitous that his unlikely partner in this nonsense, Fraser Carmichael, had disappeared from the scene at the same time.

Right now the world thought Turcot had made all the right moves but other people in power were convinced it was all unsustainable, reckless and maybe even un-American. Washington had to be put back on an even keel, a predictable course where vested interests dictated the outcome. Hal Turcot's follies had to be left behind as a failed experiment as fast as possible. It wouldn't be long before all the lobbyists were back in business. The new President, former Vice-President Frank Osgoode, was just the man to take things back to the predictable path they had been on before Turcot had tried his little end run or 'economic experiment'.

Uncertainty in the business world was deadly, and a rogue agent with power like President Harold Turcot was their worst nightmare. In the short time he had been out of office the stock market had started to stabilize.

Mary was not alone in her confusion. Why he had taken this path at this time was a puzzle to even the most knowledgeable insiders in Washington. Sure he was a liberal and many of his changes had a radical liberal slant to them, but still he had gone completely off the political rails in the last few months even according to his own supporters in the Senate. Now that Turcot and Carmichael were both gone they realized it was likely they would never know the true reason behind it all.

Earlier in St. Matthew's Cathedral, she had watched as more of his political enemies took to the microphone to extol his virtues. She couldn't bear to look at these bald-faced hypocrites.

Investigations on why the viewing stand had collapsed were ongoing but even most of the crazies thought it had to be simply an untimely accident. After all, they had multiple close-up HD angles of the catastrophe which left little to the imagination.

One of the more popular shots replayed almost incessantly on the major networks was the scene of congressmen gasping, calling out and even crying when the news was announced in the House. After a few moments they were crawling over each other to get to the microphones on the floor of the House of Representatives and later in the Senate to sing his praises. This from the people most now considered unabashed hypocrites, who it was rumored had vindictively come within an inch of impeaching him and throwing him out of office by way of secret meetings only days earlier.

The majority thought Turcot had clearly sized up the opposition and resigned to save the country from a drawn-out impeachment trial in the Senate. Of course there was Ann's illness, but Mary knew the truth of the forces lined up against him. Those last few days had been crazy and her head was spinning when Hal Turcot broke the news of his resignation decision to her.

Even Mary, his trusted personal secretary and as close as she was to the family, had no idea of the real truth of the matter.

As the funeral procession came to a close she just couldn't stop weeping. In an attempt to gather herself, she turned her attention to the immediate future. She wasn't looking forward to it, but it had fallen to her to take charge of closing down the family home in Baton Rouge.

She had a big task ahead of her. Maybe she'd find some of the answers going through all of the President's papers and personal effects which was now her sole and final responsibility.

There was no way for her to know that the real reasons for Hal Turcot's bizarre behavior and death could never be known, for it would terrify every living human being.

Baton Rouge

The shock of the entire family's passing still hadn't worn off. Now, a week after the funeral, it was time for Mary to sort through the Turcots' belongings in their family home just outside of Baton Rouge. She planned to transfer all of his important papers and mementos to the new Harold Turcot Presidential Library Foundation which like others before it, would set about the task of raising private money and finding an appropriate location, theme, architect, and board of advisors for the library, to memorialize his contributions to the country. The advisory committee for the future library had already been formed and they were anxious for Mary to report back to them what materials would be suitable for display.

Her job was to sort through a mountain of personal and professional belongings to determine what items were related to the President's career and should be donated to the library and what was possibly too personal or controversial and needed to go into storage for his estate. An estate that had no heirs, save for the very generous and surprising gift he had left for her. She had not seen the will but according to the lawyer, they had surprisingly made no provisions for their daughter Ann. The only explanation the lawyer had offered was that they must not have expected the will to come into force before Ann succumbed to her dreadful disease.

The family had not been rich but, apparently only very recently, had changed their wills to include her and the rest of their funds to go to a few charities they supported. All materials not donated to the library would be kept sealed by the National Archivist until the twelve-year presidential moratorium on his belongings expired.

Turcot had been an only child, and with his parents gone and his wife's small immediate family estranged, there was no one closer to the family, so this tedious and emotional job of going through their belongings had fallen to her. While dreading the challenge she had to admit that she alone would know the significance of many of the items to be considered.

Now a couple of weeks after vacating the White House, everything they possessed had finally made it to the home and was crammed into what the press had called the 'Southern White House'. It was a sizable home but nothing compared to the space they had in Washington. Unopened boxes and crates were in every room, the basement and even the garage. Most of them had arrived only after the accident in

Arizona so the family had not even witnessed the chaos of their southern home.

The inconsolable family maid was still on medical leave almost two weeks after the family's demise. She had not attended the funerals and it was doubtful she would be available any time soon to lend a hand. So Mary had brought in her niece Kylie, a recent history grad from Georgetown to assist her. Washington had expedited her security clearance so she could participate in the project.

The opportunity for a history major to riffle through a president's personal home was just too unbelievable and she jumped at the opportunity, especially this President who had engendered such strong feelings, been so secretive in some ways and been so thoroughly attacked by the Washington crowd.

Turcot had seemed to make major news daily just before his tragic death. Kylie knew there had to be some nascent history here and maybe some answers as to why he took on all of Washington in the last few months, risking his entire presidency. It remained an unsolved mystery for historians and politicians alike.

They arrived together to start the work just after nine a.m. As Mary opened the front door she said, "Now Kylie I must insist we wear these white gloves at all times. Some of these papers and materials will end up in a museum and frankly some might end up being subpoenaed for whatever reason, so we don't want our fingerprints all over everything. You don't want to become a witness in something you know nothing of. We need to be very delicate as well.

"I will do the first pass on everything as I should have some idea of what it is. Your primary role is to tag, catalogue and help package everything."

Kylie nodded, "I have the software set up on my laptop to keep track of everything and I'll back it up daily. How long do you think we'll be here?"

Mary sighed, "By the looks of this place it is going to be weeks for sure."

Kylie suddenly realized that even the smallest thing relating to a president was serious business and they had exclusive access to his materials so that she herself was making history through this very effort. Still any personal gain had not been her intent when she agreed to work with her semi-famous aunt on this amazing project, but she had to realize this was all new to her and if anything she was likely underestimating the import of the task and anything they might find.

She turned to her aunt, "I honestly hope we don't find anything TOO interesting. I'm not looking forward to testifying to Congress based on any of this work."

Mary simply smiled. This was all new for Kylie but Mary had essentially been walking on eggs ever since she linked up with Hal Turcot way back even before his Louisiana gubernatorial days. Political foes certainly kept you ensuring you crossed every T.

There were a few boxes from the Oval Office itself but Mary decided to start with what came from the residence area of the White House. Going through boxes labeled 'Master Bedroom' they found all manner of personal items. They found an old pair of rollerblades that by the size had to be Hal Turcot's. Mary smiled and shook her head as she just couldn't see him rollerblading.

A little later, digging further she came upon an old shoe box with no markings on it. Kylie came to the bedroom door just as Mary lifted it out of a crate. Inside was a strange looking apparatus that looked like a set of headphones but they were all white and had no wires, dials or buttons. As she picked the item out of the box it disintegrated into a puff of talcum-like powder and slipped through her fingers.

Kylie could see her aunt was shocked at what had just happened and put her hand on her shoulder, "What was that thing?"

As the tears began to flow she said, "I have no idea. I've never seen it before but it just dissolved into powder when I picked it up. It was so light and fragile. What could it have been?"

"Well if you've never seen it before it's unlikely to be anything important so I wouldn't worry about it. It'll be our little secret."

Through her hand on Mary's shoulder Kylie could feel that the woman was shaking. Then the tears came again and the sobbing started.

She eased her over to the bed and sat with her arm around her sobbing aunt.

Between the sobs Mary finally said, "You know I loved him. Not in that way. You know what I mean. He was an amazing man. I've been with him for over twenty years. I can't believe he's gone. I loved them all. His wife Ev was one of the most charming and pleasant people I have ever met and then his poor Ann, struck down at seventeen with ALS. How does that happen? I remember holding her just after she was born. She was almost like a daughter to me. And then they all die in a freak accident three days after he is forced out of office? It's all just too much. It's all so unfair!"

She wiped her eyes and nose as she continued, "He wasn't a particularly religious man no matter what his public image was, but something got him through those horrible months of Ann's illness and then the mutiny as I like to call it. It was unlike him to keep me out of the loop but he never shared with me what was really going on through those awful months.

"Those last few were torture but I couldn't find any way to help him. I swear it all started that infamous crazy crazy night about three months ago. The night that started with that billionaire, right-wing blowhard Fraser Carmichael coming to see him with the survivor of the mine disaster. With Hal gone we may never know why that Glass character and Carmichael suddenly became so important and got unfettered access to the President, why he made all those big changes to the military and why his Chief-of-Staff had to resign."

Kylie suddenly realized the stress her aunt must have been under and felt for her. Many people had suggested Carmichael's arrival on the scene with the mine inspector had been the turning point for the President for some mysterious reason, but who could know better than Mary Trudel.

Mary was still on the verge of sobbing as she spoke, "I just know it was all Carmichael's doing. I never trusted that snake and as you know, I normally refrain from speaking badly of others.

"Even though it seemed to everyone that Carmichael was close to the President these last few months, you must remember the things he did and the things he said to attack Hal before that. I was completely shocked to find out he was on that trip to the Grand Canyon with the family. Like a lot of things in these last few months, that made no sense at all."

She started crying again.

"Listen Aunt Mary, I know this has been very hard on you. You were closer than probably anyone to the family. Just think of this as his last assignment to you and we just have to get through it for his sake. We have to do the best job possible for him. Remember, you were the only one he chose to name in his will and you're the only one left who can do something this personal for him."

Mary stopped sobbing for a moment and in a cracking voice said, "That's just it. I'm not at my best right now. I don't even know what that thing was and I broke it. It's lost forever now and it must have been important."

Kylie hugged Mary even tighter and gave a little laugh, "I doubt that very much. After all it was in an old shoe box. If it was important it would've been in his vault or in the National Archives or something.

"You know what it looked like to me? It looked like one of those things that comes out of a 3D printer. The old ones were made of a material like sand and break easily. They were only used for prototypes for manufacturing or samples and such. Probably someone the President knows gave him a sample long ago and he didn't want to throw it away in case they came to visit again. It must have dried out and would've disintegrated as soon as anyone touched it. I wouldn't worry about it."

Neither of them noticed that by the time they threw the powder in the trash, half of it had somehow disappeared.

The Mine

(Four months earlier)

As BREAKING NEWS faded from the screen, CNN's latest eye candy Natalie Lelievre appeared, "We've just received word from our affiliate in Boise that there has been a mine collapse at a very deep silver mine just outside of Wallace, Idaho."

The TV screen switched to a two shot with a pretty journalist and the logo reading ...

KTVB Boise

Idaho's First in News: Jane Diaz Reporting

... across the bottom of the screen. Jane looked a little out of breath standing in front of a sun-bleached sign that read 'Culpeper Industries - Deepest Silver Mine in the USA'.

Natalie spoke first, "Jane, we've heard there was some sort of a collapse at the mine. What can you tell us?"

"Natalie, we've just arrived here but I can tell you that somewhere about two miles below my feet there was a major accident this morning. Miners are still coming out of the mine so the good news is, there are survivors. The most recent report says that two miners are unaccounted for. I have with me Jim Wilson who is the day supervisor at the mine. Jim what do we know at this moment?"

Jim, looking a little perturbed, given he really wanted to be leading the recovery effort, looked at Jane instead of the camera. "Well Jane, I think we were very lucky. We were just changing shifts at eight a.m. so most of the men were on their way out of the mine. The foreman on the shift says that almost all of the sixty-eight miners were well away from the collapse and we think sixty-six of them have been accounted for. There are no injuries among them, but there were two other men working near the ore face when this happened and at the moment we have no contact with them as the collapse apparently took out all our communications. There's every reason to believe that they are safe because it looks like the cave-in happened some distance away from the ore face, but we can't be sure until we get some communications gear down there."

Jane interrupted, "And will that not be very difficult?"

"Well it could be. First, we have to determine how large the collapse is and whether there is a safe way to clear it. Using GPS, we will also start a small drill hole right near the ore face as soon as we can get the equipment here. Our safety plan says that we should be able to reach the face in about a week with a three-inch hole if we can't get to them quicker by clearing the debris. That will allow us to communicate with them confirming they have survived and also allow us to provide key provisions to our trapped miners."

Jane jumped in, "Can they survive that long?"

"We have safe zones down there stocked with water, food, batteries and oxygen so if they can get to one of those they should be able to hold out easily for a week. Those safe zones have provisions for dozens of men."

Jane heard "wrap it up" in her earpiece and turned to the camera. "There you have it Natalie. More than sixty miners are making their way to the surface as we speak, but the fate of two missing men, twelve thousand feet below us, is unknown at this time."

***

Fraser Carmichael, Fortune's 'Entrepreneur of the Decade', in his massive penthouse office overlooking Central Park in New York, flicked the ash from his expensive cigar, lifted the phone and pressed the speed dial for his broker as CNN returned to their normal programming.

"Harry, get me into silver in a big way. If I remember, that mine was a major contributor to silver reserves and they are going to be closed for a while," he mumbled, cigar now in his mouth.

"What mine?"

"Never mind Harry, turn on CNN. Just get me into silver mines before you do that."

As he hung up he realized he had done it again. He was trying to clean up his act and his assistant had told him people didn't think it was cool when he mumbled to them with his frequently present Montecristo #2 in his mouth.

He was trying to cut down and had it under control at three a day. He had them flown in weekly from Montreal on one of the company shuttles and not declared as Cuban. Cigars from the communist island were again non grata in the US, no matter what the Obama

Administration had tried to do.

Growing up poor, first in Glasgow, Scotland and then on the outskirts of Buffalo, he now had a taste for the better things in life. Things that had been denied him as a child and learning to appreciate the best cigar he could get his hands on started as more of an experiment and guilty indulgence than anything else. Now he was hooked. His two ex-wives had not allowed him to smoke at home, but now he was free of them, if not their alimony checks.

As he looked down fifty-seven floors to the street below opposite the massive treed spaces of Central Park, he tried to imagine twelve thousand feet below the earth and trapped in a dark, confined space … if they were even alive. He shivered at the thought of not knowing your fate and being trapped so far from rescue.

***

TV coverage of the unfolding drama of the mine disaster now promoted by CNN as the 'Idaho Interment' was nonstop over the next week, complete with a big digital countdown clock graphic to the anticipated breakthrough of the tiny exploratory drill hole. They, other networks, world media, and some of the local stations had set up shop at the entrance to the mine that now looked like a tent city.

October in the Idaho mountains meant the tents were only used to keep potential snow off the coffee machines and the camera equipment as well as housing some powerful electric heaters for the technical crews, who usually worked from a comfortable studio. With limited seating in the satellite trucks, the tech teams had yielded to the lightly dressed, on-air talent so they could keep warm when not live on TV. The few hotels, motels and the tiny Rent-all place in Wallace nearby were enjoying a major boon.

Interest was piqued due to the amazing recovery years earlier in Chile of miners trapped for four months at a similar depth. Live broadcasts from the Culpeper mine with little to report, went out on the twenty-four hour news channels as Breaking News at the top of each hour. With only scant details on how the drilling was proceeding, most of the air time was taken up by background pieces on the two trapped miners. Everyone wanted the first video of the miners coming up from the depths in a steel cage just like in Chile. A ratings peak was guaranteed for 'Rescue Day'. That was on the assumption they had survived.

If both miners had died in the collapse, CNN was ready to go with their 'Final Interment' memorial tape of the two miners and their life stories.

The local roads around the Culpeper mine were jammed with satellite trucks, lighting rigs, reporters and a gaggle of hangers-on including some news junkies and wackos who were camped out across the road from the mine entrance with signs that read "Conspiracy – Watch Silver Stocks" and "SAVE OUR MINERS – OSHA DOESN'T CARE". The Occupational Health and Safety Administration always seemed to take it in the neck when there was any kind of mine event and their on-site people had been told to avoid the press where virtually anything they said was likely to get them into trouble with someone.

At the morning briefing Jim Wilson, who had now become the public face of the collapse, announced that they were hoping for a breakthrough to an open space just in front of the ore face around noon.

Right around eleven a.m. Idaho time, CNN broke into scheduled programming with their familiar "BREAKING NEWS – Idaho Interment" banner, count-down clock and theme music.

Again it was a two shot of Natalie in CNN headquarters and Jane on site. Natalie took the lead, "Well Jane, we must be getting close to some answers after a week of holding our collective breaths. What can you tell us?"

"That's right, Natalie. Eric Lawrence and Bob Glass have been down there for almost a week now and their photos are familiar to the whole world. I'm reporting to you from a new clearing in the woods where the rescue effort was set up above the ore face and where they have been drilling what they call an exploratory shaft.

"I saw shift supervisor Jim Wilson a few minutes ago and we can report that his team has just broken through with their three-inch drill hole in the last thirty minutes. They are into what they hope is an open space near the ore face where they think the men might be. They had to abandon the idea of clearing the collapse as the mine in that area was too unstable.

"As you know we had been told that the cave-in seems to have been far back from the ore face. The two missing men, one of them a civil engineer who is a mine inspector, had planned to inspect the ore face between shifts so there is every hope that they may have been far away from the collapse.

"Mr. Wilson reported that from the three-inch rescue hole that was completed just minutes ago, we now know that the area near the ore face is clear and has breathable air but we can't be certain how far back the collapse was and whether it covered up or cut off the safe zone containing life supporting supplies. They have no evidence yet of the missing men.

"They have just sent down a tiny headset with a highly sensitive microphone to listen for any sounds of life. They also sent down a device that makes a loud pinging sound and has a strobe light to attract anyone down there, and a tiny fiber optic video camera.

"If the safe zone is clear they would've had food, water, oxygen and lighting from batteries but the power at the ore face would've been cut out by the collapse so it is pitch black down there and there is no telling how far they could be from this tiny hole that has been drilled, if in fact they survived the initial collapse."

Just then there was a loud cheer from somewhere off camera.

The camera followed Jane as she ran towards the cheering and caught Jim Wilson as he came down the stairs from the temporary trailer set up near the hole for rescue operations.

She was first to the stairway and Wilson paused for her at the bottom of the stairs, "Jane, we have mixed news. One of our miners is safe but unfortunately the other didn't survive the collapse. We aren't identifying the deceased until we notify next of kin but our other miner is well and in good spirits. We'll be getting fresh water and some hot food down to him within the hour. Today is a sad day but also a day for rejoicing. I want to thank everyone who worked incredible hours to get us to this point."

"Jim, how long will it take to get him out of there?"

"Well as you remember the Chilean miners were trapped for nearly four months while a shaft big enough for a rescue capsule was drilled. We're in the same shape here. We've determined that we can't clear the original collapse without jeopardizing more men but the good news is that we learned a few things from Chile, we have different geology here and we have better equipment now but we're still looking at several weeks, not days. We have a very deep mine here."

"Thanks, Jim."

"There you have it, Natalie. Unfortunately one miner didn't make it but there are high hopes for the rescue of the second."

Fraser Carmichael caught the news about the trapped miner on his giant matrix of TV screens in his office when CNN repeated it at the top of the hour just as his phone rang from Carmen, his personal assistant. "Sir, I have Jim Wilson on the phone from that mine in Idaho. He says it is critical that he talks to you."

This was totally unexpected. Carmichael paused for a moment staring out the window at Central Park. He had just seen video of the man on TV with the local reporter and now he was calling? "Put him through."

He heard the click as the connection was established. This time he placed the cigar in the ashtray in front of him. Smoking was not allowed in the building ... for everyone else.

"Mr. Carmichael, my name is Jim Wilson. I'm the day supervisor at the Culpeper Silver Mine. You may have heard of our predicament."

"Yes, I just saw you on TV. Congratulations on getting to the missing miner."

"Well Mr. Carmichael that's the reason for my call. He refuses to speak to anyone except you. Confidentially his name is Bob Glass, and he's a mining engineer and was inspecting the mine when the collapse happened between shifts. He has only told us that he is in good health and that Eric Lawrence didn't make it. As you may know we haven't identified the name of the deceased until we connect with the family, but Bob insists on speaking only with you. Do you have any idea why he wants to talk to you?"

"Sorry, Mr. Wilson, I've never heard of the man until now. It baffles me why he would want to talk to me but given his situation I'd be glad to talk to him. Are you able to patch him through?"

"Yes, and thank you, Mr. Carmichael. We've no idea what this is about but it is good of you to assist in keeping his mood up. Our best guess is that he is going to be down there for at least four weeks as we drill a much larger escape shaft. I'll patch you through now."

After some pleasantries Bob Glass started right in, "Mr. Carmichael, I called you because I've discovered something that I think you'll value and I want millions out of this. I want to live the life I've dreamed of with my fiancée, and believe me you'll want me to be a happy man too.

"Right after the collapse Eric and I saw some light coming down one of the passageways. All of the regular light was out and this light looked weird, kind of a bluish light.

"We headed down the shaft and were shocked to find one of the walls had collapsed and we were in a computer room of some sort. You must remember we're near the face of a mine that is about two miles deep so no man has ever been here or at least no man you or I have ever met."

Carmichael listened transfixed as his breathing quickened.

"Immediately we noticed what looked like workstations and chairs that were too big to be for humans. Maybe made for something half again larger than us. Then we noticed four what we would call robots that had two arms and legs and a head but were bigger than us. Clearly they were not alive but some kind of mechanical invention with what looked like a semi-transparent plastic or rubber skin over their very intricate mechanisms. Looks to me like the robots can use the chairs but they seem too comfortable to be made for them."

Carmichael was thinking fast. The most likely scenario was that this guy had gone crazy after a week in the dark. This could also be a silly hoax or prank but he trusted that Carmen had checked out the source of the call before passing it on so at least the call was coming from near the mine.

Glass continued, "One of the robots seemed to want to protect the equipment and approached us putting itself between us and the equipment.

"Eric, one of the mine supervisors, took this as a threat, panicked and took a swing at it with a shovel he was holding. He dropped dead before the shovel got anywhere near the robot. Since then I have made no aggressive moves towards the robots and they have established something of a relationship with me. They seem to want to protect me, not hurt me.

"I've now established a sign language with them but they haven't tried to communicate verbally so I suspect they're mute. From a machine in the wall of the computer room they've offered me fresh water and some kind of really bland edible thing."

Carmichael had heard enough, "I'm sorry, Mr. Glass, but you have to understand my position. This all sounds a little TOO incredible. Why should I believe any of this? How do I know this is not a prank call and why did you call me instead of let's say the FBI or the Defense Department if what you say is true?"

Glass had thought of this, "Call back to the mine after we finish and see if the mine supervisor put this call through to you. As for me, I hold a Masters in Civil Engineering from Caltech and after a week down here I am in no mood to be playing pranks. I'm only working as a mine inspector to be near my fiancée who has family reasons why she must stay in this part of the country. I know what I'm seeing here. I've lived with these things for a week now. These are, or were, aliens of some kind. The room seems cut off from the rest of whatever is down here by a collapse near a doorway on the far side of the room, so there's no telling what's beyond that. The technology in this room is fantastic and for some reason it seems to me that it has been here for a very long time, maybe thousands of years or longer.

"As to why you, I've had time to think about my predicament and appearing on CNN and touring the late night talk shows isn't my ultimate goal. If I involve the government I would probably be muzzled over the finds anyway. I want something out of this from someone who values these technologies and is able to compensate me for exclusive access to this discovery, and that isn't the government or the TV networks. It's someone who has the wherewithal to make massive profits from these futuristic technologies.

"Now why do I think you would be interested? Apart from these amazing robots, I see lighting that seems to have no source. I see what must be electronic equipment with no wires. I see a machine that dispenses fresh water and food. I see flasks containing a pink liquid on each workstation that I'd have to guess are some kind of immense storage device. I can call the feds or one of your competitors and they can have this or you can have it all to yourself and make me a rich man. I think you get the picture."

Carmichael was stunned. This guy seemed lucid and if he in fact had an advanced degree in engineering then he probably had a good handle and interpretation of what he was looking at. While Glass had been talking, Carmichael had typed his name into LinkedIn and now it reported there was a Robert Glass living in Wallace Idaho, working at Culpeper and who had a Masters in Civil Engineering from Caltech. The scenario made perfect sense, call the first billionaire you can get to, if you want to cash out.

"OK, assume for a moment that I believe at least some of what you've told me. You've apparently had time to think this all out. What do you want me to do?"

"First I want an ironclad contract with you that I will be a very rich man and live a life that is comparable to yours in creature comforts if I give you exclusive access to this mine, meaning I will tell no one else while you exploit it.

"I need no capital and I don't want to build my own empire. I just want all expenses paid on the lifestyle I want to live including any taxes. Use your own personal expenses as a guideline. You would know more than I, on what that lifestyle costs. I'm thinking homes in a couple of spectacular locations, unfettered access to a private jet, lots of toys, and a sizable boat for parties. I think you get the picture. My guess, and it is only a guess, is that a locked in annuity or the guaranteed perpetual interest on a few hundred million for life should cover it, but you'll know better than me. You might even make me an employee with a massive expense account. The mechanisms are up to you.

"Secondly, I want you to keep all of this strictly between the two of us until that contract is signed and in my hands. This is critical to me and I'm not flexible on that term. We must have a signed contract before you can tell ANYONE. My recourse would be to find a different buyer or tell the feds what is down here and then even if you own the place, you'll lose it. I'd lose the benefits I mentioned and worst case I may have to live on the book and movie rights but it's more a matter of principle and I'm a principled man."

Carmichael had no doubt he would carry out his threat. Nerdy engineers could be that way. He knew a few of them in his own companies.

"Next, and you'll know more about this than me, lock up this site. Buy the mine, get me out of here as quickly as possible and find a way to keep all of this secret so you can exploit the technologies to your heart's content.

"I will cooperate in any way I can with my limited resources. I will take this secret to the grave and I will take steps to ensure you keep your side of the bargain.

"If this isn't acceptable to you then I think Donald Trump is still rich enough to make this happen for me or maybe Bill Gates. As I said earlier, if I can't find a buyer, I'll turn it over to the feds. You get the picture. You're the lucky one because I think this fits your business better with your military contracts. There are definitely things here that the military will pay you for, big time."

Carmichael thought for a moment before he responded. There seemed to be little downside to this and he was starting to believe what he was hearing, "Mr. Glass, you have a deal with one condition. I will invest in this and do what I can to get you out of there fast and provide you with a lifestyle even you can't dream of but the deal is off if I can't verify your findings after we gain access to the mine, and I'll sue you for my costs."

Glass eagerly responded, "Done!"

After the call Carmichael did as Glass suggested and had Carmen verify the call had indeed started with Jim Wilson at the Culpeper mine. He then took a seat on his office couch and thought through the amazing phone call for a long time before he rose and pressed the intercom again for his personal assistant. "Carmen, I need an immediate meeting with the guys. I want operations, legal, and security."

Within ten minutes the invited members of his inner circle were gathered in his office. He stood at the head of the large oval table in his office as they took their seats.

"Gentlemen, what I'm about to tell you will go with you to your graves. I can only disclose parts of a new critical project to you now and more later.

"Will, I want very specific, detailed and airtight non-disclosures at the end of this meeting. As compensation for this agreement you'll each be given one million dollars by the end of the week with your signed non-disclosure. Now I know that isn't a life changing amount of money to some of you but a court won't see it that way. There will be much more if we're successful.

"In return, I will have your agreement to pay me one billion dollars in unspecified damages or everything you and your immediate family own, and any money you earn from disclosure, directly or indirectly, or anything you or people connected to you benefited from if you're found to have leaked anything that we'll discuss on this project.

"So, you open your mouth and you lose everything. Understood?"

Each in the room nodded slowly while glancing at the others. This had to be big!

"You'll also agree to be under constant surveillance. All I can tell you is that it will be worth it. Remember, I'll put a team on this to destroy you if you leak anything at all of this matter until I release you from the agreement in writing, which will never happen."

Will Fiskins, corporate counsel had been scribbling notes.

Carmichael continued, "Will, can you make that happen? Can you get all of that into a contract and make it ironclad and totally legal that you guys are signing away your lives to me if you even hint at what you'll find out?"

Will looked serious, "I can put all of that and more if you wish, as long as everyone understands what they're signing."

"OK," he said looking at his three execs, "do I have your complete agreement?"

Fraser Carmichael was known as an unorthodox billionaire who was fond of massive deals and even though these three men had been with him for some time, this approach was novel, obviously of the highest secrecy, a little threatening, but at the same time it promised to be very exciting and lucrative.

All nodded their acceptance again.

Carmichael waited for a few seconds to see if anyone would change their minds, ask for clarifications or back out. This wasn't the first time he had sworn them to secrecy, but the stakes had never been this high or the secret so fantastic.

"OK, just to be VERY clear. This information goes with you to your grave or else. Any leak of this could cost me billions and could potentially ruin me and if I stand to be ruined you'll be right in front of me and so will the ones you love."

He could see he had their complete attention and buy-in. The only question was, would they comply forever. Forever was a long time.

Fraser Carmichael finally took his seat at the head of the conference table, "A few minutes ago I had a conversation with the miner who is trapped in that mine in Idaho. They just broke through to him and his first call was to me."

This wasn't what the room had expected. All of them had seen some of the reports over the last week as CNN, FOX and others had fixated on it with hourly coverage, endlessly rehashing the little real news they had on the subject.

"My first reaction was that he had gone loopy after spending a week alone down there in the dark, but I checked him out and came to believe the incredible story he told me.

"It seems the collapse unveiled some amazing discoveries. He believes he has found something incredible that could be worth billions to us.

"I'm not at liberty yet to tell you what it is and we'll need to verify his claims when he is rescued. I want to interview the guy in person when we get him out, but I believe what I've heard so far and I want to secure that mine for Carmichael Industries before word gets out. He has offered to keep it all secret for the right incentive. You should understand I thought about doing this myself but I need help and I need the resources of a large company like CII, so today's your lucky day.

"He wants an ironclad contract signed and in his hands before I can tell you any more about the discovery. He's thought this out and there can be no mistakes or we'll lose everything. It must remain secret for now and we'll have to maintain that secrecy after he is rescued and we see what he has found. Legal, you'll draw up the contract for Mr. Glass from an outline I'll give you today but it has a full cancelation clause if we cannot verify his discoveries and recourse for our costs if he's been lying."

The room was deathly silent as jaws dropped wondering what it could be that had generated this excitement in the boss. He had said discoveries, plural, so it wasn't likely a giant patch of diamonds or gold, but he did say it was worth billions.

Carmichael continued, "Mr. Glass is motivated by money and having a week to think about it, decided to call me first. Under the terms of our agreement, he will become a very rich man if he keeps his end of the bargain to keep his mouth shut and cooperate with us in every way.

"Any questions?"

Jim Gardino the Exec. VP of Operations was first to speak, "What do you need us to do?"

"Good question. The owners of the Culpeper mine were likely running a marginal operation before this and now they'll be closed for a while, have diminished revenues, fines, regulatory issues and law suits to deal with. They'll eventually file for bankruptcy protection but we can't wait for that.

"Will, I want you to put a legal team together and buy them out through one of our hidden subsidiaries and any property around that rescue site to set up a security perimeter whereby our operations cannot be easily observed. It has to be a clean 'as is' sale with no recourse on their part.

"We'll need a no-fly zone too for the news helicopters. I want all legal and real estate moves disguised and secret and timed to take effect when I pull the string, which will be just before we bring Mr. Glass and Mr. Lawrence's remains to the surface. Plan on a couple of weeks max to have everything ready to go."

Will was busy scribbling notes as fast as he could.

"Jim, as Ops you'll be in charge of the exploitation of the site once we have control of it. We're going to need an expert team we can trust. Start with the basic disciplines of geology, computers, energy, etc. We can expand as needed once we know what we're dealing with. I'll give you as much heads-up as I can but I need to meet Glass's demands first. Just take my word for it that this is a big discovery and be prepared with any kind of expert we might need from anywhere in the world, not only geologists.

"As we go forward we will need others but they'll only be allowed to know the bare minimum they need to do their jobs. All will be under the similar non-disclosures and they'll all be paid well if they keep their mouths shut. Legal here will figure out the details on contracts, non-disclosures and compensation packages that will lock everything up. Remember, this site is only valuable to us if we're the only ones who know about it and can exploit it secretly for years into the future.

"Right now I want you, Jim, to get the best drill team in the world out there to help them drill the larger rescue shaft. Just tell them it's funded by an anonymous Good Samaritan. Let the local guys run the rescue until we pull the string on everything.

"The drill team and anyone in a support role do not have to be in the inner circle. Their work will be finished and they'll be gone before the serious stuff starts. We need to get Glass out of there pronto before any information leaks.

"When we're just about to pull him out then we move to phase two. Legal, we need all the injunctions and court orders we require to declare ownership and clear that property of all workers, press, emergency personnel, and even police and government agencies and that has to stick for months or years as we control access to the site. Tie them up in the courts in any way you can. Spare no expense on keeping this secret and keeping others off the site. We need to handle the coroner and cause of death on the other miner too because we have to shut down any police investigations of the mine site.

"Oh by the way, the identity of the deceased is not yet public.

"This thing has to be airtight so buy or bribe if you have to, but lock that site up tighter than a drum and make sure nothing shady can be traced back to us.

"Frank you're point man on security. I want an iron curtain of security to instantly appear around that site when we take over. In addition, everyone in the inner circle who knows any aspect of the secret nature of this operation will have to be monitored 24/7 to ensure they are sticking to the non-disclosure. Hire the best security firm you can find to do the surveillance.

"Now that's the general outline of the plan. Jim, you're in charge. Make it happen! Any questions?"

Again the room was quiet. He knew these people well. It wasn't a love relationship they had with him and even though they knew nothing of the find, they would do as they were told with such a large amount of money on the table. The best he had to fall back on was their respect for him as a business leader with the Midas Touch.

Looking at the faces in the room he suddenly realized that he had unconsciously hired them for their greed. Greedy people were predictable and therefore loyal as long as there was a big carrot just out of reach. Yes, they were an accomplished group of men, but what set them apart in the end was their greed. Something Fraser Carmichael reluctantly saw as his own secret to success. He wanted it all and when he had it, it wasn't enough. He always wanted more and he wasn't ashamed of it. In his opinion you needed a good dose of greed to be successful in today's world. Greed had made America great. Unconsciously he had picked these men because they had a similar passion for money.

***

To the rescue team on the surface, Glass explained his mysterious call to Carmichael as his effort to lock up print and movie rights for his story before he told anyone anything about his experience. The fact that Carmichael was not known to dabble in entertainment was an unanswered question.

But what really perplexed the surface team was that they had been unable to listen in on the call as it had been all static. One of the operators suggested Carmichael had access to advanced military encryption technologies and had probably found a way to scramble the call. Another said that was impossible with the simple phone they had lowered into the mine but he had no better explanation for it.

The drilling of the escape shaft went better than expected especially after some new equipment and experts turned up out of nowhere from an unnamed source but still the days passed much too slowly for all concerned.

Down below, Glass was anxious to get on with it and in New York Carmichael could think of little else.

About four weeks in, late in the evening Glass's communication system with the surface came alive, "Mr. Glass my name is Jim Gardino. I'm Mr. Carmichael's Chief Operating Officer and I'm now in charge of this operation. Just to let you know, we should be breaking through to you sometime tomorrow and we've just taken over the mine and the surrounding area and expelled all of the people who were here. When we get you out of there we will airlift you to a secret remote location, check your health, get you freshened up, finalize some paperwork cementing the deal you made with Mr. Carmichael and lay plans for what I'm told will be your very pleasant early retirement.

"At the same time but only after we get the green light from Mr. Carmichael, we will be sending our first exploitation team down through the same shaft to do a full survey and as you know, confirm your earlier claims to Mr. Carmichael. Are there any questions?"

"Yeah, first it's great to hear your voice. They had told me the shaft was getting close so I was wondering when you were going to show up. I can't get out of here fast enough. Will I get to meet the tycoon himself?"

"I believe the plan is for Mr. Carmichael to debrief you with a small team and sign the documents tomorrow if all goes well, so yes you'll be spending some time with him."

Over the crackly phone setup Glass asked, "What has Mr.

Carmichael shared with you on my situation?"

"Simply that you've found something amazing down there that is worth a lot of money to Carmichael Industries International and we are all anxious to be clued in on what it is. If all works as planned we'll have that question answered late tomorrow when you're out and we can send our team down. According to Mr. Carmichael, one of your contract demands was that he not share anything you discovered until papers are signed. I don't suppose you might want to tell me what it is?"

"Nice try. Not until Mr. Carmichael and I have signed papers."

The Meeting

Everything went according to Gardino's plan. Next morning, after Eric Lawrence's decomposing remains were transported up the rescue shaft in a body bag, Bob Glass took the claustrophobic ride himself. He was immediately choppered to a nearby private airport where he was given a quick medical examination, and allowed to shower and change into some traveling clothes they had provided. He was then flown by private jet about seven hundred miles due south to the secret location to meet the big man himself. The secret location turned out to be Mr. Carmichael's penthouse suite at his own Hawk Hotel in Las Vegas.

Back at the mine, the press and the law enforcement people were furious. It had come as a complete shock when lawyers and a massive private security team showed up with court orders to have them all removed from the property the evening before the rescue. All the government entities, law enforcement, and press on site were caught totally unprepared and they had no idea who they were fighting as the corporate ownership and property transactions had all been artfully disguised. Bailiffs and Federal Marshals had somehow been summoned to serve what appeared to be valid court orders so there was no way out.

Next morning, a heretofore unknown PR firm reported that Mr. Glass had just been rescued. A website with pictures and video of his exit from the mine was provided for press access and they reported he had requested isolation from the media so he wouldn't be available for interviews. A statement professing his gratitude to all was released along with the video.

CNN got wind of the rescue and changes at the mine from their affiliate in Idaho who quickly had Jane Diaz on camera. Jane barely had time to make it back to the site, after being expelled the previous evening.

She was unable to get up to the rescue site as the new security force was keeping everyone well back from there and the main mine entrance as well. No one seemed to know why the changes had happened, who was behind them, or why even the police were not allowed in.

At this hour of the day it was Wolf Blitzer who was anchoring the

CNN live broadcast, "Jane, we're hearing that there is something going on at the mine apart from the rescue, big changes of some sort. Can you fill us in?"

"Yes Wolf, I haven't been here long but everything has changed. Late yesterday a new company took over the mine and expelled everyone from the rescue site and the entire mine property. Even law enforcement is being held back due to a court order.

"I just got off the phone with shift supervisor Jim Wilson who is actually at home now. He tells me all employees right up to management who arrived for their shift change late yesterday were handed termination notices and told that their personal effects would be mailed to them. So everyone is dumbfounded here right now. Apparently someone has bought the mine and wants everyone kept out.

"As you know, in the last hour we were given a video and pictures of the rescue from a PR firm but we can report nothing but what was in their press release, that Eric Lawrence's remains were the first thing up the rescue shaft followed by what we see on that video, a very anxious, happy and dirty Robert Glass.

"You can be sure that many people, law enforcement, OSHA, the media, mine employees and unions are upset about this and predictably some of them are beating a path to the local courts to fight for injunctions to get this situation resolved.

"A security perimeter has appeared around not only the mine but adjacent properties as well, so whoever planned this seems to have been successful at least for the moment in dropping a blanket of secrecy over this entire area. Apparently they've even convinced a court to give them a no-fly zone over the mine. We have no idea where Mr. Robert Glass is now but one helicopter seems to have been given clearance and it left here this morning. We can only assume Robert Glass was on it. That's all we have at the moment."

Wolf took over, "That's quite remarkable Jane. Please get back to us when you have something to report."

As he turned back to the one shot he said, "CNN will stay on top of this. Stand by for further news on the rescue of Robert Glass who until earlier today was trapped twelve thousand feet underground."

Later that day, while media outlets were all kept about a quarter mile away from the mine entrance hoping for a press conference wrapping up the event, CNN headquarters in Atlanta got a hot tip to check out a house fire not far from the mine in Wallace, Idaho. They were on the air with Ashleigh Banfield's program within the hour, "Ladies and gentlemen I'm hearing that we have breaking news coming from a town near the site of that amazing mine rescue in Idaho. CNN's Bruce Donald is on the scene. Bruce what can you tell us?"

Bruce was standing in front of a home completely razed by fire and still smoldering, "Ashleigh this is incredible but this is the house of the parents of the fiancée of trapped miner, Robert Glass. The Samuels' house on this quiet residential street in Wallace has almost burned to the ground. Neighbors say there was the smell of gas in the air before there was a huge explosion and fire and you can see the results behind me. With me is Francine Delamont, a neighbor of the Samuels family. Mrs. Delamont, please tell our viewers what you just told me about who was in the house at the time."

"Well I can't be certain but I saw both David and Mary Samuels early this morning and they were very excited about the rescue about to happen. They told me they had spoken to Bob earlier before he was rescued and he had asked them not to come to the mine but to watch the whole thing on TV. Later I saw Bob's fiancée Kristen arrive at her parents' home and it looked like she was going to join them for the broadcast," she said as she started to tear up. "I guess with all the media at the mine, Bob didn't want them getting tangled up in all of that.

"The explosion happened right after the broadcast of him being rescued and it was so powerful it blew out my bathroom window."

In a shaky voice she continued, "It's so sad and unbelievable. Bob is a great guy. We've known him since he started dating Kristen about five years ago. He lost his own parents a couple of years earlier so the Samuels were like his only family and we saw him and Kristen over there often.

"Can you imagine, he's stuck down there for over a month and just when he is rescued he loses everyone important to him in the world? It's just so unbelievable. The poor man," she said as tears started to flow.

The camera focused in on Bruce, "There you have it Ashleigh, a totally bizarre twist to what only a few hours ago was such a happy story of rescue and survival but now has turned into an unthinkable tragedy. Bob Glass's future in-laws and his fiancée, apparently taken on the very day and the very hour he is rescued. As you know, his whereabouts are unknown at this time but this must come as a terrible shock for the poor man who's had to deal with so much in the last month."

As the shot came back to the studio, Ashleigh was seen to be staring into her monitor and for a moment, speechless. Finally in a pleading voice she looked into the camera and said, "Ladies and gentlemen, as Bruce Donald reports, truly a bizarre twist to what was such a wonderful story only a few hours ago! Our hearts go out to that poor, poor man wherever he is. We'll keep you posted as we find out more information."

Eric Lawrence's body had been recovered and a coroner with appropriate jurisdiction quickly pronounced the cause of death as accidental with the method being massive internal injuries from blunt force trauma presumably from a mine cave-in. The partially decomposed remains were swiftly cremated at the wishes of the family in nearby Wallace.

The family had known for over three weeks that Eric was the one who didn't survive, so it wasn't hard for the new mine owner's emissary to convince them that the remains were in no state for viewing. Further, he reported, that according to the coroner there was no evidence of any foul play, but that wouldn't stop challenges to his death certificate from the media, trying to stir up and drag out a newsworthy story. That would be followed by court motions to take possession of, or exhume the remains if the family didn't put a stop to the tabloid news teams' outrageous conspiracy theories that were inevitable in a case like this. Therefore, he argued, swift cremation was the best path for the family.

They were happy to approve the cremation and to accept the $3M settlement for their pain and suffering and the fully paid, elaborate and private 'life celebration' memorial service when the time was right.

***

When Bob Glass arrived at the Hawk Hotel in Vegas he was given his own wing of the massive penthouse, a more elaborate selection of excellent clothes to choose from and a large private buffet with some of his favorite food which curiously he left untouched. Thirty minutes after his arrival he was invited into the main sitting room of the penthouse to meet with the tycoon himself, Fraser Carmichael.

Word hadn't yet reached the penthouse in Vegas about the explosion and fire that had taken Glass's loved ones.

Carmichael, looking all the part of the billionaire mogul with his entourage in tow, was slouched by himself on a beautiful cream colored leather couch, feet up on the designer coffee table in front of him, and a large cigar in his mouth. He looked fit and wore what Forbes called his favorite billionaire's uniform; hand-made designer jeans, cream colored Oxford button-down shirt with a custom tall collar but sans his trademark bow tie, an exquisite dark blue blazer with twenty-four carat gold buttons, beige blended cashmere and silk socks and highly polished Santoni Italian loafers.

"Well Mr. Glass you look much better now than you did in that video I was shown of your recovery from that dark hole in the ground. I'll bet your first shower felt good."

Glass, standing in the open doorway to his wing of the penthouse, offered only a slight smile at the barb as he looked around the room. Carmichael had three of his closest associates with him and one, because of his build, posture and stance, was clearly security.

"Mr. Carmichael I'm afraid there is something we need to discuss in complete privacy. I must ask you to clear the room."

The man's shocking level of confidence and poise caught Carmichael off guard. He blushed a little under the smoke of his cigar as he sized up the rather slight twenty-something standing in the doorway. He wasn't used to being spoken to in this way especially from what he considered to be a well-educated grunt that he had just rescued from death.

This guy appeared to be much more put together and confident than the trapped, skittish mine inspector he had been expecting. His first thought was that this must be something to do with keeping everything secret until the signing or maybe even an attempt at renegotiating the deal. He had had a month to investigate the 'discoveries' and possibly figure out their real worth. Whatever the plan, Carmichael still needed his cooperation and his silence. Glass's threat had been to give the whole thing to another billionaire like Trump but Carmichael now owned the mine. His backup threat was to spill the beans to the feds and he was still capable of doing just that. Fraser Carmichael did not like being 'handled' like this.

He bristled as he said, "I'm afraid that the board of directors of my company would insist that I keep my head of security with me."

"Mr. Carmichael with all due respect, your board does what you tell them and not the other way around. I assure you there is no threat to you here and I promise it will be well worth your while. But I must insist on total privacy before we can proceed."

Carmichael felt cornered. He now had access to the mine but he needed this guy's silence and he couldn't risk involving the feds. This Glass kid sure was pushing his buttons and within seconds he seemed to have achieved the upper hand in negotiations. He was starting to dislike this brazen young guy.

After a long moment staring at the impertinent miner and taking another puff of his cigar he nodded to his entourage. Frank Jorgen, his head of security, started to protest but Carmichael waved him off.

As the door closed behind them, Glass took out of his pocket what looked like a small polished brown stone and held it between his thumb and index finger. He moved slowly and sat across the coffee table from Carmichael on an opposing couch as he put the stone away.

Carmichael spoke first, "So now you have me alone. What is this? I have your contract right here. I hope this isn't an attempt to renegotiate? If you know anything about me, I don't renegotiate deals once they're made."

"You may want to change your mind on that point, but we'll get to that," said the now smiling Glass.

"Am I right in surmising that the story I told you a few weeks ago struck you initially as rather fantastic and unbelievable?"

Carmichael smelled a rat. Was he about to hear that he had been conned; there was no such room with robots and computers? Had it had all been a trick by Glass to get rescued faster?

Red-faced, all he could think to say was "Go on."

"Well the story I'm about to tell you is more fantastic than you can imagine, nevertheless true."

Carmichael just sat there staring at this miner who seemed to speak in riddles. He wished the man would just get to the point.

Glass continued, "Let's start with introducing ourselves. I know who you are but you don't know who I am. For the moment let's start with … I'm not Bob Glass."

Carmichael's mind was racing. More riddles. He thought 'Had there been a swap at some point since the mine or was Glass dead and was this the other miner, what was his name again … Eric Lawrence? No, he had seen their photos and this was Glass. What the hell was going on?'

Carmichael was starting to really turn red as he said "I'm afraid I'm not following you. What do you mean you're not Bob Glass?"

"Hold on to your seat Mr. Carmichael. I have actually 'fantasized' about this moment for longer than you can imagine. I will try to make this as painless as possible," he smiled.

"I'm actually one of the beings who created the room that Mr. Glass and Mr. Lawrence were allowed to discover. For the moment you can continue to refer to me as Bob Glass. There is no translation or even pronunciation of my real name that you could manage."

Suddenly Carmichael was REALLY alert. The hairs on his arms were standing at attention and his heart was instantly racing as he stared intently at the guy sitting across from him. This 'thing' had just said he was an ALIEN! Suddenly he realized his mouth was very dry and he thought he was going to be sick. Now he wished he had kept Jorgen in the room.

But then his mind went to the possibility of other explanations, 'This guy looks human and he even looks like the pictures they had on TV of Bob Glass. What's going on here? Is this guy schizophrenic? Should I yell for Frank Jorgen to get back in the room?'

Glass or whoever he was, was still talking, "Not to fear, Mr. Glass is safe as are his loved ones. You'll be hearing soon that his fiancée and her parents were killed in a house fire but I assure you they are safe. Part of my deal with Mr. Glass.

"Sadly the same isn't true for Mr. Lawrence. He left us no opportunity to save him. I'm afraid our introduction in the mine didn't go completely as planned. We hadn't counted on the frightened and impulsive Mr. Lawrence."

He paused to let the news take its full effect on the stunned billionaire facing him.

Finally Carmichael, heart pounding as he wondered if this was at all real, spoke. "Why should I believe any of this?"

Glass simply smiled and sat up forward, "Yes, excellent point.

There's no point in proceeding if there's any doubt in your mind."

He took out the shiny brown stone and seemed to rub it between his fingers again.

It took a few moments for Carmichael to realize what had happened then suddenly he became aware that his whole body was paralyzed and his breathing was somehow not his own. His eyes could move but nothing else.

Glass simply stared at him, "Don't be alarmed, you're in no danger. I've just put your mind into a state you're not familiar with. Let's leave it that way for a few minutes while I bring you up to speed on some things. I don't need you sounding an alarm until you've heard what I have to say. Any alarm on your part would sadly put your colleagues in grave jeopardy. Just relax, you'll be fine. I think today will turn out to be a good one for you. I will release you in a few minutes but I hope this little demonstration has served to convince you of my statements so far."

Glass leaned further forward and took the cigar out of Carmichael's hand and placed it in the ashtray.

"Now, for a quick education.

"I'm actually not an alien in the common sense of the word. I represent a species native to this planet, but as you might have gathered, much more advanced than humans. We were here a long time before you so let's call my species or civilization Alpha, the first species of several human-like cousins to you. We are your only surviving evolutionary cousin and the only one that achieved much higher evolutionary development than you.

"I will tell you much more about us but for the moment you need to know one thing. Of paramount importance to us is that we are not discovered by humans. While we have coexisted with you peacefully for a very long time, there is no question that humans would have great difficulty, and would not rest, if they realized an intelligent species was living below their feet. Sadly that puts us in a bit of a predicament now. We've recently found the need to communicate with you which of course jeopardizes our concealment. At this moment only you know of our existence, but that is about to change.

"We had hoped to restrict any special knowledge of the mine but unfortunately you've raised the interest of your country's security establishment with all your rather clumsy real estate and court

36

maneuverings. At this moment, based on a CIA tip, your Pentagon is launching a plan to take over the mine because they suspect you've discovered something that might be of interest to them. So any further investigation on their part needs to be stopped.

"Revealing ourselves to you was no accident. We have a much bigger problem that we'll get to, and we need your assistance and the cooperation of another member of your civilization. So, I must convince you and the man who controls your Pentagon, that would be your President, to participate in a plan to close down any investigations and keep the knowledge of our existence a secret and to assist us in a much more important and pressing matter.

"As we speak your team at the mine is having trouble with the rescue shaft which seems to have developed a serious kink in it, precluding anyone from descending. They will soon come to the conclusion that they will need to drill a second access shaft which will give us some time.

"The situation we Alphans find ourselves in was unexpected which is rare for us. Revealing myself to you puts us at great risk and even greater risk to you because I can assure you, if eliminating humans from this planet is what it takes to protect ourselves, we're fully capable of, and intent on doing just that.

"I see you're uncomfortable so I will release you. Please don't call out as it would complicate matters for both of us and put your associates in great peril. I need your cooperation but your colleagues are somewhat more dispensable."

Suddenly Carmichael was back to breathing normally on his own and he had full control of his limbs with no noticeable after effects. As he took his feet off the table and sat up straighter on the couch, his first instinct was to cry out for help or run for the door but something told him that this 'thing' was serious and neither of those options would work. Now that control of his body had been returned to him, serious sweat broke out on his brow.

The cigar continued to burn in the ashtray and he had no desire to do anything with it. He was totally focused on the 'thing' sitting across from him which for all the world, simply seemed like the young mine inspector he claimed he was pretending to be.

Glass continued, "Now I'm sure you have a thousand questions and I expect I will be able to answer most of them without putting both of us in deeper jeopardy, but that would be redundant in that I will have to do it all again for your President. So our first order of business is for you to make an appointment for us to meet the man as soon as possible ... as in today.

"For a man of your stature, that shouldn't be difficult. I understand you two aren't friendly and I won't tell you what to say exactly but you might want to indicate to him that you're aware that the Pentagon, who have been listening in on some of your plans, has briefed him and are about to move on the mine site. Now you see why I asked you not to divulge details of the room in the mine to your colleagues. Wider knowledge of that computer room would be very problematic in terms of humans investigating and finding evidence of my civilization. Thankfully all Washington knows is that there is some discovery that has moved you to take extreme measures to control the mine.

"When you call the President I would let him know that you have Mr. Bob Glass with you and he has a rather amazing story to tell that will appease the interests of the Pentagon. He can also do a photo-op with the rescued miner. As I mentioned, he has been briefed that I've discovered something amazing and his interest level should be high. A photo-op with a rescued miner, that the press cannot find, should also act as a significant draw."

Carmichael hesitated. He felt like he was learning to breathe all over again and was terrified of this 'thing' sitting across from him. He finally found his words, "Is this really necessary? If I believe what you've told me then this will certainly complicate your contact with us. If you want to remain hidden, he may not be the best person to involve. He is the most heavily protected and monitored man on the planet.

"And besides it is not only that we are not friends, I actually detest the man and the feeling is probably mutual. I doubt if I could even get in to see him."

Bob Glass smiled, "I have confidence you'll get us in and leave the security and surveillance issues to me."

Carmichael could see there was no way out of this. Somewhere deep inside he thought it was a very bad idea to take such a powerful entity, alien or otherwise, right into the White House but what choice did he have, apparently they had already killed one human and that paralyzing trick had really terrified him.

His heart was still racing from the encounter with this 'thing' but the capitalist in him was tortured by the fact that he was pretty sure he had now lost control of the windfall he had hoped to see from the 'discovery', if any of that had ever been true. Apparently the Pentagon had been listening in and would swoop in to take over and more importantly, this Bob Glass 'thing' was now calling the shots.

The alien had seemed to indicate that all would work out to his satisfaction and seeing he had no choice in the matter he decided to cooperate, at least for the moment. All this time he was wondering how he could regain the high ground and take control of this situation as he was unaccustomed to finding himself in such an inferior position.

He wasn't looking forward to calling Hal Turcot if he could even get through to him. It was likely the White House receptionists had a list of 'enemies' and his name would be near the top.

The White House

Above all, Fraser Carmichael was a born salesman and after sweet talking his way through to the Oval Office, President Hal Turcot was intrigued by the teasing call and the meeting was set up for that evening to give them time to get to DC.

Turcot's dislike for Carmichael was substantial and he knew the feeling was mutual but he did want to find out why the billionaire was so fixated on that mine the Pentagon was watching. He had to agree that a photo-op with the miner the press couldn't find was a great opportunity to get some exclusive and positive air time.

It was a rare quiet evening for the President so he had no trouble slipping them into the schedule but still spending even part of his free night with someone like Fraser Carmichael had him scratching his head. He'd have to be on his guard, anything controversial would be in the press the next day. It was generally not a good idea to have a face-to-face meeting with someone so famously negative on his Administration, but he was suddenly feeling both brave and curious.

Carmichael was a big supporter of the most conservative wing of the Republican Party and he hadn't been kind to the President in interviews, labeling him in the press during the last election as the 'Lamest of Liberals'.

The President knew the intelligence guys had been listening in on some of the calls but apparently they had gotten in too late to have any meaningful intel on what Carmichael was up to with the mine. None of them could fathom what his interest was in a very deep mine that had recently collapsed. All they knew was that it must be big. Carmichael had even refused to confide in his own execs, had them under surveillance and had imposed very punitive, ironclad non-disclosures on them, and he had gone to extreme measures to hide his moves and secure the site.

Given his history, it was likely to have something to do with technology but the CIA and the Pentagon had no idea what could be discovered at the bottom of a very old and deep silver mine. If it was gold or diamonds or some other rare find then the previous owners of the mine probably had a strong civil case against the mine inspector or the government department that managed him if he had discovered something and disclosed it only to Carmichael. But then again, knowing Carmichael he had likely offered the previous owners a deal they couldn't refuse for an 'as is' mine and being in dire financial condition after the mine collapse they might have been compelled to take the deal. There would be a clause in the closing documents that had them signing over all rights and recourse. The intel guys had concluded it had to be more than the obvious find to get Carmichael excited. Unfortunately they still couldn't even hazard a guess as to what it might be.

***

As Glass had suggested, the flight which included Carmichael's three VPs, was a quiet one with no discussion between Glass and the others. All were aware of the awkwardness of the relationship given their boss's level of tension and they all wondered what had gone on in that room at the Hawk that sparked a trip to Washington to what they suspected might even be the Oval Office.

There was no discussion as to whether the contract had been signed with Glass but it was apparent they were not going to hear of the amazing discovery tonight. They took the boss's direction and didn't ask questions.

They landed at Reagan International where the two principals disembarked, with the rest of Carmichael's team continuing on in the corporate jet back to New York.

Again Frank Jorgen, Carmichael's head of security protested but he was waved off again and now the billionaire was all alone in Washington with this unknown quantity, Robert Glass. For Jorgen this was beyond unusual and dangerous. Carmichael was a key target for kidnapping or assassination. This would certainly come up at the next board meeting where they were all desperate to protect their moneymaker-in-chief. The fact that they carried a $100M Key Man insurance policy on him would be of little comfort if anything happened. Carmichael Industries was worth a lot more than that and it was all tied to Fraser Carmichael's celebrated leadership. The stock would completely tank if the magic man himself wasn't at the helm.

A rented, armored limo was waiting to take Fraser and his guest to the White House. They were both whisked through White House security who had been advised of their appointment, and after a short wait and Secret Service screening, they were ushered into the President's office by Gerry Hastings, the President's Chief-of-Staff.

It was now just before eight p.m. in DC.

After greetings and the President congratulating Glass on his amazing escape from the mine, they had the White House photographer get several pictures of them in front of the President's desk shaking hands. As the photographer left, Glass took the lead, "I'm afraid Mr. President that this discussion we're about to have must be the three of us only."

The President's first thought was 'This guy has balls. He's in the Oval Office and telling me what to do and what is he, a simple mine inspector?'

Yet Glass's voice was strong and confident stunning the President by what seemed almost more of a demand than a request. Both visitors had been vetted and searched by the Secret Service, Glass's picture had been all over the news so any assassination plot would likely not start by trapping yourself in a mine for five weeks. So there was little question of security, yet he had never had his Chief-of-Staff chased from a meeting before nor been told what to do in the Oval Office by a total stranger.

The President was looking for an ally and the only one there was a political enemy, "This is highly unusual. Is this entirely necessary Fraser?"

Fraser Carmichael nodded and the President could see by his face that there were no options here. Carmichael tried to reassure him, "Mr. President with all due respect to your staff, I think you're going to want to hear what Mr. Glass here has to say and I concur that in this special circumstance it needs to be in total privacy … for now," he added to soften the blow.

The President thought that Carmichael looked exceptionally tense. The discovery in the mine must be big and something very important for a man of Fraser Carmichael's famed bluster to be cowed and relatively speechless. The other man, Bob Glass seemed unusually relaxed and confident even though they all knew that he was simply a civil engineer from a silver mine in Idaho meeting the President of the most powerful nation on Earth. But still there was this tease that the Pentagon claimed Glass had discovered something really big at the bottom of that mine and Carmichael had gone to significant expense to lock up the discovery. It was starting to look like the President was going to have to play along if he wanted to be let in on the 'secret'.

Before Turcot could say anything, Hastings could see what was coming and said, "Actually Mr. President, I'm pretty busy at the moment so I'll be right next door in my office if you need me."

Still curious about the tension he saw in Carmichael and against his better judgment, Hal Turcot nodded letting Hastings go.

As Hastings closed the door Glass looked around and then at both men and instantly they were both frozen in their standing position with only their eyes left to roam the room.

Carmichael was first to notice and thought, 'Shit! I should have seen that coming.'

The President's heart rate leapt or at least he thought it did as the sense that he no longer controlled his body washed over him.

In a soothing voice Glass said, "Please don't be alarmed Mr. President, you're in no danger. Mr. Carmichael experienced this state a few hours ago and as you can see it has done him no harm. You're simply in a mental state you are unfamiliar with. Most of your body's muscular system is paralyzed except your respiratory system which I control but you're in no danger I assure you. Just relax."

Looking around casually Glass continued, "You have three recording systems in this room. I have disabled the audio on them and I will provide plausible video for your protection detail if need be."

Turcot's heart and his brain were racing. His first thought was this must be hypnosis of some sort.

Glass looked back at Carmichael who seemed to be staring at Glass's hands, "Yes, you noticed that the Secret Service took my small device but as you can see I don't need it to operate. It simply makes life a little easier. I've frozen you again just as a precaution."

Hal Turcot wasn't only shocked, he was kicking himself for allowing these two to get him alone. Why had he done that? It was the first rule he had been taught by the Secret Service, never be caught alone with someone you were not completely familiar with.

He could feel the surplus of adrenalin pumping through his body and he wondered if a heart attack was next.

His next thought was, 'I'm not breathing on my own but I feel OK. How can that be possible?'

He stared back at Glass and then thought, 'Three recording systems? I only knew of two.' His mind was racing and jumping all over the place, 'Provide plausible video? What the hell did that mean?'

Here he was the President of the United States, the most powerful man on the planet and yet completely at the mercy of this … this what? What was this guy? Who was he and what was going on? He had never felt so helpless in his whole life. He looked down as much as he could at his body and realized he had absolutely no control over it.

Glass could see the President was panicking, "Just relax Mr. President. You'll get used to the sensation quickly. You've nothing to fear. I bear no malice towards you. I simply froze you so that we can have a private moment without you setting off any alarms because what I'm about to tell you will appear to you to be rather alarming in itself. I suspect however, when this is over you'll be satisfied that I am an important ally and not a threat. You'll soon see why I asked for this audience and I must insist that anything you hear in this room remain forever among only the three of us. The lives of many people depend on it, especially those close to you and believe me sir when I say that I am very serious. You need to take what I say as the complete truth. I have no need or wish to lie or exaggerate."

Glass turned and walked around the President's desk and sat in his chair just to add some authority to the proceedings. He had skillfully arranged their placement in the room after the photo session so that both men while frozen were still facing him as he took the President's chair. He had read most of the books and seen all of the movies featuring this office and knew what that chair meant to American politicians.

Certainly there would be cameras inside and outside in the garden that would pick this up but it was very likely the President had let the odd visitor try out his seat.

"As you may have surmised, I'm not Mr. Glass but you can refer to me by that name. I essentially took Bob Glass's place in the mine on the second day of his being trapped. Your vocal cords and mouth structure could not pronounce my real name so for now, Bob Glass it is.

"It will come as no surprise to you that we are not humans. We found it necessary to expose ourselves to you at this juncture for reasons I will get into presently, so we set up an 'encounter' in the mine and staged the collapse. To fill in some gaps in events for you, I called Mr. Carmichael from the mine acting as Robert Glass and made a deal with him. I told him we had discovered an alien computer room at twelve thousand feet with amazing technology that he alone would be allowed to exploit in return for some significant compensation. That call, promising untold riches, set up my meeting with Mr. Carmichael and subsequently this visit. I needed all three of us in one room and voila.

"Mr. Lawrence sadly is no longer with us as his reaction to our presence was precipitous. He tried to attack one of our helpers which simply defended itself. Our helpers are what you might refer to as robots. You'll find out that we have what you will think of as amazing technology that we're willing to share with certain stipulations. But I'm getting ahead of myself.

"Let's start with a quick education.

"I'm actually one of an older species than yours and native to this planet so you should not think of us as aliens but more like biological cousins. Our species branched off via normal evolutionary mechanisms from a common ancestor nearly two million years ago just as any other species is created by evolution. So we have a common biological heritage starting at what you call Homo Erectus and we shared much of the same DNA. Actually our active DNA was more than ninety-nine percent identical to yours before we started manipulating it, cleaning it out of the eighty percent of dormant or potentially harmful genes, and then finally just disposing of the whole idea of DNA, but we'll get to that later.

"Comparing our species to yours, early on we had some important DNA advantages. More than a million years ago we were already bigger, stronger, had much larger brains and a much longer life span than you, even in your current state of evolution. We developed quickly and at that point in time technologically we were not too far ahead of where you are today, give or take a thousand years. So as of today in terms of development, we're a little more than a million years more evolved than you. But given we no longer have physical bodies, evolution may not be the proper term.

"We essentially ruled the surface of this planet, as you do now, well before you had discovered that living in caves was a good idea. Your direct ancestors at the time were a species, rather small in numbers as were we, and you were very limited in geography to what you call Africa, so there was minimal contact between our two civilizations. We saw you as no threat or of any use to us and of course you had no communication skills to pass on any knowledge of our previous existence. Unlike humans' treatment of today's primates, we pretty much left your species alone to develop. Our civilization has always been very respectful of life in all its forms.

"As I said previously to Mr. Carmichael, we were here first, so I suggest you think of our world as Alpha, and us as Alphans, a formerly close biological cousin. In those terms you might consider me as Alpha-1 as I've been assigned to deal with you."

Both the President and Carmichael nervously picked up on the 'deal with you' phrasing.

"As Mr. Carmichael already knows from our first phone call, as a species we were on average quite a bit taller than you. We were also less hairy and had a larger cranium. Still there were significant resemblances to man of today in terms of general body shape. After all we do share a common ancestor.

"In terms of our development, there came a point when our bodies became a significant limiting factor. A two hundred and fifty year lifespan for a creature with such a large brain and ability to learn and enjoy life was simply far too constraining. So our attention moved first to extending life through medical means, manipulating DNA and later to replacing bodily systems with electromechanical ones, then a version of cloning and finally to virtual immortality through disposing of our native bodies completely.

"We now live an exclusively electrical existence in a virtual world inside what you would think of as a network with many levels of redundancy and hidden from you, as our main physical facilities are far underground.

"Actually, in the end this wasn't a very complex calculus. All we had to do was determine how the brain worked, how memory was managed, where consciousness lived and what made up personality or what you think of as the mind or the psyche. Some of your people call it the soul. Then all we had to do was transfer that psyche into a suitable electronic 'life support' environment.

"To make it simple for you to understand in computer parlance, some of the mind is stored information such as memories, and other parts of the mind are processes or programs such as decision-making, feelings, personality and most importantly the subconscious. It turns out that feelings such as fear or love are actually processes associated with the subconscious and not stored memories or preferences. That's why many of your doctors think of them as primal artifacts like instincts. So love really is mysterious, at least to you in your present state of development. It's actually a fairly complicated process associated with your subconscious. That explains why you are often not conscious of why you love one person and not another. And contrary to what many humans think, knowing in detail how love works does not destroy it or diminish its value. One of your contemporaries noted recently that knowing the components and processes of producing chocolate does not make it any less delicious.

"As your scientists are now aware, thoughts and emotions are all electrochemical processes built up by evolution to what seems to be a very complex level. The micro-mechanisms themselves are quite simple but just like your computers that are all built with 1's and 0's and a very few basic instructions, the mind is made up of simple parts. There are just a very large number of simple parts built on top of each other and interlinked, a bit like what you call software or indeed like DNA itself; simple at the elemental level but amazingly complex and seemingly magical at the macro level. Your scientists aren't too far away from discovering some of these things about the brain and the mind too.

"The idea that consciousness is simply an illusion, the perceived serial narrative of the brain's underlying parallelism, that some of your scientists and philosophers such as Daniel Dennett have proposed is actually not too far from the truth.

"There is an old saying in our culture which actually exists in your culture too. You would know it as, 'Everything is mysterious until you understand it.' Once we understood consciousness and how the actual psyche worked, it all seemed so obvious. Again, knowing how it works does not take away from the magic of seeing it in action, of say knowing or loving another person.

"So, to make a long story short, a long time ago we figured out that particular equation and were able to transfer our entire psyche into a highly reliable and failsafe computational device, or actually a very powerful network.

"Cloning had arrived about the same time so all we had to do at first was clone ourselves and reload our psyche and bingo we had another body and another life to live.

"That wasn't long-lived. Cloning was only a stepping stone and had many obstacles like the age/psyche synchronization of the cloned body, two physical copies of a body, terminating one of them and other sticky issues. In addition, we came to understand that biological bodies are much too fragile and ineffective as ideal vessels for an intelligent being. The physical brain size is very limited even with extensive genetic engineering. But beyond that and much more important, is that a body needs to be kept healthy in so many ways. It consumes amazing amounts of resources and it's always one step away from any number of biological or physical injuries or worse.

"It also wastes about a third of its time recuperating or sleeping. There are many other limiting factors but I think you get the picture. Bodies grew and served us well through evolution but eventually the mind outgrew the body and needed a much larger, safer, more efficient and sustainable home.

"When we finally cracked the key formula for the process piece, not only could we capture and transfer the psyche, we were eventually able to emulate it for every individual in their own personal emulator. That emulator was the missing link. You would probably think of it as a personalized thought engine. We needed the ability or programming to emulate our entire conscious, subconscious and decision-making abilities, and do it individually for everyone in our civilization.

"A customized and redundant personal emulator where you can load in your own psyche and bingo you have a new immortal existence that is many times bigger, richer, more satisfying and unlimited in almost every aspect. When I say immortal that is a stretch but to clarify, we haven't lost one of our original members since we made the transition over a million years ago. Now you know my approximate age, but as you might imagine, age is a foreign concept to us now. We Alphans are relatively all the same age and in a practical sense we can't grow old."

Both men were visibly shocked at the story they were being fed. This 'thing' had just said it was over a million years old. The two of them tried to grasp that concept. What could you have experienced and learned in over a million years?

Alpha-1 was still talking, "Now that our memories, consciousness and personality could all be executed inside a much more effective electrical vessel we quickly grew tired of having a body and gradually our whole civilization dumped the cloning stage and opted for the virtual solution. The driving force was immortality or rather the fear that some catastrophe would befall our physical body. Besides, virtual life does not have to deal with aches, pains, limits on strength etc. So after a few pioneers fully tested the virtual life and reported back on it, we tweaked the emulation part of the mechanism and it wasn't long before everyone wanted in.

"Today our entire species lives in a world that is real, virtual and imaginary all at the same time. For our civilization to thrive, our culture to advance, and our society to grow we live mostly in our virtual world where we see each other in whatever form we want to take, and we communicate with each other with our emulated and highly sensitive virtual senses.

"For the 'real' or physical world, our many senses as well as our arms and legs are provided by our networked helpers, which also do any physical work that is needed. We can actually occupy one of our helpers to get up close and personal to the real world. These machines are just like friends or helpers to us but they have no self-awareness. When we occupy one of them, we can see, hear, touch and smell with their advanced senses. We do that when we personally need or want to interact with the physical world, which it turns out is rather infrequent. Generally the helpers handle all of the required physical interaction with the real world.

"Of course they are equipped with many additional sensors such as radar, echolocation, eyes beyond what birds have that see all wavelengths, such as infrared, UV, etc. So we have more and much better senses than we had when we occupied biological bodies. But even these very capable machines have physical limitations that we do not have in our virtual or fantasy world. Limits on strength and the restrictions of gravity and time come to mind," he smiled.

"But the big payoff for many of our people is the imaginary or fantasy world. Because we live in a thought engine, we can create any imaginary environment or situation we desire in the privacy of our own minds and experience it with the same intense emulated senses that our virtual and real world offer. All of this is at a heightened sensual level to what our original bodies could offer. Our senses are much more vivid than before. Imagine much greater capabilities and fidelity in sight, hearing, smell, and touch, to name only a few.

"To get back on topic, without bodies our lives are truly constrained only by our imagination. We can be anywhere, do anything, make love to anyone, taste anything, and live a life that is impossible given the constraints of our old bodies and the physical laws of the natural world.

"We each have created our own fantasy world and we have endless time to enjoy it, and of course we architected this system to have every failsafe protective strategy required to make sure nothing ever disturbs it.

"Now we have time to study all information available to our civilization. When humans became more developed we had a new field to explore. As a species you have made some very notable progress in the last few hundred years. It has been fun to watch it all.

"As an aside, I was present, although cloaked, at the Wright brothers' first flight. We can't tell the future but my American studies tipped me off that someone was getting close to flight and I just happened to focus on the right team.

"Most of us have followed humans to some degree and speak all of your languages, even a few ancient or obscure ones. Because we have been around so long we didn't need the Rosetta Stone to understand Egyptian hieroglyphics, and yes I can easily read the infamous Voynich manuscript.

"Essentially we can observe anything our satellites can snoop on and your recent installation of your own satellites and then your internet made it even easier to follow you.

"Remember because we have universal technology emulating our psyches in our thought engine, we all have the same IQ and it is much higher than humans'. We also have unlimited persistent memory so we're unable to unintentionally forget anything. We have perfect recall of any experience we've had, unless of course we choose to delete a memory and then instantly it's gone and it never happened in our private space. Intentionally forgetting is also a rare activity.

"We have our own memories both private and shared to whatever degree we wish. Over the years we have improved on the basic technology and so we can experience life at a very high pace.

"I know this is somewhat long-winded, but I should tell you that there is a purpose for this primer on Alpha as you will soon see.

"To continue, one major deficiency of our own DNA was that reproduction was often not successful and new births were barely enough to maintain our population. If it hadn't been for our long life span we may have become extinct at one point.

"By the time we had the ability to fix that DNA issue we had decided that we didn't want it fixed, especially if we were going to be immortal. Some optimum size for our civilization was ideal and as we moved to a virtual and immortal existence our reproduction went to zero. So for over a million years we have had no children. We do have a clear sense of children from memory and from watching you.

"So why have you never found any evidence of us? Let's start with 'that was the plan!'

"By the time we had started moving into what you would call silicon, we had built a rather large infrastructure on the surface of the planet, although I will say we were never large in numbers compared to humans of today. At the risk of insulting you, our higher IQ tipped us off much earlier in our development to the stewardship of the planet. Even though we had significant infrastructure, it was nothing like what you have done to our planet you call Earth.

"Still we had a sizable footprint on the planet and off planet too. We still have a large satellite network that, due to our cloaking, is invisible to your technologies, but it has allowed us to snoop, as you might say, on humans as they developed.

"Our outbound space program was essentially a bust. Before we achieved immortality, we investigated the entire solar system and had a few colonies on suitable moons and planets but none of them offered any special advantages and no one wanted to expand on it, so for security reasons we closed it all down and wiped away any evidence of our exploration and returned to this planet. At some point we know we will have to migrate to another celestial body where running into other life forms such as you will be much less likely. But now that we're network bound and the physical world is unimportant to us, we can move wherever and whenever we want.

"You are very close to a sustainability crisis on this planet with your total consumption of many natural resources and your destruction of the atmosphere. Our smaller numbers never encountered these issues but we did forecast eventual risks, so finding a way to build a much more sustainable existence was part of our drive for the immortal world.

"As you might surmise your excesses have little effect on Alpha. Our current requirements to sustain ourselves are very modest. Our manufactured products are highly specialized and self-maintaining for the most part. Helpers fix themselves and anything else we need, and they do a great job. We occasionally need raw materials for our helpers to manufacture components but the only real issue is electrical energy to support our ongoing existence and we have many redundant solutions for that resource. As a result, living inside an electrical 'appliance', we consume very little by way of resources for an entire civilization, which was a key component of the plan.

"Additionally if we were ever threatened by anything we could move easily. We could simply 'mail' our civilization to a new location once our helpers had gotten there first to build a suitably secure environment.

"We were never capable of moving outside of the solar system for the same basic reason you have not. We haven't defeated the speed of light barrier, although we have evidence it is possible."

Hal Turcot was only half listening but not sure he wanted to believe any of this. His mind was still preoccupied with the positon he found himself in and the intentions of this 'invader'.

Alpha-1 continued, "But with our new immortality there were two real threats we had to deal with. Once we had no bodies and were somewhat locked into an electrical existence, we were limited to the helpers to protect and defend us. We had concerns that if we were immortal, eventually, even if it took millions of years, aliens might arrive and we would have potential problems. We could build up our defenses in advance but what kind of defenses, and to defend against what kind of threat?

"Secondly we knew it was only a matter of time before some animal on Earth, likely a cousin of ours like you, would reach a level of complexity in the brain that they would dominate the surface of the planet and come into competition with us or at least discover our existence and likely see us as a threat.

"And just as predicted, voila, here you are. So we're now at a point or close to a point where we have to deal with humans. I will soon tell you why we have picked this moment to introduce ourselves.

"You're starting to look a little uncomfortable standing there. I assure you I can stop all your body's functions as easily as I've paralyzed you and I can do that to the whole human race if need be. In addition my psyche is stored so I can't be killed and I have lethal perimeter defenses around this body. So here is a warning, don't make any sudden moves toward me or anything that could be seen as threatening or my reflexive defense systems will stop you permanently. That was Mr. Lawrence's mistake with one of our helpers and their defensive systems aren't as advanced as the ones I possess.

"So I will release both of you if you'll quietly take your seats and hear the rest of the story. As you might have surmised, there will be an offer you can't refuse at the end of my tale."

Neither liked the 'can't refuse' jargon but both men seemed to indicate acceptance with their eyes and were instantly released, breathing normally with no negative effects. Carmichael moved immediately but Turcot hesitated and then somewhat reluctantly took a seat on one of the couches in front of the President's desk.

All the while the President had been thinking, 'How do I KILL this THING?'

Alpha-1, waiting for them to settle, rose from the President's chair and circled to the front of his desk where he half sat on its edge and continued, "Now back to the abridged history of my civilization. You need to know and appreciate who we are if we are going to be trusted partners in a project I will soon outline.

"When we realized there would be an eventual threat of discovery from either aliens or surface-based intelligence we decided to give ourselves some protection or at least a buffer against discovery by moving relatively far underground and cloaking any surface activities. This would give us some warning and time to prepare. Looks like it worked for the last million years.

"By this point we didn't need food or water, only power to sustain ourselves. The surface was full of dangers as well. Radiation, the odd asteroid, fires, tsunamis, supernova radiation blasts, and some threats you aren't yet aware of. So even though we could build multiple redundant and cloaked networked facilities as repositories for our civilization, underground offered too many advantages to avoid discovery for an extended period. As I said, one day we will leave Earth as our primary home but as you might appreciate, we have something of an emotional attachment to this little planet.

"To ensure we were not discovered and hunted we had to clean up all signs of our existence on the surface. Helpers worked for many decades to achieve that goal. Eventually you would've had questions about some of our activities as we didn't do a perfect job of the cleanup. Certain areas such as the Grand Canyon, the Dead Sea, parts of the Great Lakes and some other areas were major sites of ours that had to be eliminated. You would eventually have figured out that your current explanations didn't explain everything and that some other force or forces had to be at play. So far that has not happened and the majority of your scientists are happy with the existing explanations. Explanations which in some cases we planted by various means.

"As to fossils, that was a non-issue. Our species had always cremated its dead and on top of that we had the technology to track down anything that had anything to do with our civilization to eliminate it. Besides, this was all a million years ago and the ravages of surface erosion and a few ice ages have smoothed over any hints that we were ever there.

"One other thing I should mention is this. When you have a finite number of people in your civilization that means a finite number of ideas, memories and the like to share and that can start to run short in immortality. So to replenish our thought reservoir and stimulate our creativity we have from time to time 'invited' a few outsiders to join us over the millennia.

"It's exciting to watch a human from say four thousand years ago be given an IQ of well over three hundred and watch him learn at incredible rates. Of course the shock to the psyche has to be managed carefully.

"To the extent that our guest will share with us, we get to experience his ideas, memories, skills, preferences, etc. Every new psyche brings new areas for us to explore and build on.

"As an example, accurate spear throwing became a real interest of mine some time ago when we had on-boarded an African hunter. It is unlikely our civilization will ever need spear throwers but it's a hobby that I really enjoy and I wouldn't be able to do it without the skill and muscle memory of that particular invited member. I dare say I may now be the greatest spear thrower this world has ever seen. Believe me I've had lots of practice. Some might say that for a period it was close to an obsession.

"Anyway, we didn't realize it at first but our brains were very similar to yours even though much more developed, so any human who joined us eventually fitted into the emulator well and became one of us.

"So here we are. Fate has thrust us together but I have the very important responsibility to ensure that humans do not discover us. Some of you would certainly see us as a threat and we wouldn't want to determine therefore that you were a danger to us and have to eliminate all of you. Our current thinking is that it would be disastrous to your species if humans knew of our existence. Someone in your billions of people would try to exploit the knowledge and we would be forced to eliminate them, most likely starting a cascading conflict.

"So for our sake and yours, my civilization must not be discovered by the rest of humanity. While Mr. Carmichael here has shared a cursory tale of discovery with a few people, at this moment you're the only two humans who know of our existence. Mr. Glass and his extended family have joined us and Mr. Lawrence is no longer with us.

"As I told Mr. Carmichael earlier, his people at the mine site have run into some obstacles so they have been unable to enter the mine. They are at least a month away from solving that problem on their most likely path. Our failsafe plan for the mine is to cloak the room we have down there but we want to stop further investigation to avoid complications.

"So while we have a bit of breathing room right now, you two are the only ones with the power to keep it secret by covering for what has occurred to date and making the decisions necessary to ensure the mine isn't explored. We'll get to how we do that later.

"As I hope you can now appreciate, our civilization must keep its anonymity. We can't inherit nearly eight billion new outsiders who will naturally want immediate immortality. A great deal of personal guidance is needed at the beginning and we don't have the numbers to achieve anything near that. To illustrate, what do you think would happen if you invited say four times your number of chimpanzees to join humans with say an instant IQ of a hundred. The results would be catastrophic. They wouldn't be able to handle it and you wouldn't be able to manage or police them. So before you make the inevitable demands, any ideas of the human race joining us any time soon is a nonstarter.

"At the current state of technological development, man will likely achieve immortality himself in the next few centuries and that will be your problem to deal with.

"Your first few people in the virtual world may feel like gods. You need to ensure that they don't act like gods, and not yet having a fully functional thought engine with a fantasy option, they may be tempted to do just that. It would be easy for them to outsmart the rest of humanity and use robots to enforce their will. As I said, we never had the numbers problems you'll have, but even then our earliest experiences with the move to immortality was not as smooth as we would have liked. Good luck with that.

"At the point where you discover immortality and will live long enough to discover us in some fashion, we will need to come up with additional accommodations to protect both our civilizations. I suspect we will have seen it coming and will have moved on by then. But for the moment we're comfortable on Mother Earth as you call it.

"Now there will be time for all your questions about our civilization and I will answer them up to a point. It is critical that we build some level of trust. I will not divulge anything that I think might endanger our civilization. But for the moment, do you have any questions?"

After a moment the President spoke, "What do you want with us?"

Alpha

"I'll get to that in a moment but it's important that you have a very good grasp on who we are, what our powers are, and are completely convinced of our abilities, motives, and sincerity in these matters. We are about to depart on a critical project together so the trust factor is fundamental. Any misunderstandings could be catastrophic for both of us. For the moment, let's stick to you getting a good understanding of your new neighbors. Ask away."

The President wasn't happy with the avoidance of the subject and that the dialogue was being driven completely by this 'thing'. His thoughts were full of contempt and finding a way to rid himself of this charlatan, or whatever it was, but for the moment all he could do was play along. Maybe Carmichael had swallowed the whole story, if he wasn't in on it himself, but Turcot was not yet buying any of this, although he still could not figure out how he had been frozen. Surely it was some kind of a trick. Vegas was full of these guys that could make you believe something that was not real.

Turcot tried again, "OK, so how did you freeze us?"

"I won't go into details but I have the ability to engage your brain waves. Actually I can intercept them and their functions at will, so it is just as easy to stop your heart, or for that matter all brain waves which would cause instant death. There is no effective range on this either. As long as I know of your existence and your particular brain pattern, you're within my reach. And please understand, you possess no technology to defend against this.

"I will not get into additional capabilities my civilization has, but the one I've just described isn't what I'd call one of our more advanced or what you might think of as exotic capabilities. A million years is a long time by anyone's yardstick, so many of our capabilities will certainly seem like magic to you. Remember we were much more advanced than you a million years ago, before we moved into an advanced thought emulator, so without trying to be insulting, think of the things you could impress a Neanderthal with.

"But again, threats should not be required here. We have a win-win proposal to discuss with you. Fighting us on this is definitely not the way you want to go and I'd urge you to put any such thoughts out of your mind immediately.

"Frankly my goal here tonight is to win your confidence. You'll find that we're a peace-loving civilization and harbor no animus towards humans. So please don't force my hand. Just like you, we will go to extreme lengths to protect our civilization. I don't wish to demonstrate any of those capabilities. One person has needlessly died in this enterprise so far and we don't want to add to that.

"Remember when this is all over we want to disappear underground again where we have peacefully coexisted with humans on this planet since your tribe learned to walk. So no matter what your first thoughts were, we are no threat to you. As long as you present no danger to us!"

Even with that not-so-veiled threat, Turcot had to admit to himself that after having stood there for about ten minutes completely frozen, some of this was actually starting to sound plausible. He still thought it more likely that this was some kind of trick possibly set up by Carmichael but what kind of trick was a complete puzzle. The explanation on how he could live without breathing by himself for that long would have to wait for another day. It was enough to know that this guy seemed to be able to do as he claimed.

Turcot thought he would try one more time, "You apparently have great technology. You said you'd be willing to share it with us?"

"Yes, but your civilization, and in particular your country, being the one remaining superpower, would appear to have a real appetite for exploiting any technological advance for military purposes. We would control that by threatening to share the same information with all your competitors in ways that wouldn't divulge our presence. So the stipulation is that you personally must guarantee that any technology we share with you will not be turned into advanced weapons and within five years all discoveries will be shared with the world. We will assist in this by tweaking the technologies so that it will be difficult to weaponize them. For instance, any robots left here could not be used to build new weapons with a single possible exception we'll discuss later. Our helpers are smart enough to know the difference. And to avoid questions, we will dumb down anything we give you so that it will seem like an incredible breakthrough, but still feasible in the 21st century.

"Of course if you break that promise we will disable the technologies we shared at a most inopportune moment. So it would be in your own best interests to stick to any deal we might agree to."

Carmichael was finally getting back his confidence. He had been in the presence of this 'alien' for longer and had been completely humbled by him. "I'd like to hear more about immortality and what this virtual world you've created is like."

"Good question. It is as close to your definition of the mythical heaven as is possible. Because everything you experience goes through the same psyche emulator, reality and imagination feel the same. You can have a real conversation with a real friend, or at times it may be desirable to have an imaginary conversation with an imaginary friend. They feel the same, but we can tell the difference when we need to. We had thought this might become difficult for some to manage, but given we have almost perfected the thought engine over millennia, mental disorders, anxiety, stress, obsessions, and any other mental ailments either don't exist or can easily be controlled.

"Our imaginations are much more vivid and we have the power to act on that imagination. Our processing power and the speed of our minds is vastly increased and remember we started from a higher average IQ than you have now, so the difference has been even more dramatic for our human inductees.

"On a different subject, I must say it is a challenge beyond anything I had imagined to occupy this body and more importantly, this feeble brain. This occupying a human body is completely new to us so we've never even bothered with the data to simulate it. I'm very anxious for this event to be over and get back to my own existence which now seems infinitely better than the life you humans must endure.

"But I digress, back to your question on our thought engine or psyche emulator. Some definitions or conventions will help. When you are on-boarded into what we are calling the 'thought emulator or engine', you are living in a virtual world which can emulate your current world but with all the advantages I have described. You can appear as you like and interact with all others in the Alpha virtual world our civilization has jointly created and live the life you wish. Much like the real world but with no regard to gravity, aches and pains, longevity, hunger, money, power or any other constraints of this world you are familiar with.

"When you occupy a helper we say you are in the 'real' world with the super senses I described, yet you will experience real world constraints like time, gravity, etc. And when you imagine or create a new world of your own we say you are in the 'fantasy' world.

"Some start with the fantasy that they are the best at whatever they choose to do and then go on to develop the skill in the virtual world. Remember, we have lots of time on our hands."

Carmichael was enthralled, but the President was only paying cursory attention. He was still preoccupied with the shock of this 'thing' actually being in his highly secure office.

Alpha-1 continued, "Possibly the most important feature we built in is that it can all be as private or public as we wish. We decide what to share with others.

"We can experience any situation we want, even ones that would be socially unacceptable, illegal in the real world, or of questionable virtue, all in the privacy of our own space. I think your imagination is developed enough to surmise what some of these activities might be. Everyone has some type of deviant thoughts or fetishes from time to time. Just like humans, we all have active imaginations. We can indulge our imaginations in private and it feels completely real. The thought engine has some safety features and does not allow deviant thoughts to accumulate to the point where it might tend to bend our psyche.

"On a more civil plane, we can taste the best foods ever. Climb the highest mountains. Become a daredevil in any sport, and we never sleep.

"We actually have a set of laws protecting our environment and our privacy that can only be overridden by a meeting of elected individuals who can authorize a very limited and targeted investigation if it is found to be necessary.

"Investigations of this type are uncommon and only used when there is suspected harm to others. We are a happy and respectful civilization, but in the case of a very rare guilty finding after an investigation, the result could be the individual having only limited access to our imaginary world for some period of time. Penalties are relatively minor compared to your world but so are infractions.

"If for instance you interfered with another Alphan's virtual world you may be restricted from interacting with that Alphan and their world for some period of time. Something like a restraining order but with absolute enforcement. That is rare, but again, that restriction is the most serious penalty you can pay in our world. Bad behavior is almost nonexistent. The only area of worry in that regard is of course new invitees until they are familiar with our environment and can restrict themselves to total enjoyment that does not impinge on others.

"When you can have everything you want and can keep matters private, issues like jealousy and envy don't exist. Obviously anyone who might attempt to interfere with our network, emulators or security systems would be prosecuted but that has never happened. Our early studies showed that there would be no motivation for such interference from within. So of course we would be careful when dealing with any outsiders. That's why I will only tell you some things about our civilization for the moment.

"As for me, I was essentially elected to lead this interaction with you because another hobby or skill set I've acquired, beyond American History, is Contemporary American Conversationalism. I watch a lot of your TV. I should sound in tone and phraseology like any other modern American. Mr. Glass's vocal cords help of course."

This had been something bothering Carmichael all day. Why did this alien seem so American?

"The discussion we're having here and now is of the public or shared type. Everything we say and discuss is open to our whole civilization and I can tell you that it has the attention of most Alphans and they are very interested.

"This is the first time of course that we've dealt with humans on this level. Heretofore it was one-on-one with invitations to join us. Now we're dealing with a species-to-species interaction with powerful members of your civilization which of course has potential dangers."

As the President tried to internalize that concept, Carmichael had another thought, "How did you replace Bob Glass?"

Alpha-1 nodded, "One of the helpers silently acquired some DNA from a vessel he used and we used a materialization device we have to recreate him or clone him. For reasons of credibility at introduction we wanted an exact copy of him. It helped when we explained what was going on.

"We used something like a 3D printer to create his clone but it is much more sophisticated. We then loaded my personality into it and I approached Mr. Glass on the second day of his confinement, the day after the unfortunate Mr. Lawrence had his encounter with one of our helpers. Needless to say this was shocking for him. He wasn't expecting another human down there, especially not a perfect copy of himself.

"I froze him quickly as I did you, so as not to allow him to go into cardiac arrest and over the period of a few hours made a deal with him to swap places. His technical background that you call engineering was of great assistance in his decision to be rational about our meeting and conversation. We had serious doubts about humans being too superstitious or prone to believing in magic, ghosts or spirits and 'freaking out' as you would say.

"Appearing as our target human was an approach we had never tried before. Usually when we have approached humans we have used avatars and taken our time to gain the person's confidence before we gradually explain the concept of joining Alpha.

"Unfortunately we are under some time constraints and a more direct approach to Mr. Glass, speeding up our processes, was required in this case."

Alpha-1 turned his attention directly to the President, "Mr. Carmichael also has a scientific background and accepted our interaction rather well as predicted in his hotel in Las Vegas, and I must say Mr. President, you've been a pleasant surprise too.

"Many of your countrymen remain very superstitious, and believing as they do in various myths about the supernatural, we had concerns such a person may not have survived the shock to their belief system, if you know what I mean. At least we would've had a much more difficult time convincing them of the reality of our civilization and calming them down, if indeed they did survive the initial encounter. As I say, you have been a pleasant surprise so far.

"Mr. Glass, his fiancée and her parents are now the latest outsiders to join our civilization and he wants me to inform you that they are enjoying it immensely. Mr. Glass of course negotiated with us, but his fiancée and her parents had to be kidnapped in a fashion, and brought to the realization of their situation with great care and the help of Mr. Glass himself.

"To use Mr. Glass as an example, while we were waiting for the rescue shaft to be drilled I was his mentor for integration, again because of my contemporary American knowledge. He has already achieved one lifelong goal and he wants me to tell you that he is a 'wicked jazz sax player', at least so far in his fantasy world.

"Taking a physical human form like this was heretofore unknown to us and Mr. Glass was gracious enough to share a part of his psyche which included muscle memory as I was having trouble walking. I have perfect muscle memory for my own body eons ago but no Alphan has ever occupied a human body until now. We had never seen the necessity of storing this data when we had on-boarded guests in the past."

He turned to Carmichael, "As I said earlier, I was actually the one who made the initial call to you Mr. Carmichael. We had come to the conclusion that approaching the President directly might be difficult without raising certain alarms so we knew we would need an intermediary with enough greed that they would limit exposure with the hope of massive financial gain from the technology bait. No insult intended."

Carmichael smiled and blushed knowingly.

"I chose to divulge quite a bit of information to you on that call to whet your appetite. I needed it to be a good and convincing story, still everything I told you on that call was true in terms of the technologies and the description of the former occupants."

This time it was Turcot who had a question. "How many of you are there?"

"Good question but not one that I am inclined to answer for you at this time. That will have to remain undisclosed for now."

The fact that this 'thing' seemed to answer only Carmichael's questions did nothing to convince him that this was not somehow a setup by Carmichael.

Fraser had another question, "If you have satellites, you need to maintain them or replace them no matter how good your manufacturing by robots has gotten. How do you get them up to the surface and launch them in a manner we haven't detected?"

"That is another good observation. Apart from satellites there are rare occasions when we must use the surface. The most common reason is to acquire rare raw materials that we can't create ourselves or can't find underground. We have pretty good control over what you know as the periodic table, but not complete control. We have the ability to change many elements into others, but not in all cases without expending an unacceptable amount of energy. So we need some hard-to-duplicate raw materials from time to time.

"When we do go to the surface we have egress points for our

helpers that are well disguised and we use cloaking technology to hide them or any activities we need to engage in on the surface. Suffice it to say that launch systems also fall under that description.

"Possibly one of our most developed technologies is cloaking. Due to the necessity of hiding from humans, especially in the last few thousand years, our cloaking technologies have made amazing strides and as you'll see later, they will be put to significant use."

Suddenly Alpha-1 looked pale and seemed uneasy on his feet. Carmichael started to rise and Alpha-1 waved him off, "I told you I have reflexive protection systems so please don't make any sudden moves towards me or touch me without my permission.

"I must say it has been almost a million years since I inhabited a biological body and I don't like the sensation. I suddenly feel extremely weak and dizzy. It came on very quickly … what is this … is this a subtle attack of some kind?"

Carmichael had a hunch, "When did you last eat or sleep?"

They could see immediately that Glass knew this was the cause, "I was hoping to avoid such inconveniences but to answer your question, I haven't eaten or slept since I re-entered this body about forty-eight hours ago."

The President and Carmichael stared at each other, Turcot thinking this could be an opportunity.

Alpha-1 picked up on the look, "Gentlemen please be assured that I'm confident you can do nothing to harm me. Besides my personal protective systems, our species has a full spectrum of systems protecting me. However, I'm afraid I'm going to have to service this human body first before I reveal a very serious situation and my real mission. What we have to discuss is just too important and I feel I cannot continue at this moment. This is very uncomfortable and very distracting. What can you offer in assistance?"

The President spoke quickly, "I'll have you shown to a guest room in the residence upstairs and we have a doctor on call in the building but I suspect some food and rest is all you need. Forty-eight hours without eating or sleeping is very dangerous. A few hours of sleep and some food should do the job because we're all very anxious to hear the rest of your … presentation and this deal you spoke of."

Alpha-1 nodded looking paler by the minute, "I'm afraid I must concur as I feel like I am about to faint." He bent forward slightly and took a deep breath, "Your offer is our only course of action at the moment. This isn't something we had planned on and it's very inconvenient. I thought this human body would be more rugged than it is. I'm not used to such limited brain capacity and apparently food and sleep is what I need to be able to use it to its potential. What we have to discuss is so critical that we can't risk any mistakes or misunderstandings and right now, trapped in this body, I'm definitely not able to continue.

"One thing though, I'm afraid I can't eat most of your food. It is simply too revolting to my palate as I found out preparing for this in the mine. Our studies show the only thing I might be able to stand would be cooked oatmeal and honey. Mr. Carmichael didn't have that on his buffet in his hotel which of course was designed for Bob Glass's preferences. Is that something you could provide?"

The President found himself smiling for the first time since their arrival, "I'm certain our kitchen has the ingredients for that."

Hal Turcot stood, "Fraser, why don't you go with him until we can resume our meeting. We can get you an office where you can catch up with your people."

Fraser smelled a rat but nodded agreement to the President's suggestion.

"Just a minute." Alpha-1 was immediately on alert, "What we have to discuss here tonight is of critical importance to the entire world. I come to you with a proposal that will impact both of us and it is essential that you agree to cooperate or we could all be doomed. You've seen what I'm capable of and I can assure you that others are aware and monitoring our progress. So before I leave, let me remind you that no one else can know about me or our discussions, as that could be tragic. Also you should take no actions until I can conclude my proposal. I assure you it will be worth your while. This hiatus was not planned and is most unfortunate."

Turcot stood there looking at him for a long time, the two sizing each other up. He moved carefully to his desk and pressed the intercom for his Chief-of-Staff, "Gerry, please join us."

Gerry Hastings appeared still looking put out that he hadn't been involved in the previous discussion.

"Gerry, Mr. Glass here is still suffering some fatigue from his long stay underground and we need to take an immediate break before we continue our conversation. Please get one of the ushers to show him to a guest bedroom in the residence where he can rest up for a while, make sure he gets something to eat, he knows what he wants, and please find Fraser an office in the building that he can use."

Puzzled, Hastings wondered what was going on. A bedroom to rest up in? In the family residence? That was highly unusual but it was clear the President wasn't going to elaborate further so he simply nodded.

Carmichael left following Alpha-1. He felt somewhat like a little boy being told what to do and being led around, but by now he had tremendous appreciation for this alien's ability to get his own way. He wondered if this was something the 'alien' had done to him as his normal psyche didn't include subservience in any shape or form. For some reason he was experiencing true fear for one of the few times in his life. The helplessness he felt from that paralyzing stunt was draining. He could only hope the President had assessed the situation as he had, that any resistance to this being could be fatal.

***

On board the Carmichael Industries corporate jet the conversation was no longer subdued. Frank Jorgen, head of security was particularly animated, "Listen guys, I know he's the boss but we have a contract. I signed that non-disclosure just like you but what the hell is it that we're not supposed to disclose? We were supposed to find out what it was all about as soon as they inked the deal. Will, did they sign the papers?"

Will Fiskins looked up from the Wall Street Journal he had been reading, "Fraser had all the papers. I left them in the room for him, but I don't know if they signed them. You were there. We left the hotel in a hurry and went straight to the plane. I don't know about you but I got all the signs from Fraser that we were not supposed to speak about any of this in the presence of that kid. Something is all hush-hush so I wasn't about to ask him where he left the file. But I'll say this, if he is at the White House right now then this thing might be even bigger than we thought."

Jorgen jumped back in, "You might be right but we were supposed to hear what this was all about today but all I keep getting is, 'keep your mouth shut and don't ask any questions'. Fraser has brushed me aside at every opportunity. I should be with him in Washington. The board would go nuts if they learned he was traveling around with this mine inspector and no protection."

Gardino, COO of Carmichael Industries always felt he had to take the lead, "Listen guys, Fraser promised us a big windfall and as long as I've known him he has never gone back on a promise. He's the boss. He'll take care of us, believe me. And as for the board, they know him as well as we do. If he wants to go running around Washington unprotected then everyone knows there's no way to stop him."

They were interrupted by the voice of the co-pilot on the intercom, "Mr. Gardino, there is a call coming in for you on line two."

Gardino picked up the satellite phone receiver and pressed the proper button, "Gardino here."

His face changed and after a moment he spoke, "What do you mean it's unusable, we just brought a guy up today? … A new shaft? That'll take weeks. There has to be a better solution … where are the drillers?"

After a long pause he continued, "Get on the phone and find them and get them back, I'm on my way. When I get there I want better options than another four-week drilling operation."

As he hung up the phone he turned to the two other execs, "Sorry guys, no New York tonight. Something has gone wrong with the rescue shaft we drilled for Glass. It no longer matters if we didn't get the green light from Fraser to go down and check out the mine, we couldn't go down now if we wanted. They're talking about some earth movement or something. Apparently the shaft has a 'kink' in it and cannot be fixed or used. They've been working on it all day since we left but apparently the thing is too unstable. Right now they're saying we have to drill an entirely new shaft.

"Carmichael said we needed to verify what Glass had found down there and with what is possibly going on in Washington at this moment, we cannot afford another four-week delay. I want a solution to this before we have to alert Fraser, so we're heading back!"

He pressed the intercom button for the cockpit, "Gentlemen we need to get back to Wallace pronto. Change your flight plan. Do we have enough fuel to get there directly tonight?"

There was a pause while the pilots did some checking, "We took on some fuel at DCA or rather Reagan International, but the quick answer is no sir, we'll have to set down somewhere on the way back. We'll file a new flight plan and let you know an ETA in a few minutes but it's going to be late with that stopover. We'll call corporate travel and arrange a car and hotels and we'll try to get you in to Coeur D'Alene for tonight which is the closest airport we can land at. If it's closed we'll have to go back to Spokane."

Gardino pressed the intercom and said, "OK, quick as you can. Arrange for some food at that stopover and get someone on the ground to call our families."

He turned back to the other two on the plane and said, "I knew we should've left someone more senior there. If this thing is worth billions we can't leave anything to chance and I want us there making sure that shaft is actually dead. I don't want an avoidable one-month delay. Fraser will have kittens when he hears this.

"As for us, eat all the snacks you can find, it could be a while."

The hotel they were headed for in Wallace was definitely not the best and anything short of a five star in New York City was definitely roughing it, but knowing Fraser Carmichael, they all knew this was the only course of action he would accept. There was apparently too much on the line and in cases like this he always demanded aggressive, hands-on action.

First Strike

After Hastings, Carmichael and Alpha-1 left, the President sat nervously thinking by himself, his mind racing. He suddenly became aware that his folded hands in his lap were shaking uncontrollably.

There had been a moment just after he was elected President when he had whimsically wondered what he would do if the proverbial little green men landed on the planet and said 'Take me to your leader,' He had never dreamed that day would come and certainly this would not have been how he thought it might have happened, a political enemy introducing an alien from deep in the earth.

He was still not sure if all he had heard was believable. In particular the body snatching thing had him especially suspicious. He wondered how that was possible even if they were much more advanced than man. All he knew about cloning was that theoretically you MIGHT be able to create a baby who was a genetic double, but a full grown man with memories intact?

His thoughts turned to hypnosis which he wanted to dismiss because for the last month he had been getting briefings on the lone survivor of the Culpeper mine and he could remember rational details in many of those meetings. Some kind of dream state was unlikely he reasoned. Still this was all just too incredible.

He remembered Occam's Razor which said that all things being equal the simplest answer is usually the right one and in this case the simplest one might be that he was the victim of some kind of hoax. To him, that was definitely more simple and plausible than all this nonsense about people, a million years more advanced, living in computer networks deep in the earth.

It was all very perplexing and he could see no motive here, but then again Fraser Carmichael was involved so there definitely could be some subterfuge afoot. Still, the alien claimed there was more to his story that would 'impact' all humans and then this 'offer' he spoke of. Once he had heard the entire pitch, he might be able to see the con in it all.

But then again, all things were NOT equal in this case. He had been pretty convincingly frozen in place while fully conscious. That whole part seemed very real and he could think of no trick short of hypnosis, which he had already rejected. After rolling it all over in his mind for what seemed like an eternity, he decided that the most prudent path was to take this Alpha-1 at face value for the moment. There was no question that according to this 'thing', there was a serious threat here to himself and mankind as a whole if he did not appease it. And what if he rejected the 'offer', what then? With a superior species facing them down he could think of no 'good' offer that could be in the offing; more like a demand or ultimatum was his guess.

Often when faced with a critical question, and this was the most critical of his time in office, he would ask himself, 'What would the American people expect me to do?' In this case it might even be 'What would the people of the world want me to do?'

His mind went to a question that had come up early in his presidency when SETI was being discussed. These university academics searching for extraterrestrial intelligence had been at it for decades trying to find evidence of aliens in the universe by listening for patterns in radio signal noise in space. The question had been 'What do we do if we actually find a message coming from deep space? What would we respond or should we respond at all?'

Some worried that we had already answered that question by default by broadcasting all manner of emissions from Earth.

Many decades ago with Voyager I, man had sent a space ship out into the universe carrying a human message and it was now somewhere just outside the solar system. Worse than even that, we had been transmitting TV signals for generations and radio signals for well over a hundred years. Planets within a hundred light years could have been listening in and watching Earthly TV or listening to radio broadcasts. It was a wonder they hadn't called or visited already, assuming as the scientists claimed, that life had to be plentiful in the universe, even in our own Milky Way Galaxy.

So again, the sixty-four thousand dollar question had been, if we ever did receive a message from another life form what would we answer or should we answer?

Up to this point this had been an academic question because the message we might receive would've been traveling for many years given even the closest star system was four light years away. The majority of any life, if it even existed in our own galaxy, could be thousands or hundreds of thousands of light years away. Any answer would take as long to get back to them so a 'conversation' had never been a real option.

But then a much larger issue affecting that decision had emerged, one that was much more relevant to the situation he found himself in today. Because our planet was considered very young and orbiting a young star, what if these people trying to communicate with us were thousands or millions or even billions of years more evolved than us? Scientists claimed this wasn't only possible but highly likely, almost a certainty.

He remembered a TED talk on the matter. In terms of the universe being over thirteen billion years old and our industrial age only a few centuries old, we had just arrived at the dawn of broadcast technology and it was a slam dunk that anyone we became aware of and could communicate with, would almost certainly be much more advanced than us. We had only been technologically active for about a split second in the universe's time scale. To find some other intelligent life form that was also in that same tiny slice of time would be more than lucky, more like damned near impossible. That presented a big problem. If any alien ever communicated with us then they would almost certainly be much more advanced, dominant and therefore very dangerous.

He had always thought they would have time on their side to decide whether to engage or not but it was too late, this alien was here and the problem was facing man right now. It was no longer a question of signaling to aliens that we existed, inviting a dominant civilization to visit. Man had already passed that point with this 'thing'. It was here now and there was no hiding from it. Hell it claimed they had been watching humans for way more than a million years.

Invariably Turcot agreed with the renowned theoretical physicist Stephen Hawking. His answer to the question remained that we should NOT answer an unsolicited message because of the undisputed, catastrophic history of asymmetric encounters on Earth in the past.

He had often thought you only had to look at what happened to the native Americans, the Aztecs and Mayans, the slaves coming out of Africa and the aboriginals in Australia and every other case where a more developed, and thinking of itself as a more superior civilization, met what it thought of as an inferior one. The superior race crushed the inferior race with little regard for them, sometimes even unintentionally. Man had clearly demonstrated little tolerance or empathy for what it perceived as inferior beings. Thinking or not we had always put a lower value on the lives of what we perceived as the inferior race.

To a superior race of aliens we could easily be seen as ants to be squashed under foot, a pest getting in the way of their agenda. Man's own track record in this regard was conclusive.

No, the more Turcot thought about it the more he realized that as the chosen one to represent his country and the world, he couldn't take this alien at his peace-loving and tolerant word, see him as benign, and believe the story that they just wanted to return underground and be left alone. So given there was no question of answering aliens from afar, the question now was what to do with an invading alien force from below. There was no way he could cooperate and set the stage where humanity would surely be enslaved or annihilated. He quickly came to the conclusion that resistance was the only course.

This alien talked a good story, if he was to be believed, but what had been experienced in human behavior, spoke to the fact that there would come a time when man did something that wasn't to their liking, and he would be squashed.

All that he knew for certain was that this guy claimed he was non-human, seemed to be able to prove it and had come out of that hole in Idaho. Everything else was just words and he wasn't about to become this century's Neville Chamberlain, blindly confident on the peace deal he had made with Hitler.

Besides, it was in the nature of the American people to expect action in the face of a crisis, not subjugation. If the deal this alien spoke of ever came to light, and there were no everlasting secrets in Washington, how would he explain making a deal in the face of the threat of a superior race. After all he wasn't the leader of the UN, he was the President of the United States. Negotiation and subjugation provided no solution. Action and resistance to tyranny was the only path. Man had a God-given right to defend himself.

There was no doubt in his mind that humanity's future was suddenly on the chopping block. No matter how rational and charming this alien sounded, the facts were that a much more advanced civilization would eventually tire of accommodating humans and man's extermination would be guaranteed.

In fact it had already started. The alien had complained about how man was destroying the planet; their planet. How long would they put up with that?

He finally stood and walked unsteadily over to his desk just as Gerry Hastings returned, "I need to see Dan Westgate in here right away. Find him please and tell him to use a chopper and give me some time here to think."

Gerry saw the look on the President's face and headed off to his office to make the call.

While he waited Turcot worked himself up into a froth over the situation. His emotions ran rampant, the greatest of which being terror. Mankind was under a terrifying threat and he had to do something about it. Everything in his body told him he had to fight back to get the upper hand in this situation.

Twenty minutes later Dan Westgate, the Secretary of Defense was in the President's office with the Chief-of-Staff in tow who was abruptly stopped by the President, "Sorry Gerry, again I'm going to have to have this meeting in private."

"But Hal, I need to be in on these meetings. You know the routine. Nothing will get done when you get hauled into the next thing unless I'm in on these meetings. You need me for follow-up. What the hell went on in here with Carmichael and this miner who has been offered a bedroom in the residence of all things?"

Dan Westgate stood there puzzled. Something had been going on in here earlier and it looked like he was about to be pulled into it.

Turcot was getting impatient, "Gerry, I can't explain and maybe never will. Believe it or not, this is for your own protection. Please leave us now and swear to me that you'll turn off ALL THREE recording systems in this room."

Hastings didn't want to get into a protracted battle over this in front of Westgate and he was shocked that the President was aware of the third secret recording system he alone knew of. He wondered how the President had discovered it and why he had so carelessly disclosed it in front of one of his direct reports. Figuring retreat was his only option at the moment, he simply nodded red-faced and left through the side door to his own office.

The President ushered the Secretary of Defense to one of the couches in front of his famous desk and took a seat on the couch facing him. He reasoned Gerry had had time to disable the recording devices but started in a near whisper sitting on the edge of his seat and leaning forward, "Dan, what I'm about to tell you is for you and me alone. I may be putting you in grave jeopardy. This is of the highest national security. Our country is facing a new and heretofore unimagined threat."

Westgate was starting to breathe a little harder. This President, like most, chose his words carefully so it was highly unlikely Hal Turcot was exaggerating. Whatever it was, this was real and he could tell by the President's face that he was under tremendous stress.

"Before I start let me say that I'm not out of my mind. I am mentally well and I'm sure of what I'm saying."

Turcot took a deep breath to steady himself, "I just had Fraser Carmichael in here and he brought with him that miner Glass from the rescue in Idaho. Apparently the reason Carmichael wanted that mine is that Glass told him early on, before you started listening in, that after the collapse, he had found a computer room at twelve thousand feet with evidence that aliens had been there. There were active robots and all kinds of advanced technology for a species that was quite a bit taller than man, and the robots proceeded to kill the other miner."

Westgate was clearly shocked as Turcot paused for this to sink in.

"Well it turns out that this Mr. Glass who was just here a half hour ago is no longer Mr. Glass. He is one of the aliens who built the place."

Westgate was stunned and not sure what he had just heard, "A live one? A live alien in the Oval Office? Let's be clear, what do you mean by an alien?"

The President leaned forward and whispered, "I mean a non-human being, much more evolved than us who proceeded to paralyze me just by looking at me. Carmichael and I stood right there totally frozen for at least ten minutes, so paralyzed that we couldn't control our own breathing and somehow survived with no aftereffects."

Westgate was almost in shock, "Are you saying what I think you're saying? You mean a real honest-to-God alien?" He was starting to wonder if the President hadn't completely lost it.

"Well, he doesn't consider himself an alien because he says he is from this planet but yes a non-human intelligence. Let me continue. From your taps on Carmichael you know that they claimed they had found something fantastic down there. Now this 'thing' shows up here in the body of one of the two miners but his personal power is immense and by the way, he knows you were planning on taking over the mine."

Westgate almost laughed nervously as the old sci-fi movie 'The Body Snatchers' came to mind. Although he realized quickly that there was no humor in this.

Turcot continued, "Only Carmichael and I know about this and now you, and you're not supposed to know! The alien wants to keep it between Carmichael and me so that he can keep their presence secret and he wants to do some kind of deal with us.

"He says they all live in a virtual world inside a computer or network and he had to occupy a clone of Bob Glass's body so he could 'deal with us'. He claims Glass and his immediate family who died in that fire, are safe and they've all been incorporated into his virtual world.

"He was about to tell us about the deal when he almost collapsed from exhaustion and for the moment he's resting upstairs. He says he has personal protection systems so we can't attack him directly, or so he claims. He says the other miner was killed when he took a swing at one of their robots and it was simply defending itself.

"He threatened to kill everyone including me if we don't do as he wants. For the moment his demands seem simple and innocent enough but we're yet to hear what this 'deal' is. You might even think of him as charming but I'm very reluctant to give in to any demands they might have.

"He says the deal will have a big impact on us, and by that I mean the entire human race. If we don't agree to the deal I really believe he will exterminate all of us. But even if this deal is good, which I doubt, I think it is only a matter of time before we do something he doesn't like or we disagree with him and then the jig is up, and they wipe us out."

Westgate was staring white-faced at the President as he continued, "I think you know what the American people would expect me to do."

As Dan Westgate nodded the President continued, "I have no idea what this deal is. According to 'it', it will be to our benefit but I don't think that even matters now. They demonstrated they can kill at will, he has frozen me and Carmichael to show some of his powers and he has threatened to kill everyone if we cannot come to this agreement.

For me that's enough of an ultimatum, and I keep coming back to the issue of them being vastly superior and us eventually pissing them off somehow to our infinite peril."

Turcot continued, "Now if you remember we've theorized about this in the past. There is no question that given the chance against a more advanced foe we must strike first, and they have already demonstrated superiority and hostility. I should also point out that he did not feel he needed to offer an apology for killing the miner. So again this fits the pattern of an advanced civilization having little empathy or regard for what they perceive as a weaker race.

"We can't wait until they tire of us and destroy all our weapons and we don't even get a chance to defend ourselves. We must strike first, take them on directly, throw everything we have at them and do our best to defeat them swiftly or at least show them we mean business. We may not win but we may not completely lose either."

"My thoughts exactly," said Westgate, now fully focused on the threat. "I see no other option if what you're telling me is true. I concur with your analysis. This is an existential threat to mankind and it falls to us to act in the defense of our country and this planet. If they are superior then it's only a matter of time until we're in conflict and they're holding all the cards."

Westgate stood and paced, "If what you say is true then I think we have no choice in the matter, we must move swiftly on this. The only target we know of is the mine and we need to hit it with a thermonuclear device immediately. If he's upstairs resting we don't even have time to clear that place out. That would give them too much warning."

Turcot leaned even further forward and whispered, "Will a nuke do it?"

"Well that mine is about twelve thousand feet deep so we're not going to get total destruction but I suspect everything down there is electrical and the EMP that one of our bombs puts out will likely knock out all electrical devices at that depth as well as turning everything a couple of hundred feet down into solid glass. The shock wave through the earth should damage everything down there, so short of trying to send a bomb down in an elevator, that's our only shot.

"You said they live an electrical existence so the EMP is the best weapon against them. There is no telling what damage we could do to whatever facilities they have, hell they probably have other sites, but given this 'thing' came out of that hole and there's a computer room down there then it's at least likely that it's an important site for them.

"As you say, it's critical to fire first, show them we have some weapons that can threaten them and state our intentions to defend ourselves. We need to be prepared to go to all-out war at the same time because they should be expected to retaliate in some way. We still have lots of nukes so if they start appearing elsewhere we can take them on. At a bare minimum giving them a black eye will give us a chance at some kind of parity of threat and a negotiating position.

"In terms of provocation they've already killed one American and threatened many others so in reality we are not even taking the first shot but we need to move before they detect and destroy all our weapons, if it isn't too late already."

The President was nodding, "Yeah, I agree. I see no other way to get to them. According to this alien, everything they have is buried very deep and the shaft Carmichael drilled has now collapsed so our only chance at a first shot is a big bomb on that mine. We can't just sit around and wait for them to annihilate us.

"Oh yeah, he also claims they have a network of communication satellites that are cloaked. He didn't say whether they had any weapons but we should be prepared to respond if anything gets fired at us. We need to go to DEFCON 1 and we need that new ground-based laser system ready to hit back if needed."

Westgate was stunned, "You mean they could fire at us from space? We only have two of those lasers, one on the east coast and one on the west and their targeting is set for incoming ballistic missiles so I don't know what they would be able to do in terms of targeting invisible satellites. Hopefully they're in parking orbits like our communication satellites and not whizzing around the globe.

"You know we also have that secret space laser, 'High Octave'. It's up there and semi-ready to go but its intention was to defend against the Russian and Chinese missiles so it's on the other side of the globe and would be of no use for weapons these aliens might have stationed over the US. So right now I see us only being able to defend North America with the ground-based lasers if they shoot at us from space but there's no guarantee. We have no idea what kind of weapons they have, where they are or how to target them if they're cloaked. But as you say, we have to strike first and we have to do it fast before that 'thing' wakes up or they get wind of it. Going to DEFCON 1 will have our troops all around the world at their weapons and ready to engage them wherever they might appear."

The President was pensive, "The guy really seems friendly enough but we've been through this before, we have to assume they would turn on us and it would be too late to establish any kind of threat parity. We would be at their mercy."

After a pause the President continued, "I understand your points too that we should expect them to retaliate and we could be starting a war where they have the most powerful weapons and we don't even know if they have other sites, but what other choices do we have? They started it and as you say, they pose an existential threat to us. We can't sit here and do nothing. We have to strike while we can and simply follow-up as best we can. My job is to defend America and there is an even chance they have nothing in space with weapons. He seemed to indicate that they have never needed that kind of defense.

"They may be immensely more powerful than us but a serious bloody nose might give them pause to negotiate or even back off. According to him they are all underground which traps them in a way. He says they are small in numbers and haven't lost anyone in a million years and they have very high respect for life, so if we take out a few of them it might be enough. Either way we cannot be seen as weak and cowed. Right now we're sitting ducks."

"OK sir, we're on the same page here. We must act before they have a chance to enslave or annihilate us because we can't assume they will not take advantage of their superiority. Here is what I propose. For the alien we'll put a SEAL team on taking him out ASAP. But we must move on the mine first, in case any more of them emerge.

"If I remember correctly our four-stage Minuteman rockets can't set a trajectory of less than about four hundred miles, even the ones with the new GRP guidance systems. On a close-in trajectory like this, they have to go almost straight up about seven hundred miles to burn all three solid fuel stages and then they can turn to go after a target coming in at about Mach 30. The new active guidance systems that provide for evasive tactics I think will allow for such a steep trajectory.

"I suggest we use a bird out of Minot AFB in North Dakota. They have the latest and most reliable LGM-30G Minuteman IIIs with all the guidance upgrades and the biggest hydrogen bombs. We set the coordinates for the mine entrance and set detonation mode II which is contact with the ground versus airburst. I think it will take them about thirty minutes to spin up the bird and let it fly and it should be there in about fifteen minutes after launch, would be my guess. I wish they were faster but they have three stages of solid rocket fuel that has to be burned off and they are meant as intercontinental missiles not close-in weapons.

"The fourth stage is liquid and can be throttled so we can get the full advantage of the guidance systems. I think we need the biggest Minuteman for this target. A ship- or sub-based missile might be too small or even too slow given where the mine is. None of our nuclear assets are patrolling near our own shores and readying air assets would take some time. They no longer sit around with nukes loaded. Hopefully these aliens will never see it coming."

Secretary of Defense Westgate continued, "You know we've been watching that site given Carmichael's interest in it. It's a relatively remote and mountainous location outside of Wallace. They're in a valley so a ground burst will greatly limit collateral damage. Everyone near the mine will be killed but it's late so there may be only a skeleton crew there. Our intel guys told me this afternoon that the press and just about everyone else abandoned the area earlier today once Glass was out. Still, we'll have to come up with some really fine story to cover a nuclear attack on US soil and clearly we do not want to make matters worse by claiming it was Russia or China. We might need their help before this is over."

Dan Westgate suddenly looked pensive, "Now that I think of it, I'm not even sure you have the authority to use the military's assets on our own soil."

He hesitated and then said, "Forget I just said that.

"From what I know of the mine discovery Carmichael has been talking about, and the fact that you're completely convinced you had a powerful alien in here tonight making threats, I'd say you have no choice and would be expected to act in defense of the country in this matter. I'd further propose that we have no time to inform any oversight committees in Congress.

"Sir, it is my considered opinion that you must act swiftly and decisively in this matter. I know it breaks the rules but you'll have to write up a 3093 Presidential Finding after the fact, given we have no time for it now or any notifications.

"If you're convinced this 'thing' is an alien and represents a clear and present danger to the US then you must act immediately. The fact that he threatened you the President and Commander-in-Chief of our military is in itself an act of war. They declared war on the US and you cannot hesitate sir!"

The President thought through all of the facts for a second, then nodded and Dan Westgate continued, "Sir, I'd ask you to summon the football. I have my 'biscuit' on my person and I think we must initiate this now!"

The President stared at Westgate, realizing suddenly where they had gotten to, felt the weight of the decision upon him, decided there were no other acceptable options and this was what the American people would expect him to do. He rose slowly, walked to his desk and pressed the intercom button on his phone, "Gerry, I need the football in here."

It was like an electric shock going through Gerry Hastings' whole body, "You don't mean the NUCLEAR football?"

"That would be correct, the presidential missile launch system."

Within thirty seconds Gerry Hastings was in the Oval Office with a very nervous looking young Lt. Colonel shaking as he placed the highly secure and failsafe electronic link to the military's launch control system on the President's desk and started to link it up to NORAD. His training instructed him to treat this as real, even if the President had sprung an unexpected test on him.

Gerry couldn't hold it any longer, "What are we doing? What's going on here? Are you planning a nuclear attack on someone or is this some kind of test? I was not told of any test. I know it's not April Fools' so for God's sake tell me what's happening here, this is not a joking matter. The Pentagon and NORAD will see this and react," his voice rising in tone and volume.

The President took him aside as the young officer was setting up the communications. "Gerry, if this all works out I will tell you what happened here tonight but for your own protection I will only say that a lethal threat has been issued to our country that must be acted on immediately. There is no time for any consultations and yes I'm going to nuke the bastards."

Gerry Hastings simply stood there like a deer in the headlights, red-faced, eyes wide and mouth agape. The first thought running through his mind was 'Where did this threat come from? The President had not even been on the phone. The only people in here tonight were Carmichael and the miner and the President had called Westgate in, not the other way around, so where did he hear of this threat?'

Dan Westgate, familiar with the mine site from his snooping, had opened his specialized iPhone and was using Google Earth to get the location of the Culpeper rescue shaft about four hundred yards northwest of the mine entrance and was calling out the coordinates to the Lt. Colonel, "Latitude 47 – 30 – 51.95 North. Longitude 115 – 52 – 08.10 West."

The young Lt. Colonel turned red as he was entering the numbers. Gerry almost shouted, "That's in the continental US, somewhere in the Northwest. What the hell is going on here?" he yelled at everyone in the room.

Dan Westgate spoke, "Gerry the President is right. This is a national emergency and must be dealt with now. It's a matter of life and death for all of us. A credible threat has been made against the country and in fact the world, and a specific threat of death to the President. We must act now without delay."

"A threat by whom? Someone inside the US? I can't allow this! Nuking a US town?" yelled an apoplectic Hastings. "It's not even legal! I won't allow this! You've both lost your minds!"

The young Lt. Colonel was well trained and sweating profusely, finished entering the coordinates, drew his service weapon, took a wide stance, pointed his weapon at Gerry Hastings' chest and said in a very loud and authoritative voice, "Sir, step away from the President or I will be compelled to shoot."

Hastings, caught completely off guard, jumped backwards, hands in the air and horror on his red and suddenly perspiring face.

Dan Westgate stepped forward, "Colonel please take Mr. Hastings into his office and cover him. Shoot him if he tries to interfere."

Hastings looked like he was about to collapse and pleadingly glanced at the President who seemed to indicate he was with Westgate on this. Hastings was now staring down the barrel of a large caliber service weapon and finally started moving towards his office. Over his shoulder he yelled, "Hal, don't do this! This can't be your only option!

Use your head!"

Once he was gone, Westgate took over. He broke open his 'biscuit', entered his launch codes and punched a few data points into the device that automatically picked the appropriate silo at the Minot AFB Minuteman missile site and pressed execute. As he started to talk the President's red line rang, "That will be NORAD at Cheyenne Mountain. They'll have seen the football activated, the target coordinates, Air Force base designation and be looking for confirmation. I'll take the call and give them my ID code. You enter your launch codes Mr. President."

The President opened his desk and took out the small plastic package nicknamed the 'biscuit' because of its size and the sound it made when broken open. He had only done this in simulated runs but this time it was for real and he was shaking as he took out his launch confirmation codes.

He typed the codes slowly and carefully into the console. As he was doing this he could hear Westgate on the phone verifying the intent and telling the military to go to DEFCON 1 with an undetermined worldwide retaliatory threat profile, possibly from satellites and a demand for the tactical SEAL team on the roof of the White House to assemble just outside the Oval Office main door.

Westgate was back from the phone, "Cheyenne isn't happy as you might imagine but I assured them this was a direct order from the Commander-in-Chief and the target is indeed hostile and inside our borders. Right now they'll be verifying that the call actually connected to the Oval Office. They'll be doing voice print analysis as well. You have ultimate command authority and I am one of only three people who can authenticate your order with my launch codes so as a safety feature they cannot override you now that we have both confirmed."

Both men now took the keys from around their necks and put them in their respective keyholes on the electronic football, counted down from three and turned the keys in unison.

Hydrogen Bomb

In silo A3, nicknamed "DUCK" because of its proximity to Drake, North Dakota, the excruciating boredom of the evening shift was suddenly broken by a very recognizable alarm horn sounding. It snapped both Air Force captains from the nearby Minot Air Force Base wide awake.

No test had been ordered so they were immediately in total shock and confusion. Their first thought was that it could still be an unannounced test to try to catch them off guard. There had been concerns in recent years that American Missile Command sites were less than totally prepared to do their jobs so the alarm, even if it was a test, had to be handled 'by the book'.

They confirmed the commands were coming from one of the three possible secure sources, not NORAD in Colorado or Military Command at the Pentagon as might be expected but actually from the President's football, wherever he was. That was unusual. The President's football had never been used as the initiator for any test they were aware of.

Suddenly this didn't look like a test anymore. They immediately followed protocol and broke out their daily launch codes and entered them, got the keys from around their necks, put them in the keyholes and were just about to turn them when one of them noticed the coordinates and yelled "Halt!"

"Hell, those coordinates are in the US somewhere and we're still in ACTIVE mode! Therefore this can't be a test. We're about to launch this bird at an American target. NO WAY I'm turning this key unless I get some kind of really credible confirmation! What the hell! I don't think the military is even authorized to use its weapons on US soil against its own people. Isn't it Comi Tistus or something like that?"

The other captain stared at him, "That's Posse Comitatus and I don't think it applies to us. By the time the order comes to us it's been vetted by command. Leave the legal stuff to them, but I'm with you. I want a high-level general or the SECDEF on the line before I turn this key. Somebody wants us to bomb the US?"

Just as they went to lift the red phone it rang. The more senior of the two lifted the phone. "This is the US Secretary of Defense Daniel Westgate. Do you recognize my voice?"

"Ah, sir I'm not sure but we sure have some questions down here."

"Here is the President."

A second later, "This is President Harold Turcot. Do you recognize my voice?"

"Yes sir."

"You also know this phone is on a private highly secure fiber digital network that can't be intercepted. What does your readout tell you about where this call is from?"

"The White House sir. But sir, these coordinates are for a US target."

"That's correct. We have a national emergency and must attack immediately the coordinates we've given you. You have everything you need to proceed and you must follow protocol and act now. America depends on you so don't delay, and gentlemen, God speed."

At that the line went dead.

They both stared at each other. Finally one said, "That was all recorded and both the Pentagon and Cheyenne Mountain heard it too. I'll count down from three... two ... one," and they both turned their keys.

Stage IV of the rocket had started fueling when the alarm had first sounded. The first three stages were ready to go with their solid rocket fuel preloaded and now all safety features had been removed and the giant missile was in the final stages of preparations for launch. Targeting was loaded and being verified at the same time as the onboard computers were calculating a flight profile. The countdown clock now read thirteen minutes, the time it took for the highly volatile fuel components to be loaded and pressurized into the fourth stage and a whole series of interlocks to be checked and verified by the triply redundant launch computers.

The hotline went again and it was answered once more by the more senior of the two. Heart racing, the other captain had his hand ready to slap the ABORT button.

The President asked to be put on speaker "Gentlemen, what you're doing here is vitally important to the survival of our people. I just wanted to sit through this with you, but don't let me get in the way of you doing what you need to do to carry out your orders. Please call out the countdown periodically."

Hal Turcot had a very distinguishable voice which gave them some comfort that they were doing the right thing. About every minute they called out as ordered. They watched the panels in front of them as subsequent lights turned green indicating another step in the launch process had been tested, executed and verified. Every few seconds they tried to do a mental reset, tried to understand what was happening, make sure they were not dreaming and ask themselves again if this was all real and if they were doing the right thing. One slapped himself in the face more than once just to make sure he wasn't dreaming. Each hoped beyond hope that they'd get an abort command from the President or electronically from NORAD or Military Command at the Pentagon, but no such order appeared.

The more senior one couldn't hold it in anymore, "Mr. President, why are we bombing our own people?"

"Young man, I'm afraid that is way above your pay grade so the only answer I can give you is that we've just become aware of a massive threat to national security that requires this highly unorthodox response. I wish there was another alternative but the Secretary of Defense and I are certain this is our only option. We're actually not bombing our own people and we've done everything we can to minimize the impact to innocent Americans. This is a remote location we are targeting but all you need to be concerned with is that you're about to become American heroes," he lied. They might be heroes if this action ended it all but it was just as likely to start something.

Finally they were down to the last few seconds. "Five … four … three … two … one. We have ignition Mr. President.

"HELL, THE OUTER DOORS ARE CLOSING … I CAN'T OVERRIDE IT … THE WEAPON IS ARMING ITSELF …!"

Half a second later the line went dead.

Minot

The Carmichael Industries Gulf Stream G650 on its way to Wallace Idaho was at two thousand feet on final approach to runway 31 at Minot International to top up with fuel when suddenly the entire cabin was lit up like a movie set with white light that was so intense it even blistered some of the paint on the ceiling. As the execs all jumped at the shock, the first sound they heard was the two jet engines spinning down. As the light started to subside they realized all the plane's lights were out. They all stared out the left windows and saw a bright mushroom cloud forming about twenty or thirty miles behind them and to the south.

One of them yelled out loud, "An A-bomb?"

Suddenly the cockpit door flew open and the copilot yelled, "We've lost all power and we're going down. Strap in."

As they started to comply the shockwave and the sound hit the small jet blowing out one of the windows and throwing the plane forward at great speed. Bodies and everything else not tied down went flying through the air. With the light from the mushroom cloud and ground fires the pilots just had time to see a massive corn field mostly ablaze. Gaining some semblance of manual control over the plane, they both pulled back hard on the yoke that had no hydraulic assist, just in time for a crash landing. They had no time to lower the landing gear and they hit hard as the plane started skidding askew through the field. Fire seemed to be everywhere. And then one of the wing tips dipped and everything went black.

**

In the Oval Office the President and the Secretary of Defense stared at each other praying they hadn't just witnessed an atomic explosion near Minot. They waited in silence. Minutes seemed to go by and then the emergency line from NORAD rang and Dan Westgate being closest, picked it up. His face turned ashen white. He thanked them and hung up the phone.

"Sir, Cheyenne Mountain confirms satellite systems and seismic readings show there has been an atomic explosion southeast of the city of Minot in North Dakota. The nearby town of Drake about forty miles southeast of Minot is ground zero and is likely gone and many of the surrounding farms and villages are likely flattened. Minot itself and the Air Force base just north of town may be severely damaged but the electromagnetic pulse has knocked out much of the communications so we don't know the total situation yet. Sir it appears there is no doubt that the warhead detonated in its silo."

The President sat down hard with his head in his hands. He felt like he was going to be sick. There had to have been at least a couple of hundred people snuffed out by HIM in under a second. "What have I done?" he said out loud.

Dan Westgate stood by the phone staring at the President trying to fathom what had just happened. He knew enough about the missile systems to know that it was highly unlikely, hell as far as he knew it was impossible that this was an accident. The servicemen had said something about the missile arming and the outer doors closing just before the explosion. Both of those events seemed impossible. Something or someone had intercepted their plan and made this happen.

Less than two minutes went by in total silence until the main door of the Oval Office opened and the captain of the SEAL team said, "Sir, a Mr. Carmichael and Mr. Glass are here and claim you need to see them. Turcot nodded and Alpha-1 and Fraser Carmichael casually walked in. Bob Glass's replacement just stared at the President as the door closed behind them and then he said, "I thought you were smarter than that. You've just complicated matters for both of us. If I had the morals of a human I'd strike you dead where you stand for what you've just perpetrated on your own people."

Carmichael still had no idea what was going on but didn't want to jump into the mix.

Turcot bristled, glaring at Alpha-1 he said, "You did this? You sabotaged that missile?"

"Of course we did. Did you think for a second we wouldn't be watching you? Did you not hear anything I said before? Are you so dense that you don't understand what a million years of evolution beyond you means?

"I told you that opposing us was the wrong way to go, but apparently you either don't listen very well or I've grossly overestimated your intelligence. What kind of logic do you people operate on?

"Now your impetuous, childish response has cost hundreds and maybe thousands of your citizens their lives and you've seriously pissed off my civilization who are rethinking our entire approach to your kind."

He turned back to Carmichael, "And oh by the way, your corporate jet had turned around and was headed back to Wallace. They were on final approach to Minot to refuel when this nut job here tried to nuke your mine and the missile went off in its silo not far from their plane. Your men could all be dead too."

Carmichael just stared in horror as Alpha-1 returned to the President, "Apparently force is the only language you understand. Our people grieve for your loss and I sincerely hope you will require no more proofs of our capabilities, our sincerity, and our total commitment in these matters."

Dan Westgate had been waiting his chance and rushed Alpha-1 from his blind side. Before he had taken two steps he fell dead on the Oval Office carpet.

Both Carmichael and the President gasped as he hit the floor.

Alpha-1 hadn't even looked at his would-be attacker. Without even turning to look at the body, Alpha-1 blurted out, "THE INSANITY CONTINUES! … now you've killed your Secretary of Defense by bringing him into this even though I told you several times the jeopardy anyone else would be in. A further complication you're going to have to explain.

"What was he going to do, strangle a being that can kill him with a simple thought? A being that is only temporarily in this body to make it easier to converse with you. I AM NOT A HUMAN! I'M NOT CONSTRAINED BY THIS BODY! CAN YOU UNDERSTAND AT LEAST THAT MUCH?"

After a pause where he seemed to cool down he continued, "I must say I was ill-prepared for your lack of common sense. You and your SECDEF must have subpar IQs."

Both humans were only half listening while staring at the lifeless corpse in front of the President's desk.

"Tell me Mr. President, should I just kill you now to avoid any more of these nonsensical distractions? Or will you come to your meager senses and start cooperating? Or at least doing as you're told? You have now made us complicit in the deaths of many of your countrymen and one more misstep and we will have no choice but to do this the hard way. DO YOU FINALLY AND COMPLETELY

Turcot was still leaning forward from his position on the couch, mouth agape and staring at the body of his dead friend on the floor only a few feet from him. Tears welled up in his eyes. There was no question that Dan had died instantly. You could almost see the life being driven out of him as he fell. He had dropped like a sack of potatoes with the life already gone from his eyes. Eyes now dead but wide open and staring across the floor at nothing.

The alien hadn't lifted a finger or even looked at his attacker. It was almost as if he had some force field around him that detected any threat and somehow eliminated it. And there had been zero empathy. He hadn't even acknowledged Dan's presence in the room but had killed him without blinking an eye, with even less regard than swatting a pesky insect.

Alpha-1 could see the President was lost in his shock and grief. Carmichael, while also seeming lost and staring at the fallen SECDEF, seemed a little more aware of his surroundings. "Gentlemen, I don't want to start killing off everyone who may have known something of tonight's events or could testify to it. That would number dozens and leave gaping holes in any narrative and all kinds of speculation requiring even more people to be eliminated.

"You understand that there will be innumerable official inquiries into tonight's events. Events in this room and near Minot which sadly cannot be undone, and none of those inquiries can be allowed to lead to the truth of the matter if mankind is to survive.

"Alpha MUST NOT be discovered! I think I've made that crystal clear. So short of killing you all, the best course forward is to try to get back to where we were an hour ago in terms of who knew what. It's messy but I think we can achieve it and I think you will agree it is worth a try to save mankind."

Carmichael nodded but Turcot was still leaning forward on the couch staring at his friend, dead on the floor.

"As I understand it, there are two gentlemen whom I've frozen for now in the next room who will need the last hour of their memories erased and replaced. We'll have to do something similar with NORAD at Cheyenne Mountain and a skeleton crew at the Pentagon who were listening in. There are likely about forty people who will need some narrative that ties to the actual physical evidence.

"The SEAL team outside this door currently frozen will be easy to handle. They'll awaken to a memory of a drill having just been completed.

"That leaves only us and the dead man on the floor. So the obvious thing is to blame it all on him and his undiagnosed brain hemorrhage which caused him to acquire the football from the Colonel next door, attack the President for his launch codes and key, and order the launch of the missile. That will be the scenario we plant with the two next door and the teams in NORAD and the Pentagon. No one knows why he wanted to bomb Mr. Carmichael's mine but he was out of his mind at the time. It is simply a coincidence that the missile didn't launch properly due to some failure at the silo which also caused the subsequent detonation.

"I believe Mr. Westgate was the one who spoke to NORAD to confirm the attack and the people at the missile silo are no longer a worry. I do believe your voice, Mr. Turcot, was heard and recorded at NORAD and the Pentagon but it should be easy enough to blank out those tapes and memories.

"The two next door will be given planted memories and remember the SECDEF forcing them to hand over the football at gun point and being tied up and locked up in the Chief-of-Staff's office which they will soon escape from.

"It's messy but it will do and if anything comes loose I'll fix it. Hopefully without causing too many more deaths."

Hal Turcot wiped his eyes as the magnitude of it all and his culpability was coming into focus. Apparently this alien was going to provide some kind of cover story for everything.

Carmichael was finally catching up on what had actually transpired and worried about his execs in the company jet.

Alpha-1 looked directly at the President, "See what you've done. It would be much easier for me to just kill everyone but that is not our way. Somehow we will struggle through this mess you've created and save as many innocent lives as possible. You humans are dangerously impetuous and sadly irrational. You've already caused the death of two people trying to attack us and hundreds or thousands more with a nutty plan to confront us, and all of this before you have even found out why we are here. You, Mr. President, are really a puzzle and frankly an unexpected disappointment. I take back everything I said before about you being a pleasant surprise."

The President remained sitting, confused and dazed and frequently returning his attention to his old friend, dead and only feet away from him on the carpet bearing the seal of the United States. Dan Westgate had been a very popular two-term Republican Senator from Colorado and even though they were in different parties, he had been a close friend and his appointment to Secretary of Defense had pleased the nation. He should be seen as a hero and given a hero's sendoff yet the plan was now to blame everything on him and disgrace his memory.

The room was finally starting to come back into focus for him. The alien was right. There would be dozens of inquiries from every committee on the Hill and he couldn't bring himself to lay the blame on his old friend, but what choice did he have? This 'thing' said he could just as easily kill everyone that knew anything. Hell he was ostensibly asleep when this all happened. Somehow these Alphans had monkeyed with highly secure systems in Minot to blow up a nuclear warhead.

His thoughts turned to the carnage from the bomb itself. His first thought was of the two Air Force personnel whom he had been speaking to when it all went wrong. And the small town of Drake, North Dakota. He knew nothing about the town but it was probably like every other small town in Middle America. A church or two, a bank, a couple of stores, a gas station with a mechanic and a body shop attached, a tractor dealership, maybe a small school and possibly a combined volunteer fire department and police station with one or two cops. All gone in a literal flash. It was now likely a crater and everyone there vaporized in a billionth of a second along with other close-by towns, some innocent farmers and their families.

He felt himself starting to shiver. Now he was the first President since Harry Truman to use the ultimate weapon and on his own people for God's sake. 'How could this have happened?', he wondered. What had he been thinking? This 'thing' could do everything it said it could. And it had warned him.

Turcot was sure that when morning came and rescuers could get to all affected areas, the numbers of dead and injured would steadily climb. He had no idea how big the bomb was but even the smallest in the arsenal wouldn't be merciful to the town and its surroundings. Dan had said it was one of the bigger ICBMs for God's sake. The big ones could level a large city with an airburst. From the little he knew of hydrogen bombs he was hopeful that the fact that it was below ground level and not an airburst explosion had spared lives. The force of the bomb would've been up and out leaving a large crater but less than maximum surface wide damage.

Alpha-1 was still speaking, "Now, I don't think you want the public or your enemies thinking one man could set off these weapons so the story for the public will be that an as yet undiscovered flaw during routine maintenance caused a nuclear weapon to explode in its silo. You'll inform NORAD and the Pentagon that that is the cover story. No real physical investigation is possible because everything was vaporized. The primary narrative of the Secretary of Defense going apeshit will be classified and only divulged to secure committees."

The alien's street vernacular wasn't lost on the humans.

"You, Mr. President, will go on TV within the hour to present the case for the flaw in the maintenance procedure, quell any ideas that the US was under attack. Before you do that you'll call NORAD and Central Command, fill in the gaps in the classified narrative and inform them of the cover story for the public. I have already fixed the tapes and planted the memories. The DEFCON level was set to ONE worldwide so we'll rectify that when we plant the memories in the folks at NORAD. They'll remember setting it as a precaution due to the SECDEF's antics.

"For your information the current death toll I'm told is at least six hundred and forty-five. That is our best estimate of all of Drake, which now has a large crater where it used to be. In addition there were mass casualties in several surrounding towns one of which was flattened, the personnel at the silo, some farm families in the area, anyone on the adjacent roads and highways and some unfortunate people in the southeast suburbs of Minot who were outside at the time or caught in flimsy buildings. We also don't yet know the fate of Mr. Carmichael's associates and there will be thousands of injuries, some of them critical. Also the radioactive mushroom cloud is blowing towards Winnipeg which is much larger so you'll have to deal with the Canadians too.

"As to the two of you, I think we will refrain from changing your memories so that this evening remains as a reminder of what irrational actions can cause.

"Gentlemen, do you understand both the internal and external narratives?"

Both men, gradually coming to their senses, nodded.

Alpha-1 continued, "Now Mr. President, do us all a favor and get your Chief-of-Staff in here to call the White House medic and tell him Mr. Westgate has collapsed and is in distress. For your information I've already planted the agreed story in the heads of the two next door, who have just freed themselves. I have also planted a significant hemorrhage in Mr. Westgate's brain."

Neither man felt like asking how all that was achieved.

Carmichael could see the President was still in shock and took the initiative and unlocked the door to the Chief-of-Staff's office. He had never liked Turcot and now he looked at him with unbridled disgust given his knee jerk and stupid reaction that had just killed so many innocent people. 'What a time to show some spine,' he thought.

As Hastings rushed in and spotted the Defense Secretary on the floor, the President finally seemed to come to his senses and standing said, "Gerry, Dan collapsed and I don't think he is breathing. Call the White House medic quick!"

Hastings hurriedly complied and the Lt. Colonel immediately started CPR on the Secretary.

There was nothing either the Lt. Colonel or the doctor could do for Dan Westgate. All resuscitation attempts failed and DC paramedics who had been called in finally removed the body from the Oval Office.

To fill in the gaps in Alpha-1's narrative, Turcot explained to Hastings and the young military officer that after Westgate initiated the missile launch and locked them in Gerry's office, the missile actually misfired and exploded in its silo just as Westgate collapsed on the Oval Office floor and Bob Glass and Fraser Carmichael returned. He also filled them in on the cover story for the press.

Then as directed, the President on a concall to the Pentagon and NORAD, reinforced the narrative that Alpha-1 had planted, relaying to them the story he would use with the press and public.

The networks were already reporting a massive explosion in North Dakota and speculating it had to be an atomic bomb at one of the missile silos but due to the EMP blackout of most communications in the area, details were scant.

Hastings had called in essential personnel and the President soon had a short speech for the press which he read from the podium in the White House briefing room while Carmichael and Alpha-1 watched on the Oval Office TV.

"My fellow Americans, it is with great sadness that I must confirm to you tonight that a major military accident has occurred in the state of North Dakota. An as yet unknown problem in one of our newest Minuteman missiles caused a nuclear explosion while the missile was still in its silo. Sadly the death toll in neighboring communities from this accident is likely to be in the hundreds.

"Maintenance of certain systems was underway at the time so there is no reason to believe this was intentional or sabotage or an attack from an enemy and in an abundance of caution we've instructed the military to stand down any similar devices until a full investigation of this accident is completed. Our military alert level was briefly raised due to the accident but has now been returned to normal.

"This is a terrible accident and should never have happened. I can assure you that we will determine why this tragic event occurred with such devastating consequences. I have ordered a full inquiry into all matters surrounding this accident so we can assure ourselves we are free of any threats of something like this ever happening again.

"Clearly several failsafe systems didn't work properly but we're confident everything has now been done to ensure no further accidents are possible and these missiles will stay off line and powered down until we have corrected whatever the problem is.

"Initial reports indicate that with a southwest wind and favorable jet stream, any harmful radiation is being swept at high altitude towards the largely uninhabited Canadian Far North and the Arctic, including uninhabited northern Greenland so no evacuation orders are required.

"I've instructed all of the resources of this Administration to assist the state and local first responders in any way we can.

"In a related and very sad matter, Secretary of Defense Dan Westgate, a good friend and a great leader, on hearing the news collapsed this evening in the Oval Office. We immediately started CPR and he was attended to by the White House emergency medical team and paramedics from DC Fire and Emergency Medical Services who were unable to resuscitate him. Dan was a close friend of mine and a true American patriot. He served his state and country for almost two decades with the highest integrity and he will be sorely missed by all of us in Washington and his home state of Colorado.

"Our hearts go out to all those affected by tonight's tragic accident in North Dakota. Please join me and my family in prayer for those who lost their lives tonight, or were injured in this terrible accident. As well, we hope you'll join us in praying for our first responders doing search and rescue as we speak.

"God bless America and all who call her home."

As Alpha-1 and Fraser Carmichael finished watching the President's speech Carmichael turned to Alpha-1, "You didn't have to do that. You could've stopped that bomb."

Alpha-1 stared at him with no expression. After a short pause he said, "Yes, as I said earlier it was your President's actions that caused this and let me assure you that it pains us greatly to say that it served a purpose. He precipitated that action, not us. I'm afraid we have limited empathy for what you people will sacrifice for power and this was a pure power play. He wanted the upper hand in dealing with me and now your President has garnered an appropriate reward which he will not soon forget."

"That asshole's no President of mine," Carmichael snarled.

At that Carmichael's iPhone rang and he could see it was his office.

"Sir, it's Bill in CII operations in New York. I don't know if you were informed but after leaving you off in Washington the team on the plane received information that there were problems at the mine near Wallace and they redirected the company jet there. According to their flight plan it was their intention to refuel in Minot, North Dakota and well sir, it looks like they may have gotten caught up in that explosion out there tonight. We were tracking the corporate jet's tail number using Flight Tracker, as we always do when our execs are traveling, and it disappeared from ATC on approach to Minot, at about eight fifty-five apparently right when that bomb went off.

"The plane left radar somewhere between ten and twenty miles out from the airport and maybe twenty-five or so miles from that explosion so there is a chance they may have crash landed short of the airfield. We've informed what authorities we can reach as most communications are still down but as you can imagine they're swamped so we're contracting our own search and rescue out of Bismarck. They should be airborne soon and we'll let you know of any developments."

Carmichael, not letting on that he already knew of the crash, thanked him, asked to be kept up-to-date, asked that the HR VP be called at her home to deal with the families involved and hung up just as the President returned from his TV appearance, with Gerry Hastings in tow.

Alpha-1 seemed to nod in Gerry's direction, eyeing the President who turned and said, "Gerry, I'm afraid I must ask you to leave us again."

Hastings turned beet red, "After what has happened here tonight you're going to continue this meeting and exclude me again? Hal, what is going on here? What can be so important that it eclipses an attempted overthrow of your Administration, an A-bomb going off on our own soil and Dan Westgate's death? This makes no sense at all. Tell me what's going on here! Why am I being left out of whatever this is?"

The President leaned forward and almost whispered to Hastings, "Gerry, I'm sorry. It just has to be this way. Please bear with me and hold any calls until I tell you."

Hastings looked like he was going to explode with frustration and virtually stomped out of the room and for the first time ever, slammed the door to his adjacent office. He had half a mind to call someone, but whom? Whom was he going to call to complain that the President seemed to have lost all sense of propriety? This had been the worst and craziest night of his life. Being left out of the meetings was one thing, but having a trusted friend, Dan Westgate, stick a gun in his face and then the tragedy up in Minot followed by Westgate's collapse. And now the President brushing a national tragedy aside for a business meeting or whatever was going on in there? 'What the hell is going on?' he almost yelled out loud.

He wondered if there was any connection between all of the events, but then he thought he was starting to go crazy himself. What could the connection be between a billionaire political enemy and rescued miner monopolizing the President's time, Dan Westgate flipping out, trying to wipe Wallace, Idaho off the map, and then dropping dead, and a missile backfiring in its own silo? Nothing, that's what. No connection at all. But how did it all happen inside a couple of hours? And why all the secrecy from Hal? He had been chased from the room by the President twice tonight and now instead of dealing with the Minot mess Hal was again closeted with Carmichael and the kid from Idaho. What the hell was going on? He hoped they would wrap up soon and maybe then the President would do some explaining.

After Gerry left, Alpha-1 took over speaking in a soft and reassuring voice, "Thank you, Mr. President. I know you have a lot to do and I'm sure federal and state politicians are all trying to get to you about the events of earlier this evening but let me remind you, it didn't have to be this way. Do as you're told and we may get through this without killing thousands more."

The President bristled at being blamed for it all and being talked to in this manner but he was still furious with himself and what had already transpired. He reluctantly decided, after killing hundreds of his own countrymen and seeing his friend drop dead, that he had better yield to this 'thing' and cooperate, at least for now.

Alpha-1 directed both men to take a seat while he stood. "I must say I got less than an hour's nap but the food seems to have helped and I now see the effects of adrenalin on the human body. So as you might say, 'I'm good to go' at least for a short time.

"Before I continue, let me say that we can find no words as a civilization to express our sorrow over what happened here tonight. It has been almost a million years since we experienced real death up close and to have so many die needlessly in relation to our introduction to you is a horrendous shock to us. I suspect our civilization has learned an important lesson in empathy tonight and we sincerely hope there will be no more events like we just witnessed, but I think you're clear now on our priorities. Our hope is that your mind is set on protecting human life too. But I think you understand, we will do whatever it takes to ensure our security and survival.

"As I think you're aware, we had sincerely hoped to do this with no harm to humans. There are those in our civilization who now wonder if we should have approached you in this way.

"Nevertheless we must get back to why we have connected with you two." He looked towards the floor as if gathering his thoughts, "I told you already that we've always feared conflict with Earth-based organisms or an alien arrival. Now our worst nightmares may have arrived as we expect to be facing both at the same time."

Both men shivered and looked at each other. This didn't sound good.

Alpha-1 continued, "We are about to have visitors. And by 'we' I mean both Alphans and humans. As you may appreciate, we decided a long time ago that we would contest any alien arrival if we were unaware or unsure of their motives, intent or indeed their capabilities. Inferior civilizations rarely compete well with more superior forces or at least the gamble is not worth taking. To that end we've always taken certain simple steps to remain quiet or invisible as you might say, to wit, our move underground and our development of cloaking.

"Tonight you decided to contest a new arrival, yet you knew that we once shared DNA and have been very up-front about our intent, motives and capabilities. We're all Earthlings and remember, we have lived side by side so to speak, for about two million years. So your reaction was not one we would consider logical. I also thought it was clear after our earlier meeting tonight that you understood that any confrontation with us was unnecessary and in fact unwise."

The President was wasted and simply stared back at him not acknowledging the accusations.

"Back to the situation at hand. Part of our space program is supporting our invisibility by jamming or rather canceling out certain electromagnetic energy from escaping our solar system. We do not want to send signals to anyone out there who might be listening and decide to visit us. You humans on the other hand are very noisy in this regard and don't seem to care who detects your presence. You've filled up most of the electromagnetic spectrum with everything from TV signals and radio to all sorts of communication networks that you beam out into space for anyone to hear. Luckily our electromagnetic cloaking was in place a long time before your first transmissions but we apparently overlooked something.

"Range was a challenge. We've established a perimeter for the cloaking and shortly your Voyager I spacecraft, launched in 1977, will leave the outer edge of our solar system and it will soon exceed our cloaking perimeter and any emissions from it will eventually make it into deep space. Once we finish here, we feel we will have no problem in convincing you to shut it down before it exceeds our cloaking range limits.

"But our real problem is a much different and more serious one. You had a program about eighty years ago that was extremely secret. So secret we didn't know of its existence until early morning on July 16th, 1945 on your calendar. You might have guessed that it was the first test of your atomic weapon at White Sands in New Mexico. You did a great job of keeping it secret, even from us.

"We thought nothing of it at the time but a very recent audit of our cloaking efforts turned up a serious issue. Because it was such a secret program we were unprepared for it. We now know that some electromagnetic radiation was not totally blocked by our cloaking at the time. Certain wavelengths including Gamma rays and X-rays apparently escaped our blocking of that event. The residual signal this 'leak' caused will be about eighty light years away by now and out of reach of our cloaking and definitely detectable by advanced civilizations.

"Now we come to the tough and urgent part that has caused us to reveal ourselves.

"For many thousands of years we've been tracking a number of communication-active, extraterrestrial civilizations. Yes, they are out there and we have been keeping tabs on a few dozen of them who you might think of as close neighbors. We've discovered various 'styles' of communication, all of which we can detect but in most cases we have been unsuccessful in translating them into anything useful. A new Rosetta Stone would come in handy.

"By local I mean our own neighborhood of the galaxy which you know as the Milky Way. We survey a small sphere around the Earth of about twenty-five thousand light years in every direction. That covers only a tiny part of the Milky Way Galaxy but enough to afford us some sense of security.

"By monitoring the position and style of their communications we believe that most of these life forms live and thrive in their own star system and cannot, or choose not to travel to nearby stars. One of these civilizations of particular interest to us does not constrain themselves to their own system. This intelligent life form has been seen to move between star systems and we suspect they commandeer suitable planets. Planets you refer to as Goldilocks planets; ones that are neither too hot nor too cold and support liquid water and therefore biological evolution and life as we both know it. Of particular concern is that they seem to only go after occupied Goldilocks planets.

"We know this because we've recorded their unique communication methods and styles and we see them popping up from time to time where they didn't previously exist on additional planets where we had detected and were monitoring other intelligent life. For obvious reasons we consider this life form as a potential marauding civilization, although because we cannot decipher their complex communications, we have no evidence of their intent.

"To achieve this behavior and by following their progress, we're also convinced they have attained speeds beyond light speed enabling this interstellar travel. Our best estimate at this time is that they can physically travel at something approaching three hundred times light speed, but again that's just an estimate."

Both men seated on the couches were starting to look alarmed.

"I think you can see where this is going. Our best estimate is that some radiation from your first atomic bomb arrived at their closest proximity to Earth a little over five weeks ago. There is a high probability they detected it. There is an even higher probability that they'll investigate it using their fastest transports which will likely bring them to our doorstep in about three to four months."

Suddenly both men got the horrifying picture. If they were to believe Alpha-1 they were starting to see why Alpha had decided to reveal itself to humans. But was this just a polite warning or what?

Alpha-1 continued, "The timing is all based on two very important assumptions. The first is that for the last eighty years they haven't moved any closer to Earth because our latest readings of them are that old given that the planet we're monitoring them on is a little over eighty light years away. If they moved say last year to a planet sixty light years away then we would not detect that for another fifty-nine years.

"You already know the second assumption, that their fastest speed is three hundred times light speed.

"If they were on a closer planet, as the pulse from 1945 went by they would have picked it up earlier but thankfully as time goes by and they have not arrived, that possibility diminishes."

Now both the President and Carmichael looked nervous and all the President could think of was his earlier move to try to eliminate this 'alien' in front of him. If he had been successful then mankind might have been left alone to face possibly an even worse enemy.

"So we both face an existential threat. We could and will likely receive a visit from this traveling civilization. As I said, we have not decoded their communications so we have no idea of their motives and intent on these moves and in some fields they are superior to us such as in being able to travel beyond light speed. So to make a long story short, they fit the profile of a visitor we would contest.

"Now why am I telling you this beyond a friendly heads-up?

"We have a serious problem, we Alpha I mean. Because we're immortal we've become lazy in a sense. We're in no rush for any kind of progress in the physical world. We can do anything in the virtual or fantasy world at almost any pace we wish but the physical world has limitations and we as a society have tended to ignore or neglect it for the most part. We are normally content in our virtual and fantasy worlds so the physical infrastructure and capabilities we've built are highly effective if there are no real time constraints. Scanning the galaxy out to twenty-five thousand light years, we thought that with our cloaking, we had lots of time to react to any threat. Until now.

"What that means in the real or physical world is that we have limited helpers, limited materials for building anything and limited mobility below the surface. Heretofore this has served us well but not now. We need certain capacities quickly which we can't rectify easily without bumping into humans in a major way. So we could expose Alpha to mankind or even push humanity aside and do what we need but we think we have a better plan.

"Now you begin to see why we've introduced ourselves to humans and in particular you two. You have capabilities we are in need of.

"We need access to substantial amounts of rather rare raw materials quickly. We need a large and highly secured staging area on the surface to build and launch the defenses we will need for these aliens. And we need to do it all in the next ten to twelve weeks. Only you two have essentially unlimited access to infrastructure, supply chains, rare raw materials, transport and secure staging areas. Our analysis says it would be better to run a covert plan with a few humans, meaning you two, rather than the alternative of pushing you aside and revealing ourselves completely to humans. That is IF AND ONLY IF we can get and ensure FULL cooperation from both of you.

"You need this as much as we do and we also have that one other selfish need. If we're successful, we need to disappear back underground with no one knowing. We are not at a point where introducing our two civilizations on a grand scale is advisable. Man has to make some significant social and technological advances before that is possible if it is ever even desirable. You, meaning mankind, would instantly want access to everything we have including immortality which would be catastrophic for both of us.

"However, as you may have surmised, part of the deal is an invitation for you two to join our immortal world. Not everyone was in favor of inviting you but it has become necessary due to this emergency. You're both relatively high on the list of potential outsiders we would like to see join us but frankly, not near the top.

"Typically we like individuals with skills we aren't yet fully aware of. The last visitors we recruited were from some time ago so by now there are lots of new skills and personalities we would like to experience."

Neither transfixed human reacted to the slight that they were not one of the 'desirables' because they were more than traumatized by every word that came out of this thing's mouth. 'It' was laying out a story where the survival of mankind was clearly in the balance.

Alpha-1 continued, "However this is a very special case. In return for your unbridled enthusiasm for, and success in our project, we will offer you the following; you and a few of your closest relatives will be offered access to our immortal world at a place and time of your choosing. You can either live out your normal human life and join us then or join us at the end of this project. The choice is yours and we are neutral on which path you take.

"Mr. President, in your case that would mean your wife and your daughter. In the case of your daughter she may not have months to live with her advanced ALS but I'm afraid the project must be completed successfully before we can offer any of you the access to our immortal world or to what you might think of as heaven.

"We're a very compassionate species but our entire civilization is on the line here with this coming threat and I'm afraid we must be firm about the offer. The project must be completed and succeed before anyone is admitted to Alpha. Frankly we need the leverage over you, Mr. President, especially after what we saw here tonight.

"Mr. Carmichael, we'll leave it a little more open-ended for you. You don't currently have a significant other or children so you'll be allowed one and only one 'guest' so if you do fall in love before you take our offer, I'd suggest someone without parents, children or close relatives which they would undoubtedly be reluctant to leave behind. Of course you could not discuss the possibility with anyone without our presence. I'm afraid if you offered immortality and the person wanted to remain we would have to do an immediate memory wipe on them.

"In addition for Mr. Carmichael we will leave behind some of the helpers or robots and computing power with certain stipulations. These will be beyond anything you have seen but still plausibly developed by Mr. Carmichael's 'secret' labs in this 21st century. That's if you chose to remain as a human for some time.

"So there it is gentlemen. We believe there is a high probability that a marauding race of aliens will visit this planet soon to check out an energy pulse that emanated from your first test explosion of an atomic weapon eighty years ago. We need to work together to be prepared to defend this planet. And my species desires to return to its hidden world after we're successful.

"Questions?"

Both men sat transfixed. The President looked around his office. Only a few hours ago life was so simple. Now he was battling interstellar aliens with another alien proposing a partnership. He had already blown up hundreds of his own people and killed a good friend yet he was being offered heaven as an inducement to cooperation. Again he wondered if he was dreaming or had been hypnotized as none of it seemed real.

Carmichael couldn't drag his mind away from the idea of having Alpha's robots and computing power at his fingertips. He had no idea what they were capable of but it was a damned sight more than his competitors had and likely to be completely fantastic. Being a product nerd he couldn't wait to see them.

The President was first to speak, "What do you know about these invaders?"

"Not as much as we would like. Because we haven't mastered faster-than-light travel we can't go out there and spy on them. All we know is that this race seems to be appearing throughout the close-in galaxy. They have a pattern of zeroing in on civilizations that radiate structured electromagnetic radiation so we were convinced we were of no interest to them due to our cloaking. That hope has now evaporated.

"We track them due to their very unique communications technologies which they choose not to screen or jam. That may tell us something about their level of confidence and possibly even their intent.

"When they arrive on a planet the original communications

fingerprints tend to die off to be replaced by theirs. Now that isn't a guarantee that they have enslaved the planet or eliminated their inhabitants. Maybe they're benevolent and upgraded the indigenous civilization's technology benignly, but that is a chance we're not inclined to take given the little we really know about them.

"Believe me, since we recently discovered our situation we have had all of our resources working on trying to get more information on them with the limited data we can collect. As I said, we decided long ago that we would only attempt to meet other races on our terms, not theirs.

"We also don't know their level of technological or physical evolution except that they have us beat on faster-than-light speed travel. We do speculate that like ourselves, they may have moved from a biological existence into a technology existence to provide immortality. Our belief is that the transition to a technological existence is a natural part of evolution of intellectual beings and man itself is closing in on that eventuality. So you might think of them as highly intelligent and self-aware machines as you may already be thinking of us in those terms.

"Whatever the case, we must assume in all prudence that they will be a formidable force to deal with and true to their strategy, they are almost certain to check out any energy signals or anomalies they pick up from unexplored Goldilocks planets within this quadrant of the galaxy, meaning we're next."

Carmichael had risen and was pacing slowly but keeping a safe distance from Alpha-1 after what had transpired earlier with Dan Westgate, "What specifically can we do to help?"

"We'll get into the fine details later. You may have good ideas too although we think we know you pretty well.

"Firstly we think some of Mr. Carmichael's stealthy companies can be used to shield purchases of the specialized materials we need. We have restricted the construction of the weapons we need so that you have access to the refined materials required for this project. There are a few materials that we can reprocess once we have the raw materials from you. We also think Area-51 in Nevada could be cleared out for a staging area. It is highly secure, remote and offers other advantages as a screen.

"The President would authorize the military to act as our transport. We wouldn't use the existing buildings as they aren't large enough. Our facilities would be cloaked so they couldn't be spied on but we need the large open space and the privacy of Groom Lake and the security afforded by that secret military base."

The President spoke, "There's a problem with that. There is important work going on at Area-51 and there are lots of troops and contractors there. It would be highly suspicious if I were to simply close the place down or start flying in planeloads of materials they had no need of."

Alpha-1 smiled, "Yes we are aware of that and I'm sure it comes as no surprise to Mr. Carmichael, as he was one of the bidders on the project, that you're building the first few F-47 fighters there, or the Firebolt as it's known to the military."

Carmichael almost laughed, "Wasn't the Firebolt one of Harry Potter's best magic brooms?"

The President simply smiled. Alpha-1 ignored the comments as he continued, "That project to replace the troubled F-35 and the F-22 is in some hot water itself, you will agree. In that regard we think we have a political and economic solution for you, although this may cause one or both of you to lose your jobs.

"To get much more control over the base and open it only to our project we propose that you cancel the F-47 build at Area-51, turn the site over to Mr. Carmichael's new learning robots and supercomputer that I will provide and you will award a unilateral contract to Mr. Carmichael who will build the first ten Firebolts in record time. Two to three months would be the target for delivery. Our robots will build your planes with record quality and at zero labor cost. We'll optimize everything we can as long as it seems 21st century plausible. The extra raw materials we need for our space weapon will be buried in the shipments for the F-47s.

"Mr. Carmichael will announce that he has bought X-Wave Systems out of Vancouver, Canada and extended their leadership quantum computer architecture to build the first thousand Qubit quantum computer. With its secretly developed operating system software, not only can he run the robots, but he can cut the time of development of the Firebolt drastically because all component, system and even flight testing can be simulated in the quantum computer. X-Wave is nowhere near these breakthroughs but they are sufficiently avant-garde that their technology added to some unidentified technology from Mr. Carmichael's other investments and secret labs will seem somewhat plausible to most observers. The ones who think it is not plausible will be seen as conspiracy nerds.

"The new computer will run his new self-learning robot plant, teaching the robots to optimize manufacturing as they go. It should all sound plausible as a major breakthrough for America in manufacturing. The speed will sound too fantastic but it can all be attributed to the quantum computer which can drive the next-generation robots at incredible speeds.

"In the end, you'll both present the F-47 to the world at less than half the current estimated cost and change government contracting and the military procurement processes forever, as long as it is Mr. Carmichael's robots doing the work. To make things easier for you we've already fixed many of the design flaws in the plane with solutions that will still appear 21st century."

It was the President's turn for a question, "Assuming you have all of that figured out and it's all plausible and we can convince Congress and the press that it's all real, how will you defend against these intruders? Killing a scout ship is one thing. Defeating an entire civilization is another, because surely others will follow."

"Excellent point. Our strategy is simple. We'll hide. We need to build a very large cloaking device that will make Earth look like a burned-out cinder. We will make it look like an all-out atomic war recently trashed the planet, destroying Earth's atmosphere and oceans and what is left is a radioactive mess of little interest to the aliens. It will no longer appear to be an inhabited Goldilocks planet worth visiting.

"We think this is achievable in the time we have, IF YOU COOPERATE FULLY. We can have no more diversions like tonight. I was not joking when I said we need your unbridled enthusiasm for this project to succeed. Anything short of that puts the future of this planet as a home for our two civilizations in grave jeopardy and that of course is something we cannot abide. In addition you now know the time frames involved so we can't afford any more sparring sessions or delays.

"You also know the task and you know why we have picked you two and why we must work together. We need your cooperation to ensure success, but if we don't get your full cooperation, or if factors get in the way of you cooperating, or if we sense any reluctance or dragging of feet on any of this, we will be forced to go to Plan B to ensure the survival of our species.

"I think you can imagine what Plan B entails. Essentially it would be pressing ahead with the tactics in Plan A and eliminating any obstacles, meaning any humans who got in the way. We can push humans aside with great ease and it will not distract us from our goal. As I've said before, we have very high respect for life of any kind and would only do this as a necessary step to defend our planet and our civilization, forced on us by your actions or inaction.

"As you know, we believe humans could not knowingly coexist with Alphans at this point in time and therefore we cannot be discovered. Wiping out a few hundred or thousand humans to execute Plan B could not be done without discovery so I'm afraid that scenario would necessarily snowball into wiping out all of mankind. Obviously this is something we want to avoid. We're only too aware that this is your planet too.

"So now you've heard the proposal, what say ye?"

The Challenge

Turcot seemed reluctant to respond so Carmichael was first to speak, "Obviously I'm more than enthusiastic about this and I think that was your intention. You've come to the right man. I can get this done. Call it greed if you must but I have a burning desire beyond self-preservation, to be the best in my business and I like all elements of your plan.

"If I'm to believe what you've told us, there is only upside in this for me, assuming your plan to thwart the approaching aliens works and we don't all get vaporized.

"There will be challenges of course. I have a board of directors to deal with and a management team that has had some expectations set but if I can pull it off, it's a major windfall for me. I get a massive contract with little expense, access to new earth-shaking technology for the future, and a free pass to heaven whenever I want to use it. As they say in New York, 'what's not to like'?"

Carmichael turned to Hal Turcot, thinking he was the only one who could blow this deal. The real question was did Turcot buy the story of the approaching aliens? As he looked at the President he realized this would mean working closely with this weasel of a man that he had opposed in every way possible and the evening's events had not endeared him to the President at all. Working with Turcot was more than distasteful but the rewards were well worth it. He really wondered whether he could trust this man whom he had always thought of as the weakest of spineless liberals.

The President hesitated and after several glances between Alpha-1 and himself he finally spoke, "After tonight's false start at our relationship, and given that I now have a better understanding of your capabilities and your intentions, I feel I want to be completely honest with you."

Alpha-1 simply nodded.

"I was elected by the American people and I take that responsibility very seriously, and that weighs heavily on me. They didn't elect me to subjugate myself or them to another regime. In addition, I come from a position of having a very hard time dealing with ultimatums."

Carmichael was wondering where this sudden courage was coming from. Turcot wasn't known in conservative circles for backbone or guts. This 'thing' could strike him down at any moment yet he was standing toe to toe with it.

The President continued, "I personally, and the country I lead, have a pretty strict policy on ultimatums or bribery. That said and assuming you're open to showing me some real evidence that we're about to be under attack to corroborate your claims, I have decided to cooperate with you to the degree that I'm able.

"Let me explain. If you know our political system you'll know that we have three equal branches of government and my powers aren't unlimited. Some of the things you've suggested may not be possible given the limits of my authority.

"Even if I do find a way to do certain things, like award a unilateral contract to Carmichael Industries, there would be massive upheaval in my government. Military contracts are spread over almost every state, so bumping people out of their place at the trough isn't going to sit well and they'll fight back ... hard.

"I don't know whether I can deliver on your Plan A as you've laid it out."

Alpha-1 smiled, "Are you suggesting Plan B might be our better option? Just say the word."

The President stiffened and stood tall facing Alpha-1, "You know that isn't what I'm saying. I'm saying there may be other ways to make this work. We need to negotiate a process that works for both of us and as I said, I need some proof we are actually in jeopardy."

Alpha-1 stared him straight in the eye, and raised his hand indicating that he wanted Turcot to stop, "Let me make this easy for you. I have no evidence for you of an impending attack. What we have is beyond your comprehension and I have explained it to you in terms I think you are capable of understanding. On that note, my IQ is more than double yours. Let me take that back. My IQ is likely four times yours after what we've seen here tonight. Alpha has worked out the optimum plan and all other possible scenarios have been tested and simulated. We are secure in forecasting a threat and we've tested thousands of options and full scenarios on how to proceed. So you need to take my word for it. It's either Plan A or Plan B and our final decision will be made in the next few seconds. If it's Plan B I will be forced to eliminate the two of you first because you know too much.

"There is no point in any negotiations and your 'best efforts', or how did you put it, 'cooperate to the degree that you are able', will not suffice. What is on the table is essentially the defense of this planet which you should not look at as an ultimatum. I think you should see this as your responsibility. Cooperating with us is your only option. You've nothing in your arsenal that would be useful in combating the approaching aliens or trying to force your will on us for that matter.

"And remember, when this is all over we go back underground and no one alive on the surface save possibly the two of you knows anything of our existence. So there is no downside to you if you cooperate. That's Plan A. Or we can do it the other way.

"If it helps in terms of your Congress, you probably can't find a better constitutional lawyer than me. Remember my hobby has been watching America develop as a country since before you had a constitution. You have sufficient Executive Power to do what is needed here and yes there will be opposition but not within the time period we are discussing. The Hill does not move fast. You will almost certainly pay the ultimate political price but that in no way compares with the real risk and reward picture facing you now. Impeachment compared to my offer of immortality and saving the Earth should be an easy choice.

"You only have to make this work for a couple of months and I'd think the possibility of saving your daughter, whether you want to call it a bribe or not, would be appealing.

"As to ultimatums yes, if you insist on looking at it that way, this is an ultimatum. Your civilization would very likely die at the hands of these invaders without my ultimatum so you should be happy you have new neighbors bearing gifts. Remember the old expression, 'Never look a gift horse in the mouth'. So I say to you, as to ultimatums or bribes, deal with it.

"As I see it, it is your responsibility to take this deal to save the planet for your constituency and the world.

"Now in the street parlance of your people let me say that it is time to man up and grow a pair."

The President sheepishly smiled realizing he was trapped. After a moment of looking for some accommodation and hating to be put on the spot he said, "When you put it that way, I guess I have no choice so you now have my 'unbridled enthusiasm' as you put it. I have one serious request though. Save my daughter first."

Alpha-1 was suddenly much more serious, "As much as it pains me, we've been through that. We will save no one unless this plan is executed successfully which means we need to start work now. Unfortunately, Mr. President, you've shown yourself to be unpredictable and frankly, as I said earlier, I need the leverage of your daughter to ensure you stay committed to this project. So sadly the answer is no. Her fate is now completely in your hands. If you're successful she will likely survive, be completely healthy and enjoy all the benefits of immortality in a heaven-like world."

Turcot realized he had no leverage in this matter and finally nodded acceptance as Alpha-1 turned his attention to Carmichael, "Now that that is settled, the first step in our joint project is for Mr. Carmichael here to hire me as his new Chief Operating Officer to run Area-51 but I will only be involved in our project. You should assign all other business lines to your current COO if he survived that plane crash out west.

"You'll have to make up a story as to why you've hired a relatively junior mining engineer to run your secret government project. The outside world should not know about the project or my mission but I will have total control over Area-51 as soon as the President clears it out which needs to happen within twenty-four hours."

Both men were once more shocked at the aggressive nature of this 'thing'. The time frames totally caught them off guard.

Alpha-1 seeing their concern continued, "Let me stress gentlemen, we're already behind schedule. None of this is ideal or even within our control. Our very recent audit of signals escaping into space uncovered this massive threat to our existence. I wish I had been able to get out of that mine faster but we had decided it was the best opportunity to meet you both on the right terms. While I was pretending to be trapped there, we spent the month getting ready and building subsystems with the materials we already had. Our plan ensured we lost no time on the project but I'll say it again, we may already be out of time if these aliens are on a closer planet. So everything has to happen 'like yesterday' as they say."

He turned to a shocked President and said, "If you need help on tactics just ask but I think you can find a senior military figure, give him an open-ended budget and get it done. We're now working minute to minute as we don't know if these aliens are going to surprise us and show up early.

"Mr. Carmichael and I will use his Washington condo for a base for the moment. Apparently I need more sleep or we'd be staying here to work.

"Sometime tonight Mr. Carmichael has to buy that company in Vancouver. You have to clear out Area-51 and secure it.

"We'll set up secure communications so we can speak hourly if need be. Your job is to avoid impeachment while spending the majority of your time executing our plan. Good luck. Tomorrow when America awakens you'll both make certain press announcements that will form the foundation of our work. I'll get back to you on that."

At that he signaled to Carmichael and they headed for the door.

Turcot hardly had a moment to breathe before Gerry Hastings was in the room and clearly wanting some explanations, "OK Hal, they're gone. What the hell was so important that it trumped a national crisis with an atomic bomb blowing up in its silo? Every politician in Washington and Idaho wants a better explanation and the press has already dumped on your 'less than thorough' explanation to the American people.

"WHAT THE HELL HAS BEEN GOING ON IN HERE?" he almost yelled.

"Sit down Gerry."

Hastings rejected the instruction and stood his ground.

The President took a moment to gather his thoughts and get in the right frame of mind for his new reality. Gerry would have been a great help but after the Dan Westgate thing, there was no way he could let Gerry in on this, even though he was always included and on top of everything that happened in the White House.

The President finally spoke, "OK Gerry, two things happened here tonight. One was a terrible accident in North Dakota perpetrated by a man I trusted. I'm certain they are going to find he had a brain tumor or something but we can't yet rule out a Manchurian Candidate type affair. Personally I think that was all science fiction but who knows. Maybe someone long ago brainwashed him and planted him for this very purpose. Either way we have to pick up the pieces of this terrible tragedy. At some point I hope we will understand it all and it will make some kind of sense to us, but at this moment it's a total mystery why this happened.

"As to the press and most of the politicians, deflect all questions to the Pentagon. They have the cover story and they can handle it. When you talk to them tell them we're going to need an explanation ASAP as to why the thing detonated in its silo and of course it needs to tie back to the maintenance cover story.

"Our role is to ensure we do everything we can for the folks up in Minot. It must be total chaos up there tonight. If I can, I'll fly up there myself and meet with local leaders tomorrow. I can do a follow-up press scrum from there. See if you can make that work. I'm not even sure the Minot Airport is operational at this point. We might have to fly into Bismarck and take Marine 1 up there. Call in anybody you need tonight and make it happen. But to be frank, the deed is done and there is a limit to what we can do to put those poor peoples' lives back together.

After a pause he continued, "The second thing that happened in here tonight was some unbelievable revelations coming out of the mouth of Fraser Carmichael. This guy Glass was just an ornament; an excuse to get in here and have a real confidential face to face with me. I would've kept you in here but Carmichael insisted that no one knows any details of what he has. He doesn't want anything on this getting out until he is ready and if I'm the only one who knows then he knows where any leaks came from."

Gerry interrupted, "Wait a minute. It was that Glass kid that insisted on privacy and he was in here and heard all of it."

"Yeah, but he had been coached by Carmichael to take the lead at first, given we had surveillance on the mine and we thought he had discovered something. Also, Carmichael is going to use him somehow to roll out his new technology.

"The supposed discovery in the mine was all a ruse to get in here. Somehow they knew we were listening in. Still it worked, Carmichael got his private and secret meeting with me and frankly I can now see his point on the secrecy. I would have done the same thing if I was so far out in front of the competition. What he has is so revolutionary that it has to be secret and we're going to profit immensely from it.

"To be specific, apparently some of Carmichael's companies have made some kind of amazing technological breakthrough in the area of computing and robots that is going to shake the entire manufacturing world, and I mean big time. He is about to announce an amazing new quantum supercomputer with incredible capabilities and a bunch of next-generation robots that are unbelievably fast and learn as they work. I think he sees this as a way to lock himself into major military contracts.

"As you know the F-35 is in even more trouble than the F-22 was in terms of delays and budget overruns. It has become too common and a recurring theme with these military contractors. First they promise the moon and the stars with the lowest bid that might drive them into bankruptcy and then they manage us and the project causing all kinds of delays, add-ons etc. so they end up making big profits. Anyways, Carmichael wants me to kill the work at Area-51 on the F-47 and turn the whole place over to his robots. He'll build the first ten Firebolts in just a couple of months and sell them to us for less than half the price we're currently projecting."

Hastings was dumbfounded, "And this is what preoccupied you at a time of national catastrophe? Don't tell me you went for such a crazy idea, he doesn't even like you. He bid on the 47s and lost, fair and square. This is just some kind of unhook strategy to get the contract back. You can't believe a word out of that creep's mouth. And all of this on an evening when we had an A-bomb go off and your SECDEF died in this very room? This makes no sense. Please tell me it was more than a commercial deal that took your eye off the ball."

"Listen Gerry, I know the timing is terrible but you know what's at stake. Congress is hammering me for a new budget and they won't fund any of my social programs and you know as well as I do that those programs are critical to kickstarting the economy. I'm going to solve our total budget issue by doing something no President has had the balls to do, by taking on the military industrial complex.

"On top of Carmichael's plan to take over the 47, I'm going to kill the F-35 too. There's way more than a trillion dollars tied up in the two of them over the next decade. Carmichael is likely to give me back most of that and rewrite the book on manufacturing in this country. His technology will eventually be licensed to other US manufacturers and we'll get millions of jobs back that have been outsourced. I'm thoroughly convinced he can pull it off and I'm going to use my Executive Powers to make it happen.

"I know my focus should be on Dan Westgate and Minot but there's nothing I can do about that now. Besides that's all negative news. We can deflect all attention on that to the Pentagon. Apart from some protocol changes to eliminate a SECDEF going off the deep end, they'll eventually find out it was a ten dollar part or some software glitch that made it explode in its silo but all I can do now is try to pick up the pieces and reassure the American people.

"This other thing is something positive and new and it comes at a time when we really need it."

Hastings was beside himself, "But sir, putting aside a national emergency, Congress will never let you get away with what you just told me. Military contracts like the F-35 are their honey pot. Virtually every state will be hurt with the loss of military contracts for those fighters. And if not the fighters then they'll see the military spending cuts coming and oppose you in every way possible. They'll cut you off at the knees. Nothing will get done around here. They won't let you do it … but you already know that, so what's really going on here?"

He knew Gerry was right on both counts and starting to show some impatience he said, "Hell Gerry, I'm not running for office anymore. Time to do something lasting that will make life better for Americans. Sure there will be the loss of military manufacturing jobs in the short term but we were going to lose them anyways. Carmichael can't do the job with zero labor. He'll still need logistics and sales and delivery and maintenance people just like the others do. As things stand today, more and more of the components for even military weapons are built overseas due to cost, free trade concessions, and offsets for our allies who want to buy the damned planes. This project breaks the cycle we're stuck in and gives us some breathing space to re-architect our high-tech workforce bringing back the kind of jobs that we can make permanent in the US. And it gives us a start on the social programs, like worker retraining, that we so desperately need.

"We need to retrain Americans for the jobs of the future, not spend billions lining the pockets of the rich execs and shareholders of a few companies that own the military business and outsource the labor to cheaper countries. I've had it with those fat cats virtually stealing money from the American people. Hell most of them have off-shore bank accounts to try to hide their wealth from the IRS.

"They take all the advantages of an American-based enterprise and the profits from the tax dollars we spend on their crap, but they return nothing into our economy when they outsource most of the work overseas. That reduces their costs, gets their executives obscene bonuses, and funds big dividends to the rest of their friends and shareholders who, by the way, are less and less American. Hell the Arabs and the Chinese own large stakes in these companies now. The boards and the execs of these companies are feathering their own nests at the expense of the middle class.

"Their lobbyists call all the shots. They OWN most of the politicians on the Hill. They killed the unions and they are so integrated into the Pentagon that they engineer all of these projects to run over budget. Hell they talk us into a path, then when we're half way down that path they come up with some new study, that WE paid for, to tell us we're on the wrong path and they have to redesign everything all over again, at our cost! It's a complete racket and we're the suckers who play along with it. Well no more, I'm determined to do this.

"Tomorrow I will single-handedly freeze all spending on the F-35 … ground it if I have to, kill the current F-47 fiasco and clean out Area-51. I need to move really fast on this. I need to get much of this done before they can get organized and come after me. I need a senior military man who can get this done and who will report directly to me. Who do we have that could jump right on this tonight?"

"Tonight? … Mr. President are you losing your mind? It's after ten o'clock and you've just dumped a totally wacky idea on the table and you want to start tonight? Your staff has not vetted any of this. Hell they don't even know about it. Carmichael is likely lying about everything. I'd be willing to bet there is no supercomputer or robots and all this secrecy is to stop us from discovering that. This smells all the world like a Republican trap or some kind of sting operation.

"There are constitutional issues too on the spending. Besides that, the Democrats on the Hill have no idea this is coming. We have no idea what the political ramifications of this will be except they'll all be bad, and we're dealing with a guy whom we've never trusted and it's pretty clear he hates you.

Gerry put his hand on the President's arm, "Let's get back to Minot. You do NOT want this to be your Katrina moment. Taking a national disaster lightly, like 'W' flying over New Orleans and telling the world his buddy 'Brownie' was doing a great job. It's political suicide … but you already know that too!

"If you don't focus all of your attention and press time on Minot for the next week, you'll be making a catastrophic political mistake. You'll get killed in the media and public opinion. You cannot introduce this other crazy stuff in the middle of all of this. It will not deflect focus from a tragedy, it will make it politically ten times worse.

A couple of weeks delay to investigate Carmichael's claims will not hurt anything. Hell everything to do with these fighters is already years behind schedule."

By this point Gerry Hastings was red in the face and almost yelling again, "For Christ sake, an atomic bomb went off on American soil tonight and probably killed thousands of people. Did you miss that somehow? Have you no idea what that means? And your Secretary of Defense flipped out, tried to take over the government and died under bizarre circumstances on this very floor about two hours ago. I can't believe we're even having this conversation. What has happened to you Hal?"

Turcot could see where this was going to be painful but Alpha-1 had been more than clear on the consequences of any delays or obstacles. Gerry knew too much about the inner workings of the White House and the politics involved. It had been a major part of his job to defend and protect the Turcot Administration and he was going to fight with everything he had to save this presidency which Turcot was coming to believe was doomed no matter what. It was clear Gerry's steadfast loyalty to this Administration was going to be an obstacle in everything the President had to do.

Hal Turcot took a long hard look at his friend of fifteen years, "Gerry, are you with me on this? Are you going to be part of the solution or part of the problem?"

Hastings was thunderstruck and physically took a step backward. He knew full well the implications of that question. In a much more submissive voice he started with, "Sir, I don't know what to say. You have always listened to my advice before but there is something totally bizarre about this whole night. Like the SECDEF trying to launch a missile and dropping dead after the fact." His voice was starting to rise as he continued, "Carmichael in here with that miner who needs a snooze in the Lincoln bedroom … and then Carmichael taking up all your time? And now these totally off-the-wall plans that must be kicked off tonight. Something is seriously wrong here. I need you to stop and think about this before you destroy this Administration, your presidency and your legacy. This has to stop! Take a breath. Nothing can be that urgent that we can't take the time to get it right. I beg you sir! This all makes no sense at all and you know that I'm telling you this out of loyalty."

The President's lip started to quiver, "I can see this isn't going to work and I'm very sorry but I absolutely need it to succeed. Gerry I need your resignation effective immediately. I'm afraid I need total commitment to my plans and in all honestly I can see where that is going to be impossible for you."

Gerry Hastings stood there breathless, stunned and by now shaking. This whole night had been surrealistic and there had been no warning any of this was coming. They had been laughing about something over a light dinner together before Carmichael showed up. He had always enjoyed an excellent relationship with Hal Turcot and now, just a few hours later, inexplicably he was being fired.

He fought the tears that he knew were welling up in his eyes. Puzzled and confused did not come close to explaining his state of mind. He had loved this man and had stayed with him through thick and thin, but he had never before witnessed this type of self-destructive and irrational behavior. It was almost as if Hal Turcot was the one with the brain tumor. It needed to be something that big to explain this totally unexpected and rash conduct. Even if he was serious and determined about all this, it was a totally losing strategy. Congress was never going to let him do any of this. And here he was throwing away a personal and long-term relationship that had benefited both men enormously.

This man could not have hurt him more if he had reached forward and stabbed him in the heart which was exactly how it felt.

More than a minute went by with the two men visibly shaken and staring at each other until finally Gerry Hastings spoke, "If that's the way it has to be then Mr. President it has been an honor serving you and the American people."

Before the President had a chance to thank him or shake his hand he turned and marched back to his former office leaving a shaken President behind with his hand extended and a tear rolling down his cheek.

He had just fired his best friend, longest standing ally and the one man who would do anything for him. The worst of it was that no matter how this turned out, he was never going to be able to explain any of it to him. Gerry would go to his grave perplexed and furious with a man he had dedicated his professional life to and who had just thrown him under the bus. No matter the explanations, the press would conclude that he had been fired for some unannounced transgression and that would damage his career irretrievably.

The President swallowed hard and wiped his eyes. In some ways he had killed two of his best friends in one night. He felt like his heart was in his mouth. He had never been that mean to another human being, never mind to such a loyal friend and confidant. This situation he now found himself in was unbearable. His heart was still pounding but now he had to focus all his energy on saving the planet. He consoled himself with the thought that it could have been no other way.

… Assuming Alpha-1 and Carmichael were telling the truth.

The Start

Hal Turcot had to pull himself together. Minot was again top of mind. He had caused the deaths of so many people. Looking back, taking a crazy swing at this alien hadn't been very well thought out. He now questioned the whole idea of striking first. Clearly it had backfired in the worst possible way. Sitting behind his desk he wondered if the approaching aliens would offer a second chance at this strategy or just wipe everyone out before they could even take a swing at them.

Even though Alpha's sole strategy towards the incoming aliens could be summed up in one word; 'hide', he wondered if in this case, that might not be a better direction than the failed strategy he had employed.

Now the entire world depended on this mysterious civilization, Alpha, being right.

Given he had committed to working with Alpha-1, he had some work to do. It was getting late but there was no time to lose. He knew that after the events in Minot, half the military, especially the Air Force who controlled the ICBMs, would be at their desks.

The call to the Secretary of the Air Force, General Kirk Jenkins predictably found him in his office at the Pentagon.

"Busy night General?"

"Yes Mr. President, you could say that," he said in a faltering voice. "We're all still in shock over here at Dan Westgate's mental episode and death but even more on that missile detonating in its silo. We've no idea what caused that failed launch but we'll get to the bottom of it somehow. But sir, what really happened over there to start all of this?"

"We can talk about that in a bit. I need you over here right now. Please come as soon as you can." At that the President hung up and left a curious General to find the quickest way over to the White House. He called for his car and had him put on the siren and the flashing lights and covered the few miles to the White House in record time.

On the way over he wondered how the President was going to use him as a scapegoat for the supposed failed missile maintenance. According to the President, the SECDEF had pretty much gone nuts but the cover story for the public about maintenance gone badly had already been put out and now they would need a substantial scapegoat to make it stick. Someone had to be 'accountable' and take the fall for all those deaths in North Dakota and why not the top guy at the Air Force who controlled the missile systems. It would be easy for the President to drum up some charge that not enough care had been taken, or training was delinquent for the supposed maintenance that went so terribly wrong. Whenever shit hit the fan in any situation like this, where innocent lives were lost, it was a slam dunk they would pin it on the military and the politicians would come out of it smelling like roses.

Arriving at the Oval Office, General Jenkins tried to take the lead with, "What actually happened in here tonight sir?"

"General you know as much as I do. Dan Westgate seemed to be completely normal when he was in here earlier in the evening and then suddenly he flipped somehow. Some of what he was raving about was incoherent but when you're standing in the Oval Office with a forty-five pointed at your nose you have no time to think and I simply did what I was told. He had already disarmed the Colonel holding the nuclear football so I saw no alternatives. He was going to do whatever it was he wanted to do with me dead or alive.

"I don't know if it was better or worse that the missile blew up in its silo or if he had actually been able to launch it toward that mine in Idaho. No telling what the death toll on the other end could have been but getting back to Minot, I don't know how you're going to do it with only a crater left to examine, but we need to find out why that thing exploded.

"You may not know this but I actually had that guy they rescued from the silver mine in the Oval Office with me earlier in the evening so I can only speculate that somehow in Dan's mind that mine was a threat of some kind, who knows. We'll have to wait for the autopsy to see if they can explain his behavior. One thing I can say is we need to revisit our protocol for missile launches. No one ever thought of a scenario where one of the two principals could overpower the other. I suppose either I or the Colonel could've taken a forty-five in the face but I don't see how that would've stopped him.

"You won't hear me saying this on TV but I think we dodged a bullet here tonight, no pun intended. At least we're not dealing with the Russians or the Chinese witnessing an unannounced missile launch and reacting to it. What do you think went wrong at the silo?"

The General was shocked that the President might think he had an explanation, "Sir we have no idea. There are all kinds of interlocks that should've prevented this. Essentially it is designed so something like this can never happen. The data at the moment suggests the missile did in fact arm itself while still on the ground and not in outer space. One theory is that given the target was so close we may have uncovered a flaw in the software timing logic of when to arm and detonate. Minot is less than seven hundred miles from Wallace so there's a possibility that because of such an unusual and close-in target, the software thought the missile was already inbound, approaching the target and armed the bird for ground contact. Its sensors might have thought it was already on the ground, causing the detonation and in fact Drake is actually lower in altitude than Wallace, Idaho. You can see where they may not have tested the software for a situation like that. These are intercontinental missiles after all and not meant for short range. I'm not buying that explanation but they are looking into everything.

"The data also shows the outer doors began to close but that is also a mystery at this point. The only theory again is timing. Possibly the silo for some reason thought the bird was gone and closed the doors as it should to protect the silo. Nothing like that has happened in any of our testing so I'm not buying that either. We may never find out because it's all vaporized now but you can be assured that we will do everything to find the problem.

"Based on your earlier order we received through Hastings, we grounded all Minuteman missiles until we know more. That has caused us to go to DEFCON 4 on all nuclear subs to compensate."

From what the General said, the President had the distinct impression that Alpha-1's plan and story were holding and it was unlikely that the military would be able to piece together what had actually happened.

"General, I'm sure you have it all well in hand, and of course I approve of the heightened level of readiness for the subs, but I want to move to another pressing topic.

"Tomorrow I will be making a major announcement about the Firebolt and before you go off the deep end about your favorite child let me tell you that I think you're going to like the outcome. You'll get your F-47s."

The General was unconvinced. His heart rate soared and he bit hard into his lip. This President wasn't viewed as a friend of the military. He had expected over the last few months, with all of the F-35 problems, that something might happen but certainly not tonight with everything else going on.

This President was known to value social progress over defense and now he was taking direct aim at the most important secret weapon, which the General viewed as essential to America's security. The Congressional oversight committees knew the F-47 program was late and way over budget, and there had been immense internal pressure to get the program back on track, but because of its secrecy, the public was still unaware of the massive hemorrhaging of money on the program.

The President noticed some obvious reddening on the part of the General as he continued, "As you know General, we're under tremendous budget pressure from all sides and I want you to know that American defense is at the top of my list of priorities, and I want you to have that F-47 ASAP."

The General saw this as an obvious lie, but that's what politicians were good at. This President had never seemed to care much for any of the military's priorities. It reminded him that politicians were famous for speaking out of both sides of their mouth. They'd tell you one thing while they actually meant the opposite. They often handed you something with one hand and took it away with the other, or convinced you that the shellacking you had just taken was something you had always wanted.

The President was still talking, "As you know I'm not what you military guys think of as a hawk but seriously, I want our military to have the best weapons. A strong and capable military is a key component of a robust foreign policy. I, like you, want to carry a big stick, I'm just not as keen on using it as quickly as some others. In addition I insist on sticks that work and that don't cost me double or triple what we were promised, or what they are worth.

"Now, to get back to the plan, Carmichael Industries is about to announce an incredible technological breakthrough related to a new quantum supercomputer and a new generation of networked, self-teaching, 6th-generation robots. This change in technology will surprise everyone, especially our overseas competition. It's just what we need to get the 47s much faster and control our costs at the same time.

"I'm going to turn the entire Firebolt program over to Carmichael Industries. CII has proven to me that they can produce an exceptional F-47 with extraordinary quality and they can do it all in just a couple of months, at least the first ten of them for testing and flight training. As you know the machine is essentially designed but it's the manufacturing processes that have been holding us up. Carmichael now has that licked."

This wasn't only incredible but actually impossible for the General to believe. At least the President hadn't said he was canceling, delaying or defunding the program.

The President motioned for him to sit down, "As you know that program has been following the same path as the F-35 with unpredictable delays and massive budget overruns. The RAND report that was leaked claims the 35 is dead in the water. I can't get their report out of my head that said it 'Can't turn, Can't climb, and Can't run'. All the improvements to date haven't solved the basic flaws in the design. I'm certainly not blaming the Air Force or even the designers for this. Congress made a fatal mistake in calling for a Joint Strike Fighter and the Marines' demand for vertical takeoff hobbled the entire program. So now it's good at nothing, more like a pickup truck than a Ferrari. Hell even the ancient F-16 beat it in recent war games.

"There's no way a single airframe can ever service the Air Force, Navy and especially the Marines. You and I both know the 35 is a dead duck but I'd never admit that publicly. I'm with you that the F-47 is the right answer for the Air Force. I want to put the F-35 behind us for the Air Force and go straight to the F-47. Now the Navy and the Marines may try to continue with the 35 but the right horse for the Air Force is clearly the F-47."

Jenkins finally saw a pause in the President's rant and jumped in, "Sir this all seems fantastic. Too fantastic, if I may say so. Yes we need and want the F-47 but frankly this story seems just too ... contrived and unbelievable. You can't build that plane in a couple of months. Why would you trust Carmichael? We know he has capabilities but he does drones and cruise missiles. Those things are toys compared to a next-generation 'manned' fighter. Remember, his bid on the Firebolt was turned down way back when, partly because he has no track record on high-performance fighters, never mind anything with a pilot.

"Politically, as I understand it, the two of you don't even like each other. In all honesty sir, this sounds like a scam of some kind to damage and weaken his competition and please his own shareholders. Hell it could be a trick to send his stock through the ceiling so he can buy somebody with his shares at an inflated value, or even cash out a billion or two dollars of his own shares.

"You know the book on this guy. Personally I like him and his support for a strong American military but frankly sir, he's full of tricks and famous for his shifty deals. Some of what he has done should really have landed him in prison. He's more of a showman and ultra-rich entrepreneur than a military expert.

"What you're talking about is risky beyond acceptable. I know we're way behind on the 47 and I don't want to make any more promises or predictions on when they'll have it ready, but we'd lose at least a year or two by just letting him jump into this and stalling our existing programs out at Groom Lake."

The President was getting impatient, "General, during World War II we turned out fighters in weeks!"

The General blushed, "Sir this is hardly the same thing. These babies aren't the subsonic tin airframes with big outboard piston engines that we had during that war. They're infinitely more complex and capable and you know it. They use exotic materials, breakthrough hardened electronics and tolerances that are incredibly hard to achieve, test and maintain. Virtually all of their electronics and software is custom built. They're totally fly by wire and aeronautically unstable without their computers. There's over a million lines of code in the weapon system software alone which is all custom tuned to the airframe. And they're stealthy. This fighter alone has hundreds of high-tech advances and as you know, a few major breakthroughs over previous fighters. That's what's caused many of the delays, the new stuff."

"General I understand your concerns and I had them too. Remember, he is not designing the 47, that's already done. He is simply applying an amazing new manufacturing capability to the machine. I can only say that Carmichael has what he says he has and he has proven it to me," again he lied but he had to win this General over or find a way to replace him fast.

"Carmichael's breakthrough development will change the face of design and manufacturing on the planet. His new capabilities are absolutely dazzling. He has a thousand Qubit quantum computer that is billions of times faster than anything even on the drawing boards and they have the software to drive it for manufacturing, simulation and testing, and the damned thing drives next-generation robots directly, doing the work at incredible speeds. The only part I don't understand so far is how they can virtually skip all component, system and flight testing through simulation but he claims the first machine out of the plant will perform reliably beyond the specs for the F-47 or we don't pay for it."

Some of this he knew was speculation on his part, but if Alpha-1's robots were any part of a million years more advanced than humans' then they could probably do all of that and make coffee at the same time.

"Oh yeah, he'll sell them to us at the original estimated price for the machine, not the inflated nonsense that we're looking at now. As you know those fighters are now way over twice and well on their way to three times what we planned to pay when this all started and they haven't built a single fighter yet. I don't want you to have to reduce the number of units you're getting just to meet the budget."

The General was finally catching his breath and had to put a stop to this, "OK sir, now I'm really worried. Please excuse my language but I smell a rat here. Sir, I know it's late and I don't want to sound disrespectful but this story is just too fantastic to be credible. What Carmichael is telling you seems to me to be beyond the capabilities of this century and certainly well beyond the capabilities of CII. I don't see how I can support it."

"General Jenkins I understand your concerns and I really wanted you to be a part of this success."

There was no hiding the threat in that sentence and the General realized immediately what the President was conveying. In his clumsiness he had opened the door for the President to give him an ultimatum. Obey what was about to become a direct order from the Commander-in-Chief or resign. There were lots of Generals below him who would jump at the job even if it was a fool's errand. The military were not without their own political strategies and program failures could often be pinned on the politicians given the proper ground work. He'd have to find a way to make sure the President's name alone was attached to this one.

After a long pause where Jenkins decided he wanted to keep his job, he realized his immediate task was to get out of this room without being fired and get to some of his colleagues, politicians and lobbyists who could strategize around this nonsense.

The General finally spoke, "Sir I could be a stronger advocate of your plan if I knew more about the technology and the manufacturing plan. I hope you'll ask Carmichael's people to brief me thoroughly and quickly. As for now, what do you need from me?"

The President gave him a wry smile, "Thank you, General, for your much appreciated support."

'SHIT!' There it was. Jenkins immediately recognized that somehow the President had weaseled a statement of support from him. The man was known for his political maneuvering but this had caught the General off guard and he could see where any withdrawal of his 'support' would mean the instant end of his career, and given they were in the Oval Office, he was sure it was all recorded on some monitoring device. No matter what happened now, the President would have a heavily edited version of his statement of support to flash whenever he needed it.

What a night. One of his own nuclear missiles exploding in its silo on his watch had him so frazzled that he was no longer clear-headed, and now he had accidentally yielded to the President on a completely nutty plan. Hell 'nutty' didn't even begin to describe it.

The President was still talking, "To comply with Carmichael's aggressive plan for delivery of the F-47 we need to get moving on this now. As of this moment we're going to stop all work at Area-51 and clear it out of all personnel, except for the security team. Carmichael will be taking over the entire base to build the first ten fighters. I know that will mean furloughing many workers so we have to handle that and make it attractive for them to keep their mouths shut about anything to do with the 47 or what our plans are at Area-51.

"There are also contracts to terminate with the current cadre of contractors and suppliers so we'll need good legal support. Given the overruns in time and budget we would have no problem unilaterally canceling the contract of the prime contractor and all his subcontractors for cause but we have no time to open that can of worms and start court cases, injunctions and delays, so we'll cancel without cause and pay the full penalties.

"In addition, CII will need a secure intercontinental supply chain and I've told Carmichael we will be his transport using our C-17s.

"What I need from you this very moment is a man to run this for you and me from the Air Force. A top man that can take this assignment, get on a plane and get it done. I want Area-51 cleaned out of contractors within twenty-four hours and the entire area secured so none of the contractors or suppliers currently working on the F-47 can get back in."

Blood drained from the General's face as the President continued, "That will be his first test, and it needs to happen by tomorrow to dovetail with several other things happening here in Washington. So you're looking for a kick-ass senior officer with a keen mind who you and I can work with and who can keep his mouth shut about any of the technology, processes or anything else related to this project. He'll have to drive a bank of lawyers to get that place closed down and cleaned out fast. We need to tell him to spare no expense to achieve these admittedly aggressive goals because we all want those F-47s as fast as we can get them.

"You understand the urgency of this so I must ask you for a name right now."

This was all too much. The General had never been spoken to in this way and things at his level never moved at this pace unless the country was under attack, which it most certainly was not! This guy was hands-on and virtually taking over the F-47 program by himself. For a President who had never really seemed interested in the military he was acting like a four-star General in wartime ... and all of this on a night when he really should have had much more urgent things on his mind.

He was just about to push back when he remembered the President's earlier threat. There were no signs Turcot could be dissuaded from his plan and it would be either himself or his replacement who would be taking the bows in any success. He could see by the man's face that there was no 'discussing' this either. The best he could do for now was comply with these outrageous requests and start working on unwinding them tonight and tomorrow.

After thinking for about thirty seconds he said, "Sir this is beyond short notice but I think I have your man. Brigadier General Clay Hawkins. He is the best man in the Air Force for this job. He is currently on a short-term assignment at Tyndall AFB in Florida where he is redesigning how we train F-35 pilots. He is also our point man on the Firebolt in terms of training and deployment. He is everything you've asked for. I'll find him tonight and he'll be in Nevada by morning."

Jenkins knew Clay was the right guy for the job but he was also a close confidant of the General so he would do the President's job but Jenkins would have a direct line into what was going on.

Being a savvy politician, the President knew all of that too.

Jenkins knew that even though the F-47 was an Air Force only project, the Joint Chiefs would totally lose it over what they would view as the President pushing them out of their role and sidestepping all approved Pentagon procurement processes. Only the political establishment could reel this out-of-control guy back in and they were not in the room right now. He was going to have some explaining to do to the Chiefs as soon as he could get on his phone.

The President had predicted this, "OK, Clay Hawkins it is and Kirk, it's late, so no need to call the Joint Chiefs tonight. I already have plans to brief them first thing in the morning."

The General's heart leapt for the umpteenth time tonight. There it was, he was muzzled as well.

The President continued, "I think I've met General Hawkins. I need him on a video concall with me first thing in the morning from Area-51. Say seven-thirty my time. They have a video hook up and they can patch him into the Situation Room.

"One other thing. I've made commitments to Carmichael that his amazing new discoveries like the computer and the robots will be kept to a tiny inner circle as he can't risk any hint of what he has getting out to the competition, domestic or otherwise. So I will not be sharing the entire picture with Clay Hawkins or anyone else for that matter. Therefore you aren't needed here in the morning for that concall. I will deal directly with the General and I'll see you at our regular Joint Chiefs' meeting at nine a.m."

That did it, the command structure was being broken to keep him out of the picture, another major stab in the back. He wondered if the Joint Chiefs would've expected him to have fallen on his sword and refused to cooperate.

Still, against all logic, if there was even a one in a million chance that the President's ridiculous plan would work it would be amazing to have the plane so fast. It would solve a lot of issues and with the President out front, he could take all the heat on the cancelations of the existing contracts and any failures from the new scheme. If

Carmichael was in fact playing some kind of game and the President had fallen for it, Jenkins was hopeful that Turcot could be made to take the fall alone when it all blew up. The cost to the Air Force might turn out to be simply a short hiatus from their current manufacturing of the bird.

He rose from the couch, nodded and turned to leave when the President caught him by his uniformed arm, "One last thing Kirk, I'm freezing the F-35 as well. Obviously you can keep what you already have taken delivery of until we have a better option but I'm killing the contract for the additional units in the morning. We need that money elsewhere and I'm completely confident Carmichael will deliver the 47 even before they can produce enough F-35s to make a difference. If this plan works and you get the 47s, you can transfer your existing 35s to the Marines and the Navy. They can be retrofitted as necessary and there should be enough of them to service their needs."

A shiver went down Jenkins' spine. Somehow it all seemed too late. It would make no sense to resign now that he had already professed support for the go-forward strategy, assigned a man to the program and acquiesced to everything the President had demanded. That was all on tape too. He had been tricked into his support and now felt completely trapped. Suddenly he felt like he'd better get out of the Oval Office while he still had the shirt on his back or before something even more catastrophic was foisted upon him. How had this night cascaded out of control so fast?

There was no point trying to reason with Turcot. His mind was made up and if the F-47 miraculously appeared and nothing major happened in the world in the next few months he might even get away with this ridiculous detour but General Kirk Jenkins had been eviscerated and his peers and his direct reports would instantly know and they'd let him have it.

There were really only two very bad options, resign in disgrace after being maneuvered into supporting the plan or get behind the President's outrageous scheme and push it. As an honest man he couldn't draw himself to deny that he had intimated his support or even to claim to others that he had been tricked into it. Either of those was a failure in leadership and a terrible sign of weakness.

He realized he had to go along with it, at least for the moment. His old insecurities that he wasn't good at the political piece of his job came rushing back. Even still, he was shocked at how easily the President had seemed to maneuver him into one position after another. He thought for a moment he was going to lose his supper as he sulked away from the Oval Office.

'What a night,' the General thought again as he headed to his car. An A-bomb accident on US soil that the President didn't seem focused on, the death of their civilian leader, the SECDEF, and now this harebrained nonsense about recasting the most complicated program in the military in the next twenty-four hours. His only hope was that the political arm of the government could do what he had been incapable of doing and stop this madness in the morning.

***

The President thought he had finally wrapped up the evening with two return calls to senior Senators and one to the Governor of North Dakota. Of course all they wanted to talk about was the missile and why did the damned thing explode in its silo to which he claimed ignorance and like them he was waiting for the Pentagon's investigation.

He was just about to call it a night when his intercom rang, "Sir, I'm the guard at the north gate. I'm sorry to bother you at this late hour but apparently all your staff have gone home and I have a Mr. Fraser Carmichael here who according to our list isn't expected back, yet he insisted that you would be in your office and that you would want to see him."

"Is he alone?"

"It's just Mr. Carmichael and his driver sir."

"Send him up and tell the guard at the door to escort him to the Oval Office."

A few minutes later Carmichael was ushered back into the room that had seen so much action only a few hours before.

As the Secret Service agent closed the door behind him, the two men facing each other near the couches in the center of the room didn't extend handshakes but simply stared at each other.

The President finally broke the uneasy silence, "Where is it now?"

"It's probably sleeping by now in my condo in downtown Washington and as far as I know it doesn't know I'm here but I could be wrong on that."

The President sneered, "What possessed you to bring that 'thing' into my office? He could've easily killed me instead of Dan Westgate. You aided and abetted an assassination in here tonight and it could have been the President!"

Carmichael blushed, "Hell, you saw what he can do. He'd have killed me and maybe anyone else in his path to you if I resisted. I hardly had a word out of my mouth today in Vegas when he froze me for the first time. Don't talk to me about assassinations. You made this ten times worse with that jackass move up in the Dakotas."

The President was furious, "If I find out you set me up somehow I swear to God you'll live to regret this. You do remember I control the CIA, right?"

Carmichael was apoplectic, "Set you up? Are you crazy? You think this is something anyone could pull off? That 'thing' is real and believe me it isn't taking any orders from me. It scared the shit out of me today! And while we're on the subject, let's get back to when did you grow a pair of balls and try to kill it? You know our side, including me, have you pegged as a condescending wimp and all of a sudden you get frisky and take this thing on when you had zero chance of doing it any damage? What were you fucking thinking? You could have gotten us all killed!"

The President bristled, turned red but held his temper. He really wanted to slug this idiot and he felt he might even get away with it.

Carmichael was on a rant, "You thought a nuclear missile on that mine was going to do anything? Did it ever occur to you that the mine was a ruse? You think we just happened to dig a silver mine right up to their front door? He told you they have cloaking technology for God's sake. Hell, he could be standing next to you right now and you wouldn't know it."

Carmichael almost had to laugh when the President looked around quickly for a cloaked alien and then caught himself.

Carmichael was back to fuming, "That computer room thing in the mine probably doesn't even exist. Did you not understand anything he said?"

Turcot rethought the idea of taking a swing at this insolent prick, "Listen Carmichael, you and I have never seen eye to eye and frankly you're about the last guy on Earth that I'd take any advice from. And remember who you're talking to! I'm still furious that you brought him right here into the FUCKING Oval Office. Now who is the wimp?"

Carmichael was now red in the face too. After staring each other down and seriously considering duking it out, Carmichael continued, "Listen you moron, this is Earth versus aliens, just like in the movies. Maybe two different kinds of aliens to boot. You had better get your head out of your ass and stop seeing me as the enemy."

Carmichael took a step back and started to calm himself, "Now that I think of it, we'd better both drop this thing between us right now and come to our senses. We have to cooperate whether we like it or not. We have no choice. This 'thing' is real and this threat is real, I'm convinced of it. We're looking at a potential extinction event here. The only thing you have to remember is that we're both human and the other side or sides are not!

"Now I came back here to have a candid conversation with you and to see if you had any more crazy ideas about taking this 'thing' on. I couldn't go to bed thinking you might be sending a cruise missile our way. We have no idea what its capabilities are. Unless you know something I don't, trying to kill it or its civilization is a nonstarter in my books. They're immensely powerful, invisible and we don't know how many they are or where they are. If you try to take them on, you'll be killed and the VP will take over and I'll be telling him to cool his jets. Hell this 'thing' says he's going to save your daughter. I don't have any kids but I'd think that would be a big motivator for you."

Reluctantly seeing Carmichael's logic, Turcot was starting to cool down too. He motioned to Carmichael to take a seat on one of the couches and he sat across from him, "I'm not sure I believe that whole heaven thing or his promise to save my daughter if I cooperate. Half of me wants to believe it all, but the other half says we just can't trust this 'thing'. How can we, they're a superior species? It all sounded almost plausible when he explained the whole thing but even if I believe him, my daughter isn't out of the woods. He's chosen to hold that over me until we're successful in this thing. So I'm not celebrating just yet.

"And no I wasn't planning an attack on your fucking condo with a cruise missile.

"As to my actions earlier tonight, remember what he himself said about these supposed aliens that are coming? You don't mess with a superior species. That's pretty much his message and that's where my head was at. I couldn't just sit there and let him take over the planet and don't forget this was before he told us why he was here. Remember, I was elected by the American people to keep them safe, not to capitulate to another regime or risk them being enslaved or annihilated. That's a responsibility you have no concept of.

"My Administration and most of the ones before me came to the same conclusion he did for Christ's sake. That if we ever did run into what seemed to be a superior species we were dead. We would be wiped out. That was my thinking before we heard the full story and in fact he agrees with that strategy so he should not be surprised that we tried to defend ourselves. We had to strike. You can't assume they'll be benevolent. The only history we have on this planet says that it never works out that way. The inferior species always gets wiped out or finds themselves in a terribly compromised or enslaved situation."

Carmichael was furious, "Yeah but he's not thinking of taking a potshot at an enemy he has no intel on. He is not even thinking about confronting them. Yes, they said they would 'contest' such an encounter but look at the way they are approaching it. His strategy of hiding is the only one that makes any sense in this case."

Turcot insisted, "Yeah, but we don't have cloaking and we had no warning he was coming. Hiding was not an option for us, even if we had that ability. If we had taken a swipe at them and missed or did little damage, at least we'd have shown them that we weren't going to go quietly or at least we were committed to defending ourselves. It was a long shot and probably hopeless but we've always figured that if you don't take the first shot and provide some parity of threat then you'll never get an opportunity to take one after. They'll eliminate your weapons first and you'll never have any chance at all. If the American native people had killed the entire first wave of pilgrims and none of them had ever made it back to Europe then things might have been different for them. At least it would have given them some sense of the threat, a look at their weapons and time to prepare.

"So we had to try something and we had to try it before he came back from his 'nap'. Dan Westgate understood this and he gave his life for all of us when he tried to kill it."

Carmichael sat forward, "But don't you see, this isn't the same situation at all. We're related by DNA and we've already coexisted on this planet for millions of years and all he wants to do is go back underground and be left alone. He told you that before you tried your attack. They even have a plan for when coexistence will no longer work, they'll leave."

It was the President's turn, "And you believe all that malarkey about them going back underground and leaving when the time comes? You believe that there will not come a time when we piss them off somehow with fracking or A-bomb testing, or oil wells or something else and they just swat us like a fly? He already thinks we're destroying the planet's atmosphere and resources. He said that!"

Carmichael sat back. "I wish I had a cigar. I see your point but did you not get the impression as I did that they know how to avoid that and bear us no malice? Hell, apparently we've coexisted for around two million years. But forget all that. You had your one swing at him and it probably cost a thousand American lives. I want to hear you say that you're onside with this now. That there will be no more independent temper tantrums or attack strategies deployed. I don't know about you but I want to stay alive. You and I are in this together whether we like it or not. We're the only two people on the planet that can make this work or make it fail. I vote for making it work."

The President was really pissed at how this arrogant, punk, playboy billionaire was addressing the leader of the Free World in the Oval Office of all places. He stared at him in anger for a long time, still pissed that he had brought the alien right into the Oval Office, but he had to admit he saw nothing else Carmichael could have done. Now both of them had much to lose and much to gain in this arrangement.

Alpha-1 had indeed said he could save Annie and Carmichael would get some amazing toys and a leg up on his competition, to say nothing of the military contracts he would be acquiring … and heaven for all of them.

If he believed everything he had been told, and if they could deal with the approaching aliens, then there definitely was potential upside in this, especially for Ann. All of this dependent on a couple of massive and very dangerous assumptions … that Alpha-1 was telling the truth, the whole truth and nothing but the truth and that their strategy of hiding would be in place in time and would actually work to stave off the supposed approaching aliens.

The flip side was that apparently mankind had no tools to defeat Alpha and likely the same with the approaching aliens, if they even existed. Even Alpha-1 was not sure they were coming or that humans and Alphans could do anything about it when they arrived. It seemed like the only practical approach was to play along for now and HOPE to defeat a common enemy, and then HOPE for the best in the aftermath with a presumably grateful Alphan civilization.

"I have to say, Fraser, I've never been in a tougher spot and I'm still pissed at you putting me there. It's my solemn duty to protect the American people, but at this moment in time it would seem that working with these Alphans is the only option we have. I have a philosophical issue with you and me benefiting more than the rest of humanity. Honestly, if what that 'thing' says is true about immortality then we owe it to mankind to find a way to include them, or at least get the technology they have that allows immortality. But that's for a later discussion.

"What I need right now is your personal commitment Fraser, that you will not screw this up with some reckless grab for advantage, over and above everything that was promised you. We're not in a 'maximizing profit' game here. We're in the 'survival of the human race' game. Understood?"

Turcot continued, "As hard as it may seem, and against all of my instincts, we need to stay in complete synch. As you said, we're the only two humans on this, so that makes us reluctant partners. So do I have your word that we are in this together and the survival of mankind is the ONLY concern?"

Fraser Carmichael smiled, stood as the President rose and shook his hand. "You have my complete commitment but frankly I'm more worried about your commitment. I assume this oath is mutual."

Turcot nodded as Carmichael closed with, "Who would've thought the two of us would be the ones to be in this together? This is the real odd couple. Maybe you're not a total loser after all."

Turcot said, "I think I'm going to be sick," smiled wryly and showed him to the door.

Before he retired for the evening he made one last call to one of his closest allies and confidants, the Director of the CIA, Bill Carter. Carter had apparently left his office for the evening after all the crisis management due to the missile and the President had to leave a voicemail on his secure phone, "Bill, it's Hal. I've just initiated some activities that are going to upset the Joint Chiefs. I want you to keep a close eye on them and let me know of any unusual activity. They may try to challenge me on some of these moves. As we did that other time, step up the surveillance especially calls between them and keep me informed. I assure you this is not a political witch hunt. There are real national security concerns in play."

***

Hal Turcot finally made his way up to the residence and into his bedroom. It was now a little after midnight, the bed was unslept in and he found his wife Evelyne standing in the little kitchenette holding a glass of milk and crying.

"Ev honey, what's wrong?"

"Oh, don't worry about me. You have your hands full with an atomic bomb going off and all those people dying tonight in North Dakota. It's all so sad. Those poor people. All the networks have suspended their normal programs and are speculating on anything and everything. They've already had helicopters out there but because of the radioactivity they can't get close and all you can really see are fires in the darkness.

"Of course some of them are speculating that the story about a maintenance accident is all made up. What really happened with the missile, and then Dan Westgate dropping dead?"

Hal Turcot froze. He realized immediately that he was going to have to lie to the one person he had promised himself he would never lie to. When all else failed, his family were really the only ones in his corner but he saw no options. Knowing anything about Alpha would mean having to share everything and that would put a tremendous load on his wife that she had no way to deal with, but much more importantly, it would put her life in the same immediate jeopardy that had killed Dan Westgate.

Pissing this 'thing' off had already cost him a good friend tonight and Alpha-1's inaction, or rather clear action in Minot, had cost hundreds of lives. It could kill when it wanted to. Sharing anything with Evelyne, even though he desperately wanted to, would only put her life in danger and that was out of the question.

He took her by the shoulders and stared into her eyes, "I can only tell you this because you have security clearance. You've heard the public story about the maintenance but what really happened was that Dan Westgate had some kind of a mental meltdown tonight. He held us at gunpoint and tried to launch a missile. After it failed to launch he swooned and then dropped dead in my office.

Ev was shocked as Hal continued, "It's actually a godsend that it didn't launch or we might be dealing with the Russians as well. As to the missile, we really don't know yet what happened when he tried to launch it, and with only a big hole left in the ground we may never know."

She pushed him back gently, "Wow, that's insane. Dan Westgate did this? He's a wonderful person. What do you think happened to him?"

"We don't know yet. He wasn't himself. Some brain trauma for sure. He was mumbling incoherently just before all hell broke loose so I have to assume a brain hemorrhage or something. I loved Dan too and I'm completely shocked at what happened down there tonight. There was nothing we could have done to stop him."

Turcot swallowed hard as he realized this lie was going to be hard to keep telling. It hurt deeply that Dan had to take the fall for this.

Ev continued, tearful and shaking, "It's beyond sad and tragic. At least the ones near the blast didn't suffer. I worry about all the people in Minot and the farm country around them that must have been injured or badly burned. You're going up there, right?"

"Yeah sure, first thing tomorrow. The guys are working on it tonight. FEMA will be sending in everything they have to assist, but is that what has you so upset?"

"No, it's not that, although it could be if my mind wasn't elsewhere."

Ev started to tear up again, "I was in with Ann earlier getting her into bed. The nurse was busy with something else. She's so weak Hal. She can't do anything for herself. Nineteen years old and a complete invalid. I love her so much but I see her slipping away daily. She's having great difficulty even talking. She'll never go back to college. She'll never get married, and she'll never have kids. We'll be lucky if she makes it through the winter the way she's deteriorating.

"How is it Stephen Hawking has lasted all this time but our baby is likely to survive only three years with this horrible disease? They still have no explanation as to why her and why so young. I mean ALS is rare in young adults, especially girls, why Annie?" she said as she began to cry again.

The President pulled her closer and hugged his wife hard. His only thought was, 'could Ann hold out for another couple of months until Alpha-1 delivered on his promise?' He wished he could say something but he was terrified the Alphans would know and do something stupid like kill his wife. No matter how congenial Alpha-1 sounded, he had shown that he could dispense with humans and had declined to make an exception to save his daughter.

Alpha-1 himself had acknowledged while talking about the approaching aliens that a superior race often had little empathy for an inferior one. They would let his daughter die and they would kill his wife if she got in the way or made a big stink if she knew the facts.

If Ev got wind that there was a way to save Ann, there would be no stopping her and that would spell disaster. She was pretty level-headed but given the situation he could see her getting right in Alpha-1's face and threatening to blow his cover if he didn't save Ann, no matter the consequences.

He felt like doing just that himself, but he had learned his lesson that Alpha-1 would do whatever it took to execute his plan and knocking off the President or his wife would be simple enough for him. All he could do for the moment was lie to his wife.

Confused, conflicted and feeling trapped, his mind kept flipping back to whether it would be better to try to kill this 'thing' and its civilization. No matter what he had told Carmichael, he was still concerned that man and Alphan could not coexist and man would eventually be on the losing end. But for the moment he had no other solution.

There was no way to know if this story about approaching aliens was even true. Maybe it was all a ruse to distract him while something else was afoot. After all he had declined to offer any proof of the threat intimating that humans would not be able to understand the information they had.

He was cornered and he knew it. He was stuck taking Alpha-1's word for everything. In any other matter of State he had the power of the US intelligence community to at least give him some intel, analysis and options, but not in this case. All of this with a dying daughter and a distraught wife to deal with. Leading the US as its President had suddenly dropped to third place, behind saving the world and saving his family.

Normally overwhelming distractions like this would be grounds for resignation and in fact some in the press had suggested he do just that due to the obvious distraction of a dying daughter. Now even that was not an option. Alpha-1 wouldn't stand for it. The window of opportunity to just say 'to hell with it all' had come and gone.

When his daughter had been diagnosed almost three years ago in the middle of his re-election campaign, there had been speculation that he might drop out in favor of the VP. The external pressure had never reached a peak because the VP was a real gamble for both the left and the right for different reasons and Ann insisted she was OK and that he should continue his re-election campaign.

In those days she really didn't seem ill and even if she was, there was a good chance she would still be relatively well when his second term ended. Sadly, that had not been the way things had unfolded. Her illness had progressed quickly in the last year.

He had done his best in the intervening years to show that he was still in charge, but the pressures from just upstairs in the residence of the White House had been tremendous and he found himself from time to time actually crying in the shower, terrified of facing the death of his only, beautiful daughter. Now with the Minot issue, his daughter near death, and an alien giving him orders, as well as more aliens on the way, he feared he was nearing the breaking point.

By the time they went to bed he found he couldn't sleep. He was soon up looking for his own glass of warm milk to see if that would help. The President's job was a lonely one and carried enormous stress but all of this additional stress made him nauseous and weak in the knees. Only one other human knew the total dimensions of his predicament and that jackass had no empathy at all.

***

Across town Carmichael made it back to his opulent penthouse condo on a real high. Fantastic technology at his grasp, highly profitable government business handed to him and heaven as a backstop. Terrifying but what a day it had been.

Still, he couldn't rest yet. He had lots of work to complete and would stay up late working on the acquisition of the company out of Vancouver and also trying to find out the fate of his team in the plane crash. Earlier calls to his ops center in New York about the plane had turned up nothing.

Back now from his short visit to Turcot he was in his own wing of the suite with a tall glass of a prized single malt when his iPhone rang. He could see it was his New York operations center again, "What do you have for me?"

"I wasn't sure if you were still awake sir but I took the chance. At this point we've only been able to get one chopper in the air out of Bismarck and he doesn't have a lot of 'over the target' time because he has to commute a hundred miles each way. Due to the rush we only have a pilot on board. We're trying to get a SAR tech on the next flight. All the other air resources are being snapped up by Search and Rescue so we had to pay top dollar for this guy. They know we want continuous coverage over the target area until we find them.

"The Minot airport and all of its assets are down at this time due to the damage so he can't even refuel there yet. He's burning half his fuel just getting to the search area and back.

"They won't be flying anything out of Minot until all the aircraft are checked out thoroughly and basic services like ATC, fueling and fire rescue are back online. All the aircraft on the ground are questionable due to the EMP from the explosion. They'll need all their electronics replaced or recertified so we're stuck with anything we can beg, borrow or steal from Bismarck or smaller airports further from the blast that were not impacted by the EMP.

"I just got off the line with our chopper and he has been searching the area we gave him southeast of the airport on the approach for runway 31 but nothing so far and it isn't looking good. Apparently the light and heat pulse from the bomb set most of the fields on fire unless they were on a western facing slope and the land is pretty flat out there. His last report was that some of the corn and wheat field fires were starting to die out and visibility was improving. Hang on we have him on the other line now, I'll patch him through."

Seconds later Carmichael could hear what was clearly a helicopter pilot reporting to the ops center, "I've got it, there's what looks like a corporate jet down here. It's broken in half and the nose is badly damaged. I think it was a Gulf Stream exec jet. Looks like the pilot almost landed it in a corn field and they've ended up on the bank of a marsh or pond. It's too dark and there is too much smoke from burning fields for me to get a closer look at it and there is nowhere to put down with all the fires. I'll give you the GPS and you'll need to get someone out here. I know this area and looks like it's about four miles southwest of a village named Voltaire. There's an access road running south from rural route ninety-seven and it looks like the fire is dying down around it.

"Right now I'm fanning the flames too much but there could be survivors in that thing. The fuselage is in two pieces but there is no sign of a roll over or fire in the fuselage as they are partly into the marsh. You had better get someone out here quick. They'll need pumps for water or at least a whole lot of fire extinguishers to work their way around the pond to the crash site.

"Sorry guys, I'm already passed bingo on my fuel and I'm out of here." At that the line went dead. The pilot was clearly in no mood for any additional instructions.

Carmichael spoke, "Sorry, I didn't get your name. Who is on the line from New York?"

"George Williams sir, night supervisor."

"OK, George. I think you know what you have to do. Get that pilot back on the line and get the GPS coordinates and find someone to go out there. I suspect all the fire and rescue people are busy so you'll be looking for something else. Use your imagination and pay whatever we need to get some help to that plane and keep me informed."

"Got it sir," and he hung up. He had never had to deal directly with the 'big guy', but he knew he was famous for barking orders and expected over-the-top response to anything he was personally involved in, and this definitely qualified. The only problem was he had no idea where to start.

Carmichael looked at his watch. It was after midnight and he needed to buy a company tonight. He called back to the ops center and got a different person, "This is Fraser Carmichael. Will Fiskins our Corporate Counsel was on that plane that went down tonight. I need you to patch me through to his second-in-command, Winnie Goldstein. Get her out of bed if you have to."

About one minute later a startled Winnie Goldstein was on the phone.

"Listen Winnie, I don't care if you were sound asleep, we have a priority task that will determine what you're made of.

"You probably don't know this but your boss is missing in a plane crash out west and we're doing everything we can to get to him with a rescue team. HR is in contact with his family and we all have our fingers crossed but I need something totally unrelated done by our legal department tonight on an emergency basis and you're it.

"I need you to find a way to lock up an ironclad option to buy a company out of Vancouver, Canada. I've done some personal due diligence already. X-Wave is their name. I think they're private and if I had to guess these small companies are usually valued in the $50M to $100M bracket. I'm pretty sure we can't sign closing documents tonight but I want it in writing that we have a rock solid deal to buy them tomorrow for all cash.

"We take possession tomorrow and we will keep all facilities, IP, patents and all employees including management. No change in their business plan. They need to keep doing what they're doing. The most important piece is that I need the Intellectual Property locked up solid so make that clear to them. I don't want any engineers or ex-founders claiming they own a piece of the IP after the fact. We need it clean and clear as well as any patents, trademarks, or copyrights they have. Make sure when we buy them that they have to settle any unidentified IP claims out of their proceeds.

"Do your best but you can offer them up to five times what they can show they're worth and get them and their lawyers out of bed and have them fax a signed option for purchase to you before breakfast. If you can get that far then sign it for me and pay what you need to for the option. Tell them the offer expires at eight a.m. or the buyer will move on to a different acquisition. The money will be mine so we don't need any Carmichael Industries board resolutions or approvals.

"The buyer will be New Sunrise Tech out of Sunnyvale which is a private VC I own so they have lots of cash. Keep my name and Carmichael Industries out of it for now or the price might skyrocket. I absolutely need this done. Call me anytime overnight and wake me up if you run into any problems. If you have any legal or philosophical issue with doing this for me directly because you're a Carmichael employee, then bill your time to Sunrise, understood? I want no excuses on this."

There was a long pause and finally Winnie, who was now wide awake, shaking, and fighting off serious acid reflux replied, "Will we have to file anything with the SEC?"

"No, Sunrise is a private firm and I have a strong suspicion X-Wave is private too. Anything else?"

"No sir, I've got it,"

As she hung up the phone and tried to control her shaking she instantly realized this was the kind of opportunity people in her field lived for. A multi-million dollar rush deal in the middle of the night with everything resting on her head. She had to make sure she did it all legally. Carmichael was wise to be worried about whom she worked for and whom she was representing in this matter. Her first job was to Google the firm and see if she could figure out the ownership.

Vancouver was three hours behind New York but it would still be a surprise late night call to their Chairman. She jumped out of bed and started to get dressed.

Fraser Carmichael, the world-renowned entrepreneur and billionaire finally had one of his prized cigars lit and had a few moments to reflect on this unbelievable day.

His attention turned to his colleagues on the company jet. He had pieced this team together over his early days in high-tech. He had never really socialized with them, in fact he really didn't socialize consistently with anyone. Still he had come to know them rather well and was genuinely concerned for their well-being.

What a twist of fate that found them so close to the actual explosion. It made sense they would have to stop somewhere around North Dakota for fuel if they were on their way back to Wallace, but the timing was odd. He had to wonder if Alpha-1 had had anything to do with that and then thought it simply a weird coincidence.

On board the company jet had been Frank Jorgen, head of security, Jim Gardino, his Chief Operating Officer, and Will Fiskins, Corporate Counsel. Three key employees who may now all be dead in a burning field, after that maniac Turcot had tried to nuke the alien's entry point. He had to have realized that nuking the entry to a mine twelve thousand feet deep was going to do nothing to an entire civilization. He had always thought Turcot was a little light between the ears and his actions of earlier in the evening hadn't proven otherwise. Maybe he had shown some guts standing toe to toe with Alpha-1 at one point, but he was still a moron who had made it to the White House on his looks and his exceptional abilities as a glad-handing politician, who always seemed to be able to avoid a mess with a mealy-mouthed, populist position on almost any issue.

As to the alien asleep in his condo, he seemed to be getting invisible feeds of information. Information that would seem impossible to gather like the initial number of dead from the missile. It was clear Alpha-1 had decided to keep lots of information to himself, refusing to answer some of their questions. If this civilization, which was a million years more advanced, had any weak spots it was clear that Alpha-1 wasn't about to expose them.

He found himself yawning uncontrollably. Even for a man like Fraser Carmichael the day's activities had been an enormous strain and as he put his cigar in the ashtray beside the bed, he lay back, still in his custom jeans and blazer, and dozed off.

The Plan

The President was in the Situation Room at seven-thirty and even though it was four-thirty in Nevada, General Clay Hawkins looked smartly dressed and refreshed. Turcot knew that couldn't be real, having been given less than eight hours to close up shop, pack some things, get out of Florida, and installed in Nevada.

The President immediately recognized the General and had a favorable impression of him. They must have met at some Washington event as he hadn't been to too many military bases, "General, who do you have with you this morning?"

"Mr. President, this is Colonel Frank Kirkpatrick, base commander at this secret base."

"Good morning Colonel Kirkpatrick. I know it's early and I'm sorry I didn't recognize you immediately and I apologize for that. Thank you so much for joining us this early in your part of the country but I'm afraid this conference is for General Hawkins alone. You're dismissed and thank you for your service."

There was something in the way the President phrased that sentence that not only made the Colonel blush slightly but seriously wonder what was about to transpire, given this wasn't the normal handing over of the reigns because the President was never involved in reassignments at this level. He stood, saluted and said, "Thank you Mr. President."

Turcot saluting the Colonel back, gave him a minute to exit the scene, "Now General, I'm about to assign you to a new critical commission. This is my absolute top priority for America for the next few months and you'll be my point man on it. You'll deal only with me and none of the command structure in the military. I've already explained this to your superiors," he lied.

"Over the next few months we're going to implement a daring new plan to build and deliver ten F-47 Firebolts at your location and they won't be the three that are under construction there now.

"You know as much as anyone about the Firebolt but you will not be allowed to see the manufacturing site as Carmichael Industries will be building the entire system with a new, yet to be announced, set of intelligent robots and a new quantum supercomputer that are all proprietary to CII and must be kept secret from everyone not part of

Carmichael Industries.

"Their new equipment is so secret that no one will be allowed to view any of the machines or the processes and that is your job one; providing ironclad, top security at the base. Mr. Carmichael's Chief Operating Officer for this division is a Mr. Robert Glass who should be arriving there today and he'll fill you in on any further details on the project."

Hawkins immediately recognized the name. If it was the same guy, he had been on TV just the day before being rescued from a mine somewhere in the northwest. Surely it couldn't be the same guy.

"You'll respond to all of Mr. Glass's requirements which brings us to your second job. You'll manage a fleet of up to six C-17 transports to securely and swiftly move equipment and materials from all over the globe to your site for the building of these planes. The cargo will often be raw materials and their composition and anything associated with them is also Top Secret, for Mr. Glass's eyes only or anyone he assigns. I'm providing a blanket import waiver for the project so there will be no security checking of cargo or import restrictions. I can also tell you that none of the cargo will be hazardous.

"Timing is critical so if you need more C-17s or anything else, just say the word. Transport cannot be allowed to become a bottleneck in this project so that's why we're using the 17s. They may fly with very small loads if it is needed quickly but they must be big enough to handle anything that might come up. So spare no expense to keep the project on schedule. Go as far as pre-positioning some of your aircraft globally if potential requirements can be forecasted."

Turcot was making this up on the go and he realized that some of these requirements might be more than Alpha-1 needed but thought it best to make sure that nothing could jeopardize the work.

"Now to the really tough part and one of the reasons you've been selected for this job. This all takes place today!

"By close of business today, you will on my authorization, cancel all contracts for any work being done on any project at Area-51 even if they are not associated with the Firebolt. That base must be cleared of all civilians and dedicated completely to the manufacturing of the new Firebolt. You can of course retain a few key civilians if you deem it necessary to perform your task but they must be monitored for security.

"The cancelations will furlough, for one year, all workers and essentially clean out the entire site. Our contracts have penalty clauses that cover the compensation for furloughed workers so the actual on-the-floor workers should be OK.

"Any partially built F-47s will be moved to a holding area in a hangar that Mr. Glass will identify. You decide on a temporary solution for anything you come upon until he arrives, but I want the main manufacturing areas empty and every living soul off that base, save any personnel under your direct command providing seamless war footing security.

"To assist you I'm faxing orders to you as we speak and you'll take over all military personnel at the base who will be used strictly for the security I mentioned and the support and operations of the C-17 aircraft. You'll have carte blanche and top priority on anything you need to achieve your goals. Again this is your Commander-in-Chief's top priority for the next few months.

"Today you also need to requisition what additional troops you may need to ensure that the base meets its full Level 1 secure standing. No one gets on or off that base unless you approve it and that means no one except your team, Mr. Glass, and anyone he brings to the base. Your people can use the base facilities such as dorms and canteens under any restrictions on movement that Mr. Glass will identify. Your job is to support him in any way you can and escalate any issues directly to me 24/7.

"For reasons I will not get into, this F-47 project is THE top priority for America for the next few months and NOTHING can get in the way of its execution.

"Your first challenge starting in a few minutes will be the legal one. All government contracts as you may know have a clause dealing with 'cancelation without cause' where we must pay penalties if we decide to cancel a contract without notice and for no stated reason. This way we avoid any battles over contract performance or compliance. I will ask Carmichael Industries to assist you in any legal matters and they'll know all about that within thirty minutes of this call. Do whatever you have to do at any reasonable cost to achieve the goal of a clean site by close of business today.

"Any questions?"

General Clay Hawkins' heart was pounding and he figured that was apparent on his face. He was being ordered to bypass his command structure and lead some crazy, off-the-wall project. He had an inkling something was weird when he received the call from General Jenkins at home about eleven o'clock the night before. The General had offered no details but his voice had said it all.

His mind was racing and he couldn't think of a single question to ask.

***

Carmichael was awoken at seven-thirty when his cell phone rang.

Still groggy he said, "What do you have for me?"

"Sir, it's George Williams again from Ops in New York and I have mixed news. We found a private healthcare company who had an ambulance and with the right financial incentive they went out to the GPS coordinates we gave them and they recovered two of our execs in serious condition, Will Fiskins and Jim Gardino. The pilots as well as Frank Jorgen did not survive the crash."

Carmichael sighed, at least two of them had made it. Frank Jorgen was a friend as well as his top security guy and he would be missed. As he remembered, Frank had a young family. The pilots were relatively new and came along with the lease of the plane so he didn't know them that well.

"Where are the survivors now?"

"In an overcrowded Trinity Trauma in Minot. It's the best trauma center in North Dakota but it's overwhelmed after that nuke going off and the injuries to the guys are thought to be serious."

Carmichael didn't hesitate, "Find the VP HR and ask her to call Frank Jorgen's wife and get some grief service out there. Then get her on a company plane to Minot even if she has to fly into Bismarck and drive to Minot. I want no expense spared to do the best for these two execs. If she can get them out of there to a better hospital or at least one that isn't overloaded she should do it. I want her to call me twice a day with updates. Thanks for the call and keep me updated on any developments."

As he hung up he could hear low-level voices from the outer rooms so, still wearing yesterday's clothes, he made his way to the opulent dining room in the massive condo. Glass or Alpha-1 was at the end of the huge dining room table for fourteen, chowing down on something that the housekeeper had just rustled up.

When Carmichael entered he indicated to the attendant that they wanted to be alone and he ordered his regular light breakfast and coffee.

"How did you sleep?" he asked after they had the room to themselves.

"I'm not sure. It has been a long time since I allowed myself to go unconscious like that for hours and our sleep sensation was clearly different than yours, an unusual feeling to be sure. I must tell you, I'm alarmed at what a human body feels like when it sleeps. Your bodies become completely unconscious. I mean, how do you know you'll awaken? I know you can't answer that and actually it isn't something I want to become familiar with but for now let me just say that this body does feel rejuvenated. Still, I find it very uncomfortable, awkward and fragile. I stubbed my toe this morning and that is not a sensation I want to repeat. That may not be a big deal for you but I have not experienced any unwanted pain for over a million years and frankly long ago I deleted any memories of it."

Carmichael had been staring at the bowl in front of Alpha-1 while he smiled at the alien's recounting of his morning, "Is that what I think it is?"

Alpha-1 smiled, "Well as I explained last night, apparently this is all I can stomach from your food sources, oatmeal and honey. With limited knowledge of human anatomy, in particular the capacity of your brains, we did not load all of Mr. Glass's preferences or memories so the taste sensations are mine and you have nothing like the food we enjoy. Even though ours is virtual, the right food is still a pleasure in our world. I now regret not coming up with a better solution to this issue but for now my diet will be strictly limited. I've just ordered more but I may have to appeal to your knowledge as to how much I should eat as I think this sensation I still feel is hunger."

Carmichael smiled, "One more small bowl should be your limit. The hunger sensation only goes away a little after we eat."

Alpha-1 nodded his appreciation, "Now, to get back to our project, if the President has done his job I need to get to Area-51 to start work as Carmichael Industry's new COO for the fighter division."

The housekeeper returned with Carmichael's coffee and a plate of sweet rolls and jams along with Alpha-1's oatmeal. He waited to speak until she had left, "Only two of my people survived the plane crash last night and they are in serious condition in hospital. One of my employees and two pilots died and I will have to give some attention to that. Let me call my office and see where we are with X-Wave."

He took out his phone and hit the speed dial for Corporate. He asked for Winnie Goldstein and she was soon on the line.

"What do you have for me Winnie? It's getting close to eight."

"Good morning Mr. Carmichael. I think I have more than you expected. I tracked down the founder of X-Wave who is also the CEO and Chairman. You were right, they were private and it turns out he is the majority shareholder and their shareholders' agreement does not restrict him from a change in control if the cash portion of the deal is at least a hundred and fifty percent of their most recent valuation. He didn't even have to call a board meeting. We settled on $150M and he was so excited and afraid of the eight a.m. deadline that he got his lawyers on a concall and we've worked through the night and we have a very simplified deed of sale.

"Honestly I think the man was tired running a breakeven business and was looking for an exit. He owned about fifty-two percent of the company so now he has his money and he can continue to tinker with the technology.

"At first their lawyers wanted breakup agreements, due diligence on the buyer and such, but he put them in their place since it was an all-cash deal. I think the other things that did the deal for him was the premium we paid over their recent valuation of $95M, the morning deadline, and that all employees got to keep their jobs. He's a pretty happy guy.

"I pulled out Will Fiskins' Power of Attorney and took the liberty of extending that POA to include New Sunrise Tech and me as signing authority. That allowed me to sign the documents on behalf of the purchasing company whose ownership remains nameless on the documents, just my name as POA. I used my association with another of your hidden subs so initially they won't know it was me unless they track my cell phone or research me on LinkedIn.

"They demanded payment up front of course on such an unusual transaction. I found the account numbers for Sunrise in Will's files and again I used the POA to transfer the funds electronically. Luckily the VC you picked for the purchase has a Japanese presence and we were able to use their banks which, are open when ours are not, to execute the funds transfer overnight on Sunrise's international accounts. So they have their money and the deal is signed, sealed, and delivered.

"If this all meets with your approval then when you're here I'd like to get your real initials on a few documents. If not then I guess I'm going to jail for forgery and I owe you $150M."

Carmichael laughed, "Not only am I cool with what you did, I love the initiative and when I get back don't let me forget to give you a not-so-little bonus for that excellent work."

Winnie continued, "Thank you and one more thing sir, the founder is anxious to meet the new owner and find out his plans. I don't know how you want to handle that."

"Tell him for me that it is full speed ahead with whatever they were working on and promise him we will meet when the time is right. Besides that, I think this secrecy is all about to go away so tell him to watch the business news today.

"Now Winnie, I need you to do something else for me. You'll have heard Will is in a Minot hospital and we're trying to do the best for him, but now we're down one corporate jet so I need a plane here in Washington on standby. Get someone over there to get a leased one from around here to Reagan International if any of our others can't be here in the next ninety minutes or so. I have to go now. Great work! Call me if there is anything important, otherwise you handle it after you get some sleep."

Carmichael updated Alpha-1 who was preoccupied with his bland meal, "This is a markedly different experience than our virtual world. I could see where one could take a liking to the challenge of this type of food but as you can imagine, our version is much better. Nothing falls off the utensils and the flavor is just as I want it of course, but given these harsh conditions, I'm told the oatmeal and honey is the least objectionable, and the food seems to be helping this body."

Fraser Carmichael had to smile. He owned one of the best condos in Washington and the food was top quality, even though the basic oatmeal and honey offering was not something you would use to impress anyone. To have his condo's services described as 'harsh conditions' was just too funny. It made Alpha sound even better.

He knew they had to get going but this looked like a good time to get some questions answered, "What do you know about these aliens that might soon be on their way here?"

Alpha-1 smiled and took a break from his overindulging. "We believe they are already on their way here and actually we know very little about them. We know they come from a certain direction in what you know as the Milky Way Galaxy because they are making almost a straight line in our general direction across the galaxy as they jump from star system to star system. Frankly for over a million years our civilization has been expecting something like this just as your scientists expect some contact with intelligent life eventually. We've been aware of other intelligent life in the galaxy for well over a million years, but we thought we would have more time to prepare for any potential visits. So far this is the only civilization we've discovered within about twenty-five thousand light years that has shown the capability of interstellar travel.

"If their speed is limited to three hundred times light then they are likely from inside our galaxy unless they have been doing this for more than a few million years. The earliest we see their signal is from a system about ten thousand light years away, closer to the center of our galaxy so that could be their home planet.

"Our devices that you would think of as optical telescopes aren't powerful enough to pick up any images of them such as a ship or even any reasonable resolution of any planet they have occupied. We simply recognize their communication protocol but it is something we've never been able to decipher as it is polymodal; it seems you have to piece together several different types of patterns on several very different energy bands to capture all of it. We have a suspicion there may be aspects of this polymodal communication that we have not detected yet; a piece missing out of the puzzle you might say."

Carmichael was intrigued, "Why did you only recently find out about the pulse from the first bomb in 1945?"

Alpha-1 seemed sated and sat back as he answered, "Our systems can easily handle jamming those kinds of signals but on reflection we realized that the filters were not set for that kind of emission at the time. We had no idea you were about to discover nuclear power in terms of a bomb that sends out very large energy spikes on many wavelengths from heat and sound, through intense light, to X-rays, Gamma and everything else. Even your current weapons are very crude and messy in terms of what energy they give off and you had kept your Manhattan Project very secret. What happened was that Voyager was about to become an issue as it would be outside our sphere of cloaking and during the study of its impact we decided to do an audit of all human energy emissions.

"That's when we stumbled upon the potential problem of 1945 which we now know to be real because we've picked up a faint echo of the original pulse. The round trip would have to be approximately eighty years so we found a couple of potential echo sources about forty light years out and to our horror there it was, as clear as a bell, the Gamma and X-ray echo from 1945.

"There are a few thousand star systems within range that could've picked this up but we're relatively certain none of them have life that has evolved to a level to be able to listen in. Intelligent life isn't common in star systems but even our own galaxy is so massive that we project that there are thousands of civilizations capable of communication and a smaller number capable of interstellar travel. So far our surveys have shown that less than one in ten million star systems have intelligent life that has evolved to the point of being able to use energy to transmit information and listen but that still adds up to thousands which do. There will be many more outside of our galaxy but they are just too distant to be of concern at this time.

"The civilization that has recently been 'invaded' by these aliens is about eighty light years away so they were well placed to detect that very short pulse that escaped in 1945. It just happens that they have recently been invaded or visited by this 'traveling' civilization. When I say recently I mean in the last hundred years or so. We detected their communication protocol about forty years ago but it took those signals about eighty years to reach us at light speed. At this time your human instruments are not sensitive enough to have picked up any of these faint extraterrestrial signals.

"So we're quite sure these marauders were there when this pulse arrived, which as I said last night, was a little over five weeks ago. We can be very precise on this because we have exact distances and thankfully, light speed is a very precise constant. If they were listening then they recently picked up your pulse from 1945 and as I said to the President, we are confident they will want to check it out. I would liken it to one of your ships on an unknown ocean a few hundred years ago spotting a light on the horizon and feeling compelled to have a look. We believe it is very unlikely they would pass up the opportunity.

"So not knowing with any precision their actual capabilities in terms of surpassing light speed we have only rough estimates on when they could arrive. That is on the assumption that they have not moved to a closer star system to start with. There is one system about seventy-five light years out that might have attracted their attention but as I said last night, there seems to be a predictable delay between 'invasions', so we think they have not arrived there yet although they may have sent a scout to check out the planet. Also, if they had been on that planet and saw your signal five years ago, we believe they'd have been here by now.

"We have only been observing them for a short time, that being a few thousand years, so there is no guarantee that they will not surprise us and arrive early. That's why we must work at top speed and why we need the help of humans on the surface. They might not detect Alpha immediately with our cloaking technologies but they would certainly detect you and then Alpha would be in jeopardy once they arrived.

"What I have just given you is the 21st century version of what we know. Trying to explain beyond that would be fruitless as the concepts and systems we use would be incomprehensible to you.

"Now I'm sure this is interesting and I have no problem sharing with you some of what we know as long as it does not endanger our civilization, but I think now we have to get to work.

"On that note, we've written a speech for the President around what his plans are for the F-47 and one for you on your announcement of your new quantum-driven robots. The President will find it in his private inbox and yours is in your company email. You should of course let the President go first and then you present from your offices in New York. Part of your speech announces me as the COO of Carmichael Industries Special Projects Division. I left you the meager task of explaining why you hired a young mining engineer to lead an important division but I'm sure you'll ace that one."

Carmichael frowned, "I thought I'd be going with you to Nevada."

"Not at this time. You need to get to New York this morning."

Fraser pressed, "Then at least tell me about the manufacturing plan."

"We don't have the time right now for lots of detail. To start I will check to see that the President has cleared the place out, send you a large list of what we need to get started. You can purchase the materials and I will schedule the military to transport them to Nevada. I will also need their help to move the robots to Area-51. We can't have a manufacturing line appear out of thin air so we'll get them to deliver everything in sealed shipping containers just to keep it all plausible.

"The F-47s will be built in the hangars but the space weapon will not. The buildings at Area-51 aren't large enough to build the weapon and we need an additional buffer zone in case there is any security breach.

"All the materials we need from you must come in crated so they cannot be observed. We'll move all materials into one of the hangars as a staging area and then move the special materials cloaked and as needed to the construction and launch site which is about a quarter of a mile northeast of the end of the main runway in the dry lake bed of Groom Lake. Materials, equipment, helpers and subsystems for the weapon available in Alpha will be brought in cloaked directly to the weapon construction site."

"Will I get to see the weapon?"

"Let me think about that one."

Just then Carmichael's phone rang and he could see it was the White House.

It was the President, "Fraser, can you put me on speaker if you two are alone?"

"Certainly, go ahead, "he said as he laid his phone on the dining room table."

"Good morning gentlemen. General Clay Hawkins is Alpha-1's man at Area-51."

Alpha-1 interrupted, "I was made aware of that and I know of the man. Good choice."

Both humans were stunned by this admission. Alpha-1 wasn't kidding when he said he had studied the US. He even knew key military leaders … or had somehow been briefed on the man.

The President continued, "He has been given his orders and is in the process of clearing out Area-51 and I expect he will have it done as planned by the end of the day. He also has three C-17s on the ground and three more on the way for his transport fleet and he knows how to get any other resources he needs. I will be out of here this morning and on my way to Minot, North Dakota to quell the fears of the nation."

"I'm afraid that will not be possible Mr. President," Alpha-1 interjected. "There are several reasons you can't leave now. One is that you have a meeting with me in about thirty minutes in your office. Secondly you have a speech to make on the new strategies for military and domestic spending before Mr. Carmichael makes his announcements and third there is the issue that you have serious problems in Washington at the moment. Most of the people who can do us harm are in this town and you are very unpopular this morning with your lame story about a misfiring missile and the classified knowledge that your SECDEF blew a fuse and almost started a war last night. In addition there are already leaks on your upcoming announcements that have to be dealt with.

"You, sir, are the master politician and you need to address these issues quickly and effectively. And in the future do not make these sorts of plans without discussing them with me first. I'm afraid you're going nowhere this morning. Cancel the trip, and again speak to no one about our project and I'll be over there shortly." He reached over and pressed the 'end call' on Carmichael's iPhone.

Carmichael was shocked.

The President was apoplectic.

***

Bill Carter, a handsome man in his mid-fifties and now the Director of the CIA was at his desk by eight a.m. and got the President's voicemail to reinstitute surveillance on the Joint Chiefs.

His nickname internally was DD which was a hangover from his days as the Deputy Director in the agency where he made a name for himself tracking down and eliminating several infamous terrorists.

Bill didn't like the part of the job indicated by the President's request. Domestic spying by the CIA had always been frowned on but everyone knew some level of it was always present. Still his stomach churned any time the President wanted to snoop on his senior staff, especially the military.

Bill was ex-military himself and there was just something unhealthy in a free democracy when you had to spy on your top Generals. Even though the President had said this had to do with something he was about to announce, he wondered if it was connected in any way to the SECDEF and the missile accident given it stemmed from the same night.

He was going to have to use some of his most senior deep-cover agents to start surveillance on many levels on each of the Joint Chiefs but just to get the full picture he decided to call in the most recent audio from a bug he had planted about two years earlier in the NORAD control center in Colorado. If there was a connection then he thought a good place to start might be hearing what actually went on there last night and the calamity that followed.

Opening a protected file on his laptop that contained key numbers, he lifted the phone and hit the speed dial for the head of Tech Surveillance, "Hank, I want you to ship an audio surveillance file to my account. It's encrypted for my eyes only. The channel ID is 3417-14 and my authorization for accessing the channel is 007-45PKL. I need four hours of it starting yesterday at eighteen hundred."

Hank didn't often get a call from the Director so he sat up straight as he repeated the numbers he had been given, "You should have it within the next thirty minutes if that's OK."

"That'll do. Thanks," and he hung up the phone.

Before he went into his regular early morning briefing he left a voicemail for one of his direct reports to make sure he was marshaling the cover story of the maintenance problem with the missile and making sure the real story of the SECDEF having a medical collapse was kept within Top Secret and Eyes Only government officials. Leaks on a matter like this could be disastrous.

At a minimum each affected person would get a robo-call reminding them of their responsibilities.

***

The President had left instructions at the gate and with his secretary that when Robert Glass arrived at the White House, he was to be shown immediately to the Oval Office bumping any other scheduled meetings and that this order would stand for the foreseeable future unless it was rescinded by the President himself.

There were only a few people in the White House who knew details of the President's daily schedule and most could be counted on for discretion, still somehow it leaked within the White House that Bob Glass had carte blanche and was bumping even the most important guests. This was highly unusual and simply boosted the growing sense of unease in the staff in the aftermath of the events in the Oval Office the previous night. Some knew the whole classified story while others simply had deduced that there WAS a classified version of the events that only a few were privy to.

The President was seated at his desk as his secretary Mary Trudel ushered the young Robert Glass into the office. She knew him from TV as the miner from the Idaho collapse but couldn't understand how he now had garnered such exclusive treatment in the Oval Office.

As she closed the door behind the two men Alpha-1 spoke, "Good morning Mr. President. Thank you for waiting for me. I left the recording devices in this room disabled last night so your late night meeting with Mr. Carmichael was not recorded."

The President blushed as he realized Alpha-1 likely knew everything they had discussed.

"I will leave you with a device that will allow you to do the same for our future phone calls and any meetings you have with Mr. Carmichael. It would raise too many red flags and invite investigations to leave the recording devices permanently disabled.

"I trust you've had time to read the speech I prepared for you announcing your changes in fighter acquisitions."

The fact that he was being given travel orders, handed speeches, and being hung up on really got under his skin, but there was no doubt in his mind that this was all part of his new job description, and he needed to get used to it and demonstrate complete cooperation. Already he did not like this 'thing', found the directness and bossiness unnecessary but he reasoned he had no choice but to bite his tongue and go along with it.

The morning light had changed nothing for Turcot. Glass still looked like a twenty-something human but apparently that was a dangerous illusion.

Frowning, the President answered, "Yes I have read it and it's acceptable, but you do know that I have a professional staff write my speeches. I sent it to them to edit so they don't become suspicious that I've become an expert in speech writing overnight. I explained to them that I had some help from Carmichael's staff putting it together.

"My plan is to use the daily briefing at one p.m. to reiterate my condolences to the people of Minot and to make this announcement. Before that I will brief the Joint Chiefs."

Alpha-1 smiled, "All in agreement. That gives Fraser some time to get to his office in New York. However, you need to know that opposition is building and problems are appearing. Nothing is sacred in this town and some who know the classified story about last night have leaked it to some others in Congress, who are not cleared Top Secret in this matter. Some have simply been told that the public cover story is a fabrication. Others have gone as far as to intimate that it had something to do with the Secretary of Defense having a breakdown and trying to launch missiles from the Oval Office.

"In addition, I suspect the juxtaposition of the tragic events of last night and your announcements today of changes in military spending will confuse and even infuriate some. I think Gerry Hastings' input to you was on point. The timing of your announcements could not be worse. This was not part of our plan but your actions of last evening have put us in a very awkward position. We cannot jeopardize the project so we'll just have to press on with these new challenges you have afforded us."

Again, Turcot realized Alpha had somehow snooped on the private conversation he had the previous evening with Gerry Hastings and Alpha-1 probably had all the details.

Alpha-1 continued, "Lastly, I'm afraid General Kirk Jenkins has briefed his counterparts on the Joint Chiefs about your discussion last night against your direct orders. I'm afraid he wasn't as supportive as he may have led you to believe. You cannot of course reveal that you know this but you have your work cut out for you to keep our plan on the rails, keep your Generals in line and maintain your position as President.

"As we suspected, you're going to have significant opposition to everything we're attempting and it will start this morning and build after your speech."

The President was continually surprised by this alien, "How do you know all this?"

"I think you know we can monitor all your communications and for the rest of it, well I'm not prepared to go into that for the moment. Trust me, very soon this opposition to anything you do will grow to disturbing proportions and important scenarios will have begun. You'll need your best political skills to remain in your job and keep moving forward on our project which you know is critical for the survival of our two civilizations. Failure to comply or succeed will trigger regrettable actions. It is still far from certain that humans will survive this entire event. Many things can go wrong and as you know, I will not jeopardize my civilization. You MUST be successful in executing your role in this and that means staying in office and avoiding any interference with our activities at Area-51. We have no guarantees that our defensive strategy will work but it is all you and I can do to defend this planet."

The President thought he detected less confidence in the newcomer this morning. He hoped he was wrong.

Alpha-1 rose, "So in the parlance of the day, there is about to be a total shit storm in Washington starting today and as you can see now, this isn't a good time for you to be thirty thousand feet in the air winging it to Minot. That can come a bit later. You need to be here this morning extinguishing fires. Frankly I hope you now appreciate that your popularity, legacy and political future are no longer relevant beyond keeping your job for a few months. So you need to get a new mindset going, one that reprioritizes everything. Your only political moves should be those that advance your chances of staying in the job for three months. Believe me, if we are successful and your family ends up in Alpha, none of your political wins or losses will mean anything to you.

"Now I need you to get me a chopper to Andrews and a fast jet out to Nevada."

Hal Turcot was stunned once more with both the predicament he was in and the fact that he was taking orders like a junior officer. The fact that this 'thing' looked like a twenty-something engineer didn't make it any easier. Every time his mind ended up in that place he quickly reminded himself of the fate of Dan Westgate, the fate awaiting his daughter, the fact that this alien could freeze him and blow up a nuclear missile in its silo. But the biggest concerns were Alpha going to Plan B and the proposed real threat of an impending alien invasion.

After Alpha-1 left Turcot was distraught and furious. He consoled himself by the thought that this was the sacrifice he had to make to save the world. This arrogant alien just made it really uncomfortable. And working with that right-wing clown Carmichael, who almost seemed giddy about his good fortune and his new toys didn't make it any easier either.

Due to Alpha-1's meeting he had been forced to postpone the Joint Chiefs' meeting which he was sure only made them angrier after being briefed by Jenkins who would have certainly put everything in the worst possible light.

Mary called ahead and told them he was on his way. Word had already reached them that it was the young miner Robert Glass who had bumped their meeting and that just further enraged them.

Turcot was itching to tell them he knew of Jenkins breaching his orders and briefing them in advance but there was no way he could do that or he'd have to explain it.

These particular military leaders had been rumored to dislike any Democrat occupying the Oval Office but his sense was they disliked him even more than was customary and the events of the last twenty-four hours just added to that. These guys knew the American people would blame them for one of their 'toys' going awry and killing hundreds of Americans while the memories planted in their heads said the President had actually stood there and did nothing while Dan Westgate tried to launch a weapon.

Turcot realized it was a blessing they did not know the real truth that he had initiated the missile launch himself.

Entering the room he walked briskly to his position at the head of the table, "Gentlemen, thanks for waiting. Instead of you briefing me this morning, I'm going to brief you."

A few of them squirmed in their seats. They were honor bound to do what they were told by this liberal 'dove' but they didn't have to like it and Jenkins had already given them some idea of what to expect.

The President continued, "Firstly, there is the accident last night. It is critical that we stick to the cover story of a maintenance procedure gone south. I'm hearing there are leaks from those in the know relating to the SECDEF. I don't think we want the American people worried that one of us could have a stroke or a senior moment and start World War III. So please do your best to put a lid on any leaks.

"General Jenkins, the minute you know anything more about what went wrong at that silo, I want to know. I'll be up in Minot later dealing with the aftermath and providing assurances to the American people. I'd be a lot more confident in that task if I knew we were on to the reason it all went so wrong last night. Keep in mind it could've been much worse if the damned missile had actually launched and someone thought we were starting a war. Knowing the Russians and

Chinese, many more Americans including all of us, might not have survived last night.

"I am convinced what we will find is some fixable issue and not that there was any sabotage or basic design flaw because just like you, I sleep better when those missiles are wound up and ready to go. I want them back on line as soon as possible. Hopefully they will never be called on but I do believe they are an effective deterrent to the few bad actors out there who could pose a nuclear threat. We don't need that idiot in North Korea getting any weird ideas because one of our key nuclear systems is down.

"Now on to a new matter. Repeating things I've heard you gentlemen say, the US military remains the strongest in the world by far. Most of our weapon systems are the best in the world and they should be, because we still spend more than the next ten players combined.

"We have the best and often the most when it comes to aircraft carriers, fighters, bombers, tanks, drones, smart bombs, nukes, satellites, subs, intelligence networks and on and on. From time to time the opposition has better small arms like the AK-47 that is still being used around the world, but you get the picture.

"After the Bush wars and Obama's ISIS actions we've gradually built our forces back into a position of being able to handle a war in two separate theatres at the same time as we did during the Cold War. Some, primarily on the Left, consider that to be an unaffordable luxury or a waste of money but I, like you, think that we, as the remaining superpower in the world, need the overkill that is provided by such a massive military capability. Our overpowering strength is a deterrent in itself to anyone starting anything. I just wish it didn't cost so damned much.

"We may have fewer naval vessels afloat today, but we all know each warship carries more power than most navies. The existing fleet of fighters are still vastly superior as a total force to anything out there and we have the best-trained and best-equipped Army on the planet."

The Generals were girding themselves for the expected attack. They already knew from Jenkins what was coming, but the President had decided to try to 'sell' them on his plans.

Turcot was still talking, "The Russians have a couple of real showoff planes like that crazy Sukhoi 47, but no quantity to provide any real competition to our Air Force and the Chinese may be a threat when they mass produce the J-20 or the 31 but not for quite some time.

"To put this in perspective, our military goals for the last fifty or so years have never been to have the best team. It's been to have the dream team of all the best players in the league on our squad totally dominating everyone else and this may come as a surprise to you but that's exactly where I want us to remain."

The men in the room knew not to challenge him while he was on such a rant. Typical of a liberal to take this slant. Clearly the US military was so far out in front because that was the way the American people wanted it. But liberals never saw it that way. They would rather save some money, yap about the military industrial complex and take a gamble on the country's security.

Turcot continued, "Safe to say the military is in very good shape for the moment."

He could see by their faces that they knew what was coming.

"Our domestic situation is much different. We are no longer leaders in the world in many important categories. Now we even hear that we're probably tenth in what the surveys call 'upward mobility' or what we used to call the 'American Dream'.

"This country has complex challenges and only some of those can be helped in the short term by money, but they can be helped.

"Now I briefed General Jenkins last night because I needed his help but I want to let you all know now that I have some revolutionary plans.

"Let me start by acknowledging and thanking General Jenkins for his support for my plans. General, that was very much appreciated. I know this may cause some short-term challenges for the Air Force but it is a big man who is willing to make personal sacrifices for the good of the country."

Jenkins was red and livid as the others glared at him. It was apparent to Turcot that Jenkins hadn't told them the whole story including his early support for the program.

"Now to the plans. You know that I'm no political friend of Fraser Carmichael but gentlemen, he is an American gem and I never thought I'd find myself saying that. Like other famous American entrepreneurs, he is always pushing the envelope of what is doable.

He is a master in so many domains and currently builds some of our best drones and cruise missiles. But like Henry Ford, his real penchant is for innovative manufacturing and man has he come up with an amazing breakthrough.

"Last night I started out as a skeptic but by the end of the evening I became a convert."

This stunned the room. Jenkins had gotten it right. This had all happened in one night. A night that earlier had featured a massive hydrogen bomb going off on American soil killing hundreds and injuring thousands and somehow this wizard had the time to discuss manufacturing with Fraser Carmichael? How was that even possible? Any sane man would be so shocked at the catastrophe on his watch that he would've canceled everything else for the rest of the week. Yet Turcot seemed to be reveling in his new-found interest or 'hobby' in manufacturing.

The President was still talking and becoming animated as he went on to give them a detailed description of Carmichael's breakthroughs and capabilities with his new supercomputer and amazing robots.

The Joint Chiefs were not buying it. Hal Turcot wasn't known to be a manufacturing guru and was most likely just parroting what Carmichael had told him to say. Why he was suddenly embracing Carmichael, a political enemy, was yet to be revealed.

He continued, "Before General Jenkins arrived last night, Carmichael took me through how he came upon this development. Then realizing what he had and what a strategic advantage it could be to America, he decided to keep it secret and offer it to our military where he saw that not only could he give us a big leg up on weapons but he could save us billions in the process. A win-win for the country, our military, and of course himself.

"Our contracts are massive so it was a great place for him to start. He can't take over all manufacturing in one fell swoop so he decided to focus first on the area that would give us the most advantage. Eventually I believe he will move his new manufacturing architecture into the commercial space, but for now it's ours to take advantage of.

"Now make no mistake, Carmichael's goal is to lock up virtually all military weapons manufacturing as soon as he proves himself on this first project. This morning I'm canceling all contracts on the F-47 and awarding the entire program to Carmichael Industries."

The lack of visible shock in the room confirmed that Jenkins had already told them of his plans.

"I have no problem with him going after lots of military business if it's limited to us and if everything comes in at half price or better. His sacrifice in this is that he is limiting the availability of this new manufacturing to US military projects where he could have just as easily gone off and licensed this capability to Honda for billions to produce cars, jet skis and the like. I have to reluctantly recognize here and now that the man is indeed a genius and a patriot.

"That said, Carmichael has committed to delivering the first ten F-47s for training in about three months, which is realistically three years earlier than what has been committed by the team building them now. He claims he can come in at really low cost for the planes and he'll beat all of our goals for ease of maintenance and lifetime cost of ownership."

General Hawthorne, Chairman of the Joint Chiefs and Jenkins' predecessor at the Air Force was incensed that this seemed to have gone so far so fast. Still miffed at how Jenkins had let this get out of control the previous evening he just had to jump in, "But Mr. President, so far we have only Carmichael's word about his incredible advances and these unbelievably crazy deadlines and costs. He does not have a stellar batting record. Remember when he tried to take on Trump in the resort business. He closed that down and lost billions within a few years."

"General this is not the same thing. Carmichael knows or at least knew nothing about the resort business. He is arguably one of the world's best at manufacturing. Apple may have him beat in the consumer space but in his domain he has always been much more innovative than the rest. And believe me, this is a bigger breakthrough than anything you've ever seen. It's a complete paradigm shift in how you approach manufacturing. He described it to me as a 'tipping point'", he lied, "when suddenly you make a massive breakthrough and everything becomes really simple."

The others just sat and stared incredulously at the recklessness of the President's intended path. They had been discussing this amongst themselves before his arrival and he was right that the US Air Force was in relatively good shape at the moment, even if the F-22 and the F-35 both had certain problems and were coming in at nearly three times the projected price on a per unit basis.

Hawthorne thought he needed to do something but it was looking like there would be no talking him out of this crazy idea at the moment. Even the tone of his voice left them no doubt he was a man on a mission. At least this crazy, reckless experiment appeared to be limited to a three-month window. That would definitely slip, but it might be best to step back and let this thing fail and be ready to pick up the pieces. A few months of a hiatus would turn into a much longer delay in terms of restarting the program after his failure but with some concerted effort it might be manageable and tolerable.

On top of that, Congress would be furious and would see the threat as they were all lining up to get a piece of the pie for their state when real manufacturing of the Firebolt kicked off. There was no way Congress would stand by and let Turcot and Carmichael get away with taking over the entire project, which thankfully would put them out front and avoid a confrontation between the Joint Chiefs and their boss.

CII was never going to deliver and take all of the manufacturing of the fighter away from Congress. Even if somehow he stumbled over the finish line with a single, half-baked fighter, Congress couldn't stand for it. They all stood to lose too many jobs, too much influence, too much in campaign contributions, and too many perks from the defense industry. The only issue was that Congress tended to move slowly. Turcot might still get his three-month experiment after all.

Turcot could see the resistance building and he had to put a final point on this as he continued, "Gentlemen, I have a busy morning as you can imagine from the disaster of last night. Let me finish by demanding all of you support the plan. Last I checked, the American military is led by an elected civilian representative and that would be me, and I've made my decision on this."

This was WAY out of character and out of bounds for a President to bring this up in such a crude fashion in this room and every man was shocked and repulsed. In effect it questioned their loyalty and commitment to their oaths. They looked at each other as if to say, 'you say something' but before anyone could object, the President continued, "I will have a press conference today where I will announce changes in the processes for acquiring military weapons but I will go further than that. I will announce the suspension of work on the F-35 based on some technical issues in the design that must be worked out before we continue. In reality that plane is dead. It may have been dead for years if you listen to the RAND Corporation. We lost any chance of a leadership fighter when Congress insisted we use the same airframe for the US Air Force, Navy and the Marines. Joint strike fighters that try to be leadership platforms in many roles were always a bad idea and dead on arrival in my opinion and I know at least some of you feel the same.

"Now the 35 may have a role with its VTOL in the Navy and Marines so eventually all planes already delivered will go to them as the Air Force takes delivery of the 47s. The Air Force desperately needs the 47 for their changing requirements in warfare."

Jenkins had warned them of this piece but none of them thought he would actually cancel the F-35 until he had the magic F-47s in hand. This had just gone beyond reckless.

The President seemed on a roll, "I've canceled construction of the first three F-47s at Area-51 but of course that was a secret development and no specific announcement will be made except to allude to a new way forward in design and manufacturing and the resultant savings of billions to be put to use for underfunded social programs especially retraining any displaced workers. This is a great day for our military and you'll get more than you were expecting from the new fighter but you won't need all that money to do it."

Hawthorne was furious. There it was; a master political deal between political enemies. Carmichael would get the contract for the F-47s and Turcot would get to funnel lots of military money to his pet social programs. The real danger was that even if Carmichael and Turcot fell flat on their faces in Groom Lake, it would be near impossible to take the money back for the military once it was earmarked for the President's social programs. And there was no way Congress or the American people were going to vote for a tax increase to put the lost money back into military spending once it was gone. It would take an all-out political war and likely years to resolve that issue.

Hawthorne being the most political of the group realized that all of this could be challenged under the constitution but if Turcot executed fast enough then he might just get away with it. In fact that was likely the master political plan; start a bogus fighter program as a screen to move money to social programs and once executed, it would be hard to reverse.

Congress's only recourse would be to freeze the money or even impeach him but that would take time and the way he was moving it would be too late to address all of the damage he could do. He would likely pay a massive political price for this but who knew his actual motive, his defense for Congress, or even his end game.

There was no telling how he was going to pull this off, but just in the last twenty-four hours he had shown his political skills by apparently tricking Jenkins into a statement of support that was no doubt recorded on the Oval Office tapes and laying a plan to get his way on social programs. And all of this at an inopportune moment when the people, Congress, and the press were all focused on a national tragedy. It almost seemed like he might have been waiting for a suitable distraction and used the missile disaster to slip in his crazy plan. Yet every man in the room could see that that was political suicide.

The others felt for Jenkins and his Air Force who had basically been told to sit in the corner and do as they were told. None of the others made eye contact with him. His resignation couldn't be long in coming. They all wondered what Turcot could do to put the rest of them in the same position but for now his focus seemed to be confined to fighters.

"Gentlemen, I'm convinced this is the right direction for our country and it will put our military even further out front than it is today. Good day," and he rose and left a stunned audience.

As he closed the door General Hawthorne, Chairman of the Joint Chiefs spoke, "Well gentlemen, that was completely unexpected. I for one had no notice that he had any of these plans in mind and we are led to believe it was all cooked up last night, in his office, in the middle of a national catastrophe. If I didn't know better I would say he has lost his mind. And you can't repeat that.

"Jenkins, he just eviscerated your career and your legacy as head of the Air Force. For the good of the country you need to get on top of this and derail this nonsense or we'll all be doomed. You're his target today but the rest of us can't be far behind.

"I suspect he'll set up a direct line to Clay Hawkins at Groom Lake and do an end run on normal military channels but you can't let that happen. Until you are officially dismissed from your command, you have the responsibility to manage anything under you. That's not insubordination, that's exercising the constitutional duties of your office. He didn't release you from your command, so it's your duty to keep a close eye on what's going on out there. Our command structure is firmly based in law so you cannot be pushed aside while you're still Secretary of the Air Force, and it's a command not worth having if you can't get control over it.

"Gentlemen, this man, although he is the Commander-in-Chief, has never shown the ability or penchant to lead the military. It is our duty to remember our oaths to the constitution and do what is best for this country and therefore I suggest that vigorous opposition to these plans is called for, within the law of course. The only way we can change his mind is through the political process so I would suggest you brief all of your Congressional contacts on the implications of this crazy plan. Advanced fighters in three months; who is he kidding?

"Good day," he said as he rose, took his brief case that had never been opened and left.

As the other members filed out they realized General Hawthorne had waited outside the room and he pulled General Jenkins aside for a private meeting out of earshot of anyone else. "Kirk, you're in big trouble here. If he actually goes ahead with this whole thing then it's imperative that you find a way to scuttle Carmichael's plans. I don't think I have to tell you what our lives will be like if Turcot gets away with directed tenders and farming business out that is ours to allocate. We'll have lost total control of the procurement process and you know there are powerful people in Congress and industry that won't stand for it. There is way too much money and way too many very important people involved here. Things will get really crazy if we don't put a stop to it. This plan of his is a total showstopper. You need to find clandestine ways to disrupt and destroy any of Carmichael's initiatives. Let me be clear, you need to take extraordinary measures or your position will be untenable."

He left Jenkins wondering what the chairman actually meant by 'extraordinary' measures.

Nevada

General Clay Hawkins was used to tough assignments, but laying off several hundred workers with no warning was an entirely new experience for him. Some of these guys were unionized and that was also a concern.

He was on unfamiliar ground and trembling slightly as he walked up to the microphone on the temporary stage in hangar #1 at Area-51. As an ex-fighter pilot he had faced the enemy in war with courage but this was different and scarier on some level. The only weapons available to him were his words and they were untested.

He had sent secure notices canceling contracts to the legal departments of all the contractors involved but that would certainly not be the end of it. Even though the government was well within its rights to cancel without cause, law suits and injunctions were likely but at least he had informed them before he spoke to their people. The mumbling from a couple of small groups in the crowd seemed to indicate that some in the audience had already heard from their HQ's and they were spreading the news.

To add some gravitas and security, he had called in all but essential perimeter military staff on the base. Four of the largest of them in their fatigues, were on stage with him and the rest were spread throughout the hangar. He knew unionized employees could, from time to time, get frisky when it came to their employment conditions and many of these workers fit that profile.

He had just enough time to grab a coffee to give him a boost after getting less than two hours of restless sleep on the tiny military executive jet out of Florida.

He knew that the expectation of many of the rank and file was simply that Colonel Frank Kirkpatrick was being reassigned and this was the new guy heading up the program for the military. Most were expecting the pro forma pep talk.

The crowd looked even larger than he had expected and he wondered immediately if his troops would be of any help if discontent devolved into aggression.

"Ladies and gentlemen, I am Brigadier General Clayton Hawkins. I'm the new commander here at Groom Lake. Colonel Frank

Kirkpatrick is off to another important assignment.

"First off, I want to thank all of you for the incredible work you do and express our gratitude that the world remains unaware of the fantastic work that goes on here. You've done an excellent job in building our next warplane and an equally excellent job of keeping it secret.

"However, the President and the military brass have decided on a different direction for the moment."

He could see the agitation building in the crowd.

"The current plan is that the fighter you're building will be put on hold for possibly one year. Everyone on this base will be furloughed for that period of time. I've canceled the contracts with your companies this morning and made the standard provisions, by contract, for them to pay your salaries for the furlough period."

Someone yelled out "You can't do that." Another yelled, "What about overtime and vacation pay?"

"I'm sorry, I will not respond to heckling. Your contract is with your respective companies so you should speak to them about how you'll be treated as individuals. As I said, in legally canceling their contracts we provided for up to one year of severance or furlough pay for every worker which is a standard part of all these contracts. That is more than I'm authorized to tell you so I'd suggest you take up any questions on these matters with your respective companies. Whether your company allows you to transfer elsewhere inside your company, seek employment elsewhere during the year or whether they have a termination option is tied to your agreement with your company. So for some of you this might turn out to be a fortunate event."

He realized he had just set the companies up for some trouble but he knew these military contractors and they were more likely to keep the furlough pay for themselves and give all their workers two weeks' notice. At least he had done his part to protect the workers by letting them know up front the companies had their money.

"It's my solemn duty to remind you that all of you remain under federal non-disclosure agreements for life as this is Top Secret work and I know I can count on you to honor those agreements.

"Anyone breaching these non-disclosures will be prosecuted to the fullest extent of the law governing Top Secret government work. Any breaches of confidentiality will be treated as treason and I know I don't have to remind you that in a case like this we will be successful in prosecution and sentences for treason are severe.

"It would pay you no dividends to speculate on what we're doing with the fighter in its current state or any plans going forward. That is also covered under the non-disclosure. To remind you, you cannot tell ANYONE what you did here, what we're doing, anything about today, anything about this place, speculate on what we might or might not do or even that you've ever been to this secret base. The safety of our nation depends on your commitment to keeping these secrets.

"Now that you all know the facts and that there are provisions for you to be paid during this furlough there is no reason to delay the change. I've ordered the planes up from Vegas and they'll be here in the next thirty minutes. Please empty out your lockers and leave no personal items behind. Take no souvenirs from here or anything that isn't yours, and board the planes as soon as they arrive."

A few pockets in the crowd seemed agitated. There was always someone who didn't like change or more likely didn't trust the company to pass on the furlough pay.

"Let me close by saying that to protect America the government must do what is in the best interests of our military strategies. You've assisted in a very important way towards this goal and we thank you for your service. You all possess critical skills that we require and maybe one day we will work again on important projects for our nation.

"It is unlikely the need for advanced weapons will go away any time soon, so there is a good chance we will see you back here someday. That is why we've made these efforts to treat you fairly and compassionately, and to part on friendly terms.

"On behalf of the President we would like to thank you once more for your invaluable service to our nation.

"Best of luck to you all, and God bless."

He left quickly out the back door with his escort. Within seconds he had a call from one of his direct reports on the hangar floor indicating there was lots of grumbling but the conversations seemed to be centered on what they were going to hear about severance or furlough from their various companies. Other than that they seemed to be filing out calmly and heading for the locker areas.

The planes came and left without incident except for a few who screamed something in the direction of the military barracks on their way up the gangway.

By noon Hawkins had his troops dismantling manufacturing jigs and moving half-built airframes to the smallest hangar on the base that would keep them out of the elements. He needed more manpower, so to speed things up he had, with the help of the Pentagon, requisitioned a planeload of airmen from Nellis AFB in Las Vegas and a busload of airmen from the drone base at Creech AFB, about sixty miles south in Indian Springs.

All of the big stuff was quickly out of the four main hangars, but he could see it would take more than a day to dismantle all of the manufacturing jigs and really do a full and complete cleanout. He decided to wait for Glass to see if he needed to rush in even more help. The President had said by the end of the day was the target, but he had so many men on the job now they were virtually running into each other and this guy Glass wasn't even here yet.

Generals Jenkins and Hawthorne, for their part, had put out the word that Hawkins was to get whatever he wanted.

There had always been the opportunity to hold back some of the contractors to assist but from his experience, you didn't want people who had just been furloughed working on your site. Sabotage was almost guaranteed. In the end, on the recommendation of the departing Colonel Kirkpatrick, he only kept a few of the kitchen staff.

***

The President had only arrived back at his office from the Situation Room when his secretary Mary Trudel grabbed him at the door. "Mr. President I heard through the Secret Service that Gerry Hastings resigned last night and I'm trying to pick up the slack until you find a replacement. To be very frank sir, if you don't return some of these calls from Congress they're going to storm the Bastille as it were. There are lots of concerns about the explosion yesterday but more to the point, I think someone on the Joint Chiefs has already leaked some sort of news and excuse the expression, but whatever it is, they're going nuts over on the Hill. I've never seen anything like it.

"If I may, I think you should at least return the calls from the leaders of the House and Senate. But before I go, I must say I'm sure you must be beside yourself with grief for the hundreds of people killed in that accident. I was in bed early but I was shocked when I turned on the TV this morning. I should have come back in last night but no one called."

"No Mary, there was nothing you could do. Listen, please get Gerry's deputy in here to take his seat for a while. He can work out of Gerry's office."

"I'll do that immediately sir. Can I get the Senate leader on the phone for you? Better to start with your own people before you talk to the other side if you know what I mean."

"Yeah, get him on the line. Thanks Mary."

Hal Turcot made it over to his desk and pressed the line for the residence. Evelyne was up and took the call, "Ev, I left before you got up and just wanted to let you know that today is going to be a horrendous day. I'm going to make several announcements and it's really going to get tense. I know Ann watches a lot of TV so please make sure she is aware that I'm OK and this is all part of the plan. I love you both. Talk to you later." He hung up only to realize he hadn't let his wife get a word in.

Line one lit up and he grabbed it, "Bob?"

"Yes Mr. President. What the hell has been going on over there for the last twelve hours? Yesterday was a slow day until a bomb went off and they just seem to be going off hourly now. I'm hearing all kinds of ridiculous stories about the White House."

"Well Bob tell me what you heard and I'll tell you if it's true or not."

Bob Downey, the senior Democratic Senator from Massachusetts and leader of the Senate didn't like these guessing games. "First there is the bomb. Did Dan Westgate really have a breakdown, take over the Oval Office, threaten people and try to launch a missile at China and subsequently drop dead or did someone take him out?"

"No, no one took him out! And no, for God's sake the target wasn't China. Where the hell did you hear that?"

"I don't know. Some rumor started around the Capitol that NORAD made up the story about the target being some silver mine. I know the public think it was a maintenance issue but what about all the rest of it?"

"Well for starters, shut down that rumor about China, we don't need that complicating things and yes, all the rest of that is true.

"I haven't heard the autopsy results yet but there must have been something wrong with him. He was babbling and incoherent and we didn't feel like storming him with a gun in our faces.

"Thank God the missile didn't launch or we might have seen a reaction from the Chinese or more likely the Russians. Excuse me for saying it, but that was an unbelievable stroke of luck in the middle of a catastrophe, but it puts our entire missile program in question. Maybe one of the guys at the silo pressed the wrong button. We've never been able to simulate the full measure of stress these guys would be under if they had to press the button and now we can't ask them what happened. Remember, they would have known Dan had set the target as Idaho and that would have added to the stress."

"Look Hal, this all sounds wacky to me but I have a million questions on the bomb and what we're doing about it, but I know you're busy so I'll just rip through these other rumors. Did Gerry Hastings resign and if so why?"

"Yes and it was based on the fact that he couldn't support me unreservedly on the path I've chosen."

Downey cut him off, "OK, to this path you speak of," his voice becoming more urgent, "are you actually contemplating a press conference to announce the cancelation of the F-35 and the F-47 without coming to Congress first?"

Wow! Either Jenkins had spread the news overnight or the Joint Chiefs had gotten to their contacts on the Hill in the time it had taken him to get upstairs to his office. Then again, Alpha-1 said Jenkins had briefed the Joint Chiefs last night so it probably all spread out from there.

He paused to gather his thoughts, "Yes to the cancelation of the F-35 because we're getting nowhere with that. It's bleeding billions by now and the word is out that it's weak. That RAND report is a few years old but still valid. We need the 35s replacement and we need it fast, and we don't need to be throwing good money after bad.

"That decision of Congress to force the military to share a fighter is the culprit here so you can blame your buddies over there for causing the death of the F-35. You can't build a machine that is simultaneously fast and powerful yet at the same time needs a giant fan in the middle of its body to accommodate vertical takeoffs. The military told us that when Congress insisted on a Joint Strike Fighter, but we didn't listen. Now we have a pickup truck instead of a Ferrari.

"And no I didn't cancel the Firebolt. I just restarted the program with new people. I've canceled the existing contracts and given it all to Carmichael Industries who have this amazing new technology. They have built a giant quantum computer with free-moving robots that learn and speed up as they go. They believe they can ship us the first ten fighters in about three months. I have Jenkins' support on the matter and I've demanded the other Joint Chiefs get behind it too."

By his tone it was clear that Downey was furious, "Yeah, that's not the way I'm hearing it. Jenkins thinks he was tricked into supporting it. He called me himself late last night and got me out of bed. Right after he called his buddy Williams in the House I'll bet, and you DEMANDED the other Generals support it? But forget that for a moment. WHAT THE HELL ARE YOU TALKING ABOUT DELIVERING STUFF IN THREE MONTHS? THAT'S CRAZY TALK," he yelled into the phone.

"In twelve hours you've turned the whole world upside down and at the time of a national emergency to boot. Have you lost your mind? An atomic bomb just went off on American soil. Did you miss that somehow? And now you're planning a press conference on what, fighter jets? The whole world will think you've totally lost it. And besides that, you can't give out contracts without going through the Pentagon's official bid process.

"Forget about the press who will think like most Americans that you've totally lost your mind focusing on this today, as opposed to the mess in North Dakota.

"Forget about the American people and the world worried about an atomic bomb going off on American soil and what REALLY happened.

"Forget that you had a cabinet member that tried to take over the government and dropped dead in your office.

"Put all of that aside for a moment. With these announcements you're planning today, we'll be completely frozen over here on the Hill. Nothing will get done. This nonsense will suck all the air out of the room. You can't even do some of these things by yourself. You may think they're all the purview of the Executive Branch but I can guarantee you that absolutely no one over here will agree with that.

"Killing the 35 and restarting the 47 will put thousands, hell tens of thousands of people out of work in most of the lower forty-eight states, kill the stock market in high-tech and it will likely cripple some state economies who depend heavily on military work.

"Every damned Congressman and Senator will want your head when word spreads and believe me, bad news travels fast over here. Have you forgotten that you are first and foremost a politician because you sure seem to have totally lost that whole skill set?

"You must have been in a coma to miss the fact that Congress will never let you get away with this. I've had about forty calls from Senators already and it isn't even ten o'clock yet. The markets will collapse for God's sake. What were you thinking? And what the hell do you mean that nut job Carmichael will have 47s in three months? Are you out of your mind? He can't even build a single landing gear in that amount of time."

Turcot was first and foremost a skilled politician indeed, and he had already considered all of the angles and pitfalls Downey brought up, but there was no turning back and there was no way to explain in any rational way what he was up to, "Listen Bob, of all the people over there, I need you on side with this. This is going to get really dirty and I need you in my corner."

Downey was close to speechless, "For a nutty plan like this? Are you kidding me? You're throwing away your career and your legacy and now you want me to jump in with you? For a start you could've warned me about the 35. I had no idea twelve hours ago that you were even thinking of doing anything with it, never mind canceling the entire program."

Hal Turcot didn't want to admit that a little over twelve hours ago HE had no intention of taking this path.

Senator Bob Downey was still ranting, his Boston accent growing by the minute, "OK, again, forget all of that. Forget we have a national emergency on our hands. Take a minute and do your best sales job on me for your change in focus and these changes you plan to announce. Why should anyone like this? Hell I can't believe we're actually discussing this. What were you thinking? Your timing makes no sense to say nothing of this nutty, half-baked fighter plan. But just for shits and giggles, go ahead, try to sell me on it."

Downey's vulgarity and heavy Boston accent told the President the Senator was beside himself. Downey had never spoken to him in this way with or without the vulgarity. But the President had no choice. No matter how crazy this all seemed he had to press ahead. The survival of the planet depended on it.

He realized he may have pushed too far on the cancelation of the F-35. He hadn't even told Alpha-1 about it yet but he had his reasons to go beyond the F-47, although he was already questioning the political wisdom of the move.

There had been no pressing reason to kill the 35 right now, but when he got 'handed' the idea of an F-47 in three months, his knee-jerk reaction was to kill the 35 too. While this could solve his budget problems, he was forgetting that he was the only politician who at least partially believed the F-47 delivery date to replace the 35s.

He was personally convinced the F-35 was no longer needed by the Air Force but he was the only one that saw a different path and he hated losing so much money on a bad and massively expensive fighter when he couldn't scrounge up enough money for the simplest of his social programs.

His own projection was that the current F-35 would probably cost well over $250M a copy by the time it was finished, including all the support services, and that could fund lots of programs that were even more important to Americans.

Now, he realized that politically, that part of the plan had been rash and unnecessary, putting even more pressure on his increasingly fragile presidency, but changing his plan now was a bad idea. Backing off on the 35 would open the door to killing the plan for the 47, clearing out Area-51 and the whole house of cards could come crashing down. He could not show weakness to either the politicians who already knew of the plan, or his military leaders. If he could survive the plan for the F-47s then he could survive with the F-35s rolled in. After all, if he believed Alpha-1, he only had to survive a few months in office.

All he could do was press ahead and try to stay in control until this invading alien challenge was met and to do that he had to start building support for his decisions.

Downey would be the first test, so he gathered his thoughts and started, "OK, it's a great idea because it solves our budget problem and gets us the money we need for important social programs. We are frankly WAY over-invested in our military hardware and grossly under-invested on what really matters to the middle class and the poor and you know that.

"Call it a pilot program if you want. I'm not attacking every piece of military hardware, just the next fighter. They're still spending hundreds of billions a year on aircraft carriers, subs, tanks and everything else, so don't buy into this nonsense that states will go bankrupt or our defensive posture weakened.

"This is a bold and necessary move to start to get control of that cursed military spending and takes on that juggernaut once and for all. It saves the American people hundreds of billions, hell nearly a trillion over the decade on the two fighters by my calculations.

"It's a smarter approach to how we spend the peoples' money. I don't need a tender or bid process because it's a directed tender. Carmichael's the only one who can do it. And we're making Carmichael build it with no guarantees. If he achieves his goals it puts America back on top not only in fighters but in manufacturing too. Hell we might even be able to wrench back other manufacturing sectors from overseas if his processes can be licensed to US companies alone.

"This is a win-win. You need to break a few eggs if you want to make an omelet. There you go, that's the cliché Americans will connect with. Make sure you get that into your talking points for any TV interviews."

Downey was thinking, 'That's it? He wants me to go with eggs and omelets?'

"OK Hal, if we put the Firebolt aside for a minute because it's secret and the Republicans can't beat you over the head with it, I see your point and there could be some good stuff here if ANYONE besides you could be convinced to believe Carmichael, but Hal you've lost your political touch, and on a day like today with a national emergency in play? It can't be done!

"Even though the plan might have some merit in YOUR mind you cannot bypass Congress like this. They'll kill you. Even our side will want your head. You have no allies on this. We all get most of our campaign contributions from the very companies you've just damaged. Hell Raytheon is the biggest commercial employer in Mass. What the hell am I going to tell them? They're not going to be happy finding out that you're having a love affair with a competitor, Fraser Carmichael of all people. Last time we talked you thought he was a clown.

"Listen, you didn't think this through Hal. This won't fly. They'll have the whole White House in public hearings on the Hill within a month if you go down this path and this would be the textbook case for Congress, under their constitutional oversight role, compelling you to testify yourself, in public, in front of every American household and they'll make you look like a crazy man.

"They'll go to the Supreme Court and SCOTUS will side with them and compel you to testify on how this all came about. Federal courts in virtually every state will issue injunctions to stop you from canceling the contracts and that will work its way up the ladder to SCOTUS as well, and I just can't see them coming down on your side. This is a classic self-inflicted wound. Hell it's political suicide!

"Congress controls the purse strings, not you. I guarantee you'll lose eventually in the Supreme Court and all of this will be undone and you'll be left the massive loser. Your presidency will be finished. You can write off your last two years in the White House because you'll get nothing done after pissing off the entire Congress.

"The Joint Chiefs must be apoplectic over this. They are all well connected to big Republicans. They'll be feeding them all the scoop on where to look and who to subpoena. The files over at the Pentagon will all be open to anyone who wants to kill your programs."

Turcot answered, "You know I won't testify and they couldn't compel it. That won't fly under Separation of Powers."

Downey was shocked, "That was the only thing you heard? You won't testify? SCOTUS will not agree with you, but even if you're right, that won't stop them from trying. Taking it to the Supreme Court will make you look like an ass for not explaining your moves. There's no question in my mind that in this case, because you took it all on yourself, SCOTUS will find in their favor. They'll hold you in contempt if you don't testify and that will be the start of impeachment on the basis of abuse of power.

"I'm serious. This is big. If you don't bend on this they'll go for your head. Your only out MIGHT BE, and I say might be, if you do something completely amazing with public opinion where right now you are doing the exact opposite due to your neglect of the Minot accident. As of today you'll look like a total jackass to Joe Six-pack if you try to move their attention away from Minot to some cockamamie plan for secret fighters that you can't even explain because it's all classified.

"Your best hope is that the Republicans will drop the 47 issue for three months until Carmichael falls flat on his face but then they'll find a way to get that on the table and accuse you of gross mismanagement of a critical defense program. But in the meantime they'll crucify you on the 35 and Minot.

"The fact that Carmichael is a big Republican activist and contributor to the GOP won't save him from their wrath when they find out he won't be subcontracting much to their districts. They'll fry him too. He'd better watch his stock price and double up on his personal security.

"But Hal, you're a smart guy. What's going on here? You know all this! You know you can't do this today. You must be laser-focused on Minot and that's all there is to it."

The President had heard enough. He wasn't going to convince Bob Downey any more than he had already so he decided to cut it off, "Look Bob, I can't wait. The horse has already left the barn. I need to strike before they organize against me and find a way to stop me.

"Listen, I have to go. You know the routine. You brief as many as you can get to, and take some of the load off me, and give them something to think about. They won't want to get too far out in front of this when they realize the American people rarely object to massive savings in taxpayer dollars, and giving a black eye to defense contractors is just the cherry on the cake.

"Part of my announcement today will be a tax cut for the middle class funded by this change. Let's see them try to attack that. A Democrat cutting costs and lowering taxes? How could they be against that? And let them know on the Hill that I can't run for a third term so this is legacy stuff. I have the biggest balls in the room! Talk to you later."

The President hung up on a furious Bob Downey before the Senator could remind him that he himself wasn't on side with this and couldn't support the cancelation of the F-35, to say nothing of the crazy plan for the F-47. This was a career limiting issue. The President didn't have to run for re-election but everyone else on the Hill did.

Downey was shocked by the bravado he heard coming out of the mouth of a President most thought of as a little timid in a fight. Something had changed. This President had clearly found some kind of misdirected courage somewhere and Downey didn't like it at all, even if it did serve some of the goals of the Democrats. He really wondered who had the ear of the President these days and was giving him such insane political advice. Surely it could not have been Fraser

Carmichael who was a sworn enemy.

His last thoughts were of the bomb in Minot. Something crazy had gotten into the President in the last twenty-four hours. An actual atomic bomb had exploded on US soil and instead of focusing exclusively on that, he was off on some nutty plan to revolutionize what, the military, US manufacturing? It made no sense at all.

Bob Downey's blood was boiling and he could hear his throbbing pulse in his ears. The bomb was a national disaster and something that would be seen as much worse than Katrina, which had been an act of God, not a failing of our revered military. The investigation, he was sure, would conclude that it was an avoidable calamity. Even though the loss of life would likely be smaller than Katrina, it was an A-bomb for God's sake and we had somehow done it to ourselves. Downey seriously hoped the cover story of a flaw in a maintenance procedure would hold because there would be real consternation if Americans thought mentally ill people could press buttons in the White House to wipe them out.

No, Harold Turcot wasn't going to escape this one unscathed unless he changed his mind before his press conference and it sounded like there was zero chance of that.

***

Sheriff Sam Worthington of the Shoshone County Sheriff's office had just gotten back to the office in Wallace from the mine site where he had wrapped up and dismissed all of his police who had been managing traffic. Given there was no one left to talk to and the miner was rescued, the media quickly beat a path out of town. Many of them were on their way to Minot to cover real news, the aftermath of the horrendous missile accident.

Sam was still pissed that bailiffs carrying court orders had been able to keep him and his men off the mine property. The county's lawyers apparently were not as tough or as fast as whoever was pulling the strings on this and there would be hell to pay as soon as he could chase down the town manager.

There had been no FBI involvement for a simple mine rescue and casualty, so he had retained jurisdiction, which made it all the more puzzling how some judge could issue an injunction to keep him from investigating a suspicious death. It made no sense.

He had just gotten to his desk with a coffee when Frank Racine, one of his deputies came in carrying some papers.

"Well I know where Glass is. The White House posted a picture sometime last night of him with the President and none other than that billionaire, Fraser Carmichael. I'm willing to bet Carmichael is the one behind all of that injunction nonsense out at the mine. He must be the invisible owner.

"My plan was to get a new subpoena, get down in that mine and investigate the death of the other guy," he shuffled his papers and found what he was looking for, "Yeah, Lawrence, Eric Lawrence. But guess what? The mine shaft they drilled has apparently collapsed and is no longer usable, according to some press guy out there that knows one of the security guards. He says it might cost somebody a million to drill a new shaft. I think someone doesn't want us investigating this death.

"And, wait 'til you here this. A coroner has already ruled Lawrence's death accidental even before a police report. Not only that, the body was cremated yesterday only hours after it was removed from the mine."

Sam Worthington was exhausted and just stared at him. Right now he was just too tired to give a damn. The trapped miner had been saved and as far as he was concerned, everything could now move back to a snail's pace as the courts worked it out.

Racine was still talking, "I don't recognize the name of the state coroner and his office says he has suddenly left on vacation. Add to that the fact that Glass's whole extended family disappears in a fire at the same time as he's being rescued and man something is totally wrong here. Somebody is orchestrating something massive here but for the life of me I can't figure out what or why."

The Sheriff sneered, "So go call Geraldo Rivera if he's still around, or another one of those famous investigative guys on TV. Get them out here. Sounds like you've got a great conspiracy there. They could make a big TV special out of it. Maybe even Pay-per-View."

He continued, "I know we're expected to believe it's all a coincidence but how you gonna investigate this? Start with motive. Who had motive to do anything criminal? Until you come up with something else I see nothing here. Don't waste your time on it unless something pops up. I just came back from there and they'll tie us up in knots with injunction after injunction. Let the dust settle and let's see what else turns up. At least we can still investigate the fire, maybe we'll find something there. Until then as far as public statements are concerned, it's all coincidental and we don't comment on conspiracy theories.

"Hell for the moment we don't even have a crime to investigate. You find someone who thinks a crime has been committed here and can tell us what it is and you'll get my attention."

Frank could see that he wasn't getting anywhere with the Sheriff but he was pretty sure this wasn't over. Some piece of info was missing that would tie this all together.

The Press

Hal Turcot had spent most of the morning on calls to senior politicians on the Hill which had made his call with Bob Downey seem like a cakewalk. There was no question, as Alpha-1 had warned, that he had stirred up a hornets' nest. The only thing that surprised him was how fast it was escalating.

The press had all been given the two-minute warning. The President was about ten minutes late when he entered the briefing room in the White House where his press secretary normally gave the daily briefing at this hour.

He started in his best somber tone, "Ladies and gentlemen, I have a short statement and I'm afraid I have no time for questions today.

"First let me say that we all woke up this morning to the aftermath of the tragic event I spoke of last night. A terrible accident near Minot, North Dakota has taken the lives of an estimated seven hundred of our fellow Americans and many more are injured. All Americans mourn for those who lost their lives, were injured or lost loved ones in that terrible accident. They are all in our prayers.

"Search and rescue teams report good progress in rescuing the injured and early reports are that the fallout will not present a significant risk to any populated areas so no evacuations are in order.

"I can assure you that the military will discover how this could have happened but for the moment missiles of similar design have been powered down. This does not jeopardize our defensive posture as the US has many systems in backup for these missiles, including those on submarines and cruise missiles deployed around the world.

"These weapon systems are complex and by their nature they can be dangerous, but they are a necessary element of our defensive capability. Sadly we need these weapons to keep America safe. We thought we had every angle covered but apparently not. I can assure the American people that we will get to the bottom of this and there is no reason for concern. Just like the two shuttle disasters, our teams will discover whatever caused this and we'll fix it.

"Again our hearts and prayers go out to the brave people of Minot, North Dakota who have woken up this morning to a terrible disaster. I have ordered all branches of the Federal Government under the leadership of FEMA to provide any and all resources required in supporting North Dakota. After I leave here I will be on my way to Minot and we will do everything we can to get them back on their feet because that's what Americans do.

"Now briefly, on a separate but in some ways related issue, I'd like to advise you of something that I had planned to announce to the American people before the tragic events of last night. It is awkward to be addressing this at this time but it is important and I feel I must do this now as certain changes I have been working on will start taking place today and you need to know about them.

"I have just wrapped up a personal review of our military capabilities and budgets. We find ourselves in the enviable position of having the strongest military in the world by far. You may be aware of reports that show that the US spends as much as the next ten countries combined on defense.

"We have the best in the world in virtually every weapon class whether it is fighters, subs, aircraft carriers or any other weapon. As such, this is an excellent opportunity to reap the benefits of that position. Certain changes to take advantage of new capabilities will be made immediately by Executive Order that will ensure we maintain and extend that global leadership in the area of air power while at the same time saving us about a trillion dollars over the next decade."

That was an unbelievably large number and the press who were not privy to the leaks and rumors coming out of Washington this morning, immediately knew something big was coming.

"Of course I can't say too much about the future of what we have planned for strategies in air power but let me assure you our plans will maintain and increase our leadership in the world and the changes we are implementing today will accelerate that leadership.

"Sadly, as I think you are aware our domestic report card isn't as rosy but we're about to change that. Our unemployment rate, wealth disparity, incarceration rates, K-to-twelve education, infrastructure and many other sectors no longer lead the world in excellence. Inadequate education and training, unemployment and low wages are at the heart of many of these issues.

"That trillion dollars of savings from our military spending will trim our deficits, fund a much-needed reduction in taxes for the middle class but also provide funding for some sorely needed programs here at home especially in the area of 'Work as you Retrain' programs to assist displaced workers in meeting the needs of the world today.

"Our industries are always short of people in the STEM fields. For those of you not familiar with that term, it stands for Science, Technology, Engineering and Math.

"Some of you know that we have seven of the top ten universities in the world and there is a large and steady flow of foreign students entering this country every year just to take advantage of these great centers of higher education. And guess where these foreign students are all focused? That's right, on STEM education. Look at any graduating class in Engineering and Physics and you will find it's mainly made up of minorities from other countries here on student visas. Sadly some of our top universities are even reporting that current graduating classes in engineering and medicine have no American-born students.

"We've been promoting these fields and trying to entice American students to focus on the opportunities in STEM where starting salaries are higher and the need is great. At a time when many university graduates in other disciplines are finding minimum wage jobs, STEM offers a much brighter path. Technology grads are having no problems finding great jobs with exceptional starting salaries and business leaders call me daily asking for the government's help in promoting STEM education.

"College tuitions and student debt are a major concern in this area so we will introduce a series of programs where American citizens, registering in accredited STEM programs can count on the government to cover up to twenty-five percent of their tuition and books. Students in the top twenty-five percent of their class will automatically qualify for even more. This will make a STEM education much more affordable and help American high school students who have the right skills to make the proper choices in their education. So to all the kids out there, study hard on your math and science subjects. The government wants to help you get a great education and start a rewarding and well-paying career.

"At the same time, our existing work force is in need of retraining in these fields. The fields of renewable energy, robotics, medical research, financial services and various kinds of software and simulation are critical to our leadership in the world. Some of the money we're saving will go where it is most needed; new programs to promote and incentivize STEM 'Work as you Retrain' programs where you can earn a decent wage while going back to school.

"Some of these initiatives can be implemented immediately through Executive Orders but others will need Congressional approval. So please call your representatives and let them know you support this sensible military modernization and STEM education.

"So, how will we save all of this money and maintain our leadership position?

"Because I'm convinced of this path generating what we need to keep our military the best in the world, I'm announcing today the suspension of all manufacturing of the current F-35 Lightning II fighter, saving billions of American tax dollars. Certain long-lasting challenges in that program have come to light and it is only prudent to halt that program while we rectify the issues or find an alternative. It's a wonderful platform for today's needs but it is incapable of growing into what we need for the future."

At this announcement all of the insiders in Washington virtually fell out of their chairs. This guy was off his rocker. There was no way this was going to fly. The markets would crash. If he got his way dozens of military contractors doing work in almost every state had just had their contracts canceled for the planes and everything that supported their design, manufacture and operations. Those on the inside knew Area-51 was working on a replacement but even the most optimistic estimates had it years out.

The President looked directly into the cameras at the back of the room, "We have enough of these planes in service to satisfy the immediate needs of our military forces who depend on it, but the Air Force in particular, needs a better and more capable fighter to live up to their role in the future.

"So today I'm announcing that a single very unique contract has been awarded to Carmichael Industries with heavy punitive terms, for the ongoing design and manufacture of our next-generation fighter which of course will remain Top Secret. Mr. Carmichael will soon hold a press conference to explain further, but our expectation is that he will surpass all of the goals for cost, performance, and delivery time, given some amazing advances in manufacturing that he will be announcing.

"From these changes to our military procurement I expect to see one trillion dollars in savings over the next ten years. And this is only the first of many programs I expect to change in this regard.

"This switch represents a complete change in how we fund

military weapons development. For too long America has spent an inordinate amount of our budget on weapon systems that the military did not need or in some cases, did not want.

"Even if they are needed, these programs seem to never meet their goals, often come in at three times the contracted price and fill the pockets of rich industrialists whether the projects succeed or fail.

"That will end now with this new procurement process based on performance-to-contract that I'm piloting with Carmichael Industries. Watch for further changes along these lines. The days of the USA spending twenty percent of its budget on the military are over. We want better paid troops and much more competitive and functional weapon systems. And we won't be spending money on things that don't work or don't do the job."

The press were dumbfounded and were scribbling notes as fast as they could. Putting aside the nonsense surrounding the timing of his speech, this announcement was unheard of and would start a war in Washington. There was no way the President could do this on his own. Congress controlled the purse strings. Besides that, Carmichael was a Republican who hated the President and no company had ever been 'given' an exclusive contract, skipping the Pentagon's normal bid process. This broke all kinds of rules and there hadn't been a single hint that it was coming.

Throughout the Capitol, TV's were tuned and politicians and lobbyists alike were fixated on Turcot's every word, and they were horrified by what they were hearing. It was much worse than the morning's rumors. Not only was he completely canceling the 35, he announced he was going after other military weapon programs by himself, without Congress, and apparently without a bid process. Many thought they were witnessing the birth of a dictator or the end of a presidency where Turcot thought he could single-handedly award massive military programs to whomever he wished.

The lobbyists were particularly shocked. How could they exert any influence if buying Congressional votes got them nowhere? Congress was who they relied on to get their clients the contracts they wanted. And a no-bid process? If there was no bidding then they lost the ability to rig the specs and requirements in the bid documents to direct the contract towards their clients.

Half of the insiders were wondering why they had never heard of any of this or saw any signs it was coming. Things just didn't happen quietly like this in Washington. No one had reported Carmichael was up to something and no one thought Turcot was even looking at military procurement. Lobbyists in particular would be under the gun to explain why they seemed to have no clue on what was going on.

The President was starting to wrap up, "Under the terms of our contract, Carmichael Industries will only be paid for finished and working weapons. Then if it meets our specs in every regard Congress still has to authorize the actual purchase saving billions of taxpayer dollars. Under our Constitution, Congress controls the purse strings but I control the execution of the procurement process, although I must say I suspect Congress will have a tough time saying no when Carmichael Industries has the solution they want, ready for delivery at the price they wanted long ago.

"The Executive Orders I have signed today are all well within the power of the Executive Branch, no matter what the Washington lobbyist community is going to tell you over the next few weeks. I don't expect they will be happy now that their manipulating of the procurement process has taken a big hit. But as my grandmother used to say, 'you can't make an omelet without breaking a few eggs.'

"I think every American will see this as a smart fiscal move and hopefully you'll help me fight off the special interests in Washington. They'll undoubtedly try to scuttle this new method of government acquisition by spreading all manner of misinformation, which is something they're really good at.

"This is the way our democracy was meant to work. I'm simply putting the Executive Branch on steroids and the high-spending and lobbyist-addicted Congress on a diet. And I don't think the middle class will object to a tax cut either. I'm taking tax money out of the fat-cats' pockets and putting it back where it belongs, in yours."

Somewhere in the press room there was a smattering of applause from the newer members of the press corps, a highly unusual scene for this room. The old-timers were not clapping because they knew this would get really messy, making for good news but trouble for the country. He couldn't do this without Congress even if he claimed he had not breached the bounds of his office. He had just declared war on Congress. A war between branches of government was never good for the country. Some of the most astute observers in the press corps thought, but did not say out loud, 'impeachable offense'.

The President continued, "Again, Mr. Carmichael will be holding a news conference in New York within the hour to elaborate on some of this from his perspective. He will explain why he has been awarded this unusual directed tender.

"My fellow Americans," he said, no longer addressing the press but looking directly towards the bank of network cameras at the back of the room, "I'm leaving now to go to Minot, North Dakota, the scene of that terrible accident last night. But let me leave you with this thought. In today's world we're in competition with all other countries in a race to achieve leadership as a nation for ALL its people, not just the ultra-wealthy. We've spent too much of your tax dollars on poorly managed military programs. I want the US to extend its lead in defense but no longer overspending for what we get. It's time we made some serious investments in domestic programs that touch real people.

"In my last few years in office I plan to extend our privileged position in the military by cutting out the middleman, the lobbyists and eliminating all of the graft and project mismanagement games. We will use the money we save to pay down our deficit, reduce taxes on Middle America, retraining our workforce and start the long process of working our way back to the top in all our domestic challenges. I know I can count on your support.

"God bless America and all those who call her home."

Again there was a smattering of applause from random members of the press as he turned and marched briskly out of the room, with some members of the press yelling questions as he left.

This was raw meat for much of the press. Some of them loved it. A big war in Washington had just been declared and Hal Turcot may even have put his job on the line when he started it. His last couple of years in office now promised to be amazing from a daily headlines point of view.

The general feeling in the press was, 'Who would have thought this President would have done that?' It showed tremendous courage or complete recklessness but on the day after a national disaster? Totally bizarre and the height of insensitivity, even if he had actually planned this announcement much earlier, as he claimed.

It didn't take long for the TV talking heads to jump on these amazing revelations. CNN had their regular news anchor on camera, Candy Crowley, who was back leading the Washington beat.

The broadcast was handed over to her to chair, "So ladies and gentlemen, am I wrong or did we just hear a power grab from the Executive Branch of our government or is the President within his rights to take each of these actions? Sally let me turn to you first. Is your President out of bounds with some of these moves?"

Sally was Politico's most recent hire and had proven to be an able spokesperson for the Left's take on any political situation, "Candy, he's everyone's President, not just the Democrats' who I'm afraid will not be unanimous in their support for his really surprising actions announced today.

"But let me be the first to say, even though I support this President and think there are some real gems in what we just heard, I find it completely unthinkable that he chose to address this situation today."

Everyone at the table and split screen to other studios was seen nodding their heads in disbelief.

"I know he said it had been planned for today some time ago, but I mean really! I don't think there is a single person in the US today who cares much about military spending given the unspeakable national tragedy we suffered last night.

"But you asked, so as to his announcement, military spending as most of us know is spread pretty evenly across the country, and apart from the contractors working on the F-35, and our next secret weapon the F-whatever, who will all lose their contracts, every military contractor, and maybe some in other areas where the government spends lots of money, will be really shook up about this new model pioneered by Fraser Carmichael of all people, where they must guarantee performance up front. The way I read it, Congress does not have to buy this new plane if they don't like it. So I suspect Carmichael's stock will be under scrutiny for a while. He'd better say something in that announcement that comforts his shareholders.

"Some government contracts already have performance bonds but this is way beyond that. This new model is a 'build it and we'll buy it if we like it' model. This is really big. Looks like in the future any government business may be a 'bet your business' endeavor and only the very biggest of companies with the financial resources to take the risk, will be able to participate.

"But to answer your question directly, Hal Turcot may be on solid ground in that he doesn't need Congress if he isn't spending their money now. They'll get the chance later to vote on whether to buy what Carmichael comes up with but realistically, if there is some new whiz bang fighter flying around Washington and shooting targets out of the air, and with the F-35 dead, Congress is going to have a hard time saying they don't like it and want to start another ten or twenty year program to build their own fighter, even though we know they would never be able to agree on what it should be. Most would agree they stuck their collective noses too far into the design of the F-35."

Bret Garfield, the conservative pundit from the National Review jumped in, "Now wait a minute Sally. Are you trying to say he didn't break any of the rules in that speech? I can assure you, no one on our side of the House or the Senate has heard ANYTHING about this. It seems like he pulled this idea out of thin air. There is a basic separation of powers in this country that includes all kinds of checks and balances covering the Executive Branch. He's not our king and he doesn't run the country by himself. Hal Turcot will never get away with this. There are many ways Congress can strike back and it isn't only the funding for the development of the F-47." He immediately turned red and prayed the CNN editor bleeped out the secret fighter's proper name on the six-second delay to broadcast.

He continued, "At least that's what all the techie blogs are calling it these days.

"Congress's oversight responsibility will play out with endless subpoenas for White House staff to testify as to how this decision was made. Who was consulted? What guarantees have been provided? What is Carmichael's real deal? What government money is being funneled to the development and what was the military's input to these decisions? And finally, did anyone get paid off here with some kind of under-the-table deal? That's what oversight is all about.

"I'm already hearing some people claim that he announced this today to take attention away from Minot and the dramatic failure of this Administration to keep people safe."

More than one on the panel wanted to scream, 'What people? How could you know what others think of this when the announcement was made about thirty seconds ago and you've been here the whole time?'

But none had the courage to put him on the spot as he continued, "He is not keeping us safe when all the world's nuclear powers know our missiles are off-line right now.

"No, this isn't over, not by a long shot. As Winston Churchill once famously said, ' … this is not the end. It is not even the beginning of the end. But it is, perhaps, the end of the beginning.'

"I don't know what Hal Turcot actually believes he is going to achieve with this but all he has done is put thousands of hard-working men and women across this nation out of work and for what, his legacy? That's the height of insensitivity and arrogance on the part of a man who has always claimed he represents the working man."

Sally was furious, "What he has done, in the face of mountainous opposition, is finally taken on the military industrial complex that your guy, Eisenhower warned of and Hal Turcot told them today the gravy train is over."

Candy interrupted the two squabbling pundits and said, "We'll have to leave it there. We want to take you now to New York where Fraser Carmichael must be a pretty happy man and is about to make a follow-up statement to what the President announced."

***

Carmichael had caught the President's broadcast from his office and told his assistant to give the press a five-minute warning in the lobby of the Carmichael Tower, where a temporary stage and podium had been hastily set up. The cancelation of the F-35 caught him by surprise and aside from the fact that it might complicate the political situation it actually could be helpful given it would now be much more difficult for Congress to reject his new fighter.

Alpha-1 was almost in Nevada and caught the speech on the satellite TV on the small military corporate jet the President had provided out of Andrews Air Force Base. Unbeknownst to the President, Alpha-1 was aware of the addition of the F-35 cancelation but had allowed it to go unchallenged to see what happened. There was a chance the cancelation of the F-35 might actually help their cause by steering attention away from the F-47 and Area-51 and by legitimizing the President's cost-cutting campaign against the military contractors.

Alpha's analysis was that the addition of the F35 cancelation could be a net positive to their plans to get away with the building of the space weapon, by reducing overall risk. It would definitely increase the chances of Turcot being impeached but not in time to hurt the project. Still Alpha-1 would have to remind the President that they needed to agree on any major moves like this that could jeopardize the project. Turcot's penchant for running things to his own agenda might get in the way.

***

General Clay Hawkins watched it all unfolding in his new office in Area-51 and was impressed. From what he could tell, the first the Joint Chiefs had heard of this was last night just before he got the call and here they were less than eighteen hours later and it was all a fact and announced to the world. If he was right, the speed of this thing was uncanny and Turcot sure knew how to get his ass in gear when it was needed.

According to the President's earlier call, this guy Robert Glass was on his way here now. He was anxious to find out if it was in fact the same guy, a trapped miner a little more than a day ago, and now the project manager for the F-47. 'How the hell did that happen?' he wondered.

He had hoped Carmichael was going to be with the new guy when he landed but according to the President's statement, the billionaire was in New York preparing for a press conference. At least Carmichael had a kick-ass reputation. Not all of it positive though.

New York

With all the attention focused on him by the President's speech, Carmichael was in his element as he headed for the microphones. The room was nearly full. Earlier in the day, rumors that his press conference would be tied to the President's hadn't been denied by the Carmichael press office so the turnout was exceptional. The press all knew it wasn't above Carmichael to have started the rumor and now the President had just confirmed it.

Blinking into the bright TV lights he said, "Ladies and gentlemen, thank you for coming today. I will make this brief. As the President stated, we have an exclusive contract to design and build the next-generation fighter for the US Air Force," he lied. Somehow they would get a contract signed but that was all just administrivia now that the President had made it public.

Carmichael continued, "Design is a strong word as there has been lots of design work completed since the program was started years ago but we will take over the job of building it at a secret location. I could tell you more but you know what they say … I'd have to kill you."

He suddenly realized he personally, and Bob Glass, didn't even have Top Secret clearance yet for the fighter or access to the secret base. More minutia, but sharing Top Secret information with people not sworn in could get the President into some really hot water.

"This contract is a very special new concept in government acquisition and procurement. To elaborate on something the President alluded to, we will fund the entire project out of non-government funds and sell the final product to the military when it is accepted. As an example, the F-35 was in development for almost twenty years and cost nearly $400B just to develop and that is more than the value of my company. So before my stock goes to zero on the New York Stock Exchange, let me explain.

"Essentially the long and expensive design and development phases of the next-generation fighter are complete," he lied. Experts knew that some of the development invariably happened after the first planes were flying.

"However the major factor making our strategy feasible is a tremendous breakthrough that is exclusive to Carmichael Industries in the area of Harmonized Manufacturing, a term that will become more familiar as we go forward." A term he had invented on the elevator ride down to the press conference.

"Our revolutionary new technology is what makes this contract a great day for Carmichael and ensures our success and profitability.

"Over the last few years we've spent enormous resources on perfecting a new highly integrated, self-learning manufacturing system. This system has two major components; a supercomputer and a fleet of incredibly intelligent self-teaching and networked, free-moving, robots.

"The computer is the first thousand Qubit quantum computer which makes it about a trillion times faster than anything else on the planet."

There were gasps and a few snickers in the crowd of reporters. Some had no idea what he had just said. Some knew that the biggest quantum computer in operation was about thirty Qubits and the real techies didn't believe a word he was saying. A thousand Qubit computer was out of range for current technology and possibly would remain that way for the next thirty to fifty years, especially the software to drive it efficiently.

He continued, "The computer was developed on the back of work done at X-Wave Systems in Vancouver, Canada which is now owned by me through a sister company of Carmichael Industries. That acquisition and my own skunkworks in several think tanks throughout the world have provided an astounding breakthrough in quantum computing, operating software and robot development. We actually used the computer to design the new robots and even some of its own operating software." Carmichael was tickled with himself for making most of this up on the fly.

Now the techies all sat up straight. X-Wave had some of the world's best experts and they were thought to be prone to making outrageous claims about their hardware and software. Here was Carmichael either buying their story or confirming it. Either way he now owned them. That put their breakthrough technology together with potentially more breakthrough technology that Carmichael had just confirmed was coming out of his rumored secret labs, along with a very big pile of money and now an amazing contract. This could be serious after all.

"As you may know, quantum computing is especially well suited to optimizing solutions that have large numbers of competing variables like in this case, optimizing a complex manufacturing process and directing robots on what to do next. Simulation is another sweet spot for quantum computing which is another major requirement of this type of manufacturing.

"We now own X-Wave, as we needed to tie up the IP or intellectual property. In addition to their hardware and software, Carmichael has developed a breakthrough operating environment that is integrated with a fleet of 6th-generation autonomous robots producing a system that can teach itself at incredible speeds to do almost any task. While this is all proprietary and we're unwilling at this time to demonstrate our capabilities let me just say that these aren't like robots you've seen before. They are a generation newer, free-standing, self-powered and mobile unlike the machines you have seen bolted to the floor in manufacturing in the past. They have much higher fidelity in all of their actions and they are many times faster. That combined with their self-learning capabilities and being linked wirelessly to a massive computing platform gives us a startling advantage in manufacturing, design, simulation and testing."

The techies were incensed. More statements that begged credibility. There was nothing in the literature or on the web that said Carmichael had any interest in developing robots, never mind claiming to have a fleet of breakthrough 6th-generation autonomous robots.

"Humans give the system a design to work with. The system then optimizes the design through various simulation routines to make it meet all performance specs. It plans the build to six sigma standards at the end product level, which also makes it easier to manufacture and cheaper to maintain. In this case the end product is the next-generation fighter for our Air Force.

"The robots then teach themselves how to build it optimally and improve on the processes as they learn."

More unbelievable statements and maybe the craziest yet. Six sigma was an unreachable goal in a complex mil-spec fighter even at the component level. This guy was claiming the whole plane would be virtually perfect, not just most of its individual components. Those who knew the quality assurance term knew that it meant less than one manufacturing flaw in every hundred thousand 'planes'. He had just announced he would build only perfect fighters. No high-tech manufacturing process in the world could promise an end-product as six sigma, even on much simpler products. Those in the know knew that the math on how six sigma was calculated, was against them. A virtually perfect fuel injection system on a car was one thing but a perfect car where every component had to be perfect every time was exponentially more difficult. That one statement alone could not be true in the estimation of anyone who knew anything about quality control.

Carmichael continued, "You can imagine that this is a highly proprietary system and for the moment will be used in secret only on Carmichael's military projects but at some point I'd love to have a discussion with a leading Formula 1 racing team," he joked.

"I think now you see how the President was able to award us a directed tender for this product. No one else on the planet has anything close to this capability and we'll deliver an outstanding product in record time.

"So, before the stock market hiccups let me just say that I expect the net of this project will be a modest positive influence on our bottom line for this fiscal year even if I sell these to the President at a third of what he was going to pay my competitors. The bigger profits come later when we can take over full projects from design on up.

"I'll take a few questions."

The screaming started and he had to listen carefully and point to one reporter at a time to hear the questions.

"I'll repeat the question. 'Where is this computer?'

"You'll never know and you'll never find it. The labs we've used to develop the hardware and the software for both the computer and the robots are hidden as part of one of the many subsidiaries owned by either Carmichael Industries International or by me directly. Some portion of all of that will definitely be at secret military sites where the 6th-generation fighter will be built but that is of course secret too. The development of our new manufacturing capability is spread all over the world in companies I like to think of as a stealth network. And none of the above will be in Vancouver.

"X-Wave will continue with their development and commercial contracts for their client base and over time we will augment what they have with some of what we've developed.

"As I said before we simply bought them to lock up some important IP and avoid any lawsuits from them. So please don't go harassing them. Everything they know about our developments and this new project they'll get from this news conference.

"I'm sorry I'm going to have to cut it off right here but I do have two other items that you may find newsworthy. Firstly I must leave now to head to Minot, North Dakota where two of my execs were injured in a plane crash last night and three other Carmichael employees lost their lives. Sadly they were on a corporate mission and on approach to Minot's airport for refueling when that explosion happened last night.

"Secondly, as you may have seen from White House photos, I met young Mr. Robert Glass in the Oval Office last night. He was the trapped mine inspector from that Idaho mine disaster.

"Both the President and I were completely smitten by this young man who by the way has an advanced degree in engineering from Caltech and for personal reasons was working as a mine inspector in Idaho.

"Both the President and I were immediately taken by his intelligence, candor and poise. To make a long story short, Bob Glass will be heading up the new military project from a management perspective, and reporting to me and the President. He is an employee of Carmichael, in fact he is Chief Operating Officer of our new division."

Mouths were left agape throughout the gathered press. For many this had been a most bizarre twenty-four hours. A nuclear weapon accident killing hundreds, the President freezing the F-35 and canceling the F-whateveritwas and awarding a contract to a political foe with a scary new manufacturing process including learning robots and a fantastic supercomputer, and to top it all off, putting a trapped miner in charge of it all. Many of them thought the headlines would just say 'WOW!' Or maybe even 'SKYNET IS HERE!' referring to the Terminator series of movies where the robots take over.

Carmichael had to do his best with his security team to exit the room full of reporters screaming questions at him.

All the insiders in Washington had been glued to their TVs to see what Carmichael would announce and now they just sat there stunned. One senior Martin Marietta lobbyist turned to an influential Senator in his office and said, "He's really going to do it. Turcot, that madman, is actually going to try to do everything we had heard rumors of this morning. He has either gone totally mad or Carmichael has launched the biggest con in history.

"Did anyone believe a single word coming out of Fraser's mouth?

"Somebody please pinch me and wake me up."

***

It had been a slow news day in Vegas. Andrew McPherson, or Andy to anyone who knew him, had been camped out at McCarran International on a boring assignment for the RJ, the Las Vegas Review-Journal. He was waiting for some rumored celebs to arrive commercial from the Big Apple for a special fundraising concert that night on the Vegas strip. None of the planes had anyone of interest and he was starting to think it was a bust. Trying to work his way up the ladder as a rookie, he had no regular beat and was considered a roving reporter by the RJ, but he was starting to build a good reputation for sniffing out a story.

Today his only hope was to get a candid photo of some star arriving and maybe get a question or two answered. There were no other press in sight so if it was some celeb he knew something about, he would try for a quick exclusive interview using all the charm he could muster. That typically didn't work, but if they were also promoting something like a new movie they might oblige.

In reality he found this stuff boring, but he looked on it as putting in the time to build a reputation as an investigative reporter. He'd have to do this kind of grunt work until he found a real story to make a name for himself in his new profession.

His career change had not impressed his ex-girlfriend who thought he was throwing away all his education and a budding career. With an advanced degree in physics, pure materials research had turned out to be a giant yawn for him and after a couple of years at it, investigative reporting seemed like a much more exciting career, even if it meant starting at the bottom by hanging around the airport on puffball assignments to earn his stripes.

Getting through security with his press pass, he had stationed himself between two gates where most of the New York flights came in. He was really getting tired of it all when two unmarked 737s landed, one after the other and taxied to the end of the terminal building. It was generally thought that these planes ferried staff and workers to a secret military base called Area-51 somewhere north of Vegas. He thought it odd that they would both come in together and at this time of day. 'They must be returning empty,' he thought.

To his surprise, a few minutes later, hundreds of mostly men in work clothes emptied out of the two gates at the end of the concourse and headed in his general direction. They didn't look happy and were grumbling to each other under their breaths. One particular group who all seemed to know each other stopped just past Andy's position as one of them turned and looked back down the concourse.

"Where's Fritz? He was right behind me getting off the plane. There he is. Fritz, over here."

The man apparently nicknamed Fritz worked his way through the busy concourse and arrived with the group of seven or eight men. "Let's get a beer and talk this over. What about that dive, Wendy's just outside the airport?"

Fritz and the others indicated they were in. They all disappeared down the concourse as Andy waited at the gate where the next New York flight was just starting to deplane.

As luck would have it there were no celebs on this flight either. He was still thinking it was odd that if these guys were from up north then why were so many of them coming back in the middle of the day, so on a hunch and given he had nothing else to do, he decided to grab a beer at Wendy's, a hole-in-the-wall he had been to once or twice himself.

At this time of day Wendy's wasn't particularly busy and the eight guys from the airport seemed to have picked up a few more of their friends and easily made up more than half of the occupants of the dank lounge. Andy had only patronized Wendy's a couple of times at night when it was hopping. Now the more subdued western music sounded like a backdrop instead of the main attraction.

The guys from the airport were gathered near a pool table further into the lounge as Andy took a place at the bar and ordered a beer. He could just barely make out some of the discussion that was clearly hushed and not loud like one would expect in a bar with a bunch of guys. He kept his back to the group and pretended to be interested in a brochure he had picked up on the bar.

Over the next forty minutes and two beers, picking up a word here and there, he pieced together that they were not happy, seemed to have been let go with no warning, wondered what the hell the military was up to, speculated it had something to do with the nuclear explosion in North Dakota and wondered out loud if the 'companies' were going to treat the workers right.

One of the guys who had been doing much of the talking headed for the men's room and Andy saw his chance. He waited a few seconds and then followed the man.

Straddled beside him at an adjacent urinal he said, "Hell of a deal. No warning at all. I don't know about you guys but my company better come through for me?"

The other man looked suspiciously at him, "You from up there too? I don't think I've seen you before?"

Andy took a chance, "Been there only about three months in final assembly but hell I wasn't lookin' to be out of a job so fast."

The other guy looked around to ensure no one was near, "Yeah. You might be able to find a job but man I'm a titanium welder. Those jobs don't grow on trees. At least they tell us we're covered for a year. My bet is the project is dead and they're going to trash everything we worked on. Maybe a hundred million or more into the garbage would be my guess. From what I hear that F-35 is no prize either so it's hard to figure out why they decided to ditch the only replacement they had for it."

He paused and then continued, "Listen we shouldn't even be talking like this."

"Yeah, you're right," Andy said as he zipped up, washed his hands and made a quick exit. He was back in his car before the other guy returned and before questions started about who he really was.

Andy knew the political guy at the RJ and headed back to the office to find him.

Jim Burrows was often a snarky type always wearing suits and sticking pretty much to himself, but something made him look approachable today as Andy took a seat beside his desk.

"Jim, what are the rumors about what goes on up at that secret Air Force base north of town?"

"You mean Area-51?"

"Yeah I think that's the one. They fly planeloads of guys up there daily, right?"

Jim nodded, "Unmarked 737s as I remember. Well it's one of the most Top Secret bases in these United States. Pretty much every secret flying piece of gear started its life up there or over in Palmdale.

Some of the gear stays secret even after it's active. I think the SR-71 Blackbird flew originally out of there for years before we even admitted we had it."

Andy smiled, "Yeah that's the place. What have you heard about what they're working on up there now?"

Burrows shrugged, "You probably want to ask Walt. He's the conspiracy guy but from what I've heard, the rumor is that one of the big projects up there is a replacement for the rather sickly F-35, so it could be anything from the F-36 to the F-1000 the way the Air Force numbers things. But yeah, that's a pretty good guess. Why do you ask?"

"I think something's cooking up there. I was at McCarran this afternoon and a couple of planes brought back what looked like a bunch of disgruntled workers."

Burrows squirmed in his seat and returned his attention to something he had been reading on his computer screen, "Probably, nothing. We'll hear something useless about it in a week or so. They're always dumping one contractor in favor of another up there."

"Yeah, you're probably right." Andy could see there was nothing more to get out of the irascible Burrows so he headed over to his own temporary desk he shared with another roving reporter.

'Still,' he thought, 'there were so many of them, they seemed to be from multiple contractors and they seemed to think whatever they were building up there just got trashed. Why would the government trash its next whiz bang fighter?'

He decided he would do a little more digging on this. His technical background had piqued his interest in Area-51 and he had always wanted to find out more about what they did up there. The word was that you couldn't get within miles of the place with all the security they had and apparently it was buried deep in the massive Nellis Air Force Reserve of over five thousand square miles that included several bombing ranges. Still he had a hunch something was changing and there might be a story if he could find a way to dig it out.

Part of the answer came when he caught the rebroadcast of the President's and Carmichael's press conferences on the internet.

He mused to himself, 'So Carmichael Industries is the new tenant at Area-51 and he's bringing a supercomputer and a bunch of freaky robots, and a guy who was a mining inspector yesterday is in charge of it all. This just got really interesting. I wonder if those furloughed workers hang around Wendy's all the time?'

A New Home

As prearranged by the White House and the Pentagon, Alpha-1's small military executive jet was directed to snake its way through various bombing ranges and land at Area-51 where he was met on the tarmac by Brigadier General Clay Hawkins. They shook hands and introduced themselves. Hawkins who was in his late forties, thought this kid sure didn't look the part of a Chief Operating Officer of a Carmichael division who was taking over the 6th-generation fighter program. Carmichael had earlier confirmed in his press conference that the kid was in fact the rescued mine inspector after all. This was starting to look weirder by the minute.

Bob Glass/Alpha-1 wanted to see the main hangars first so the driver took them quickly around the largest of the hangars, all of which were a beehive of activity still cleaning out all of the work that had been in progress. The buildings were almost completely vacated except for the smallest which held three partially built airframes and lots of manufacturing jigs, hastily crammed into the building and filling every corner.

As they left the last hangar Hawkins said, "I understand from General Jenkins that Carmichael Industries does not want to start with anything that was already in the process of being built. As you saw, there are three planes here that are at least partially built."

"The General was correct. Please continue to move everything out of the other four hangars into that storage area we just saw. Your second job, General, is to get on to your predecessor or the prime contractor and find all of the design documents. I need a comprehensive list of what exists, how I get access to it and what computer format it's in. I know these were commercial contractors building the planes but I also know the military has access to all the documents in a case such as this where contractors are swapped out. I also know that the US government has ultimate intellectual property rights over the development of these fighters and all of their component parts so there is no legitimate claim by the previous builders on the IP, including all design docs. You own it and I want it as per our contract with the President."

Glass continued, "My first task is to load all of the existing design data into my computer which will be available remotely later today. Once you've cleaned up these hangars and found the design docs, I need you to put complete focus on firming up the perimeter security which will extend two miles in every direction from the center of the main runway and five miles off the ends. It needs to be 24/7 impenetrable, so get whatever tech and manpower you need in here today to achieve that. I think you have overlook areas and they need to be covered too, so long-distance photography is not possible. Do you understand?"

An alarmed General Hawkins reluctantly nodded yes. He hadn't been expecting this kind of interaction. This guy was very comfortable barking orders to a senior military officer. Too comfortable for Clay Hawkins' liking but he remembered the President's words about cooperating with all of Carmichael's people. He'd just have to suck it up.

Glass was still talking, "Once the perimeter is secured we will start moving in equipment and materials and here is a critical point, General. No one other than Fraser Carmichael and I will ever see the manufacturing floor so we need a second security perimeter at least one hundred yards away from the hangars to keep even base personnel away. Part of our deal with the President is total secrecy over our equipment and processes to the point that if the building catches fire you must stand back and watch it burn to the ground. Under no circumstances will anyone be allowed to observe our operations. Our whole manufacturing process, all of its components, the supply chain and anything else related to this project has been classified Eyes Only," he lied. "Is that clear?" he said forcefully.

Hawkins was already getting a real hate on for this insolent pup. After a long pause while he stared down what was apparently his new boss, the General said. "Yes Mr. Glass, perfectly clear."

"Now General, I need you to instruct all of your team in this matter and anyone else who may be allowed on the base from time to time. Not only is it forbidden to observe any of our operations, we will have our own countermeasures in place and they can be lethal. Please make sure your people know that too. They should not approach these hangars for any reason whatsoever."

Glass continued as they rode up the flight line outside the four bigger hangars, "You need not have any safety or security concerns inside the hangars. For one thing there will be very little human involvement in there. All our control is remote. Within the hangars, our robots, environmental systems and security systems run by our robots will ensure safety and security. Our robots can handle any emergency requirements without assistance. By the way the site will be active and monitored 24/7."

The first thought that the General had was, 'When did this guy have time in the last day after escaping a mine to amass all this information, project plan and the like? It was as if this guy had been preparing for months for this operation. Was the whole mine thing some kind of ruse?'

He knew Carmichael was in the Oval Office with him last night and he had read a bit about how the rescue had been totally taken over and orchestrated by unknown entities and hidden from everyone. Had Carmichael staged the whole thing somehow and this guy really wasn't a rescued miner? There was no way this guy got briefed in the last eighteen hours to the extent that he now was leading this project like a pro.

As he remembered, there had been a big flap about a new PR company releasing the video and photos of his rescue. How could they be sure this was actually the guy that was trapped, or if anyone was trapped? This guy could be a plant.

And it wasn't as if his relatives would miss him. While he was waiting for the Carmichael jet he had done a Google search on the guy and found out that his fiancée and her family, his only living connections, had been wiped out in a fire the very hour he had been rescued. Besides that being a very suspicious coincidence, maybe this guy wasn't who he said he was.

Something was definitely weird here and now all of this incredible secrecy about a bunch of robots? Yet he was under orders from his command and directly from the President to cooperate. He decided that wasn't good enough. He was going to have to look into this a little deeper.

Glass was still talking, "So General, now maybe you can show me to my office. I'm not sure what your plans were but I want to be near the work."

Hawkins nodded, "We had two choices so given your preference, there is a suitable office in hangar #1 for you. I also have a senior officer's bunk in the main building for a living space but I was not informed of the size or office requirements of your staff."

Glass finally smiled, "I have no staff. This operation is all run by our robots and they don't need offices or bunks. For me your preparations are fine. Now do you have any questions?"

The General thought for a second and then said, "If we can't see your equipment, how will we get it in here?"

"Good question. When the time is right I will give you a location where two C-17s can land at an airstrip in the US and pick up a series of flight containers. They'll be delivered here and moved into place in hangar #1 by your ground crews who will then leave and I will personally tow them to the right manufacturing hangars and start the assembly. We'll use hangar #1 as a staging area where your folks can get access at prescribed times to deliver and remove containers."

'Wow', Hawkins thought to himself. 'This guy is going to set up a manufacturing line for ten aircraft by himself? And this with equipment he wants me to believe he has never seen before, given he was trapped in a mine? I sure hope the assembly instructions are well written. There's no way this is happening.'

Even if the mine rescue was all a ruse of some kind, there was no way one man could build a production line for even one plane in less than six months and he had been told this project was time critical. Something didn't jive here. HELL NOTHING made sense here. Suddenly he thought that maybe he had become party to some massive fraud being perpetrated on the American people.

"OK one more question. How will you do all of that work by yourself?"

"That's actually part of the beauty of our new systems. One of the robots per hangar will come in completely assembled. I unpack him, he unpacks another and assembles it, they do the rest of the unpacking and assembly of the robots and then they unpack and assemble all of the manufacturing jigs. I predict it will take about a day and a half. Remember, they don't sleep and with their advanced vision systems they can work in total darkness. These are robots like you have never seen before. They work much faster than what you typically see on TV. They can do everything any 5th-generation robot can do, but they're as much as ten times faster and much higher in fidelity, adaptability, accuracy, balance, etc. They have a large tool repository so they simply snap on the tools they need for a particular job and go at it.

"Now you see why this all has to be secret. Carmichael Industries doesn't want the competition finding out what we have. We've made breakthroughs in many areas with these robots such as on-board power systems, vision systems, dexterity, microbalancing, microtolerances, self-learning, artificial intelligence, tool flexibility and speed. As you might expect there is a tipping point in computer and robot development. There comes a point where they can design themselves better and faster than a human can and we reached that point with these robots but not to worry, they're not self-aware so there is no possibility of them taking over. That's only true in sci-fi books.

"Back to the task at hand. As we build these fighters the robots will get better and faster with every operation as they find ways to optimize processes, and they share their findings with each other. That's what quantum computers are good at, optimizing a solution from many alternatives.

"But before all that begins we need the design docs. We could of course take on the full design and build an entirely new F-47 but one advantage the current design has is that it has already set expectations and has been preapproved by the Air Force. So we may as well build something that looks familiar to the customer even though lots of technology and even many of the requirements of the fighter have changed since the plane was conceived some years ago.

"Both the Russians and the Chinese have made progress on their fighters, but Mr. Carmichael and the President want to prove a point; that we can deliver this thing, as originally specified, in record time and record low cost. So to accommodate this 'shock and awe' strategy, we'll skip the intensive redesign phase.

"I think you can see one of the political objectives here. If we can prove to the Russians and Chinese that we can build anything we want in record time, then that is a very big deterrent for them to cause any mischief. Kind of walking softly and carrying a big stick. That's apparently President Turcot's mantra and another reason why we need to meet the schedule and keep our capabilities Top Secret.

"A key Carmichael breakthrough is that our quantum computer can simulate the actual flight characteristics of the fighter from previous fighters' performance and the F-47 design docs. This will allow us to make minor changes to the design to improve performance and test flight characteristics in all modes of flight. We can also optimize all manufacturing steps as the robots learn more to make the whole system much easier to maintain by introducing small changes to the design and manufacturing with future maintenance in mind. We'll produce a fighter that is better in many ways than what the Pentagon was expecting and we'll make it much easier to maintain, which by the way is of no benefit to Carmichael but will reduce the lifetime cost of ownership greatly.

"Of course when the military see this Carmichael expects to cash in on future contracts for easy to maintain, leadership weapon systems. If I were you I would consider buying Carmichael stock. Now that the existence of the technology is public there are no concerns about insider trading."

That did it for General Clay Hawkins. This kid had been on this for months if not years, not eighteen hours. He didn't even talk like a civil engineer or mine inspector. He must have come out of the lab that developed the computer and the robots that Carmichael had spoken of in his press conference. What the hell was all that mine disaster and rescue stuff about? This guy had not spent the last month at the bottom of a deep mine, no way! He felt even more wary now and suspected that something bizarre and probably malicious was afoot.

Hawkins realized he was not a political animal but he was going to have to tread lightly on this project until he could find out more about what was really going on. Generals Jenkins and Hawthorne needed to know about this so they didn't get blindsided no matter what the President said. 'Or were they in on it?', he wondered.

Hospital

After the press conference, Carmichael jumped on the company chopper over to Teterboro and took the backup company jet to Minot.

This plane wasn't as opulent as the Gulf Stream G650 he had lost the previous night but with full tanks it had just enough range for Minot, it was fast and comfortable and he had lots of room as he was flying alone.

With a couple of hours to kill he sat back to relax and reflect on where he was, given the roller coaster of the last day.

He had made his mark on the world as a bit of a wheeler dealer. Even though he had an engineering degree, business had initially interested him more.

Using a method his now-deceased father had used, he sought out what the market considered as undervalued companies and bought them. In the early days it was with his father's money or at least his leverage. He often split them into more lucrative 'pure-play' companies and sold them usually within eighteen months. As his dad had discovered before him, some companies dabbled in too many areas and didn't know if they were fish or fowl. They were underperformers as far as stocks were concerned. This made them a great flip target.

He replicated this a few times making lots of money until he became bored and realized that a products company that could invent something entirely new and reap big profits was what he wanted to run. Newer products and higher profits made the share prices soar. Even in these cases, flips were what he was after and he made his fortune in just a few years.

Over the next decade he bought, cleaned up and sold several products companies by relaunching old products or identifying new products the market wanted or splitting the companies into more viable entities. This is where he found his true passion, innovation, so he held on to parts of these companies instead of flipping them.

He loved working with the techies, dreaming up new products and bringing them to market. This taught him to be very attuned to the market and more importantly, to be very secretive about product development. Competitors always wanted to steal your ideas and get to market first.

His new empire grew steadily until he had amassed a sizable fortune.

He was so diversified and spread out around the globe that no one knew exactly where all the money was coming from. He had developed a stealth empire of private companies that was impervious to some of the tactics he had used to get ahead. His own motto was 'keep it small, private, dispersed and invisible.'

Carmichael Industries was the big exception. To win large government contracts he needed mass, gravitas and reputation. He joined a few of his smaller companies and did an IPO to take it public to reap a windfall and provide himself with a building with his name on it on Central Park and true mogul bona fides. By this time 'Carmichael' was a brand unto itself and the IPO exceeded all expectations and gave him a big personal payday. These days he had the wealth and power to make just about any deal happen, but self-funding the F-47 was something he would never have attempted himself. Only the availability of Alpha's technology made sense which raised a problem. As President, CEO and Chairman of the Board of the largest of his companies, Carmichael Industries was a public company and therefore he now had a boss, his board of directors.

Winging his way across America on his way to Minot, he suspected the board was going to be a challenge as he was making big moves, hadn't consulted them and clearly couldn't tell them anything about Alpha-1 or anything that had happened in the Oval Office. Still he was almost giddy about the future. The only man on the planet controlling technology that was thousands or hundreds of thousands of years more sophisticated than the best of the 21st century and a 'Go to heaven, do not pass go' card he could cash in any time. Invincible came to mind. The only downside was having to rely on that idiot Turcot and the possibility of approaching aliens. If Alpha's plan didn't work then they were all in tremendous jeopardy and the more he thought of it the more real it seemed and the more terrified he became. Unlike most of his life, there was little his wealth or power could do about approaching aliens outside of what Alpha-1 had planned.

Still, if all went well and he got to Alpha, his first thought was to live out his boyhood dream and become Superman and relive everything from that comic book series. As an obsession in his younger years he still had an almost complete collection of the

Superman comic books. If Alpha-1 had spoken truthfully then that would all be possible in the fantasy part of his consciousness and it would all feel totally real. He could live every episode of his hero's conquests. Some of the more spectacular story lines came to mind.

A beeping noise brought him out of his daydream. Thirty thousand feet over Lake Erie on his way to Minot, his iPhone told him he had an urgent text message from one of his board members that simply said CALL! It was surprising that it had taken so long for the board to react after his press conference a few hours earlier. He suspected there had been a few urgent phone calls between board members leading up to this text.

This particular board member was the one they all called when they had something delicate to discuss with the 'Whiz Kid'. Carmichael laughed whenever the moniker came up. Some form of the term had been used on the covers of both Forbes and Newsweek when they had done exposés on him. Maybe at one time he had been a young whiz at business but now in his mid-forties, he saw himself as much more seasoned.

Still the board knew he was the brains behind all of the exceptional deals the company had pulled off. Each board member cashed a pretty handsome monthly check for their participation in the company, but they would never dream of telling Carmichael how to run his business. The SEC mandated a board to protect minority shareholders rights but everyone in the business knew there was a category of company where the top guy did whatever he wanted, within the law, because he was just that good. Carmichael Industries was the current poster child for this setup.

Lately and now with this project, he had been climbing into the realm of Gates, Olsen, Ellison, and Jobs in terms of visionary corporate tech leaders that boards would generally not interfere with.

He decided to avoid the 'Call' demand for the moment. Rollie and the rest of them would all be quaking in their boots after the press conference and furious that he hadn't called to tell them what he was up to. In the end they would all accept his plans but he realized they had been put in a precarious position by not being able to answer any questions from the press on where, why and when. The boys and Lucie, the lone female on his board, would just have to wing it until he had time for them and until he had decided how to cover his tracks as it pertained to Alpha-1.

He was in an awkward position too. Alpha-1 had made it clear that nothing was up for negotiation. He and Turcot were simply expected to do as they were told. That was an unusual and uncomfortable position for Carmichael, but he had resigned himself to the fact that he was just going to have to play along in order to be rewarded with the benefits he had been promised.

This idea of 'heaven', whenever he wanted it, certainly felt foreign. He wasn't certain what it would feel like for a man like himself with billions to blow, where he could essentially have a piece of heaven on earth whenever he wanted it. What worried Carmichael was the rush he got from business and making the 'deal'. It was the battle of minds and the chance that you could lose that made his heart race. A setup where you always won might be fun for a while but could it really replace the adrenalin rush he so craved from business?

He was also worried about how he would feel being only as smart and talented as everyone else in Alpha. He didn't feel that he looked down on his fellow humans but he certainly thought of himself usually as the smartest guy in the room and with his credentials he always carried lots of invisible yet tangible power and gravitas into any gathering. In Alpha, even if he could have anything to make himself happy, how would he handle everyone else being on the same level?

Great wealth and power had many benefits, one of which was being able to set your sights on some outrageously expensive icon like a yacht, a painting by the masters, or an island and besting everyone else in acquiring it. But, again, according to Alpha-1 that might only be possible in the Alpha fantasy world.

When Alpha-1 had told him he could live out his human life, with the toys that he would be left with, he immediately thought that was the path he wanted to take. But that wasn't a decision he had to take now. He decided he would let that one ride and see how things went. If in fact, it was all true.

Just after takeoff the pilot had told him they had to land in Bismarck due to the damage at the Minot airport and the fact that its only operating runway's navigation aids were out and it was being reserved for search and rescue missions and medivac. Now the copilot clicked on the intercom and said, "We're starting our descent sir. We have a Bismarck Helicopter waiting at the Executive Terminal to take you up to Minot. I just received a message from them that they flew your VP HR out of here earlier this morning and she plans to pick you up with a limo at the helipad at Minot International as anything closer to downtown is currently reserved for emergencies. They also say that both men have been upgraded to satisfactory."

Later on the way up to Minot in the chopper the first signs of trouble were burnt fields. Then he saw the first signs of the blast wave from the bomb. Anything that would topple in a hurricane like highway signs that were facing southeast, were down. There was still plenty of smoke in the air from smoldering fields off to the southeast but properties that were on the northwest side of hills were better off. There was very little traffic on the roads and then he remembered the EMP. Anything within a certain range would've had their electronics knocked out.

As planned, Hazel Cooper, Carmichael's VP HR picked him up at the helipad and briefed him on the limo ride to the hospital. When they arrived, the hospital was a beehive of activity with bomb victims stacked up in the hallways. He found that Hazel had arranged to have both men in a small semi-private room. They looked much better than he had expected. He asked to speak with them alone and she left them.

"Good to see you Will, Jim. How are you both feeling?"

Jim Gardino, standing beside his bed and wearing a hospital gown and sling spoke first, "Well I'm the lucky one. All I had was a sprained ankle, a stiff neck, a dislocated shoulder and some cuts and bruises. Will and I were both thrown clear as we were at the very back of the jet. As you know the others were not so lucky. That pilot did an awesome job and it looked like we were going to get away with it skidding across that field but we must have hit something hidden like a big rock or a tree stump that ripped the plane apart and started fires everywhere, although some people are telling us the bomb started lots of fires too. Both Will and I ended up on the bank of a big pond."

Carmichael turned to his corporate counsel, "You look like you've been in a war."

"Yeah, broken leg, broken arm, damaged vertebrae in my neck and burns on my good leg. Unlike Lucky over here, I passed out and when I woke up my good leg was on fire. I'm really sorry we couldn't help the other guys. As Jim said, the pilot was amazing. After that jolt we got from the explosion the plane was virtually flipping through the air like you threw a stick or something. We were pretty close to the ground at that point but somehow they got control of it and set us down in that field. At first I thought we were just going to skid to a stop but … well Jim's right, we must have hit something."

Gardino interrupted, "Hey the President was just in here touring the place and said hi to both of us."

Suddenly Will Fiskins teared up, "I've known Frank Jorgen for a long time and I know his family. Has anyone spoken to Jane? She must be devastated."

Carmichael was unsure. The last twenty-four hours had been horrendous, "I think HR has but I haven't had time myself. I should get to her and the families of the two pilots right away.

"Well I must say I was expecting much worse when they said you were both in serious condition."

Gardino answered, "I think that's what they call it until they examine you thoroughly looking for hidden injuries, but I'm getting out of here as soon as they can find a doc to sign the release. They need these beds apparently and I certainly don't need it. Hazel said she is organizing a chopper to get me down to Bismarck where I can get a flight home."

It was Fiskins' turn now that he had regained his composure, "Fraser, we both saw the President's press conference followed by yours. What the hell is going on? Apparently we now own a company out of Vancouver, a supercomputer with a fleet of amazing robots and a contract for the next fighter? This all happened last night after we dropped you off? And why did you hire the Glass kid?"

"Gentlemen that is a second reason I'm here. Firstly I wanted to make sure you were both OK. Anything you need, really, don't be afraid to ask. We want to take care of you both and get you home safely.

"My second reason is you're the only two remaining that know that we thought there was something discovered in that mine. All I can tell you is that it wasn't what I had expected, Glass wasn't what I expected and there is nothing worth pursuing in the mine, in fact as you know the escape shaft collapsed and so I'll be putting a stop on digging a new shaft.

"After that, one thing led to another, the President and I had some very meaty but classified conversations last night and the result was the press conferences you saw which I can't elaborate on because it's all Top Secret. All I can tell you is that I have made a deal with Turcot that has nothing to do with that mine. It involves Carmichael

Industries as the frontman and some other companies I own personally building the next-gen fighter. So sadly, the mine opportunity is a dead issue.

"That leaves me in an awkward position with the two of you. I had projected big things coming out of that mine and now with the change in company direction with the President's Top Secret project and your knowledge of things in the past, I'm afraid we're going to have to amicably part ways. Frankly you know too much of the inner workings of the company and could be a handicap moving forward. Due to federal secrecy rules, I can't explain it any clearer than that but I need to buy you both out of your contracts.

"Now in terms of a severance, I'm willing to consider the chance that the two of you may never work again. That is unrealistic but I want to make sure you're protected and see some return on your commitment to that mine opportunity. Of course you get to keep the million I gave you initially on the mine deal.

"So what I'm saying is, you two discuss it and tell me what the numbers are for both of you and Jane Jorgen and I'm likely to agree."

After an awkward pause, an apoplectic Gardino spoke first, "You're firing us? Did I just hear that right? You came all the way here just to fire us?"

"Gentlemen, please don't make a big thing of this. I want to do this amicably. You've both been major contributors to the company and you'll be very difficult to replace. The company is headed in a new direction. Because of the deal with Turcot I need to buy you both out of your contracts with that non-disclosure still in place, i.e. you owe me everything if you mention ANYTHING about the mine, your jobs or this parting of ways. The outside story might be that you both had a life-changing moment in the plane crash and decided to resign and rethink your priorities. If anyone asks you about the computers and the robots I announced this morning, just tell them you're under non-disclosure. After all you know nothing about them anyways.

"I'm not even going to insist on a non-compete. You can go work for the competition if you wish. Your only restriction is you can NEVER talk about anything to do with Idaho, my deal announced with the President, what you know and don't know about it, as well as any other normal company confidential information you may have. And that includes talking to the board. I need you both to resign and honor our deal."

Gardino was shocked and close to tears. He had dedicated a fair part of his life to Fraser Carmichael and his company with the hopes of some future major payout especially after what they thought was a fantastic discovery in the mine, and now this? After surviving a plane crash on Carmichael business? This guy was standing there firing him after all of that?

Fiskins assessed the situation very differently and saw an opportunity. Given they knew nothing about the 'project' with Turcot, he couldn't fathom why gagging them and termination was necessary. As far as he could tell they knew nothing that would be of interest to anyone. Even so, they could both get a great payday out of this termination without cause and he'd make Carmichael pay. There had to be a lot of money in this deal with Turcot or Carmichael wouldn't have jumped into it with two feet. It was clear for some unknown reason that he had to dump the two of them which spelled the perfect recipe for a giant payout and Fraser had already indicated he wanted to be generous.

On top of that there was something very secretive about it because Carmichael seemed particularly interested in the board not interviewing them. There was no telling what that was all about but for the matter at hand it was probably irrelevant. While it was unlikely to be anything illegal, he wanted them muzzled and he could be made to pay for it. With his own résumé of being on Carmichael's inner circle he could get a great job elsewhere, after he took a few months off to mend and do some travelling and fishing.

Fiskins waved to Giordano to sit down, "Sir, I understand completely your position and these things happen in business, let me talk this over with Jim and we'll get back to you very soon. I think we'll be able to work something out."

Gardino was staring at him like he was mad but he realized Fiskins was the legal guy and he probably knew what he was doing. Still the shock of surviving a plane crash, expecting untold millions from some amazing discovery in a mine and now sitting here being fired was almost too much to take. His first instinct was to lay Carmichael out flat, if only his good arm hadn't been in a sling.

Fraser had been right. Fiskins would see this as an opportunity and talk Gardino into it. He thanked them for their service to the company, wished them well in their recoveries and exited the room leaving one smiling and one furious.

As he left their room he took a deep breath. There had been just no way of leaving his closest advisors and executive team in place with this Alpha-1 character calling all the shots. It would take zero time for them to smell a rat and start investigating all of the moves he was about to make. Terminating them quickly had become a must.

Fiskins waited until he was out of earshot, "Jim don't worry. Your ship just came in. You are going to get a massive settlement out of this and a great paragraph in your résumé. I'll see to it. You'll still get millions. You just won't have to work for it.

"The only thing that puzzles me is that we know nothing. All he told us was there was something discovered in the mine that he has now closed, so we must assume there is nothing down there. Then why does he have to buy us off? What secrets do we have that caused this?

"Hell what am I talking about? Who cares what it is? He has some secret deal with the Turcot Administration and we're not part of it so it's going to cost him heavily for us to exit quietly."

Gardino just hoped he was right.

Before Carmichael left the hospital he phoned Jane Jorgen to give her his heartfelt condolences and to tell her not to worry about money, 'Fiskins had something in the works'. He had the ops center in New York patch him through to the homes of the two pilots where he delivered a similar message without alluding to the money situation. He had really not known them well and they actually worked for the company they leased the plane from. Their firm had insurance policies on them that would probably compensate their families properly.

He headed back to the chopper as he wanted to get to Nevada before it was too late to see Alpha-1 and meet the new General in charge of the site. But just as he entered the small chopper at the airport he was informed by the pilot that they were grounded.

Apparently the President was in the area on Marine 1 viewing the damage and all aircraft were grounded until he was out of range. Carmichael smiled at the irony of crossing paths way out here yet again. Just missing him at the hospital after the twin news conferences was probably a good thing as he would have had a full press entourage with him and neither of them wanted to get further into detail on the 'project'.

About fifteen minutes later the helicopter pilot announced that the President was over Drake, or what once had been Drake and they were cleared to Bismarck but if Carmichael wanted to get to Nevada tonight he would have to hurry because Air Force One was on the tarmac and flights would be grounded once the President returned.

Wallace

Deputy Frank Racine caught up with Sheriff Sam Worthington at the coffee machine.

"I know you were a bit impatient with me yesterday but I'm not letting this thing just fizzle away.

"I drove past the site of that fire at the Samuels' place and you won't believe it. I know Wallace is a small town but would you believe that's the house my aunt used to live in. I didn't recognize the address yesterday."

Worthington finished stirring his coffee, "Yeah, so what."

"So guess what I did one summer about ten years ago. I helped my uncle remove an old gas furnace from the place and he had the gas capped. It's a small house so they switched over to a pellet stove for heating. I walked up to the side of the house this morning and the gas pipe is untouched and sticking out of the ground with the cap still on it. So how does the thing blow up from a gas leak?"

Worthington just shrugged.

"OK, I called the coroner's office back. As you know he certified the death and left town so I asked them to fax me over the papers. They did, and get this, before he left he didn't only sign the death certificate for Mr. Lawrence, he released the remains before the police had a chance to investigate and as you know, the remains were cremated.

"What's even more suspicious is that he did not release them to a family member. Some guy apparently showed up with a Power of Attorney for the remains. The signature on that document is unreadable and the printed ID info on the form is completely bogus.

"I called the Lawrence family and they say it was all arranged for them and the guy they dealt with only gave them his first name, Bob. Apparently the new owner of the mine took care of everything and they settled out of court for an undisclosed sum. No papers of any kind except for the POA they signed which they didn't even get a copy of. The whole transaction was done in person and they have no contact information for this guy. They got their money and they were told the ashes will be delivered to them by courier.

"I'm tellin' you Sam, something stinks here and I think it is our responsibility to get to the bottom of it. I want a full investigation into Lawrence's death and the cause of the fire that took Glass's future in-laws and fiancée and I want to get subpoenas for Glass and Carmichael."

Sam smiled, "And what? You're going to drill your own shaft at the mine, and you'll serve those subpoenas where exactly? And how are you going to get them back here to be interviewed under oath? Start state extradition procedures with no crime in mind? I agree there are lots of unanswered questions here but I see no way for a small county sheriff's office to pursue this. If you think you need to chase this down you'll need more and you'll need to draw in the FBI to get any traction on drilling mine shafts or extraditing big shots. So don't involve me unless you have a lot more than this."

Racine was red-faced. The Sheriff was right, but that did not make it right just to drop it. The Sheriff was also right that they needed the FBI and he didn't have enough yet to involve them.

Drake

Hal Turcot couldn't believe what he was seeing. They had been warned that airborne radiation was now minimal only if they remained above fifteen hundred feet where they wouldn't stir up any of the radioactive ash. They'd also have to limit their time over the site.

It had been a long day and the sun was getting low in the sky as the helicopter circled over an enormous crater where Drake, North Dakota, had been. It had been a small town of nearly three hundred people living quiet country style lives. His first thought was, 'Where did all the earth go?'

Suddenly over their headphones they heard the pilot, picked from Minot AFB for his knowledge of the area, say in a shaky voice, "Sir, we're over where Drake used to be. My family used to run a farm about five miles south of town and I actually graduated from Drake High School which was at the north end of town closer to the center of the explosion.

"The missile silo was a little less than a mile north of the center of town but as you can see, the whole community is gone. All I can recognize is what's left of the old Soo Line Railroad tracks heading east and west at the south end of town. There isn't even debris left from the big grain elevators alongside the track."

Aside from the massive hole, which had to be more than a mile across, there were signs of a couple of scorched cement slabs where houses would have stood, beyond the pit and near the south side of what was once Drake.

Roads approaching the town from the four points of the compass gradually disappeared as they neared the massive hole. Everything was scoured clean and painted an ashen grey in the dimming light, which he reasoned must be scorched earth or ash from the fireball. There were no vehicles in sight anywhere, nor remnants of buildings or even grass, just a massive smoldering pit almost like a huge shallow volcano caldera.

There was nothing recognizable for miles so it was hard to get a scale of the disaster except possibly for the few tiny cement slabs where houses had been and some pipes sticking out of the sides of the pit leaking water on the south side. From that he realized the total size of the crater and the scope of the disaster. It reminded him a bit of flying over lava fields in Hawaii but this scene was smoother and even more desolate and colorless.

He had never given much thought to the power and destructive capability of nuclear weapons. It was hard to imagine how smashing a few atoms together could do this. It had been a long time since Americans had felt that threat and imagined what it would look like so he was totally unprepared for what he saw. He realized quickly that the damage was actually much more limited because the missile had been below ground, yet the devastation was still overwhelming and immense.

General Hawthorne, Chairman of the Joint Chiefs and the Governor of North Dakota were with him but none of them had anything to say. They just stared in silence, each man not wanting the others to see the tears in their eyes. It was just so totally devastating in scope and gravity.

The pilot circled several times slowly. The sight was beyond anything he had ever expected. Like himself, he assumed his passengers needed a few minutes to take it all in and maybe say a prayer for their fellow Americans who had done nothing to deserve this. It had been ten years since high school but he knew there had to be names on the list of the dead from the town that he would recognize. He had flown over deserts in Afghanistan and Syria but he had never seen anything as void of life as this.

In the distance, about ten or fifteen miles out, in what seemed to be a perfect circle Turcot could see smoke and the first signs of trees blown over and still smoldering. Nothing within twenty miles could've survived the initial blast and then the fires afterward.

On the way to Drake the Governor had told him that more than a half dozen other small towns, one even larger than Drake, within twenty-five miles of ground zero had also been flattened and casualties were as high as one hundred percent in some of them. Earlier Turcot had seen what the intense light and fire of the explosion had done to the outskirts of Minot that was at least forty miles away. The scale was completely unbelievable.

His mind went to the folks in Drake. Just after eight p.m. the previous evening, they had probably been going about their business, cleaning up after dinner, getting the kids ready for bed, doing homework or watching a favorite TV show when in an instant they were blown into the stratosphere and vaporized into non-existence. A deep sadness crept over him as he returned to the realization that he had essentially pushed the button to make all this happen.

He was sure Drake could never be rebuilt. Hell it would've taken millions of tons of earth just to fill the hole if the radioactivity of the site was not an issue. Some memorial would have to be erected at a safe distance because the whole area was probably off limits for a long time, like Hiroshima.

Earlier he had seen burned and blinded victims overflowing the hospitals in Minot. He stumbled upon the two execs from Carmichael Industries when a doctor mentioned two patients from an aircraft accident. He wished them well but declined the opportunity to get into a discussion with them about Fraser or the project. Carmichael could deal with that touchy subject.

The light was getting low and the pilot figured one more pass was enough before they headed back to Minot. After they returned from looking at the bomb crater the President landed once more near the largest hospital and addressed the press as had been the plan.

After a long pause as the cameras rolled he said in a very quiet and subdued voice, "I've just returned from viewing the destruction caused by the missile that accidentally exploded last night. It's a terrible sight and one can only think of the lives that were snuffed out in the blink of an eye.

"As I said before, the federal government will do all it can to assist the good people of Minot and other towns near ground zero to rebuild their lives. The sights we saw this evening remind us that these weapons are totally insane and can never be used. I hope all nuclear powers in the world, and their citizens, will take a very close look at the photos we will see over the next few days. I'm more committed than ever to eliminating nuclear weapons from the arsenals of the world. Civilized people have no need of these senseless weapons and sadly, as many people have said, they are only an accident waiting to happen and unfortunately we now know that to be true."

He surprised himself at just how well he could pull off such a lie. There had been no accident here. It had been his futile and misguided attempt to attack Alpha and their refusal to spare the citizens of Drake and the surrounding towns.

***

It had been a long day for Alpha-1 who wasn't used to how tired his new body got. He was starting to recognize hunger and had found the canteen on the base for only his second meal of the day as the sun was setting. He reminded himself that he'd have to get used to this feeding routine. Hawkins had briefed the cook on Glass's strange diet and his oatmeal and honey were awaiting him.

He thought he might be able to try some native vegetation. He had memories of some fruits and vegetables when he had a physical body but he was only mildly surprised to realize that none of it was the same over a million years later. Apparently those that he remembered were all extinct or had either evolved or been bred into things he didn't recognize and even the smell of the fruits and vegetables the cook had on hand, was off-putting. He realized, at least for now, he was stuck with the oatmeal and honey regimen which wasn't too distasteful and seemed to keep this human body fueled.

Facing the prospect of eating the same thing at every meal, he was starting to wish he had loaded at least some of Glass's food preferences into the memory of this body. He was starting to think he might need to use cloaking to sneak some Alphan food in but then they only had the virtual version of it and even if they could manufacture it there was no telling if it could sustain this body, or maybe worse. Alpha had no experience in creating the physical versions of their foods so that was a moot point and he didn't have the time to start a trial and error cycle on foods, or spend the time to zip back to Alpha to have some of Bob Glass's food preferences loaded.

He smiled as he remembered lying to Carmichael about the helpers providing food. In reality the real Bob Glass had had access to the mine's emergency provisions but within forty-eight hours Glass was sampling the good virtual stuff in Alpha. How he wished for some of that for himself now.

As he was eating alone a young staff airman came in, "Sir, General Hawkins wanted me to let you know that we have an inbound aircraft claiming to be carrying Mr. Fraser Carmichael and he thought you would want to approve his landing here and wanted to know any restrictions Mr. Carmichael might have."

"Thank you Sergeant. Mr. Carmichael is always welcome on the base and has no restrictions. When he lands please let him know where he can find me."

"Yes sir," the young sergeant caught himself as he almost snapped to attention and saluted realizing only at the last second that he was facing a civilian and a pretty young one at that. As far as he knew Carmichael was the big boss yet this guy who was about his own age hadn't jumped and headed for the flight line to welcome him. This guy had balls.

Fifteen minutes later as Alpha-1 was on his second helping, Carmichael entered the austere cafeteria sporting one of his favorite cigars, "I hope you've found us suitable rooms for the night because I've had a long day in Washington, New York, Bismarck, Minot and now 'Nonexistentville' Nevada."

Alpha-1 seemed incapable of humor, "It may have seemed like a long day but there will be many more and frankly we're no closer to our goal. This room has no listening devices so we're clear to speak as long as we aren't too loud.

"I saw both press conferences and while they departed in some ways from the speeches I gave you I think they achieved their purpose. The President's canceling of the F-35 was not in the script so I sincerely hope it does not complicate matters.

"As to here, General Hawkins has made reasonable progress in setting up security and clearing out the areas for the manufacturing lines. I have most of the design documents loaded on to our computer and it appears that building all ten fighters in twelve weeks will not be an issue. I will give you a list of materials we need from your companies in the morning.

"Soon I will give the General the GPS coordinates of an airstrip where our manufacturing line and our robots for the F-47 can be loaded. They are being crated as we speak so they can't be observed during transit. We could simply have cloaked them and walked them in here but then there would be the question of where the production line appeared from. All materials you will source for the fighters and the space weapon will come in by his transports. Materials we already have for the space weapon will be brought to the construction site under cloaking.

"To that end, as he cleared everyone off the base we started setting up our primary site for the manufacture of the space weapon and the launch pad. Take a walk with me."

Dusk was behind them and they were only about a hundred yards from the mess hall when they ran into the first sentry whose job it was to keep everyone away from the hangars. He hadn't been expecting anyone coming from behind him in the direction of the buildings,

"Who goes there?" he said rifle pointed at Glass's chest.

"Young man, I'm Bob Glass, project leader for this entire base and this is Fraser Carmichael, CEO of Carmichael Industries. Do you recognize us?"

"Yes sir I do. We were given photos of you both, but the protocol is that I still have to challenge you for the password."

"That would be 'Potomac'."

"Thank you sir. Have a nice walk and if I were you I'd make some noise as you may run into other sentries and they may not be as cool as me. Please stay away from the active runway." The two men could see the sweat that had broken out on the young airman's face.

As they moved on Alpha-1 looked north and south and seemed happy with the sentry coverage he could see with the light of the base in the background.

Carmichael broke the silence, "I like a walk in the desert as much as the next guy as long as we don't run into any snakes. What are we doing out here?"

"A couple of things. One we just completed. Checking to see if security is in place and functional. There is another perimeter out there about two miles and five miles off each end of the runway. The second reason will become apparent in about another three hundred yards. I've disabled the runway incursion alarms so we can take a short cut over the end of the runway. I also know there are no planes in the vicinity to worry about."

Carmichael assumed they were going to see the area where the weapon would be assembled and launched but in the darkness he could see nothing but sand and the odd sagebrush on the dry lakebed stretching out before him.

It was a moonless night with only minimal light coming from behind them on the base and he was starting to trip over the odd stubborn plant when suddenly he was in a massive brightly lit dome several hundred yards in diameter and more than a few hundred feet high. Many times bigger than the biggest enclosed stadium he had ever been in. He stopped in his tracks and let his eyes adjust to the light as Alpha-1 proceeded further into the room. He took a step back and was in total darkness again. As his eyes adjusted to the darkness he could barely make out a fading image of Alpha-1 about ten yards in front of him in near total darkness. He took one step forward again and he was in the lit dome with Alpha-1 again about ten yards in front of him, but totally lit up by the bright light that seemed to be everywhere but he could see no source for it.

The next thing he noticed was that the floor, which had been desert sand, was now bright white, flat and hard. According to Alpha-1, they had started the construction of this dome only hours ago when the base had been cleared of contractors yet it was immense.

Alpha-1 turned and looked at him, "We'll start loading cloaked robots in here tonight. They'll bring materials with them to get started so the real work will start in about an hour when the construction scaffolding is installed and tomorrow the C-17s start delivering planeloads of raw materials.

"Much of the material from Alpha will come in just as the equipment for this dome did, under cloaking. For the raw materials you are ordering, the military will transport them in crates and flight containers directly into hangar #1 which we will think of as our staging area. Some of the shipments are for the F-47s but the rest will be moved out here by our helpers, cloaked and as needed.

"As for moving materials on the base, that's my job. When they bring containers from the C-17s to the staging hangar they'll leave them on trolleys that I can tow as required to each of the hangars, bringing back empty containers for Hawkins' team to reuse.

"For this launch site, we picked a spot in the desert where no one has any reason to go. We've watched this position for the last five weeks and it seems ideal but we have a strategy to deal with anyone that walks through that invisible wall by accident.

Carmichael asked, "OK, but will I get to see at least some of the robots and the process in action?"

"Well given that part of the deal is that you'll own some of these things you had better become familiar with them so yes, whatever time you can spend out here and away from New York you're welcome to work with me and the team of helpers on the 47s. We could also bring you out here to the launch site for the weapon development but any movement to and from here uncloaked is just asking for trouble so you'll have to be cloaked and I'm not sure what good it would do you to be here. You will not recognize anything. All I can tell you is it will be massive. You won't even recognize the materials being used or the advanced helpers that will be in use here.

Much of the work will be happening at such a pace that your eyes would likely not be able to pick it up.

"I have no concerns about you seeing our contemporary robots because you'll have access to them in Alpha assuming we're not all dead if we are unsuccessful in repelling the aliens ... or if we have to go to Plan B for any reason," he smiled.

"The work in here will be going on 24/7 at a pace even faster than what's going on in the hangars. We will be using our latest helpers at this site and advanced materials and processes. The production line, the robots and the computer for the F-47s are all dumbed down to a level where it will be plausible that you, with your brilliant 21st century mind, created them all. Still, don't fret, they'll be generations ahead of what's used elsewhere by humans today."

Carmichael nodded that he understood the tradeoffs, "When do we get started on the big stuff here?"

"Maybe you didn't understand. As I told the President, we may be too late already if those aliens have moved closer, or if they can travel faster. We started more than a month ago. At one of our sites we've been building additional helpers, manufacturing scaffolding, and subassemblies for the space weapon since we discovered the problem which was the day before Mr. Glass experienced a mine collapse. So we've been busy for over a month on this. As I said, the work of installing the manufacturing jigs will start in about an hour.

"Right now there is work going on that you cannot see. This room was just completed but has to be cleaned to less than one part per billion in contaminants, surfaces are drying and hardening and other preparations are going on to accept the machinery we will use. We can't stay long because all of the oxygen is being removed as we speak and replaced with inert gases. Oxygen is a major corrosive and combustion element as you may know and the robots don't need it. I'll have a portable breathing apparatus for this human body when I'm in here. Within a day the scaffolding will all be in place and we'll be assembling parts of the weapon.

"For the F-47 Firebolts, after we ingested all of the specs this afternoon into your new quantum computer we made thousands of changes for optimization already. Even where you choose to tie down wiring harnesses can improve manufacturing time and maintainability.

"Right now at one of our own facilities we're packing your helpers for delivery in the morning."

Carmichael knew he had become a bit of a nerd and in love with technology. The high-tech portion of his business empire had always attracted him. He was thrilled but still curious, "OK then, what is the plan for the aliens?"

"As I have told you we will simply hide. We are building a massive cloaking device at this site. We haven't tested a full-scale cloaking device of the scale we're talking about but our simulations seem to indicate it will work. You should think of cloaking as the ability to mask any or all energy, or make it appear to be somewhere else and to change that energy making it 'look' different on all energy levels. We could make the Earth look like Venus for instance and place it somewhere else in the solar system. You wouldn't know it was there unless you physically bumped into it.

"We actually considered that exact strategy but we don't have time to mask the gravity of planets and the adjustments that would mean to the entire solar system just in case these aliens might detect even small gravity inconsistencies.

"As you'll come to see there are several important assumptions in our model but we think we have the best plan we're capable of and it has a fair to good probability of success.

"We expect them to enter the solar system at sublight speed until they get their bearings. We believe and hope that they are blind while exceeding light speed.

"The plan is simple. Make the Earth appear as a burned-out, radioactive cinder with no water or atmosphere. Something we believe they will choose to ignore as a place to visit or exploit in any way.

"Of course we don't know what they have for eyes but in any case it is much more likely the first ship or scout will be unmanned, to use a term you're familiar with, and we have the entire electromagnetic spectrum cloaked, so they shouldn't see anything we don't want them to see. The tricky part is handling scans. We expect them to use various energy waves to scan us and we need to pick them out and reflect them in a way that is consistent with all the other energy beamed to them. For instance if we project a burned-out mountain range in visible light then they have to see the same thing as a reflection from anything like a radar scan. As I said, that's the tricky and risky part of cloaking."

Carmichael could see the logic of it all but he was even more worried now, "That's your only plan? You're basing this all on your ability to hide even in the face of their unknown scanning technology?"

Alpha-1 smiled, "We're open to suggestions."

Carmichael simply smiled back. He recognized that it was unlikely humans could come up with anything to improve on Alpha's plan.

There was nothing yet to see in the dome, massive as it was yet invisible, sitting on Groom Lake just northeast of the main runway, so they headed back to the hangars and ran into the young sentry one more time.

"Hope you enjoyed your walk. No snakes out tonight?"

Carmichael answered, "Nope, just a great night for a walk to work off all that outstanding food in the mess," he joked. He had actually eaten on the company jet on the way out.

As they walked on they heard the sentry report in that the two men were headed for the hangars.

When they arrived General Hawkins was waiting for them at hangar #1.

He introduced himself to Carmichael and said, "Gentlemen, I'm afraid it will take us the rest of the night to completely clean out the hangars you wanted for production and this one for staging. Once we're finished everyone will be evacuated to the line we agreed on and no one save yourselves and anyone you designate will be allowed inside that perimeter. Are we on schedule Mr. Glass?"

Alpha-1 responded. "Yes, very good work General but we definitely must finish the cleanout tonight. I sent you an email with the first transport schedule. When I get back to my office, I will send you an email for a key US site where we have material ready. The airport designation is 03UT and it's a private airstrip. The good news is that it is only about three hundred miles directly east of here in Utah. Roughly 37-07 north and -109-58 west. The bad news is that the five thousand foot private runway is not the ideal strip for your birds but if you pick the right pilots I think your C-17s will have no problem with it. Nav charts say it only has about thirty-five feet of usable runway width due to some crowning for drainage but it is actually closer to a hundred feet wide. If your pilots have any concerns about the runway point them to the 535th Airlift Squadron who have used tighter runways in the Red Flag exercises in Alaska."

Leaving Hawkins even more puzzled as to his background, Glass/Alpha-1 continued, "The elevation is 1621 meters and the prevailing winds will give you a simple approach for runway 24. There are of course no navigational aids except for temporary lighting which we've provided for, so you'll have to go on the GPS coordinates I'll provide for the runway 24 threshold. All of the crates will be just off the downwind end of the runway and each is marked with its precise weight in pounds and lined up in order for your loadmasters to confirm load balancing.

"You'll need to take forklifts with you but two C-17s will handle the load. The materials are ready now and you must pick them up before daybreak to avoid any prying eyes although it is pretty desolate out there. Your men should be able to file a flight plan from what I'll send you but if they need any other information, I'll provide it."

Again General Hawkins was shocked. Now this kid knew everything about loading C-17s. Who the hell was pulling the strings here and where was he getting all this info? He had an idea of the pick-up area which he knew was open desert and wondered how they had gotten that much material out there, and why a desolate private airstrip? They had either flown the stuff in or used semi-trailers to get it within spitting distance of Groom Lake. 'Why not just get access to the base and drive it in here themselves?' he wondered.

The General looked at his watch, "I'd better get the transport crews briefed, the planes ready and flight plans filed. If that's all there is gentlemen, I have lots of work to do."

Glass/Alpha-1 nodded. Carmichael just stood there looking a bit lost. Hawkins didn't miss this. The official story was that these two met just yesterday and Carmichael had hired Glass on the spot to run this massive new F-47 program.

But there it was again, this puzzling behavior. The body language, postures, and presence said the twenty-something Glass, supposedly a recently trapped mine inspector, was actually the one calling the shots in this duo even though Carmichael was the bigger-than-life celebrity business tycoon. This in itself was way too bizarre. It sure seemed like this kid Glass was the boss and Carmichael simply along for the ride. Some kind of subterfuge was afoot and he was more certain of it now than ever. It looked like Glass could even be the center of it all or the mastermind in some way.

Thinking there was nothing he could do about it at this moment,

Hawkins excused himself and headed off in the direction of the main office building on the base, radioing ahead to gather the team he would need to brief.

Alpha-1 waited until he was out of earshot and said, "Maybe you shouldn't be seen here too much or at least with me. I don't know if you picked up on it, but that man is very confused by our seeming reversed roles. Am I right or am I reading things into human behavior that's not there?"

Carmichael nodded, looking after the departing General, "No, you're definitely right. I only hope he keeps it to himself and doesn't alarm certain others like his superiors."

He smiled as he turned to face Alpha-1, "As for me, I suppose I will have to act a little less humbled in your presence. You must understand, I haven't had to deal with a superior being before, or at least that's the way you seem to me. I'll do my best to play my part and maybe you can just try to keep things sane around here. I'd say your level of authority, poise and confidence is confusing that man. Remember he is a General and is more used to ordering others around, and you're supposed to be a young, junior mine inspector, not a million-year-old advanced alien … no offense intended."

Alpha-1 smiled and nodded as Carmichael continued, "Anyways, we just have to do our best to keep up this charade. I'm going to head back to New York tonight. As I understand it the first job here is to set up the manufacturing line and I'd love to see that, but maybe it would be better in a day or two when things are a bit more established."

Alpha-1 nodded again, "We don't need you here and when we do get around to discussing how you're going to manage these technologies, I think you'll be pleasantly surprised. The learning curve may seem steep to you but it's actually quite simple, so don't agonize over that.

"Now my message to you and the President again is this, we need you both to continue to control this site and keep everyone out. That means you must stay in charge of your company keeping the raw materials flowing, and he needs to avoid being thrown out of office and losing control of this site. We don't want to have to start over with new people. You in particular will have a big job keeping up with the emails I'll be sending you on materials we need, so don't let that become a bottleneck.

"I understand you terminated your two executives who knew there was something going on with that mine and I sympathize with you having to do that to loyal employees, but it was the right decision. For your information, Turcot had an even tougher job dumping Gerry Hastings. You need to ensure you close that deal with your guys and keep them quiet."

Still wondering how Alpha-1 knew all that, Carmichael changed the subject, "I'm still worried about the President. I've always thought that at his core he's a weak man. He and I had a conversation last night and while he says he is on board one hundred percent I think he may need some coaching to keep on plan. Remember he feels he has to protect the American people and that weighs heavily on him. He's also a bit altruistic in his personality. In fact it wouldn't surprise me if he tries to find a way to bring all Americans or all humans into Alpha."

Alpha-1 nodded, "Yes, I'm aware of that possibility. I will reiterate my earlier message to him. I already gave you both a scenario of what would happen if humans could invite chimps to join their ranks. On-boarding any entity is a big job. The jump in IQ is not as big for humans but it takes lots of coaching to help the full psyche catch up with its new-found environment.

"If coaching is not handled properly over an extended period of time the results can be disastrous. Almost a million years ago we had the near catastrophe of introducing the fantasy world to our own people and we didn't even experience as big an IQ jump or have to deal with the massive numbers of people you would have. Some of our people became hopelessly lost in fantasies and it took us a very long time to settle the entire civilization down.

"Believe me, you'll love it when you get there but only if you take it slowly and listen to your coaches.

"As to the President, I too had a conversation with the President earlier today and I'm convinced he is properly motivated now and we have taken additional steps to ensure he will stay on track. I wouldn't worry about him. You just worry about your own challenges and let me worry about him."

Carmichael wondered what that all meant but decided not to push it. He simply nodded and went to shake Alpha-1's hand who awkwardly responded when he saw the outstretched hand.

"Remember what I said about sudden moves towards me or

touching me. You don't want an unexpected handshake to cause your untimely death, do you?"

Carmichael shivered, smiled and turned to leave saying he would be back in a few days.

Alpha-1 stopped him, "Oh, one last thing, you need to get on to the President and get landing rights for these guys at that Utah airstrip. It's called 03UT and it's owned by A. Z. Minerals which is actually controlled by the Navajo Nation. It's just outside of Mexican Hat, Utah, it's unmanned and almost never used but it is on their property and they are the owners of record. It's remote and desolate enough for us to sneak our cloaked shipping containers in there if we use it only at night.

"It's in Monument Valley which gets its share of tourists during the day. Should be an easy enough task for the two of you to get landing clearance since I'm doing all of the heavy lifting here. Remember the first planes could be there in about three hours."

Carmichael boarded his jet wondering if the Navajo Tribe would be in a good mood with this short notice, but that would be Turcot's issue.

The Build

The two big C-17 jet transports had no trouble with the Utah airstrip and were back by eight a.m. with their full loads, each making a perfect landing to the south in the early morning desert sun. Everything was unloaded and in the staging hangar by nine-thirty and the area cleared of all personnel. Glass was left alone with his two planeloads of crates and flight containers. He was seen from time to time driving a tug and towing baggage cart trains of shipping containers to the other hangars. No one got a glance at what he was moving but Hawkins from his second floor office reasoned at least some of the crates had to contain fully assembled robots as noises started emanating from each hangar shortly after the tug dropped off containers and Glass left.

The next time any of the hangar doors were opened it became apparent that large heavy curtains had been installed which revealed nothing of the darkened hangar's contents as Alpha-1 entered and exited with his tug and carts.

Pretty soon the sounds, often high-pitched squeals and squeaks, could be heard coming from all three of the assembly hangars. This seemed to the observers as the sounds of high-speed drills, impact wrenches or other tools working at high frequency. The sounds were uninterrupted and gradually built through the day to the point where it sounded like at least a hundred workers were at it full speed in each hangar. Everyone on the base was soon sure there was something amazing going on in those hangars and wished they could get a look at it. For Hawkins, the noise from all the activity seemed to offer some credibility to the fantastic stories he had been hearing about Carmichael's new Harmonized Manufacturing, but did nothing to explain all the other concerns he had.

Alpha-1 had decided not to cloak the sounds so that a legitimate manufacturing process could be assumed. The troops had been told it was a 24/7 operation and they were all glad the dorms were far from this incessant noise.

Around noon Glass appeared in the General's office in the main office building, "We will be ready in a day or so with the production line. Mr. Carmichael's robots work VERY quickly. Faster than anything I've ever seen and I can see why they must be hidden from view. They are amazingly advanced and you don't want to get in their way.

"From the specs for the planes you gave me yesterday the computer has established the materials lists and prioritized them. Mr. Carmichael's companies are sourcing the materials now and I need you to watch your email for the flights we will need. The first loads will be Pittsburgh, Baton Rouge and Taipei, Taiwan. Some of the materials are coming from China but as you know, they won't allow a US military aircraft to land there so private commercial cargo flights will deliver materials to Taoyuan International near Taipei where you'll pick them up at the cargo hangars specified in your emails.

"Again we're on an incredibly tight schedule so even though we don't yet have confirmation of an ETA for materials in Taipei we need you to get a couple of transports headed that way now. When at all possible, you need to forward position your aircraft to cut round-trip flight delays. So some of the flight plans I will send you will not yet have their load manifests, they will follow as soon as we have details. Tell your pilots that they now live by ACARS. They'll get flight plans, refueling plans, load plans, weather forecasts and anything else they might need directly from our computer into their cockpits on the ACARS system. We'll also let them know of any facilities issues like catering, housing, material handling equipment, etc.

"I think we have thought of everything but I have given you my SAT phone number by email where I can be reached 24/7 if there are any questions, and I do mean 24/7. Even I cannot become a bottleneck in this operation."

The General glanced at his computer screen and he could see the emails pouring in with detailed titles. As Glass was talking he opened one of the emails with Taipei in the subject and was shocked at the detail.

There were transport tail numbers, diagrams and descriptions in terms of the pallet sizes and weights, a load plan already done for his loadmaster to ensure the right center of gravity on the big transports, fuel calculations based on forecasted high altitude winds, and even a flight plan file with target takeoff and landing times and climb and descent profiles as well as the current cycle AIRAC information, SIDS & STARS and both the commercial and military NOTAMS for the target airports and their alternates, including in-flight refueling plans or stopovers in Hawaii for fuel.

All the fuel plans were laid out with prepaid confirmation numbers for the fuel providers when the provider wasn't military. The plans also included forecasted weather for the entire flight and contact information for all aspects of the flights. He even had a table that looked like it was updated dynamically with the schedules and flight hours of crews so Hawkins could decide whether he needed relief crews on long flights.

The last item on the email was the ACARS flag indicating when all this information had been or would be sent to the right plane. Apparently Glass had taken the initiative to pre-assign Hawkins' transports for him. All he had to do apparently was assign the crews.

Blushing he looked up at Glass who was still standing in front of his desk, "How is this possible? I've never seen anything like this. I'm sure the best commercial airlines don't have this capability even for daily scheduled flights. You have everything the pilots will need here. Are these details all real, checked out and verified? This would take a team of ten or more people to put this together and even then it would not appear in this condensed and organized fashion."

Glass smiled, "Sir, we have the world's biggest and fastest computer working exclusively on this project and we're a completely interconnected world with the internet. Big 'Q', as I now call him, is capable of doing this, running all of the robots and anything else we throw at him. For your information he is running at about five percent capacity at the moment. And yes, I'm informed that everything is checked out to at least six sigma level. The flight plans in particular have just been filed so in some cases we do not have confirmation from the designated airspace but as these flight plans are accepted or modified we will update them on the in-flight ACARS systems."

The General hesitated, still red in the face, "Mr. Glass, please explain to me how a man who was recently trapped in a mine for five weeks, who's education is civil engineering and whose job was inspecting a silver mine, gets offered a job in the Oval Office and is capable of everything I've just seen? Because I just don't understand you or this production line you speak of, or a promise to deliver ten of the most complicated machines man has ever built, and do it all in a couple of months. Please explain any part of that to me because none of it makes a bit of sense and I want some assurance that I'm not participating in anything nefarious."

There was no hiding the concern on the General's face. Alpha-1 had known this would be a critical issue on the project but had not completely appreciated just how much of a shock this must be to the man. In reality it was almost like having to explain a GPS receiver to

Columbus. This man was definitely on the critical path and could easily become an obstacle. Underestimating the shock to the man of the speed and all the changes for the project was a major oversight.

A little TLC and finesse was about due. "Listen, here's all I can tell you. I was in top form in the Oval Office. I was on a high. The high from just being rescued after more than a month alone in a dark hole. I hadn't heard about the fire in Wallace and Carmichael insisted we go directly to a photo-op with the President.

"Who was going to say no to that?

"Anyways, Carmichael had offered me a lot of money for the book and movie rights to the entrapment story. I think his working title was 'Unbreakable Glass'. So I was feeling rich and lucky and I was all spruced up and sent in to meet the President. Seems like Carmichael was actually using me to get time alone with the President and one thing lead to another. They were treating me as some kind of hero and we were like three peas in a pod when Carmichael comes out with this idea to take over the Firebolt project because he has all this new stuff that he wants to try out.

"You know most of it. He claims he has this new supercomputer and amazing robots that he has been working on for years. Eventually he gets around to some of the capabilities and blurts out that he could build the first ten Firebolts in three months and the bet is on. He goes on to claim that these robots are so autonomous and can learn so fast that anyone could run the damned program, and that's when he turns to me and says, 'Even him'.

"Well honestly I don't know what they were drinking but the conversation just got weirder and weirder until it's a done deal. I get the job to talk to his master computer, feed it all the specs, unpack the first robot and tell you what emails it's spitting out. I'm running about five minutes ahead of you on this thing. If I stumble I'll be run over.

"Those flight packages looked pretty impressive to me too. You and I are in the same boat. I don't understand how Carmichael achieved this or why he put me in charge but man I'm telling you, that manufacturing setup is like nothing I've ever seen. There has to be a massive team behind this somewhere running that damned computer. We have a computer here on site but my guess is that it is only a node on a network and the real compute power is in the cloud or in a bunker somewhere. I know a little about this kind of tech and I think he's using some kind of spread-spectrum satellite comms for the linkup like a massive Wi-Fi network in the sky that must have incredible bandwidth to achieve these kinds of results and drive all those robots.

"I don't know what the President's motivation was, but from his speech it looks like he is trying to teach the military procurement people a lesson and find money for his domestic programs. At the end of the day it may only cost him a three-month delay in the F-47 program if this all falls flat. As far as him agreeing to put me on the project, I think his only requirement was that I have some brains and no political agenda. So he figured that a guy who has an advanced engineering degree and was trapped in a mine is not a Carmichael political plant.

"But let me say, from what I have seen of those robots building the manufacturing jigs, I would not want to bet against Carmichael pulling this off. That computer ingested the entire design and started spitting out results in the form of material requirements emails within seconds.

"Last night when Mr. Carmichael was here he looked like a different man. I think he woke up after that meeting at the White House, and the two press conferences, and must be wondering what he got himself into. He runs a public company and it looks to me like he is flying by the seat of his pants and I would not be surprised if his board isn't all over him on the risks involved here.

"I must say, now that I've seen the machines and worked with that computer, I can see where his enthusiasm is coming from. How they built it all I haven't a clue but it is a generation beyond anything I've seen or heard of and they're amazingly fast.

"Maybe one day you'll get a look in there but those robots move around at incredible speeds and I'm told they have complex vision systems that pick up much more than our eyes, like infra-red and UV so they don't even need lighting. Hell they probably have better night vision systems than the military.

"The first time I walked in there when they started to build the manufacturing jigs I thought I was going to get run over by them but they are so fast and accurate that they just swarm around you and don't come close to running into you, if you don't make any sudden moves. There must be nearly a hundred of them spread across the three hangars but they move so fast it sounds like a lot more.

"They're truly amazing and if I was to guess, I'd say in about a week or so we'll see the first subsystems of ten F-47s starting to appear."

Hawkins wasn't buying it all but thought the kid knew how to tell a convincing story.

Glass continued, "Before the White House I only knew Carmichael as some kind of miracle billionaire whiz kid like Jobs or Gates. Now I work for him on an amazing project. This incredible manufacturing technology he has is a big competitive advantage, and I can see why it has to remain so secret.

"So if you think this whole thing is strange, think of my position. Two days ago I was stuck in a mine for more than a month with a dead guy. Then my fiancée and her parents are wiped out on the very day I'm freed. Not only that, they burned in the house so there aren't even bodies to recover. I took this job before I heard about the fire and now if I try to go back there I'll be swarmed by media. So I may as well just tough it out here and bury myself in my work."

Hawkins thought it was a good show and almost credible right up to the bit about the fiancée. It was a masterful attempt to cover up whatever the truth was but he still wasn't buying it. The crowning doubt was the lack of distress or any emotion whatsoever with regards to his personal, monstrous loss. He talked about it like it was something he read in a newspaper about some other poor family. Who knew what his relationship with her parents had been but this guy just lost his fiancée in a fire and there hadn't been a solitary sign of grief.

Who could think of a loved one being blown to bits or burning to death and not be tormented and crippled with grief? There was the old adage that everyone grieves differently but not like this. Not by ignoring it and taking a new exciting job and burying yourself in it within hours of losing the love of your life. And not even going to the site of her death or where they had lived? There was always the possibility of an acute case of denial but he just brought it up himself. He was not in denial. He just had no emotion tied to it at all.

But that was a big part of the mystery too. What did it even mean that he had no thought for his fiancée? How could that happen? Was this Bob Glass some kind of a plant or substitution for the real Glass? That didn't make any sense either but this guy was clearly working hard to sell his story.

No, this made zero sense, but he was pretty certain Glass would stick to the story and he wasn't about to get much more out of him; much more of the truth anyways.

Something else was going on, Hawkins was convinced of it. Glass was a bright kid for sure but not bright enough to be driving a project like this and with the complete confidence he displayed? Not a chance. He knew too much too fast and was way too confident. You could hear it in his voice and the way he was comfortable giving out orders ... and Carmichael, he had almost seemed cowed by the kid. Hawkins was sure of one thing, this kid had been on this project for months if not years. There was no doubt at all in the General's mind. This whole thing, this whole setup was some kind of a ruse. Glass was a nice kid but the General didn't believe a word that came out of his mouth.

.

A Call

Somewhat to avoid the press in the back of Air Force One, the President had taken a nap on the way back from Minot and it was very late by the time he got to the White House. He felt suddenly refreshed and headed to the Oval Office knowing there would be at least a stack of letters for him to sign.

This was something he traditionally didn't like delaying. While Autopen was used for most presidential signatures, he had asked for special letters to be left for his personal signature and the odd personal note. Some of these were for the families of veterans who had died recently from wounds they had acquired in combat, some of them passing away years after they were wounded. He had been to Bethesda and Walter Reed military hospitals several times and his staff had left yellow post-its on the letters if the President had actually met the veteran or their families, along with a note on anything that had been discussed so he could add a personal touch in handwriting on the form letter.

Everyone else had gone for the night and he was alone, and about a third of the way through tonight's stack when his 'red' line rang. He immediately grabbed it fearing the worst.

A familiar voice said, "Sir, my name is Bob Glass. I'm the real Bob Glass as I think you've been introduced to a new Mr. Glass."

The President immediately was on alert, "How did you get on this line? This is a secure military emergency line. You're breaking multiple federal laws by even using it."

"Sir, I really am Bob Glass and I'm no longer a human you might say and this is definitely an emergency that you need to be involved in."

The President decided to let him go on, "Prove to me that you're who you say you are."

"Well not sure how I'm going to do that but here goes. I was replaced in the mine by what we would think of as an alien. He replicated my body and left the mine in the escape tube. I on the other hand was converted and adopted into a new civilization which is real, virtual and fantasy all at the same time. I live somewhere now in a network of computers.

"Is any of this helpful?"

Turcot paused and then said, "Yes. I think only you or someone from that world would know these facts. How were you able to call me?"

"Well, I'm an engineer and I know some things about technology and with my increased IQ and some data I've been able to find, I was able to connect with you on this line. Don't worry, no one is listening in, I made sure of that.

"I can now connect with you this way when needed but if you have to talk to me, that's more difficult. I think I can rig up something that looks like a communication headset, but I don't know yet how to get it to you, so keep your eyes open for a shoe box where you might not expect to find it. Inside will be a device that you can use to connect to me. Just put it on and I'll be with you immediately in a private space.

"You must know that I'm breaking some of the cardinal rules here by connecting with you. Contact with humans is forbidden without approval of the governing body down here which brings me to why I'm calling you.

"I don't know what you call him but I don't think the other Bob Glass is everything he says he is."

Turcot wanted to hear more, "Please continue. By the way we call him Alpha-1 and his world Alpha."

"OK, Alpha-1 told me the story of their offshoot from a common ancestor about two million years ago and then them becoming immortal about a million years ago. He also told me they had from time to time 'invited' certain humans to join them but frankly I have yet to meet an original entity from Alpha other than this Alpha-1. So far he seems to be the only one. Everyone else I've met is ex-human. In fact, this governing body, that approves human contact, is nowhere to be found.

"Add to that the fact that he seems to have powers that are greater than anyone I've met. When it comes to higher-level functions, he seems to somehow control what we can see and do. For instance only he can control inviting humans and doing the transformations with special helpers only he controls. From talking to others they claim this is a 'right' claimed only by original Alphans but again I can find no one who has ever met a native Alphan besides him. He was the one who on-boarded everyone I have met so far, and frankly this setup does not seem to alarm anyone here.

"So while this world is everything he promised me and more, and while I tend to believe his story about approaching aliens, I have no confidence he is telling us the whole story. There is something very odd about the fact that he seems to be more of a benevolent dictator than an equal resident of this world."

Turcot was anxious to get more, "This is fascinating and if I'm to cut through all of this, your message to me is caution. He may not be what he says he is and Alpha may not be what he says it is. Is there anyone there who has witnessed any malice from this being?"

"No sir, they all think highly of him but many here claim to have been here for a long time and culturally they have all accepted his dominance. I'm the newcomer and this all sticks out as a red flag to me. Then again I come into this with a modern education and a penchant for inquiry and liberty which may not have been true of African spear throwers of a few hundred years ago. But again, that might all be a mirage created by him. At least the piece about my fiancée and her family seems to be true as I see them here and I know humans are reporting their deaths in that fire."

The President pushed for more. He wanted to see how much Glass really knew, "OK, you've given me lots to think about, do you have any idea where you are now?"

"That's very hard to say in terms of physical location. Frankly I agreed to the swap because I was terrified of those robots and worried the surface might not find me or rescue me in time and eventually his story was very compelling.

"As I know he told you, he shares most of his interactions with you folks as public, but apparently not everything. A big issue for me is that he lied to you and Fraser about the discovery in the mine. That apparently was all a ruse to get Carmichael involved. There was no computer room so I'm afraid Mr. President that you were tricked into thinking that was a key site for them before you tried to nuke it. I know that must be resting heavily on you.

"But let me answer your question. The helpers did show up in the mine seemingly out of nowhere and Eric did take a swing at one of them. It was not long after I established something of a hand signal thing with them that he appeared in my body. He froze me and eventually made the swap deal with me, but again there was no computer room and my sense was they had recently built access to the mine just to get to Eric and me.

"Anyways, there was a new opening at the end of one of the mine shafts and we walked down a short corridor that seemed to me to be freshly bored and entered what I'd call an underground train line which ended at the mine, so I think that whole branch of the train line was built just to get to us. My guess is these trains are used elsewhere by the helpers, as this civilization no longer has bodies.

"I'm calling it a train but there were no train tracks and the capsule was aerodynamic and just big enough for the two of us and two helpers.

"It was very spartan but two chairs had apparently been added for us. The two helpers that accompanied us anchored themselves to attachments on the walls for transit. This thing had no windows and took off like a rocket and accelerated for about three minutes at something close to three Gs so we were going really fast. Based on G-forces I know we made some gentle turns and probably joined a main line at one point as I heard sound changes from outside the capsule like other vehicles flashing by. So we were going way beyond the speed of sound I believe, just on the basis of some math. After that, we glided at a constant speed for about another five minutes, making more gentle turns and then decelerated at around negative three Gs for another three minutes so a quick calculation says we were between three and six thousand miles from Idaho.

"Of course I had no sense of direction so we could have been going anywhere but given their story of wanting to stay hidden, my guess would be we're under the Pacific or the Arctic somewhere.

"The last few minutes in the capsule we did make some tighter turns and rose and fell sometimes so I think we were negotiating some kind of a network at a central site for these vehicles. We ended up in a small loading and offloading area. We walked through another few short corridors. They were all rounded tunnels with smooth flat floors with invisible sources of lighting and I found myself in a much larger, ultra-modern facility and then in a hospital-type setting with what looked like special purpose helpers. Alpha-1 explained what was about to happen and they sprayed some kind of mist near my mouth and nose. I gradually lost consciousness and then woke up in Alpha as you call it, which if I believe Alpha-1, is in a network of computing devices that could be anywhere. In this digital state they could have mailed me across the solar system for all I know.

"But it seems like I'm in a real world which I'm told is fashioned after the world they knew nearly a million years ago. All I can say about that is that it looks hundreds or thousands of years beyond what humans have accomplished to date in terms of buildings, technology and the like but remember it's all in a thought simulator.

"Sir, if this is anything like the way they lived a million years ago then humans are nowhere near that today.

"So according to Alpha-1 my psyche now lives in a network of computers, possibly duplicated for redundancy all over the solar system but it sure feels like I'm walking around in a marvelous new world and I feel like myself but much lighter and euphoric.

"Everyone here is represented by an avatar or a creation of their own making that represents their body and let me assure you, there are no unfortunate people when it comes to good looks in Alpha. Most I'm told chose like me to go with an idealized version of their former selves. Apparently the psyche prefers seeing a familiar face in the mirror, at least initially.

"That's what got me wondering about native Alphans. The helpers in the mine were close to nine feet tall and that's the way Alpha-1 described their species to Fraser but there are no nine-foot avatars walking around so I started asking questions about where people came from.

"Anyways, that's a long-winded version of I don't know where I am now and I know of no other native Alphans here."

The President thought for a moment and then said, "How are you and your relatives fitting in?"

"Good question. My fiancée and her parents are the first people here who had no warning they were coming. They in fact didn't have a vote in the matter but I made it a condition of the deal I made with Alpha-1. There was no way I was leaving my fiancée behind and I knew she would not leave her parents.

"To ease them into it they were apparently frozen in mind and body until the conversion and then placed in the exact environment they left, watching my rescue on TV in their home in Wallace. I entered the room to their surprise but not enough to give anyone a virtual heart attack. Over the next few hours I gradually explained the whole thing to them. Not long after they were kissing and hugging me for making the deal to include them. It's tough to turn down immortality and this amazing world we now live in.

"You'll love it here but we must survive this alien arrival first, I think you'll agree.

"Listen Mr. President, I think we've pushed this far enough for a first call. I'll call back if I find anything new and soon you'll be able to call me. My only advice is to keep a close eye on Alpha-1 and I'll keep investigating."

After the President signed off, he sat there going over what he had just heard. The call had been completely unexpected and raised some important issues. A deep yawn told him it was well past his bedtime.

***

Bill Carter, CIA Director, sat there staring at his PC mouth agape. It had taken him all day to quietly orchestrate the various modes of keeping tabs on the Joint Chiefs and it had been after ten p.m. when the office quietened down enough for him to pull up the audio file from his secret bug in NORAD.

But what the hell was going on here? This was nothing like what he had been told about the evening of the missile accident. The audio file captured all of the communications between the White House, the silo team and NORAD, with the Pentagon on the line as well, but after listening to a section of the recording three times he still could not believe his ears. The classified narrative was that Dan Westgate had blown a fuse in the Oval Office, stolen the football, held the others at gunpoint and tried to launch a nuclear missile at Idaho but nothing like that scenario was supported by this recording. There was no mistaking the clear voice of the President himself talking back and forth with the silo team and waiting through the countdown with them. And when he did hear Westgate's voice it was clear and as calm as you might expect in the middle of such a crisis. There was no sign of any mental health issues or subversion on his part. Yes, Westgate had done most of the talking on the phone to NORAD and even ordered DEFCON 1. Westgate had also been the one to order the SEALs to the Oval Office for some unidentified threat but no mention of a 'drill' as the SEAL team remembered.

According to the secret recording from NORAD, the President had been driving the whole thing and did most of the talking to the silo crew. Neither Westgate nor the President had explained throughout the event what the actual threats were inside the White House or in Idaho, but there seemed no question they were in agreement on bombing that mine.

But that was impossible. It did not jive with the known facts. There had to be at least thirty people in the NORAD control center and the Pentagon that night listening in on this, and then there was the Lt. Colonel with the football and probably Gerry Hastings, both in the Oval Office who had to have been standing next to the President when this was going on. Even the SEAL team was in on it and yet no one had offered up this version of the events.

On top of that, the President had mentioned nothing of this to him when he called about monitoring the Joint Chiefs, yet he was clearly implicated as the leader of whatever transpired according to this bug.

This just did not add up and any possible explanations were really limited. He could only think of three scenarios and they all seemed impossible.

Either there was a massive conspiracy afoot where dozens of people at NORAD, the Pentagon and the White House including the President himself were lying, or they had all been completely brainwashed into believing a totally different version of the facts, or somehow this digital recording had been intercepted and doctored to tell an entirely different narrative. A recording that as far as he knew, no one other than himself and a trusted tech, now stationed in Hawaii, knew about. A digital file that was not only secret as to its existence but using the best encryption the intelligence services had. Encryption where he had the only key for access.

But the last troubling piece of information, adding to the mystery, was that he knew about the meeting the previous evening between Jenkins and the President. One of his agents had been dispatched to track down an audio of that meeting so he could find out what issues relating to the Joint Chiefs the President was worried about.

Late in the afternoon his agent reported back that he had the audio of that meeting by way of the White House staff, but they had revealed, without explanation, that the system had been experiencing outages and there was no audio record of what had transpired around the time of the missile disaster and Dan Westgate's death. Other pieces of the evening were lost too and on both independent systems. For unknown reasons the Oval Office tapes had switched off and at several times during the evening. He thought to himself, 'Am I sitting on the only real and valid recording of what actually happened that night?'

A shiver went down his spine. This was the most serious and the most mysterious event he had ever experienced in his long career at the CIA and it was on his shift as director. Something very strange had happened or was still happening and none of the alternatives he could imagine made any sense at all, or were even possible as far as he could tell.

Suddenly his focus was no longer restricted to spying on the Joint Chiefs. If the recording was real then outrageous crimes had been committed here, causing the deaths of over seven hundred innocent Americans. But that meant people in very high places were implicated in some unknown way, either as co-conspirators or brainwashed victims. Again, IF the recording was real then whoever was behind this did not know of his secret bug at NORAD, so for the moment he was on his own in figuring out what was going on.

The worst scenario was if the recording was real and the President was involved in some kind of subterfuge and had ordered the missile strike that had somehow failed. That meant Dan Westgate was likely innocent and had probably been taken out as part of a cover-up. Another question was how and why had the Secretary of Defense been killed after it was all over? According to the recording he had not tried to stop the event. It appeared that someone in that room might have killed him but the autopsy had said it was an internal brain hemorrhage. The last piece on the secret recording was NORAD informing him of the failed launch and explosion in the silo. Westgate had still seemed lucid and 'in' on whatever plan was afoot and then presumably hung up shortly before he died ... or more likely, was killed.

For this whole scenario to be true, everyone that had been in the Oval Office, NORAD and the Pentagon had to be lying or even more ridiculous, brainwashed. That all sounded just too crazy. People in three very different locations all brainwashed at the same time? Yet how could someone have gotten to this secret encrypted digital recording and doctored it to make it sound like the President was the culprit? And why?

The bigger question left open was, what was the purpose of it all? Or worse, was this some kind of ongoing deception and the events in the Oval Office were only part of a larger scheme that was still playing out?

He physically shivered. This was terrifying and he would have to move slowly and deliberately. He was on his own and for the moment he could involve no one else. Who was he going to trust if possibly the President was involved in this? If any of these scenarios were true then Turcot had to have accomplices.

A terrible thought came to him, 'If all the scenarios he could think of were impossible then there had to be another scenario he hadn't thought of.' He racked his brain but nothing he could think of came close to dealing with all the conflicting facts he had.

His first task was to decide whether to copy the recording, making sure it was secure, or destroy it.

***

After the surprise call from the real Bob Glass in Alpha, Hal Turcot climbed the stairs to the residence and entered their bedroom. The bed was unused and he found Ev once more in the tiny kitchenette, still dressed, red-eyed from crying and holding a warm glass of milk.

Nearly sobbing she said, "I can't sleep ... don't want to sleep. I was just in Ann's bedroom watching her and wondering how long we have left before she is gone."

He pulled her close and tried to reassure her with, "Don't worry Ev, everything will be OK."

She was furious. Was he insane? Nothing was going to be OK! She pushed him back to arm's length, "What do you mean 'everything will be OK?'... You'll be OK? ... I'll be OK? Our family isn't going to be OK!"

Realizing he had stepped in it he pulled her close and simply hugged her.

She was ready to hit him. Was he in complete denial? Their daughter was dying and the way things were going, very soon. She knew he had the weight of the world on his shoulders but this was just too much. He was never around to see the daily deterioration and at the very end of his daughter's life, for God's sake.

She wondered if it was a man thing, to bury your head in the sand when close relations were in peril where you could do nothing to save them. Did he think it would somehow go away if he didn't acknowledge it?

She thought for the first time that he had a heartless side to him if he couldn't see and share in her pain. He was pulling away from her and Annie at the worst possible time.

After leaving a sobbing and confused wife he made a detour and ended up sitting at the bottom of Ann's bed listening to her labored breathing. It was worse than he had expected. Ev was right, Ann was really struggling. It was quite clear she was in jeopardy of not making it to the end of the project.

It had indeed been a long day and he decided to sleep in the guest bedroom so when Ev did come to their bed it was empty, which only increased her angst and overwhelming sadness. This was further evidence to her that he was avoiding their problems.

Through fits of absolute sobbing, she cried herself to sleep in their massive bed, more alone than she had ever felt in her life.

Next morning he was gone before she rose leaving her to fret alone all day about Ann. She had long since canceled any engagements outside of the White House so she could spend all her time with her daughter, but given that Ann slept most of the time because of the morphine, she was alone again with only Ann's nurse to keep her company, and although the woman was an angel, she was running out of encouraging things to say to keep Ev's morale up.

As Hal Turcot marched into the Oval Office, Mary Trudel, his personal secretary of over twenty years, and Kyle West, filling in for Gerry Hastings, were hot on his heels.

Kyle was first to speak, "Sir, we really put Jim Knowles on the spot yesterday for the press scrum. You had no time to brief him and after that press announcement yesterday he was peppered with questions he couldn't answer. He did an adequate job of sidestepping everything but you'll need to brief him this morning so he can be prepared.

"On second thought I may have embellished how well it went yesterday. Frankly, according to Jim, it was a complete disaster. He didn't know the answers to nearly all the questions and he feels like he has lost much of his credibility with the press corps.

"To add to the chaos, he felt he had to announce Gerry Hastings' resignation as it was all over the building and again there were lots of questions he couldn't answer, so we'll have to do damage control and prepare him for that. I need to know the party line too. I tried to call

Gerry but I don't think he's answering the phone. Why did he resign?"

Mary interrupted, "Sir, not only Jim and Kyle here are in a funk over this, a couple of your cabinet members want some answers too. Could I suggest a short meeting to brief them all this morning?"

Hal Turcot had been staring at the two of them. This was a mess that would only get worse, so he needed to bring them all up to speed and try his best to get them onside with all of the changes and the challenges to come. "OK, if you can find an opening on the schedule this morning get all the ones affected, and only the ones directly affected into the room. No more than forty-five minutes though."

Just as they were about to break up, the Press Secretary Jim Knowles himself, burst in holding some papers, "The Chinese just announced that they know that China was the target of that missile and they've raised their military readiness level putting all of their forces on high alert."

The President sat down hard in his chair. "Shit!" He looked at Mary, "Get me the Secretary of State on the phone and the Head of the Navy."

Before anyone could move a special line on the President's phone lit up from the Joint Chiefs.

As he went to lift the phone he turned to Mary and said, "No need, here they are."

After the Chief had informed the President that he had the full Joint Chiefs with him, Hal Turcot said, "Listen guys, I think I know why you've called. We have a crisis. I told you yesterday there were leaks. According to Bob Downey there's been a rumor running around the Senate building that China was the target of that missile, which is obviously false, and it looks like someone leaked that to the Chinese because they have just announced they KNOW our real target was them and they have raised their readiness level."

Hawthorne, Chairman of the Joint Chiefs confirmed the reason for the call.

Turcot continued while waving directions to Kyle, "OK, I'll get the Secretary of State on to their embassy first and set up a call with the Chinese Minister of Foreign Affairs. We need to assure them China was never the target. I'll talk to the Chinese President if I have to."

Kyle, as acting Chief-of-Staff, rushed out of the office to deliver the President's directive leaving Mary and his press secretary.

"Walt, as to the Navy, I don't know where all our carriers are right now but make damned sure none of them are near China, headed that way or even at anchor pointed in their direction. Pull all the subs back a reasonable distance too.

"General Hawthorne, tell all bases in South Korea, Taiwan, and Japan to suspend any exercises near the Chinese border. I don't want anyone thinking we're in preparations for anything. The slightest misstep could cause a flare up.

"I'll brief the National Security Advisor and have him make sure there's nothing going on with North Korea. They could throw a wrench into the works here and start something or just try to stir the pot. We don't need even the appearance of hostilities right after I've stopped two fighter programs and taken our ICBMs offline. Hell, knowing the Chinese they'll probably twist my actions to make it look like a feint to catch them off guard."

Admiral Walter Gibbs of the Navy spoke, "In addition sir, I suggest we go to DEFCON 3."

The President wondered if these guys had been listening, "Hell no! We need to de-escalate this situation now! Hopefully our diplomatic assurances will be enough in the next few hours but I don't want to do anything that could be seen as aggressive!"

The military leaders on the other end of the phone all looked at each other with an expression of horror.

The President picked up on the total silence and continued, "I do understand of course that we must be prudent so make sure we have all eyes on China and then if we don't see a reciprocal de-escalation from them in the next twelve hours then we may decide to change the DEFCON level, but it has to be seen as a reaction to their moves, not a provocation on our part. Understood?"

In unison he heard "understood" from the Joint Chiefs. What he couldn't see was them all shaking their heads in disgust.

"Gentlemen, please stay on top of this and inform me of any developments," he said as he hung up.

Turning to Mary he said, "Please set up that cabinet meeting we discussed ASAP and as to the press, Jim get the word out immediately that the Chinese rumor is nonsense and anyone reporting it even as a rumor is highly irresponsible. I'll accompany you into the daily briefing and take questions on everything but don't warn them, that just gives them time to work up some awkward gotchas. You and I will get on the same page before we walk in there so you'll be prepared for follow-ups."

Jim seemed relieved and headed off leaving Mary.

She looked sympathetic as she said, "Sir, I know these are terrible times for you with Ann sick and all. If there is anything I can do to take some of the load off, please don't hesitate."

Turcot smiled, "Thank you Mary. There is one thing you could do. From time to time maybe you could run upstairs and just check in on Ev. She's having a really hard time right now and a few kind words might go a long way."

Mary nodded acceptance but was shocked that he didn't seem to realize that he should be the one running upstairs for a few minutes throughout the day to comfort his wife and check in on his sick daughter. She was only too aware that even five minutes was hard to find in his schedule, but this was his dying daughter. She felt he was making a mistake and figured the first lady had probably come to the same conclusion much earlier.

***

At the Pentagon the Generals were left looking at each other after the President signed off. This was the first time in their memory that a potential foe raising their threat level was not instantly answered with the US raising its DEFCON status. They had all come to their jobs assuming that that was an unwritten rule. The US had likely initiated this episode with the missile explosion but still, this lack of action signaled weakness as far as the military was concerned, and one never displayed weakness in the face of the enemy, especially the Chinese.

General Bill Dean, the toughest guy in the room, Secretary of the Army and the most outspoken of the bunch just couldn't resist, "Now you know why I call him President Turtle. When he feels threatened he stops and pulls his head in."

Hawthorne sneered at him, "Bill, keep that shit to yourself for God's sake!"

***

On his way home from Groom Lake and after his late night call to the President to get landing clearance for the C-17s in Utah, Carmichael had slept a bit on the plane and got into New York very late. He was awoken right at eight thirty the next morning by Winnie Goldstein who had rung his cell phone.

"Yes Winnie, what's up?"

"Sir, the board called an emergency meeting for noon today. Can you get here for it?"

He realized she had no idea where he was and he wasn't ready yet to face the board. He needed a bulletproof story to feed them and he needed some time to put that together.

Winnie was waiting so he said, "What's the agenda and how can they call a meeting on such short notice?"

"Sir the rules allow for a meeting without the normal twenty-one day notice if a majority of the board agrees to waive the notice period and they did. Also, they said nothing about an agenda."

"Well, tell them I can't be there. I'm unable to attend due to pressing business matters and find a way to kill the meeting even if they have a quorum."

"Sir, I'm not in those meetings. Will Fiskins is the secretary of the board but he is still in the hospital out west."

"Listen Winnie, you're not supposed to know this yet and I need you to keep it quiet, but Will Fiskins is resigning and I need to find a replacement. For the interim you're my point man in legal and I want you to attend that meeting representing Will.

"Will and I are the only two company execs on the board and we have the right to send an alternate if for a valid reason we can't be there in person. You're Will's stand-in and I'm not attending and I'm not assigning anyone as an alternate. See what you can do to kill anything happening in that meeting."

He hung up knowing he had left her with a very sticky problem walking into a board populated by some of the biggest names in American business, but after how she had handled the X-Wave acquisition, he had a feeling she would do OK.

As soon as he hung up the phone it rang again. This time it was Joe Riser, VP Finance, "Joe what's up?"

Joe sounded concerned, "I just got off the phone with this guy Glass you hired. He has sent you and me a list of materials for the project out west and he says you've preapproved all of it. It's massive and expensive."

"He's right. Anything he needs, procure it for him and follow his every instruction in terms of purchases and delivery instructions."

"Listen Fraser, this is MANY millions of dollars and we have no established budget in the approved company plan for any of this. I can't in good faith sanction any of this without a board-approved budget; it's too big. This guy said he had more orders coming and if it keeps up this way, our contingency fund will be gone by noon so there's no way to bury this.

"I saw what you said in the press conference but I have no paperwork supporting such a massive corporate investment. We don't even have any guesstimates to forecast the effect on earnings for the SEC which I must file right away because you made material statements in that press announcement. I need to do that filing today and besides that, the stock took a hit yesterday and it will tank if we can't show the market some numbers that make sense. Either way, I need to give the SEC something right away."

Carmichael could tell that his normally placid VP Finance was freaking out about this as the man continued, "I thought you'd be in the office before I had to deal with approving massive expenditures like this and cooking something up for the SEC. I mean this guy is a racehorse and just by his tone I expect an avalanche of purchases in the next couple of days.

"I understand he is the COO of that division but if I approved these acquisitions without the proper approved budgets I could be hauled in front of the board and fired. You know I have a key fiduciary responsibility here and I think you can appreciate that I'm totally exposed."

"Listen Joe, I'm the only one who can fire you and the only way that is going to happen is if you do anything to get in the way of this project. Write up any budget documents you want. Take the original published target for the selling price of the new planes off the internet. We're building ten of them so multiply by ten in terms of the revenue. For the expenditures divide the selling price by four to cover material costs because our direct labor costs will be close to zero. Apply the average corporate overhead numbers. All of this will happen in the fourth quarter so there's your EBITDA forecast to give you profit and tax forecasts. So now you know what the budget has to be. Write that all up as an approved budget from management and I will sign it when I see you. Get Winnie to sign it if you must because she has my POA, but DO NOT delay anything required for this project, and do an appropriate summary of that for the SEC filing.

"The numbers I just gave you will yield at least a small net positive impact on our bottom line just like I announced so there will be no surprises for the SEC.

"Glass has carte blanche on anything he needs. I trust him completely. Now, I can't talk right now Joe, just do whatever it takes. Increase our credit line if you need cash flow relief but make it happen. If there's any issue getting money to cover this then I'll back it up with my own wealth. I have other private companies involved in this so I'll work on sharing the expense load with them so that this is only a short-term issue for CII.

"Lastly, I'll get board approval on this, not you. I will send you an email in the next few hours documenting all of this to give you some cover," and he hung up.

Joe was left staring at the phone. Fraser could be rash and fast moving but never like this. Make up a budget in the hundreds of millions from newspaper articles? He had no idea of the terms of the agreement with the President. When would they get paid? Who had authorization to make purchases or changes to the project? Was there a real contract? Did he need to make provisions for possible overruns, cancelations, delays, bad debts and the like? Some of Glass's requirements were from overseas. He didn't even know what currency all this stuff would be in and whether he needed a hedge contract to cover currency fluctuations which in something this size could be millions. None of this was known and any budget he could write up would be a sham at best. None of it would pass even a cursory look from the company's external auditors.

As for Carmichael's instructions, yeah he could probably throw something together making lots of assumptions and that might stick for a day or two, but if the board or the SEC came sniffing it wouldn't be worth the paper it was written on and no matter what authorizations he had from the CEO his ass was still sticking out a mile. If it all blew up he would never work in finance again. He needed the real thing and from what he had just heard it was a pretty good bet Fraser Carmichael had no idea how to paper this deal either.

Fraser had cut him out of the inner circle about a month ago, when some big deal about the mine in Idaho had been cooked up in his office with a couple of the other execs. Being VP Finance he knew three of them had been given a million dollars each to keep quiet about the new 'project' and the fact that he had been left out burned him.

Now with Fraser AWOL, and the two other surviving VP's in a hospital in Minot, he was left alone to hold down the fort. Earlier he had tried to get to Will Fiskins in hospital to get some legal advice, but for some reason Fiskins was refusing to take any calls. Now he was being asked to write up phony budgets in a publicly traded company, potentially a career-ending proposition. If Fraser Carmichael could not do a better job of filling in the details when they met, he was going to have to consider reporting everything to the board, with resignation in hand. Otherwise he would never be able to find work in a position of financial authority again. The only thing that kept him from doing that today was that it was not the first time Carmichael had taken SOME shortcuts and this job paid well.

***

As all eight of the external board members filed into the boardroom on the top of Carmichael Tower overlooking Central Park, Winnie Goldstein was already seated with her laptop open in front of her. She rose and reintroduced herself to each of the men and the one woman on the board, indicating she was taking Will Fiskins' place today given he was unavailable. The accident, which had been ignored by the press, came as a complete surprise to an already unsettled board. No one had thought to tell them that a company plane had gone down and several company execs were out of commission and one had died. This did nothing to relieve the obvious tension in the room.

In the past Winnie had been brought into a couple of board meetings to make presentations so they all recognized her as one of Fiskins' people.

Rollie Winston, the most senior member of the board started to call the meeting to order as the Chairman hadn't shown up yet and asked Winnie where Fraser was. It was Fraser Carmichael's habit to make a grand entrance after the board was all in attendance.

"I'm afraid Mr. Fraser is unreachable at the moment and very busy on company business. As Will Fiskins' stand-in I've been asked to perform the secretarial duties for the board. I don't have an agenda for you as the company didn't call this meeting but that point is now moot. It is my duty to inform the board that we don't have a quorum for this meeting and therefore the meeting cannot be called to order."

Rollie Winston interrupted, "Sorry, but I had my legal people look at CII's board rules and I'm satisfied we have a quorum of more than half of the elected board members present."

Winnie interrupted again, "Yes you had a quorum to schedule the meeting and to waive the notice period but the rules state clearly that to call the meeting to order and deal with the business of the company you need the presence of the Chairman or CEO, both being Mr. Carmichael, which you don't have. So as acting secretary I declare this meeting postponed and not adjourned because it is not an official meeting, until such time as we can achieve a quorum."

Several of the board members started to protest before she cut them off, "I know that is an unusual point in our bylaws but apparently Mr. Carmichael insisted on this rule when he took the company public. I suspect we've never had to exercise that rule until now but it is quite specific, anything discussed or decided here would not be legal or binding on the company or even make it into the minutes for that matter. Of course there will be no minutes for today as we have not had an official meeting."

Before the objections could fly Winnie interrupted again, "On a separate subject, and as I mentioned to some of you when you arrived, Will Fiskins was injured in a plane crash in Minot and will be unavailable for board meetings for some time. The company plane was nearby that explosion in Minot. We lost three employees and two were injured. We lost our head of security Frank Jorgen, and two pilots. Will Fiskins and Jim Gardino, our COO were injured but will recover.

"I will leave it to you gentlemen and lady to connect with Mr. Carmichael in the hopes of finding a time when the board can meet with a proper quorum."

Rollie Winston, red in the face stood, "Ms. Goldstein, I think we would all have preferred it if you had warned us of Mr. Carmichael's absence and this quorum issue before we wasted our time coming here today. This is most inconvenient. We're all very busy people and provide our time to this company at great expense to ourselves and our other business interests."

Winnie remained seated, "I'm sorry sir. As you can imagine things are in a bit of flux because of the recent deaths and injuries of several of our key executives in that plane crash. I had very little time to prepare for this meeting and just in the last few hours I heard of Mr. Carmichael's unavailability. Then I only discovered in the last few minutes waiting for you while reviewing the secretary's duties and the company bylaws that we didn't have an official quorum so again I apologize for this unavoidable inconvenience."

The female board member, Lucie Coultard spoke, "Ms. Goldstein, of course we understand your predicament but you must understand that we all have significant responsibilities and only one of those is the welfare of this company. I do hope Fraser isn't avoiding us. He made some very outlandish announcements to the press including some very large financial commitments and I'm quite certain none of the board was informed or consulted in advance. Even the CEO has limits on financial commitments. Please get a message to him immediately that the board would like to meet with him in person at his earliest convenience. I think in this case a call-in on his part would be unacceptable to most of us. You understand there are Securities and Exchange Commission issues here and the company is exposed so this meeting cannot be put off for long."

Several of the other board members nodded.

"I'll do my best. Please excuse me, we're rather busy at the moment," she said as she closed her laptop and hurriedly left by the rear door of the boardroom.

***

As the time for his meeting with his cabinet approached Turcot realized he had been running hard and was less prepared for this meeting than he wanted. He couldn't share anything of Alpha with them and he hadn't had time to think up a complete and convincing cover story either. In his new 'circumstance', he found more and more he had to make up lies just to get through the day.

His heart seemed to be racing as he focused again on the specter of aliens arriving at any moment and zapping all life out of existence. This load would cripple most presidents. After all, up until a few days ago, the job as president of the most powerful country on Earth had been comparatively straightforward. Now the presidency had been turned upside down, all the normal trusted advisors were out-of-bounds and he was left to wing it alone. No amount of preparation would have helped in this case.

The press briefing was only a couple of hours away and he was sure that with their combined efforts he would definitely be put on the spot. Suddenly his confidence waned and he felt on unfamiliar ground, and completely unprepared for the encounter. The press could be like a pack of wolves and there was definitely the scent of blood in the air putting them into a feeding frenzy. The White House press corps were the cream of the crop from their individual media outlets and there were lots of them. They were either proven veterans or favored up-and-comers trying to make a name for themselves by catching the President in a lie or feeding him a 'gotcha' question that was so awkward he looked like he was hiding something when he tried to walk a tightrope on a politically correct answer.

Sadly, he who could make the President squirm created the news snippets and sound bites and got lots of kudos from their colleagues. That was the way to move up the ladder fast. The sides were nearly fifty to one when the inevitable sparring started. His biggest fear was one of them catching him in one of his many lies about the project.

Mary had gathered his inner circle in the Cabinet Room. He had State, Justice in the form of the AG, the CIA and FBI directors, Defense, NSA, Treasury, Commerce and Homeland Security all represented by their respective cabinet members except of course Defense where Otto Harding, Deputy Secretary of Defense was standing in for the recently deceased Dan Westgate.

Kyle West, acting Chief-of-Staff sat directly next to the President with the VP on his other side. Jim Knowles, press secretary, sat just behind him.

The White House photographer and a media pool photographer took a few pictures of the meeting that would be released to the press, highlighting the President and his cabinet staying in lock-step over all recent developments. The President nodded to Kyle to clear the room so he could start the meeting.

"Well ladies and gentlemen it has been a very busy few days. Let me just jump right into it and bring you up-to-date with what has been happening around here. We all need to be on the same page."

CIA Director Bill Carter sat forward in his chair. Maybe now he would get some answers as to what was really going on. He seriously wondered if there was something the President would say that would provide any kind of explanation as to why the recording he had locked up in his desk bore no resemblance to the completely different classified scenario that had been put out on what had actually happened that night.

A quick call earlier to the 'fired' Gerry Hastings had provided no new information. Gerry was nervous, upset and confused as to how things had gotten so crazy, so fast, in his relationship with Turcot but when asked for his version of events, he had offered nothing different from the classified narrative. That meant he was either a brainwashed victim of events, a co-conspirator, or the audio recording was bogus which left Carter right back where he started.

Still Gerry's sudden and puzzling departure was additional evidence that something very strange had happened that night.

Turcot was still talking, "Before I start let me remind you that this is all classified and the narrative we have given the American people is necessarily quite different than the reality. There have already been leaks on this matter and because of that, we now have something of a crisis with the Chinese so I need to ensure everything I tell you here stays confidential.

"The other night I was hosting Fraser Carmichael and that miner who escaped from the mine collapse out in Idaho. It started out as just a photo session and some small talk but grew into something much larger as I will get into in a moment. Just as we broke up Dan Westgate entered and briefly shook hands with Mr. Robert Glass whom he seemed to know. Some of you know Dan and the Pentagon had some suspicions about a possible discovery and had been monitoring the goings-on at the mine.

"After they left I noticed immediately that Dan was looking very ill and agitated. Within a minute or so he seemed to have a complete breakdown and pulled out a gun. I've no idea where the gun came from."

Bill Carter made a mental note. The evidence showed that the only gun in the room appeared to belong to the Lt. Colonel. Where was this gun the President spoke of? How did Westgate get it into the White House where only the Secret Service, military on special assignment like the Lt. Colonel, and the SEAL team could carry weapons? No one had recovered a second weapon in the Oval Office and no one had reported any stolen weapons. He sensed with increasing horror that some of this was being made up on the spot by Turcot. That, or again brainwashing to make him believe that.

The President continued, "He ordered Gerry Hastings, in my name to call for the nuclear football and then held all three of us at gunpoint while he commenced to set up a launch. There was no opportunity to alert the Secret Service and I'm sure a few of us would have died, had we tried. It looked to me like he knew where he could be observed through the windows and planned it so no one outside knew what was going on. I have been told recording devices were not working so he must have done something to them before he entered."

Bill Carter took another note. Gerry Hastings claimed there was a third recording system in the Oval Office that only he was aware of until the President indicated he knew of it. So how did Westgate know of it and how to turn it off?

Turcot continued, "I think we all thought the missile wouldn't launch somehow with all the checks and balances in the system. I didn't know then that NORAD and the Pentagon couldn't override the football once it was activated.

"In his incoherent mutterings we came to understand that he had some problem with Mr. Glass and intended to bomb the mine in Idaho. No one knows why. He knew where in my desk I kept my key and the launch codes. We all stood there a few feet from him, frozen and frankly scared to move. He was completely out of his mind and could just as easily have killed us all. You know the rest. He tried to launch the missile but something out in Minot backfired and it exploded in its silo killing hundreds in the immediate vicinity."

This had been really bothering Bill. Not only was there the mystery of the secret bug and the competing stories of what happened but a highly secure atomic weapon had somehow armed itself and detonated in its silo basically saving America from what might have been an even worse scenario. That in itself was thought to be impossible on top of all the other impossibilities in this puzzle and there was no way that was a coincidence.

This was all linked somehow. Every piece of it was impossible yet it had happened. The story the President was recounting, which was the internal classified version, had giant holes in it. It was lie on top of lie meaning that there had to be an even chance that the audio he had stashed away was at least part of the real story. Whatever or whoever was behind this was unbelievably sophisticated in their capabilities and he visibly trembled at the thought.

The other scary thought was that this event, whatever it was, was more likely only a piece of something bigger. Surely the ultimate goal of conspirators at this level could not have been to wipe out a tiny town in North Dakota? But that just raised the terrifying question of what the real target was.

Turcot continued, "Of course that is not the story we have been forced to create for the outside world. We don't want Americans, or the Russians and Chinese for that matter, getting the idea that one man can snap and launch nuclear weapons. We will come up with a better plan to secure these weapons but for now the story is that a maintenance procedure went bad.

"I haven't heard yet what the autopsy showed but it must have been some significant brain trauma that caused a psychotic breakdown. When he realized he had failed he seemed to completely lose it, grabbed his head and keeled over. I think he died instantly and all attempts to revive him failed."

Carter wanted more, so to kick it off he asked the first question, "Was there no way to rush him? I mean there was an armed Colonel in the room right?"

"No. Dan was standing near the door to Gerry's office and as they entered, the Colonel was disarmed with a gun in his face."

Carter had been right. The President was in fact claiming there was a second gun in the room which no one else knew anything about. The question remained, how did Westgate get a gun into the White House and more importantly, how would you get rid of the gun once you're dead? Either Westgate had an accomplice in the room or Hal Turcot had just made up the second gun story. The only accomplices could have been Gerry Hastings, the Lt. Colonel or Turcot himself. Still Turcot had never suggested one of them was involved in smuggling a weapon out of the room.

As Bill looked around the gathered staff he realized he was the only one there who knew enough details of the event to catch Turcot in this probable lie. The only other one with enough detail to question this narrative was the President himself, so now it seemed more likely that the President was in on this subterfuge than a victim of some kind of brainwashing. The audio in Bill's possession was now looking more like a possible witness to the actual events around the Minot disaster.

Turcot was still talking, "There was no way to rush him. He kept us at a perfect distance where he couldn't miss us with a shot and we couldn't get to him in time to disarm him. In retrospect maybe all three of us should've rushed him but one or more of us would likely have been killed and you don't know your willingness to sacrifice your life until it's staring you in the face. I for one did not find that kind of courage within myself. We were all simply frozen waiting for an opportunity that never came and I think we were all hoping that Minot would cancel the launch somehow or that NORAD would override it once they saw the target, but now we know that the system is set up so that they can't override it. Something we need to take a hard look at."

Carter sat back so as not to draw too much attention to himself fearing the President would see something in his face revealing his disbelief in the story. If this investigation had been perilous before, it just became much more so.

If the President had been brainwashed and thought he was speaking truthfully that Dan Westgate had done this alone then the recording had to be doctored or everyone involved brainwashed. But if the recording was real and Turcot had been driving the launch, then he was either lying or again, brainwashed. That meant dozens of people in NORAD, the Pentagon and the White House had to be lying with him or brainwashed. This still made no sense. And who jimmied the missile to make it explode? How was that part even possible given the military security around that ultra-secure remote site? That probably meant there had to be co-conspirators with access to the controls in the missile silo.

Turcot continued, "Only people such as yourselves or other Top Secret cleared people know the truth so I need you all to reinforce the public story and watch out for rumors such as the one going around the Senate that got to the Chinese that they were the target.

"The military are working hard to find out what went wrong at the silo but they have no ideas yet on how that happened.

"Listen, I don't have much time. I would love to stay and discuss this more but I must prepare to meet the press soon. You now know everything I know about that terrible accident. Let me move on to the deal with Carmichael.

"I think him showing up with this young guy Glass, who by the way is beyond impressive as a person, was just a ruse to get to see me alone. As you know, he and I are definitely not friends and I can't see myself granting him an audience if it wasn't for his offer to introduce me to the young Mr. Glass, who has captured the hearts and minds of Americans over the last month. We did get a photo-op that you might have seen."

Turcot went on to explain what he had heard and seen during his interview with Carmichael and why he had jumped on board with the idea for the F-47, finishing with, "There is a real national security concern and opportunity here. For now he has it all locked up at one of our secret military bases but who knows if he has a backup somewhere else. So Bill, the CIA should do what they can to track down his secret labs and overseas operations and decide what we need to do to protect any of those facilities from falling into the wrong hands."

Bill wondered if Carmichael was the clue he needed here. Two things Gerry Hastings had said came to mind. That the whole night had revolved inexplicably around Carmichael and the miner before and even after the missile accident and that the whole F-47 thing had been hatched in that one single night. All these amazing things happening in the same room in one night might be related in some way. He'd have to take a closer look at Carmichael and his project. But he realized that he was just adding more variables to an equation that already had no solutions.

Turcot was still addressing the room, "So, Carmichael being the consummate capitalist came prepared with a full pitch. Basically he would fix our fiscal deficit gap and give me funds to support the social programs I can't get Congress to move on. Although, as you know, he is one of these Republicans who are always harping on the 'handouts to the takers'. So that part of his pitch must have been hard for him to swallow, but he is a salesman after all.

"The main complaint of the Republicans has been expenditures and the growing deficit. Well that argument is now gone and I want to put pressure on them to move on programs such as STEM grants to American students who will register and graduate in the technical subjects which is key to our future. We must ensure that not even one grant goes to an illegal or an overseas visiting student or we'll get fried politically.

"In the meantime, I'm a second-term President who can't run for office next time around, and I'm determined to get something done even if I must go around this do-nothing Congress. So I signed an Executive Order canceling quite a few Air Force contracts and awarding a sole source contract to Carmichael for the next-gen fighters. Congress won't like it but I have all their arguments covered.

"On the subject of money for the changes to the two fighters, over ten years that's close to a trillion dollars. From what I've seen, our operational costs estimates for the new fighter will be much lower too, given the quality and maintainability I expect out of Carmichael. His new computer not only optimizes the manufacturing process but also tweaks the design to make the fighter easier and much cheaper to maintain.

"So as you see, it was a deal I couldn't pass on. Even if it turned out to be a massive hoax or he fell on his face, all we are looking at is possibly a three-month delay on the new fighter. We've already survived much longer delays in weapon systems and nothing that has been done cannot be undone. The cherry on the cake is that we give a big black eye to all those military lobbyists on the Hill who get things their own way all the time."

The Commerce Secretary was the first out of the gate, "Sir, if I may, the elephant in the room is that Congress will not let you get away with any of this. It upsets the applecart in so many ways. Even the Democrats are dependent on military spending in almost all of their states and if they aren't affected by these cancelations they'll surely see the writing on the wall that you've declared war on military contracting. There is no question we must find ways to reel in military spending in favor of social development but these changes will be seen as rash and even reckless.

"You have awoken a sleeping giant in Congress. They may be a 'do-nothing' Congress now but just wait 'til you see how fast they move on something like this. I don't think impeachment is out of the question. You're risking being driven out of office and your VP will become President for the next two years." He looked around the room at some startled faces, "I'm sorry, but with all due respect sir, someone has to put that particular stinking fish on the table."

Frank Osgoode had been an almost invisible VP and blushed as attention turned to him. Osgoode was a 'do as your told' type but several suspected he might spur on the idea of impeachment in the House where he had many old friends. There was no way he was going to get elected as the next President but this impeachment idea was a strategy Congress would support because they all knew Osgoode could be made to return things to the status quo. A couple of Executive Orders and life could be set back to normal for the massive military industrial complex.

The President smiled, "As to Congress, bring it on. I'm doing this for the benefit of the American people and I trust in their judgment. The big mouths in Congress are going to have to go up against the American people and promised tax relief if they want to take me on. And frankly, they don't scare me anymore. I'd rather go out fighting than whimpering.

"So I want and demand the support of everyone in this room. I don't want to hear about any back-channel griping going on. You're either on my team or you're not. If you find you can't support me in this then you need to do the honorable thing like Gerry Hastings and resign your position."

The look of shock was universal around the table. Some thought to complain about the open threat, but thought the better of it as they all worked at the pleasure of the President and, at the end of the day he was the elected one, and he deserved to be surrounded by people who believed in his vision. But he was asking a lot and this demand was very unlike Hal Turcot. They had never seen this 'in your face' style from him before.

The question for all of them in the ensuing hours would be, would it be better to stay and hope for an impossible outcome, or leave now and save their careers? They all knew they had to make up their minds fast because it was likely a microphone would be thrust into their face very soon, where they would be asked on camera by some sharp reporter if they supported the President's plans.

Hal Turcot felt he had delivered the message he wanted and stood to leave, "Kyle, I need you and Otto for a few minutes in my office."

He turned and exited leaving a stunned room. What shocked most of them was that he hadn't gone the extra step and demanded an on-the-record, up-or-down indication from each of them in terms of support before he left the room. This was a high-wire act indeed. He had no assurances from his senior cabinet members that they were on side. They were free to walk out of the White House and declare him a madman if they chose. That showed either complete confidence or amazing political recklessness on his part.

The truth in fact was very different. Hal Turcot didn't care which side of the argument they came down on because he had a different sense of the timing. Much bigger concerns had his attention now. He had only weeks to worry about his presidency, and a desertion of one or two wouldn't mean much in the big scheme of things, even if they did fry him in the press. Whether or not he had them on record as supporting him, they could be made to look like traitors if they mutinied and again timing was everything.

His little dog-and-pony show in front of his cabinet was simply to arm them to talk to the press and avoid the possibility of them ALL resigning en masse. Now at least the most loyal ones would stay the course and give him the cover he needed.

The most confused man leaving the meeting was Bill Carter. The President's bravado in the meeting had only stiffened his resolve to get to the bottom of a situation that was not only confusing but terrifying. Something happened in the Oval Office that night. A mass murder eclipsing anything since 9/11 had likely been perpetrated and no one was being held accountable. That or a phony recording was on a USB flash drive in his desk and either scenario was shocking. But neither of those theories addressed how a highly secure nuclear weapon could be jimmied. He just didn't believe in a coincidence of this magnitude. Somehow the events in the Oval Office and the missile backfiring had to be connected, but how?

He would have to redouble his efforts to get to the bottom of it. The problem was that it was so big and consequential that senior people had to be involved because the President was either behind this or a victim of it. He didn't know whom he could trust, even within his own organization.

His only hope at the moment was that the Air Force would come up with some explanation as to what had happened in that silo. That might lead him to who or what was behind all of this.

Conflict

Kyle West and Otto Harding followed President Harold Turcot into the Oval Office.

The President turned to face them before he reached his desk, "Gentlemen, please take a seat."

Kyle was relatively new in the White House and had been forced into Gerry Hastings' Chief-of-Staff role very quickly. He was intelligent and competent, but in his early thirties, quite young for such an enormous job. Hal Turcot suspected he would have to coach him and Mary would be a help too.

Otto Harding was another story. He was a career Defense Department wonk. In his fifties, he had come up through the ranks and probably handled half of Dan Westgate's job before his sudden death. His loyalty might turn out to be a challenge given his linkages to the old guard in the Pentagon and lobbyist groups.

The President addressed them as one, "The two of you are key to the success of the next three months. Kyle, I want a lid, as much as possible, on any Executive Orders until I signal the information can be released. I've made a few in the last couple of days but there are likely more to come and I don't want them broadcast until I'm ready. Only those who need to know should be informed and they need to be told to keep it quiet too. Clearly there are some changes where people directly affected by any order might tend to leak it for political purposes, but see what you can do to minimize that.

"Otto, I know you haven't had much time to grab the reigns at Defense but I need you to run interference to make sure we stay on plan. One area we're likely going to have problems is patents and IP.

"As you well know, for national security reasons, all government contracts like the ones for the F-47 have clauses that allow me to cancel any contract and to build anything we want by ourselves or farm the work out to others. We always insist on owning or controlling the design, patents and the intellectual property for all military procurement. That's a safety valve so the weapons cannot be sold out of our control and so that in times of war or great need, we can sidestep manufacturers and farm out manufacturing to additional suppliers or in fact to anyone we choose. In this case we may have several instances of this.

"Take the engines for the F-47 as an example. If Pratt & Whitney can't furnish enough engines for these fighters or meet the quality specs then I'm going to give Carmichael the green light to build them himself. I'm sure his robots can manage it. There would be an issue if we used standard off-the-shelf P&W engines, but there is always some customization for each fighter so we need to use that wedge to deflect any patent or copyright challenges. Either way, we have the right to build our own special engines."

Harding was shocked, "Sir, you think Carmichael could tool up and build engines in time? It requires all sorts of specialized equipment. They even have specialized plants for some of the components. It takes P&W months to build an engine and likely many months to set up a production line. I don't see Carmichael making any of that happen any time soon. Hell, the titanium and ceramic turbine blades alone in any jet engine are a major specialized manufacturing undertaking in themselves. They have their own dedicated design and fabrication facilities just for turbine blades."

Turcot was becoming impatient, "An old-style production line is what they have set up over at Pratt, not a next-generation autonomous robot line driven by the world's smartest robots and the world's biggest computer. And besides, that's Carmichael's problem. As far as I know he is going to buy whatever he can, such as hydraulic pumps, tires, avionics and of course turbine blades or even whole engines. He needs to spend his time on the assembly of the fighter but if he cannot get delivery of quality components to meet his goals and he needs to build canopies, or ejection systems, or glass cockpits from scratch, he has all the design documents under non-disclosure and he tells me he can build them all himself," he lied.

"I had to yield to that demand given we've demanded an impossible delivery date and he's funding it all. He can't build P&W engines and sell them commercially outside of the program but our terms and conditions on military equipment allow me to let him do it for this program."

Otto could see the boss was not getting it, "But sir, he's a competitor to many of these companies. He builds drones and cruise missiles and they have engines too. If he has access to Pratt's design docs he could steal key patent-protected technology. They'll never stand for it. I know in times of war we can brush that aside but vendors will scream bloody murder if you start allowing their competitors to see their detailed designs, never mind build an advanced capability to compete with them on their own products."

"Listen Otto, two things. One, I've signed Presidential Findings on this," he lied. "I've declared this as an urgent need to fill the gap left by the F-35 fiasco. I intend to give Carmichael whatever he needs to meet that deadline. Secondly, these companies have been raping us for years with their overpriced components. Their investors are sitting fat and happy on the backs of the middle class who can't make ends meet because of all the taxes we collect to pay these leaches for the overpriced crap they dump on the military. I'll bet if Carmichael had to, he could build a P&W engine for a fraction of what we pay now.

"But don't get all excited. If Pratt & Whitney can deliver the engines or any other supplier delivers their stuff in the right numbers and the right quality then we don't have an issue. Anyways he can only build stuff for this project so he is not going to be competing in the market with anyone."

Otto knew he was on thin ice trying to argue with a President who seemed more liberal and anti-business every day. "Sir, I must warn you, ever since your press announcement I've spent ninety percent of my time on the phone with Senators, Congressmen, lobbyists and major manufacturers. They're all lined up against these moves which they see as a complete power grab by the Executive Branch, and throwing a monkey wrench into a system that's working.

"Stomping on intellectual property rights and patents is guaranteed to push them over the top. As soon as this gets out they'll have buildings full of lawyers petitioning the Supreme Court. Maybe CII can't use their designs to compete with them in the commercial market, but Carmichael is still going to see all of their trade secrets and how do you put that genie back in the bottle?

"These guys are all interconnected and belong to multiple industry trade groups, so any move in that direction will spread like wildfire and you'll bring the full force of the industry down on you."

The President, hands on hips, was growing quite frustrated with all this pushback, as Otto pressed on, "Remember most states get a big chunk of military spending, so right there you have most of Congress and the Senate lined up against you even if some of them are liberal Democrats who want to see defense spending reeled in. Just not in their state and not while they're in office. We have a system that is working and everyone out there is against any unilateral change."

Turcot straightened showing his impatience, "You think I'm not aware of this? What you don't get is that I'm determined to stay the course. And as a matter of fact, the system you speak of is NOT WORKING and I mean to change it. Now, I need a team helping me on this 24/7. Do I have your commitment to support me or should I hurry up the job of replacing Dan Westgate, leaving your name off the list? Are you in or are you out?"

Young Kyle had been watching this quietly and wished there was a rock he could hide under. He had never seen Turcot dress down a cabinet member before. Clearly Otto was new to the job and most likely temporary, but this ambush on the part of the President was very uncomfortable to witness. None of the staff, including his old boss Gerry Hastings, had ever indicated Turcot could be like this.

Otto paused for a moment blushing beet red. This headlong rush of the President's was much worse than he had suspected. On top of everything that had already been announced, the guys on K Street were going to have a total fit when they heard about a plan that might brush aside intellectual property rights including patents. Hell, they'd probably storm the White House when this got out, yet his sworn duty was to support this President in good times and bad.

Gathering himself he finally said, "I work at the pleasure of the President. In all honesty sir, I'm very concerned about this direction and I can't see it working, but that's for this room only. I will drive your agenda right up to the point where I can no longer and then you'll be the first to know. I owe you that much. I don't like the two-faced operations of some in Washington so you have my undivided support and loyalty. But I won't shut up in this room about the challenges and what we're up against. You are the elected leader and you get the final call."

"That will do for now," was all the President had to say.

They seemed to be at an awkward moment staring each other down, so Kyle jumped in, "Sir, I've never been read into the new fighter program and given I'm holding down Gerry Hastings' chair I think it would be helpful if I knew something about it."

The President hesitated still staring at the outspoken Otto and finally turned to Kyle, "Otto here will bring you up to speed but essentially it's the first 6th-generation fighter which means it's a big leap over the F-22 and the F-35. In terms of outward appearance, it looks more like the F-22 than the 35 which had a body shape issue due to the vertical takeoff demands of the Marines. The 22 was a better starting point and for the first time we'll have a fighter sporting canards."

Kyle looked puzzled, "Canards?"

The President smiled, "No, nothing to do with mistakes or ducks. Canards are small highly maneuverable winglets near the cockpit. The Chinese have them and most of the recent Russian fighters use them. Among other things, they provide for very high maneuverability at low speeds. Unlike the competition we have relied solely on vectored thrust for maneuverability on our most recent fighters, which is just what you want in higher-speed scenarios but with the expected developments in ground-to-air defenses and low-speed ground support combat missions, we find that we now need the canards to get out of the way of incoming missiles. The Russians and the Chinese use both vectored thrust and canards for low-speed maneuverability but until now we thought high cruise speed and over-the-horizon kill technologies with smart bombs and missiles from high altitudes combined with stealth was the ticket.

"But recently the biggest need has been for close air support and ground attacks against mobile terrorists which often means going much lower and slower where we're very vulnerable to shoulder-held missiles.

"Let's say you're doing close ground troop support. Even though we have great stealth as far as radar goes, newer surface-to-air missiles or SAMs can track heat, radar and even movement with their latest vision systems.

"So if an enemy gets off a shot, our first option is a new kind of flare that is super-hot, radar-attracting and now sends out a large smoke screen to try to defeat the tracking of the missile. If that fails we have a system in the 47 that calculates the close rate and just at the right moment does a modified blackout button routine with the aid of the canards to basically step out of the way of the incoming missile. You can repeat that move even if the SAM reacquires the plane, until the missile runs out of fuel. Just like a bull fighter stepping out of the way of a charging bull."

"What's the blackout button?"

Otto took over, "The F-22 was the first to have it. In an emergency where a missile is closing the pilot can hit a button that executes up to a twenty-two G U-turn depending on the speed of the fighter. That causes the pilot to black out and the fast moving missile to miss.

"The plane can take that many Gs but he can't. The plane then flies straight and level until he wakes up and takes control again. There are very few pilots that have ever tried it and no one wants to volunteer testing it again, so there was always concern they would wait too late or not press it at all.

"Even a one hundred and fifty pound, fit fighter pilot in a form-fitting seat suddenly weighs more than three thousand pounds. Apart from blacking out, that does nasty things to your body and you're likely to be off work for a while if you're lucky. Also the turn isn't a guarantee that the missile wouldn't be able to reacquire while the pilot is snoozing, and firing two missiles at a calculated gap might catch the fighter in level flight before the pilot awakens.

"With the canards and putting all of this under the control of the plane's automatic defensive systems, we predict much higher theoretical survival rates. At lower speeds it doesn't have to be a twenty G turn to sidestep an incoming missile. That's the theory anyways, until they come up with missiles with their own canards, bigger steering fins and better tracking software I guess."

The President jumped in, "You might have seen those popular YouTube videos of the more advanced Russian Sukoi fighters doing backflips, frontflips, flat spins and the like with the use of their canards. Well slow-motion dogfights where you might want to use that will be rare we feel but not so the close ground support requirements.

"The highest vulnerability of fighters is landing and takeoff because they are low and slow, so a guy, five miles off the end of a runway in Afghanistan, might just get a shot off while the plane is coming in for a landing or taking off. If you remember they got a DHL cargo plane and a C-17 in Baghdad. To avoid that we prefer using aircraft carriers or bases in friendly countries far from the front lines and guys with anti-aircraft hardware.

"Now with this technology we can base them closer in and do jobs like fast-response close air support that was problematic before. The step-out-of-the-way thing works just as well during takeoff and landing.

"Of course the Firebolt has many more advances but from the outside the canards will set it apart from anything else we've flown.

"So back to the project at hand, you two are critical to making sure Carmichael achieves his deliveries. The very fact that we have the first ten Firebolts flying and more on the way will put the Chinese and the Russians back on their heels for a few years and give us some breathing space. The fact that he saves us loads of money is icing on the cake. So you see this is a win-win for the Air Force and the American people and when they see that, it will be tough for Congress to take me on. That's the major reason this all has to happen so fast.

"Now I must get moving. Kyle, ask Jim Knowles to join me so we can go over my remarks to the press," he said looking at his watch.

"Otto, I'm counting on you! Don't let me down," he said, his finger poking in the air at the man's chest.

***

Andy McPherson was antsy since he had seen the planeloads of workers coming back from Area-51. His new career was going nowhere unless he could find a juicy story so he figured it was time to pay that bar at the airport a follow-up visit. He had gotten the impression from the first time that Wendy's was a late afternoon watering hole for some of them so he waited until just after five p.m. hoping to see if anyone showed up.

The door opened after he had been there about ten minutes and a chubby fellow entered. Immediately three of the men Andy had guessed were workers from up north rose and greeted him, "Hey Charlie. Where you been? Man we miss your food. Best gumbo outside of New Orleans."

Charlie joined them at the bar, luckily within earshot of Andy.

He seemed to be happy to see some familiar faces, "Still workin', still cookin' up the best chow in this godforsaken desert of a state."

One of the men seemed surprised, "You got a new job already?"

Now it was Charlie's turn to be surprised, "No, I thought you knew. I'm still up there. I didn't get furloughed. They still have to eat and I guess word had gotten around about my grub so they decided to keep me and a couple of the kitchen staff. But now the whole place is filled with military guys with all that formal salutin' and shit. Hey you guys are still under non-disclosure right?"

One of them patted him on the back, "Yeah sure, don't worry about that. We know we have to keep our mouths shut," he said in a barely audible whisper, "So they brought in troops? Are they doing our work?"

"No way. The day you all left they cleaned out the big hangars and stuffed everything into the little one down at the end of the flight line. From what I've seen and heard from the troops, there is no one in the hangars. All the guys up there are on security detail and man are they taking it serious. I can't walk anywhere without getting challenged. They're all staying on the base in those barracks. The kitchen staff are pretty much the only ones coming and going. I almost had the plane to myself this afternoon. It's Kathy's day to do dinner. They put a small puddle jumper on the route just for me and a couple of my guys. I noticed our old 737s still sittin' off to the side over at McCarron."

"So what are they doing up there?"

"Hell if I know. There are weird sounds coming out of the hangars like I've never heard but I've never seen anyone coming or going from there except this one guy. They're flying in lots of stuff though, maybe too much for a couple of fighters. All I know is I see it all in big containers going into the hangar closest to the admin building. I overheard someone call it the staging area but the only thing I've seen is this one guy driving a tug and towing containers in and out of the other hangars. I think it might all have something to do with that billionaire guy Carmichael and probably he has all those robots he talked about in there. I swear I saw him in the mess one night talking to this other guy and according to Kathy she thinks he might be that guy they rescued from that mine up north.

"There are certainly no new faces on the grounds except for the guy that met with Carmichael. The guy is a weird cat too, will only eat oatmeal and honey, turns his nose up at all my creations even though the troops love the stuff like you guys did," he said mocking a pout.

They all laughed as he continued, "There's even more weird stuff goin' on up there. They're flyin' in so much cargo 24/7, much more than when you guys were up there and I'm getting all of my supplies from these big cargo jets they're flyin'. I overheard one of the cargo handlers sayin' there was too much material for even a dozen new planes but who knows.

"Just this morning one of the pallets of food set off the radiation alarms when they brought it in through the loading dock behind the mess. I had them check it out but they said it was very low level and it wasn't dangerous to anyone.

"I'm told those alarms were installed way back in the fifties when they were doin' underground nuclear testing a few miles away and as far as I know they've never been used. I almost jumped out of my skin when that damned horn went off. At first I had no idea what it was. So I'm askin' myself, how come the food is radioactive?

"Then get this, I'm unloading these big restaurant-sized cans of tomatoes we use in soup and pasta dishes when a couple of knives stick to the cans. Turns out all the same cans that are radioactive are magnetic too. The stuff inside seemed fine but the cans are all really magnetic."

"Did you tell anyone?"

"Not yet but what are they goin' to do, demagnetize them somehow? Doesn't affect the food as far as I know. Worked out fine though 'cause I have a couple of the cans on a shelf right over the grill and I keep all my clean utensils sticking on them," he said laughing.

"Wow, and you say there's noise coming out of the hangars but no workers in there?"

"Yeah, that's right. Man if they've replaced all you guys with robots then you're screwed and last I checked, robots don't give a shit about good gumbo," he said laughing.

Just then one of the two interrogating Charlie looked over at Andy noticing that he was close enough and may be listening in. Andy took a last sip of his beer, nodded to the four of them who had now all turned and were staring at him, and he promptly left the bar.

He drove down the side road a few hundred yards and pulled off into an area where he could park.

If he was right, Carmichael had installed his robots in record time and they were already busy building F-47s at Area-51. He took out his phone and Googled 'materials radioactive magnetic' and within a few minutes he figured the best explanation was 'rare earths', which he recognized from his materials research days. Another couple of minutes and he had it. His memory was correct; rare earths were materials that were semi-metals in that they had some of the characteristics of metals and some of non-metals and they could be both magnetic and mildly radioactive. A little more research and he found that they might be used in small quantities in electronics, engine parts, and lenses. The cook had said they had infiltrated his food products which had to be on a different pallet and likely in a different shipping container. That meant there was either a large quantity or they were super-concentrated and highly refined. Certainly not what you would expect from tiny amounts in a few components buried deep in an engine or some electronics.

A little more research and he found out that rare earths were found usually in ores in almost every part of the world with China having the biggest commercial deposits by far, and some of the rarest ones. Apparently China had cornered the market on almost all of the rare earths. He remembered from university that they were difficult and dangerous to mine and even more difficult to process. Each processing plant had to be custom built to get the most out of the local ore.

He thought to himself, 'why would Carmichael be bringing lots of rare earths into a site to build F-47s?' From what he knew and had just researched, there were miniscule amounts of the stuff in certain components but nothing that could explain large quantities, enough to contaminate a nearby pallet of cans of food. And why so much material being flown in?

Well whatever it was, he was pretty sure now his hunch had been correct. The project the President had alluded to, and the contract awarded to Carmichael, was all happening about a hundred and fifty miles north of Vegas. As always, everything out of that base was secret, but all of these changes and the strange clues had piqued his interest. The press were desperate to get to Carmichael to find out more about his 'Harmonized Manufacturing' but Andy suspected there might be a bigger story to do with the rare earths and excess cargo. Either way, he had to find a way to get an exclusive.

***

Fraser Carmichael had congratulated Winnie on her excellent handling of the board situation. He had forgotten about the stipulation that he had to be present for the meeting to be called to order. He was still trying to avoid them for the moment, so he had been working from his penthouse in New York for a few days, when his cell phone rang showing it was from CII.

"Sir, its George Williams from the ops center. We had a call from an Andrew McPherson. He's a reporter from the Las Vegas Review-Journal and he claims to be writing a story about you and an Area-51 which he claims is a secret military base north of Vegas. I assumed this might have something to do with your new military project so I decided to alert you."

Carmichael simply said, "Go on."

"He says he knows what you're doing and he knows about the 47s and the … 'rare earths' from China, whatever that is. And also that the weight totals don't make sense? I've no idea what all that is, but he says you might want to give him an interview before he goes to press with what he has."

Carmichael hesitated only a few seconds before answering, "Ignore him, but it was the right thing to alert me. If you hear anything more from him let me know," and he hung up.

After thinking for a moment he called back to his ops center, "Tell security I want a full run up on that reporter and I want it pronto."

***

A few more days had gone by and the natives seemed restless again so President Turcot decided it was time to take some pressure off Jim Knowles and take over the press briefing for a change. He realized he was the best one to get his message out there and keep the wolves at bay.

The press felt Turcot was avoiding them so when he walked into the briefing room, questions were still focused on the A-bomb and how could such a thing have happened with all of the safety interlocks. He even got a question on whether he was considering unilateral disarmament after such a tragic accident and his remarks from outside the hospital when he visited Minot.

As the briefing went on he sidestepped most of these questions with his fallback position that it was still under investigation, that the US needed its nuclear arsenal as a deterrent and again expressed his condolences to all affected by this horrendous accident.

The questions then moved to the fighter jets and became more aggressive. For the first time the word impeachment was put on the table by a reporter from FOX News, "Sir what is your reaction to some people on the Hill who think you've committed an impeachable offense by scrapping the F-35 and assigning military contracts without the due process of a full procurement cycle?"

The President hesitated before answering to a suddenly hushed room. He decided to have a little fun and to do something he had never had the guts to try, "I love these questions about 'some people on the Hill'. Would you care to elaborate? Which people … or is that total speculation and you just made that up?"

In a hushed room, the FOX News reporter was stunned, caught off guard, clearly red in the face and embarrassed at the pushback and could think of nothing to say, to the delight of many of his contemporaries who had him pegged as a lightweight hack. The thing with gotcha questions was you needed a fallback position.

Turcot waited just long enough and then continued, "I thought so. But let's give you the benefit of the doubt. Any challenge to my presidency would have to be based on a violation of the Separation of Powers doctrine and I think most constitutional experts will agree that the Executive has all the power it needs to affect the changes I've made. Moreover I think the American people all realize that you don't have to spend as much as the next ten players combined in defense to maintain a lead. Ideally you just have to spend more than number two but I would never propose going that far. I want the strongest military in the world and I want them to be the best equipped.

"We're simply making sure we get the maximum bang for our buck. We'll have even better fighters than we originally planned and we'll have them faster but at a reasonable price. One that will allow us to spend more in areas where we no longer lead the world.

"The changes I've made will still have us spending more than at least the top five or six nations in the world combined so I think there is no reason to pass up on an opportunity to save a trillion dollars, reduce our deficit, invest in our future, and give a tax break to Middle America. To extrapolate on something a famous Republican, Everett Dirksen once said, 'a trillion here and a trillion there, and pretty soon you're talking real money.'"

The Press Gallery to a person was scribbling as fast as they could and the network anchors had the couple of sound bites they were hoping for.

"I'm making these changes within the powers of my office and they are the right moves for this country. It is incumbent upon government to spend the peoples' money wisely, so I call on Congress to enact the legislation I've requested that reduces our deficit, gets tax breaks to those who need it the most, begins to make major investments in our future by making college affordable once more. It gives students a real incentive to register in the STEM fields where our future is the brightest, and where jobs with the best salaries await.

"And most important, we need to retrain our existing workforce for the jobs of today and allow them to earn a wage while they're learning.

"Congress are the ones who need to act now to remove this excess spending from the Pentagon's budget and redirect it because our Air Force doesn't need it any more but our deficit, our middle class, our students and our displaced workers do.

"You've all seen the very positive polls on my announcements so let me say today that if the legislation Congress comes up with does not have some version of all the elements I've just outlined, I will veto it. In my opinion this requested legislation is a no-brainer. I've done the heavy lifting by securing the savings and the American people demand that Congress does its part. What are they waiting for?

"Now if there is anyone over there on the Hill that thinks I have overstepped my authority I would urge them to check with some constitutional lawyers and then if they are still unconvinced, I say, bring it on. Otherwise, do your job!"

At that he stepped away from the microphones and exited the room swiftly as reporters screamed follow-up questions.

He was back in his office and turned on the TV. To his dismay the only sound bites they seemed focused on was his referral to other nuclear powers as 'players' as if it was some sort of game, predictably the 'trillion here, trillion there' quote which they seemed to give him some credit for, the veto threat, the 'What are they waiting for and do your job!' quotes and finally the 'bring it on' phrase where they likened it to W's famous bravado with the 'Bring 'em on' taunt to Iraqis attacking Americans during the Iraq war.

He had been hoping for a bit more empathy from the press and disappointing as the coverage was, his attention quickly returned to why he was making these changes. He activated the device which blocked any listening devices and dialed a number he had recently memorized.

Fraser Carmichael answered his iPhone, "Yes Mr. President."

The President assured him, "We're on a secure line so we can speak. I don't know if you saw that press conference but between the press and my own cabinet I'm not a very popular guy these days.

"But more important, you heard Alpha-1, these aliens could be here anytime and that worry trumps keeping our jobs which in my mind is no longer a long-term goal, so please tell me you're keeping up your end of the bargain and we're making stellar progress out west."

Carmichael hesitated. Until what seemed like only a few days ago he hated this guy and now they were in business together. He was still having a hard time dealing with someone he considered half moron, half weakling and mostly wrong-headed on just about everything, but he reminded himself reluctantly that he had to put all that aside. They had to work together and he was just going to have to find a way to do that, even though the more he thought about it the more he despised the man. Even thinking about the man made him nauseous. Part of him still wished he could scream to the world that this nut had blown up hundreds of his own people in Minot.

"Listen Turcot, calling me isn't going to make this thing go any faster and believe me, I haven't forgotten about the aliens, how could I? I can think of little else. But to answer your question, I've only been out there once so far and this Alpha-1 character seems to be true to his word and has everything under control. We're in contact almost hourly with his steady stream of demands for materials.

"All the robots and manufacturing gear for the fighters and the space weapon were due to arrive as I left. Hawkins seems to be behaving. I saw the beginnings of the site for the space weapon which is massive out on Groom Lake about a quarter a mile from the runways and if I had to guess, he's on schedule, but every time we talk he too is quick to remind me that they could be wrong on an arrival date so we must make this work with zero delays.

"He has me running off my feet trying to keep up with his demands for materials and frankly I'm starting to have big issues with paying for it all. Also, it's not like I can delegate this to anyone, so essentially I'm his logistics guy these days, chained to my computer screen, chasing materials, POs, and shipping manifests all over the world. I would like to get out there again but my chain doesn't reach that far.

"By now on his end, they must have the F-47 production lines up and working. All of the operations were to be 24/7 and there is no question Alpha-1 is focused on the urgency and will do whatever it takes to succeed, even if that puts some humans in jeopardy. As far as I can tell he hasn't killed anyone lately.

"I spoke to Hawkins yesterday and he says Glass drives himself really hard and needs to remember to eat and sleep. Apparently he is putting in really long hours, sometimes all-nighters. Remember he has two projects out there and he must be splitting his time between the hangars and that massive invisible dome he built on the lake bed.

"Other than that I think things are progressing as he planned.

"Oh yeah, and he wasn't too impressed with the fact that you canceled the F-35s without talking to him first. I must tell you that it doesn't make sleeping at night any easier when you're going off plan like that."

The President let that one slide, "Listen, clearly I can't jump on Air Force One and wing it out there to check on progress and I can't ask the Joint Chiefs for a briefing so I'm counting on you to keep me in the loop. My big challenge will be staving off impeachment for the next couple of months or you may be dealing with the VP, who to appease the Hill will likely cancel everything at that base and we can't have that. My cabinet and FOX News have already put impeachment on the table and we're not much more than a week into this."

Carmichael interrupted, "In the vein of potential obstacles, a reporter out of Vegas has somehow pieced together a few data points and is asking some awkward questions. He seems to have figured out that not all of the shipments into Area-51 are for the fighters or at least there is something mysterious about some of them. How he did that I have no idea, but I'm pretty sure he doesn't have much. There must be a leak out there but my best guess is he's speculating and trying to get me engaged to confirm or deny his suspicions. It's not like I can call Hawkins and ask him to start an investigation for a leak because if he heard the rumors on shipments he would start investigating that too.

"Normally I'd expect you to put the FBI or CIA on his tail but we can't do that either. What would you tell them was the reason for investigating the guy? There's a high likelihood they would find out little about him, but more about his theory that something is going on out there that isn't above board, and we don't need your security services snooping around on this. I'm sure you have your hands full just keeping the military out of our hair.

"So for now I have asked my security people just to do some background on this guy. At least they'll have no way to look into any of his accusations about Area-51."

The President reacted quickly, "I see your point but this is more than alarming. We can't have a reporter snooping around. Somehow we need to neutralize or eliminate the threat this guy represents before he stumbles on something more tangible. We absolutely cannot let that happen. Keep me informed. We can't let this thing get loose on us. We need to take any and all measures to contain this and if that means involving the CIA with some cover story to get them involved, then so be it. So if you get to the point where you think this guy is a tangible threat, I'm your first call."

Carmichael wondered if he was reading the President correctly. He hadn't thought of taking the guy out. Apparently for the President that was a possibility and he suddenly saw the side of the picture that a sitting President has to deal with when thinking of national security. He had never come across a situation in business where killing an obstacle or kidnapping him had ever come up. Not only that, Turcot had gone to that scenario pretty quickly. Maybe he wasn't as much of a wuss as Carmichael thought he was. Still he was shocked and wondered if he had actually read Turcot properly.

They signed off committing to staying in touch daily on developments.

***

As time passed, Carmichael was still hiding out in his penthouse in New York handling everything by phone and his laptop. Several voicemails had been left by a couple of the board members but he had ducked even listening to most of them.

That and the stress of the developments of the last few weeks had finally caught up with him and he was frazzled. It was times like this that he realized that being completely alone in the world with no family or significant other to lean on was a major handicap. He had a few occasional girlfriends he could call up for some 'company' on short notice but the 'project' had kept him too busy to even think about a social life. Besides what help would a confidant be if he could confide nothing?

He realized also that he was putting Carmichael Industries in great jeopardy without the approval of his board and he was going to have to face them. Given the SEC exposure it was going to have to be sooner rather than later. The filing he had approved for the SEC was holding for the moment but it would not survive any scrutiny. He had put off facing his board far too long already.

He knew he couldn't tell them the unvarnished truth so he was going to have to come up with some plausible and very convincing story for the whole thing. These board members were all very accomplished in their fields and could probably see right through any story that wasn't airtight. He wondered if Alpha-1 or even the President had any appreciation of the predicament he was in. Unlike the President who could order staff and the military around, there was no giving orders to a board of this stature.

Normally he wouldn't be worried about them but this situation was different. Up to now he had had his way with them but the commitments he had made in the press needed board involvement. On top of that, the massive material purchases his company was making would eventually be leaked to the board by some do-gooder, likely in his finance department. Delaying facing them only made matters worse.

The board had pretty much always given him carte blanche on his business dealings due to an almost flawless track record, but this was way beyond what he could expect them to leave completely to him with no explanations.

He had handpicked his board to impress Wall Street when he took the company public and they were heavyweights in industry which was definitely a two-edged sword. Their own reputations were on the line and he knew that was paramount in their minds. He had to give them some sort of cover for his moves or he'd be faced with either a board revolt, a vote of non-confidence which would replace him at the helm, or mass resignations on their part. None of these would do the stock any good, but Alpha-1 was the much bigger issue. What would he do if Carmichael's hold on the company was to come loose?

Any of these scenarios would also alert the Securities and Exchange Commission who would likely launch an investigation and he couldn't have the SEC in on this either. Even a cursory look at the financials and contractual arrangements around the project by either the SEC, the external auditors or even the board would be disastrous.

He had to head that off so he realized he'd have to polish up his song and dance routine, call a board meeting very soon and pitch a great story.

This life-changing 'thing' coming out of a mine shaft in Idaho had been completely unexpected and very stressful on many levels. He felt he was no longer in control of his own destiny to the point that he now found himself hiding in his condo and hardly sleeping at all, which just made things that much worse.

He was taking orders from a being that could kill him if it wanted and he was being forced to work with that moron Turcot. On top of that he was putting his biggest investment, Carmichael Industries International, in jeopardy with what by now amounted to well over a hundred million dollars in purchases with no immediate revenue to support them. Worse, he saw no way to reduce the stress. It wasn't like he could dump the project, resign his position, take off on a vacation or even confess all his concerns to a therapist.

Still, there were rewards to be sure. The promise of world domination in manufacturing with the new technologies was indeed exciting but still Alpha-1 had indicated that wouldn't be open-ended. At some point its plan was to level the playing field by leaking information on the robots and the quantum computer to other countries and even his domestic competitors. It was up to Fraser to make the best of the early start. His thinking was that when that day came he would take the promised exit to 'heaven'.

As to the project, according to Alpha-1's plan, with zero labor cost and flawless execution, his company was bound to make obscene profits on the first ten F-47s. Yet the up-front materials bill was for both the fighters and the secret space weapon and it was mounting fast. Alpha could probably drum up cash but how would he explain where it came from. A money laundering investigation would not help.

For the short term the project was a massive drain on the company's resources. Fighter jets, it turned out, used very expensive components, space weapons even more so. He had tried to offload some of the expenses by directing purchases through other subsidiaries and even some private companies that he owned. That meant he was funding some of the project out of his own pocket. Much of the time in his Manhattan condo was spent liquidating personal assets and moving money around to cover the bills Alpha-1 was racking up. Still his hope for a positive outcome and the promised rewards made it all worthwhile.

Yet unless he could affect delivery of the jets and declare revenue, there would be no offsetting effect on the company's P&L which would cause the stock to tank, even if only briefly. In the event that he couldn't declare revenue, he would have to be prepared to explain a massive unforecasted negative deviation from plan to the board and Wall Street and that was never easy, simple, welcomed or a positive influence on his reputation. His newest and biggest fear was that the fighters would be perfect, but Congress would drag its heels beyond his fiscal year end on approving the acquisition just to penalize Turcot and CII.

There was no way he could get any guarantees up front as Congress was against the whole strategy from the start and without a contract with Congress he couldn't even declare deferred revenue. The plan was that they would have to buy them if they were flying around the capital building but that didn't mean they couldn't hurt him badly with a few well-placed delays. His only hope might be to weather the storm if the board and the market saw he had a winner, a large Finished Goods Inventory number, and that it was only a matter of time until the revenue flowed. Still Wall Street could be ruthless with missed targets.

Just to add to his problems, this reporter out west was sniffing around and had some damaging information. He was pretty sure that much of what he claimed to have was speculation, still it sounded as if there was a leak. These reporters always tried to convince you they had much more information than they actually had to force an interview and then they'd try to trick you into confirmations or denials on complete guesses on their part. He knew the tricks well and usually avoided those types of interviews, but in this case the stakes were enormous.

Somehow between Alpha-1, the President and himself, there was no way they could allow someone to snoop around and piece together a story that something more than F-47s was going on in Nevada. He would have to stay close to this issue. It was a pretty good bet that the reporter didn't have enough to go to print, but his interest in rare earths was alarming. Best to let him stew for a while until CII's security team had a chance to thoroughly check him out.

As he looked at his stock tracker on his iPad he noticed the stock was already down ten percent based on the nervousness left after his press conference where he flat out told the world he was taking a gigantic leap of faith with his new government contract by funding it from internal resources until complete. He had been forced to leave out the details on the duration of the contract due to its Top Secret nature. Still he would have to share some unclassified version of it with the board.

The board, he reasoned from the few voicemails and emails he had looked at, must be going out of their minds with angst so he called

Winnie Goldstein and asked her to call an emergency board meeting at the earliest possible time. At the same time he asked her to track down security and tell them he needed that report on the press guy out west.

It had taken a little time but now there was no question in his mind that Alpha-1 was telling the truth. The fact that he was putting in all-nighters out west demonstrated Alpha-1's own angst over the situation. The survival of humans was at stake whether it was from the approaching aliens or Alpha itself, if the President and he himself were somehow unable to comply with their part of the deal.

Never in his life had the stakes been so high, death of the human race on one hand and life in a real heaven on the other.

'If only I could get a full night's sleep, without two different sets of aliens zapping me,' he thought to himself.

Telling a Story

The President's days were almost completely occupied by hosting Congressmen and Senators in the Oval Office and trying hopelessly to convince them he was on the right path. If they were not in his office they were on the phone and occupied almost all of his time. So much so that he realized he was really neglecting his other duties and none as obvious as his wife and terminally ill daughter.

His announced 'plan' or cover story, even he had to admit, while it had been well rehearsed by now, was weak and had holes you could drive a truck through. One area he had no good answers for was the fact that he was putting tens of thousands out of work in the defense business with no strategy to replace the jobs in the short term and all his antagonists knew it. To make things worse, there were still no 'Work while Retraining' programs coming out of Congress. No surprise there. They would throw every obstacle they could think of in front of him to try and derail his plan.

His defense that deficit reduction, tax breaks and promoting STEM education were the upside of his strategy just wasn't cutting it and Congress had made no move to implement these offsets either. But he had no choice, Alpha-1 needed Area-51 and so the cover of robots building super fighters was a necessity. The shelving of the F-35 added some credibility to that part of the story and did give him the deflection of the deficit reduction as a legitimate goal, but it was that move that had cost so many jobs in the short term. In retrospect, the F-35 thing was probably a badly timed political mistake, but he was stuck with it now.

His strategy for the moment to avoid impeachment was to be available to both sides of the aisle trying to find allies and gradually he got better at the narrative he had invented.

Part of the game in politics when you were losing was just to keep the ball in the air. Don't let it hit the ground. Don't let anyone make any final decisions. Keep inventing distractions to keep your opponents off guard, give your supporters something to parrot and hope the neutral players would think the jury was still out.

That tactic had worked for years for the tobacco lobby and more recently the climate change deniers and creationists; stall, stall, stall, and keep everyone thinking the jury was still out. Paint it as an ongoing controversy, or unresolved science, years or even decades after the facts were settled.

He was even losing at this juggling game, and more of the people he had been able to count on in the past seemed to be deserting him. Either it was the fact that, like the good Senator from Massachusetts, they had massive military spending in their state which also translated into big campaign financing from special interests, or politically they all smelled a failing cause and like rats were abandoning the ship.

The word impeachment had now made its way onto the mainstream networks and print media. None of them save FOX News was promoting the idea but all were speculating that only a massive shift in public opinion could stem the tide moving in that direction.

So it was a welcome relief when the day finally arrived when he was able to turn his attention briefly to a different aspect of the job, international relations.

Violeta Michaud, the three-term Liberal Prime Minister of Canada was in town for a prearranged meeting and was going to do the usual photo-op in the Oval Office just before a private thirty-minute meeting with the President and a State Dinner recognizing an upcoming anniversary of NAFTA.

Vi, as she was known to many who knew her, was a mixture of French-Canadian and Japanese parents, and as well as being quite the looker, she was a real political power, punching well beyond her weight on the international scene. She had been in power in Canada for more than a decade and had established excellent relations with the right world leaders.

Her unusually high international credibility stemmed partly from the fact that she had done a good job domestically for Canada but it was her stature as an articulate, charismatic leader that had really put her on the international map. She was immensely popular in her own country and Americans loved the straight-talking beauty who seemed to be able to speak her mind and yet never pay the price from her critics who were often afraid to take her on, given her political prowess. Being very photogenic, she seemed to always be on the cover of magazines and was often seen on the red carpet at various awards events.

She was singlehandedly credited with the modern approach to Islam, its followers and the various nut jobs who hid behind it. Her rhetoric and leadership on the subject had set the Jihadists back by defusing their argument that the West was in a war with Islam. Her message was so succinct that many politicians and even internationally known modern Imams had taken up her mantra and in no small way she had led the way in neutralizing the terrorists' rhetoric.

While she hadn't always been in lock-step with the US on everything, she somehow seemed to come out on top on most international issues. One speech she had made to the UN on yet another round of aid for Haiti and other pathetic economies had been the oratory of legends and actually had topped out as a greatest hit on YouTube. Her name had been rumored a few times for the Nobel Peace Prize but the right international calamity hadn't presented itself where she could engage in some fashion and prove her mettle.

After the perfunctory photos in front of the fireplace in the Oval Office, the room was completely cleared as she had asked for a personal session with the President, sans staff.

Once the room was cleared and they were settled, the President opened the dialogue, "Vi, on behalf of the American people I want to personally thank you and your nation for all the assistance you've offered in North Dakota. I know you still have teams of utilities groups on the ground from as far away as Winnipeg, Calgary and Toronto. That help is surely welcomed. And at the same time I was very pleased to see you didn't make a big thing of all that radiation passing overhead. We dodged a bullet with a warm front and a helpful jet stream I gather."

"Thank you Mr. President. I think you know that the assistance and gratitude goes both ways. Our utilities groups in particular have always helped each other after disasters. Just in the past decade there have been at least a half dozen major ice storms where we've helped each other out. That's what good neighbors do, so thank you for the gratitude but that goes both ways."

Abruptly she seemed to take over the conversation, "Hal, let me move on. There is a personal matter I wish to discuss with you, so if you have the capability I'd ask you to turn off any recording devices. I think it would be best for both of us."

After a long pause while he stared her down the President went to his desk and activated the device Alpha-1 had given him. This was an unusual request in that generally world leaders discussed important international matters that the State Department needed to be fully briefed on, and generally discussions between leaders needed to be preserved for history but she had said it was a personal matter, addressed him as Hal and there was something in her facial expression and tone of voice that conveyed that this was not a trivial request.

As he returned from his desk he said, "I think you know that this is very unusual but I can assure you we're completely dark now in terms of recordings."

Vi sat back on the couch facing the President as he retook his seat across from her. Remembering he knew some French from growing up in Louisiana, she started, "Hal, nous sommes des amis depuis longtemps, non?"

Turcot simply nodded agreeing to their long-term friendship as she continued, "Back in the days when we first met and you were the Governor in Louisiana, I thought we established a certain kinship and a very open relationship. From my perspective we've always agreed on important matters and when we haven't, we've been comfortable with each other's position. I also think you know I have a reputation for speaking my mind and I see no reason to be other than forthright in this case. So please excuse me if I seem somewhat direct but we're about to discuss a matter that is very close and personal to me."

The President nodded, "You're right. We have been friends for a very long time." He wondered what was coming next. He had a sneaking suspicion and he wondered why he hadn't thought of it earlier.

She stared at the floor for only a second and then started, "This is a delicate subject but we absolutely must clear the air.

"I think you are aware of this matter as your security services would surely have informed you that your recently deceased Secretary of Defense, Dan Westgate and I go way back. Back to McGill University in Montreal where we both did our undergrad studies. He and I were something of an item back then and frankly we never lost touch. Neither of us ever married nor wanted to but when we entered politics in our respective nations, things became a little more complicated and we agreed to be discreet about our infrequent rendezvous.

"We would normally meet three or four times a year at one event or another. I'm sure you know of this and I'm equally as sure that you trusted him and hopefully me, to keep the business of our two countries out of that relationship."

Hal Turcot simply nodded.

She continued in a strong and confident voice, "To make a long story short, I saw Dan at the Defense Ministers Conference at Montebello near Ottawa two days before he died. Your Secret Service and my CSIS guys of course knew of this and I must assume you knew about it too. I was the keynote speaker at the event and as it was late, I decided to stay over and spend some time with my old friend, discreetly of course.

"What you may not know is that in our normal banter he informed me that he had just finished his annual medical two days earlier including a full body CT scan and was given a clean bill of health. I knew him to be in excellent physical condition, so this did not surprise me.

"So not to put too fine a point on it, he didn't die from a brain hemorrhage, or at least one brought on by a health condition. That, and knowing him far better than most people, I don't believe the public story that there was simply a maintenance error in Minot or the internal 'real' story that he tried to launch a ballistic missile at Idaho and I now believe there was something much more sinister about that evening."

The President was shocked that the Canadian Prime Minister knew the classified story then he remembered the total integration of American and Canadian forces at NORAD. Still there was a pretty good chance her CSIS spy agency had picked up confirming details. And here she was with additional evidence that even the classified story was a ruse. Only Alpha-1, Carmichael and he knew the real story. This woman with her outstanding international reputation could prove to be very dangerous. She could easily blow the whole thing out of the water, yet he suspected only the best of motives.

She continued, "Dan Westgate was a much greater loss to me than anyone could know and believe me when I say I'm very angry personally that he seems to have been caught in the middle of something and at least internally has been left to take the blame for such a catastrophic event. He was as close to me as any husband could be."

She paused to gather herself, "Now I'm a big girl and I know things happen at our level that need a comforting narrative, so I can see where a dead man might be forced to take the blame. I could of course make something of a stink about this including putting my

CSIS guys on the hunt for answers but I see that not offering any solution for either of us.

"I think I can still call you un ami proche and I think you know of my discretion. So as a good neighbor but more importantly as a grieving lover, I'd like to know directly from you and in complete confidence, what the hell happened that night? How did he really die and why did Dan have to take the fall for it?"

She sat there with just the hint of a quivering lip and glassy eyes waiting for an answer as ideas rushed through his head.

He had great respect for this woman, especially for the way she was handling this. She was right, he also considered her a close friend and she was definitely in a position to blow at least the Dan Westgate thing out of the water.

That and probably everything else attached to it.

If Dan had indeed had a full medical just before his death, and Turcot had no reason to doubt her, then Dan's doctors must have been forced by someone to lose the records and forget the results of the medical over threats of some sort. He did have what appeared to be a brain hemorrhage, which was likely inexplicable after just having had a clean CT scan.

Until this moment the President hadn't been informed of the CT scan issue with his doctors, which could be deadly to the accepted classified narrative if it ever got out. In addition, while Canada and the US swore they were not spying on each other, both leaders knew some of it went on and there was no telling what her CSIS guys might be able to dig up or whether any activities they engaged in would pique the interest of his own CIA.

With the little data she had, she had already pieced together the fact that the classified story was also a ruse and there'd be no convincing her otherwise.

Vi Michaud was a different kettle of fish than Westgate's doctors. There would be no intimidating this woman. He could see the grief in her eyes, now that he knew the full dimension of her relationship with his old friend. A crippling grief that she had been forced to keep to herself.

Yet he didn't want to do the same thing to her that he had done to her lover, invite her into the inner circle only to see her eliminated, to contain the knowledge of Alpha and the threat they all faced.

She was still waiting for a response and could see the President was struggling with something.

He finally looked into her eyes and spoke, "Vi, you're right. We have a friendship that goes back a ways and we both have responsibilities that we take very seriously. Let me start by thanking you for addressing this matter in the fashion you've chosen. These are extremely delicate matters and your discretion is appreciated much more than you can know.

"Let me also say that I'm inclined to tell you some of what you want to hear but only if I have your complete assurance that no one else will EVER hear of this, especially your intelligence services. I understand you have responsibilities to your nation but I want your assurance that what I tell you will never, ever leave this room. You must take any information I give you to your grave. To give you some idea of what is at stake, let me say that the survival of your entire nation and mine as well as the rest of humanity depend on your commitment to secrecy on this matter. Your own immediate survival and mine are linked at this very moment to this secrecy."

Apart from being shocked at his response and what she saw as an unveiled threat, she could see the gravity of the matter in his eyes and she was instantly sure that this wasn't a politician's rhetoric. It was a fellow human dealing with a monstrous secret that had to be preserved.

After a long pause, she nodded and said, "What can you tell me?"

The President took his time. He wanted to appeal to her with enough information to stop any investigations or spying.

"The day Dan passed, I became aware of a threat to our entire civilization. By that I mean the human civilization, not just the West. As we stand here today, only Fraser Carmichael and I are aware of this. No one else in the world is aware of it. That is why you've seen the unholy alliance he and I have formed.

"The threat is external and there is a plan to combat it but part of the issue is that no one else can know about it for reasons I can't even begin to explain. I made the mistake of bringing Dan into it to assist me. Dan by the way was a very good friend to me too for decades and I was shattered by his passing. The mistake of bringing Dan into it cost him his life and I'll never forgive myself for that.

"I can't go into those facts more but I was with him as he

sacrificed his life for this cause. I can assure you his death was quick and painless and entirely my fault for involving him. He died a hero in service to humanity. So now you know my reluctance to share any details with you. I cannot put others in the same jeopardy that I stupidly did with Dan. As I'm certain you appreciate, I'm personally racked with remorse over the position I put him in and his resulting death. I cannot repeat that mistake by involving you."

She couldn't stop a tear from rolling down her cheek and she quickly brushed it away.

Turcot averted his eyes for a moment and then continued, "I won't get into the details of the Minot explosion as frankly that is a tangential matter but you can be assured by me that Dan wasn't responsible. If there is a culprit in that matter it is me. Dan died heroically trying to defend us all but you're right, we needed to deflect attention and sadly Dan has been called to make a final sacrifice, to take the blame for something that is mine alone."

Vi was suddenly aware that her mouth was hanging open and closed it.

He paused to let her gather herself.

"The next-generation fighters and all my other controversial decisions of late are also a diversion or decoy from this matter."

"The threat is immediate and should peak in the next two to three months. There is absolutely nothing beyond what I'm doing that the planet can do to prepare or defend itself. This is all on me and Fraser Carmichael. That is all I can say that will not jeopardize your life and mine. I only hope and trust I have not gone too far already with you."

Vi sat there staring at him and internalizing this horrific picture the President had just outlined. The picture he painted was an extermination event that for some reason had to be kept secret. She realized from his cautions that asking questions was both a waste of time and treacherous.

She assumed from his words that the threat was from space or maybe one of those theoretical calamities like the Earth's poles reversing or something. Most likely it was a world-ending asteroid collision but that didn't explain why knowledge of it had caused Dan's death, or why no one else could know about it.

Still, she believed what she had been told and didn't want to push a threatening situation any further. He had said he may have gone too far already. Her intent in getting to the truth of her lover's death did not include sacrificing her own life. He was very clear that both he and she could die simply by drawing her into it. She had enough respect for this man to know that he had already pushed the boundaries as far as he could on what he could tell her.

After a very long time with the two leaders internalizing where they were and simply staring at each other she said, "What can I do to help?"

The President finally offered a smile, "I'm so glad you asked.

"One major threat to our plan is either me or Fraser Carmichael losing our jobs and control of our action plan. He needs to stay in charge at Carmichael Industries and I cannot be impeached because bringing Osgoode into this would spell disaster. The wolves from the Hill are closing in and I only need to stay viable as the President for another two months or so. After that I don't care. Hopefully the world will move on never knowing what this was all about, with or without me as President."

This really drove home the message if it wasn't already totally real for her. This man was sacrificing everything he had worked his entire life for, just to stay in office for two more months to complete something that was critically important to the entire world. This made her even more curious, but statements like she had just heard, from the most powerful leader in the world, in this very office, had to be taken seriously and she was just going to have to bury her curiosity.

Turcot continued, "As I know you are aware, you have a wealth of credibility and lots of political clout, frankly much more than the size of your nation would dictate. So anything you can say to the press out front to give me a bit of a breather might help with public opinion and delay the impeachment hawks."

"You got it," she said.

"Is there anything more you can tell me about this threat?"

The President thought for a moment, "No, I'm sorry I may have gone too far already. Please just trust me. I absolutely have your best interests, and those of the entire world at heart. And please, let me assure you, there is no possibility of America taking any kind of advantage from this."

She let that sink in, "Your plan. Is it solid or should I rush back and go to confession before I meet my maker?"

The President smiled, "Nothing is certain but my hope is that we have a better than fifty percent chance of weathering this threat."

She was shocked, "Wow, then confession it is."

They wrapped up their conversation and she took the very unusual step of hugging him hard as she left the Oval Office saying, "God speed et bonne chance mon ami! Someday, if we get the chance we should raise a glass to our wonderful friend Dan Westgate."

He simply nodded. The President's already deep respect for this powerful woman had just jumped a full notch. She was willing on his word to do what she could to help, even though they both knew she had a responsibility to her nation to protect them and any other PM might have forced the issue on that basis. He realized suddenly that this conversation couldn't have happened with any other world leader. Their relationship of mutual respect built over years had made all the difference and he was thrilled to see, that even in a case such as this, they remained close friends. She was again his favorite politician in the world.

As predicted there was the usual press scrum in front of the White House with a bank of microphones set up. Her reputation as a very photogenic, straight-talking world leader who on occasion made headlines with her pronouncements, had the microphone racks filled.

She stepped up to the microphones as the first press person yelled out, "What did you and the President discuss?"

The President watched her performance from the TV in the Oval Office.

She smiled, "I had a delightful meeting with the President. As usual we discussed a range of issues important to our two nations. The President thanked the Canadian people for their assistance on helping to get Minot back on its feet and of course we discussed the situation with the F-35 fighters as Canada was one of the first nations to sign on to an acquisition of the fighter to support our NATO and NORAD commitments as well as enforcing our sovereignty in the North. We've taken delivery of about half of what we ordered so it will be critical to fill the gap with something new, not too far down the road.

"On the subject of the F-35, let me say that I have tremendous respect for the President's initiatives to reel in uncontrolled military spending. While your military dwarfs ours in spending, we're tightly connected through NORAD and the many military exchange programs we have with the US. We've fought side by side in many battles. Our militaries are very highly integrated which means we share some of the cost challenges you have. This is unsustainable for the both of us and it has taken a true leader like Hal Turcot to take on that cost structure as he has.

"Anyone who tells you he has weakened US military posture is lying to you. You all know the US spends more than the next ten countries combined and the military industrial complex, with the help of their lobbyists and lackeys in politics, have had a stranglehold on your economy for the last half century.

"Between Hal Turcot and Fraser Carmichael, they're going to show the US and the world a better way to balance the needs of society as it pertains to both security and social progress. I salute the President for his bold and courageous decisions.

"Now I don't usually meddle in the internal affairs of other countries but let me just address the elephant in the room that the press seems afraid to pursue. Americans need to take a close look at who is bankrolling their politicians. Your recent Supreme Court rulings have opened the flood gates to special interests, and even foreign governments openly buying votes in Congress. You all know this. Hal Turcot has tried to get you all to realize this troubling and let me say, self-evident yet much under-reported fact.

"What you may not know is that this fact, more than almost everything else, sets you apart from the rest of the world. No other Western country has to deal like you do with the vagaries of the influence of lobbyists and unlimited campaign financing. If politicians are literally being kept in office by the defense industry then they are a big part of the problem of why this country has been slipping backwards in its social agenda and you all know that it has. You know the stats on where the US sits with respect to wealth imbalance, K-to-twelve education, incarceration rates and gun violence as well as dozens of other social dimensions. You no longer lead the world in any of these dimensions and I would think that would be something you would want to reverse.

"Much like us, your infrastructure is in need of a major overhaul, and you still have not established universal healthcare like everyone else in the developed world. Don't take this from me. The President has spelled this all out for you and people must start listening to him. The rest of the world 'gets it'. This money in politics is by far your biggest blind spot and it's destroying your country.

"As a nation you're being bled dry by greed, the uber-wealthy and special interests and those are not my words. They are the words of your visionary leader, Harold Marshall Turcot.

"From one good neighbor to another, you need to get your house in order and get behind your President on this. You've been waiting for a generation for a leader who will put the common man first and now you have him and he only has two years left to deliver real change. It's time to fight off the nonsensical and thinly veiled misinformation campaigns and get behind the leader you've always needed and only you, the press, can do something about it.

"I hold you, the press, completely accountable for all the confusion and misinformation out there. You need to cut through all of the lies and misdirection and do your job; investigate and report only the truth and call out the lies for what they are.

"Fair and balanced does not mean tip-toeing around the truth, regurgitating bald-faced lies or reporting recycled, debunked nonsense, and you all know what I'm talking about. So to the press in your country and mine I say you need to get back to the job of reporting the truth, the whole truth, and nothing but the truth and shame on those of you who do not."

Leaving a shocked and virtually breathless press scrum behind, she briskly turned and marched to her waiting limo, screaming reporters now chasing her with follow-up questions.

This was unheard of. No foreign leader since possibly another Canadian, Pierre Trudeau, had ever spoken their mind in such a forceful way on American soil and even his rebukes to both Nixon and Reagan had paled in comparison to the diatribe she had just unleashed.

The press loved this even though she had pointed a finger directly at them. This was revolutionary. No world leader had ever had the balls to speak their mind on US domestic issues and on the White House grounds of all places.

Turcot realized the right-wing press in the US would hammer her likely as 'the wicked witch of the North' or the 'frozen bitch from nowheresville', but not as much as the Canadian right-wing press who would kill her over meddling in US affairs and seeking the wrath of right-wing American industrialists who had significant sway over the

Canadian economy.

The TV networks caught her exit from the White House grounds with a backdrop of about half of the Press Gallery running, clapping and waving like a bunch of school kids at the Queen on her exit. A scene that was so unusual it would make up a good part of the coverage in the following days. FOX News covered it hourly with aspersions to the 'liberal press' and their adoration of the current champion of socialism and extreme liberal rhetoric and focused heavily on the unbecoming and arrogant interference in US domestic issues.

The President smiled as she made her escape and made a mental note to send some anonymous roses to 24 Sussex Drive in Ottawa. She'd gone way beyond the call of duty and while this was invaluable to him, he knew she would face a firestorm on her return to Canada from her conservative opposition.

Coverage of her remarks was on all of the political shows and news channels with the general consensus that she had overstepped her bounds but had said what was on the minds of many Americans. Many agreed that the press had to take a hard look at themselves, their frequent misguided attempts at 'fair and balanced' reporting where they had to admit they had been caught reporting nonsense, conspiracy theories and the like, and their lack of focus on campaign financing and the role of lobbyists.

A snap poll showed predictable results. About a third of Americans, almost exclusively bicoastal and northern Democrats thought she was a bold leader, had hit the nail on the head and wished she could run for President of the US after she was finished with Canada.

Another third almost exclusively southern and mid-western Republicans wanted Canada invaded, a wall built to keep out the crazy northern liberals and all financial aid to Canada cut off, even though there never had been any. And the last third never watched the news and had no opinion or even thought Canada, if they were so unhappy should secede from the union and give up their statehood.

But there was enough of a groundswell in calls to Congressmen, the polls and in the press that it set some of the purple state hawks on their heels for a spell. They were all conspicuously absent for comment to the press and did their best to hide until the dust settled on this unexpected detour on the road to impeaching Hal Turcot.

She was a tough act to follow and no one wanted to address her specific points made on the White House lawn. What were they going to say, the US was better than Canada and she should keep her mouth shut? This is of course exactly what went out on the airwaves from FOX News who were the only ones who felt they had to attack head-on the big-mouthed elitist from the wildly liberal and cowardly 'British Colony' to the north.

The incessant calls to the President to explain his moves took a major hiatus and for once he was able to get back to his normal activities if even only for a few weeks until the pressure to impeach him started growing once more to a fever pitch. All the time he was praying progress was steaming ahead on their two projects for the fighters and the space weapon.

The Gang of Three

Three nights after Vi Michaud made good her escape back to Canada, a third unremarkable black SUV pulled up to a small vacant warehouse in the shadow of I-95 in Baltimore. As with the other two armored SUVs, the main occupant left his driver/bodyguard and smart phone in the car.

As the man referred to only as Number 3 in these meetings entered the building, the other two making up what a very few people knew as 'Concierge Services' were seated at a card table at the far end of the abandoned warehouse. It was a rare occasion for these three to meet in person so Number 1 and Number 2 stood to shake hands as he approached.

Number 1 spoke first, "Thanks for meeting here gentlemen. This is the kind of thing that has to be dealt with face to face. We all need to be on the same page and there are just too many ways for others to intercept our communications otherwise. By the way, I had my man scan for electronics so we're all clear."

Number 2 spoke, "I agree, there are some things we need to deal with face to face with maximum stealth if you know what I mean.

"So, I had a feeling it would come to this. My guys are furious and screaming for action. They're all over their Congressional guys but rebuilding support for impeachment after Michaud's command performance is only half the problem. There's the issue of timing. They figure it will take a month or two or even more to get him out of there and that is unacceptable. They're all wondering what more damage is he likely to do before they can dump him."

Number 1 spoke, "Our side is in agreement. I'm under tremendous pressure to make something happen. As usual no one wants to put it into words but I think we all know what they mean by action. Only in this case it's the big guy himself."

It was Number 3's turn, "I see no way around it. They pay us to do the really dirty work and we all knew it might come to this one day. There's no getting around our responsibility in this case. No one else is positioned to do anything about this. If we don't act, no one will trust us again. We get paid the big bucks for exactly this type of eventuality. So I see no choice in this matter.

"Without saying it, our guys think if he's taken out, Osgoode would be sworn in and he'll easily commit to undoing this nonsense and booting Carmichael out. Carmichael is not the issue. With Turcot gone his board will be his problem and they'll take care of him by turfing him when he loses the deal. Therefore he's a non-issue for us.

"You both represent multiple industrial and lobbyist organizations as do I and no one wants to get their hands dirty so there is building pressure for us to just get this done fast before official requests need to be made and that means the risk of leaving trails that can be followed. I don't think any of us wants anything like that so we just need to get on with it. Our clients simply want him to go away with no fingers pointed at them."

The other two nodded agreement.

Number 3 continued, "So it's decided. We must move and we have to move fast. I have the right guy for this job. He's offshore but I can have him here in a day. This guy is a unique pro so we must leave it all to him or believe me, even though he knows me under a code name, if we try to track him in any way, he will find us and take us out. So his mandate is to get it done under his own secret plan so we can have no schemes to take him out after, and then he disappears without getting caught, agreed?"

The other two nodded.

"This is a pricey one due to his exceptional expertise and the fact that he may have to disappear completely for years. It'll cost a million each so I'll expect the deposits overseas as before."

The other two nodded, stood, shook hands and headed back to their vehicles.

***

Bill Carter, CIA Director, had been putting in even longer days of late. His tiny team of senior analysts working on monitoring the Joint Chiefs typically reported directly in to him after hours and he was reviewing the file as he waited for his key man who'd called in asking for a short meeting.

He had not shared the recording he had out of NORAD and he still had no idea what it meant or what he was going to do with it. He still could not understand how the digital recording could have been intercepted, decrypted, modified with the President and Westgate's clear voices, re-encrypted with the same keys and put back either in NORAD or on CIA's file servers after it was sent to him. He had listened to it half a dozen times and was even more puzzled than before. As a precaution he ordered a second copy from Tech Services to verify it had not been hacked on his end and decided to wipe any trail by ordering them to delete the original.

The only other scenario he could think of was that the President, the Lt. Colonel on duty that night with the nuclear football and Gerry Hastings were all lying and that thirty-odd people in NORAD had been brainwashed into the narrative of Dan Westgate busting an artery and trying to launch a missile. Again this was a crazy scenario but the recording clearly had the President pulling the strings and even sitting through the countdown.

He also knew that the Air Force still had no idea why the thing had detonated in its silo.

None of it made any sense but one conclusion was unavoidable. Something very big, very dangerous and very criminal had gone on that night or was still going on.

He closed the file just as Phil Harris, his key man on the operation walked in, "Good evening, Mr. Director. Sorry I'm a bit late. I was putting out a fire over at Bethesda and I thought you needed to know about it."

Bill frowned, "Say more."

"Turns out the coroner who did the autopsy on Westgate had requested his medical file and there is a CT report in the file from two days before his death showing a clean, normal brain scan. Apparently he had a full annual medical at Bethesda and part of it was the total body scan. But as you know, over there, to provide maximum privacy for Administration folks, they don't have patient names on files, so whoever did the original analysis on the CT scan didn't know it was Dan Westgate and wouldn't have made the connection on his death. But the coroner did."

Bill leaned back in his chair, "So that sounds unusual."

"Yeah, according to the coroner it's really unusual and he was about to set off alarm bells, but not to worry. I quizzed him a bit and found out that unusual does not mean impossible. I explained just what a can of worms he might be opening up with any speculation, like being called before Congress to testify about a conspiracy that he would be creating. I mean the guy did have a blown artery that could only be natural, given no signs on the skull of any trauma and nothing on the toxicology report. I impressed upon him the idea that speculation on anything other than natural causes is not warranted but you know these medical types. He wanted it all tied up with a bow on it.

"He admitted it was not impossible that records could have been screwed up or that Westgate could have had a clean scan forty-eight hours before so I told him to simply note the cause and manner of death and, absent any other evidence, to leave any reference to the CT scan out of his analysis which he agreed to do.

"Westgate died from a brain aneurism and that's all. I mean, we have eyewitnesses. There was no evidence of anything else and several people standing there including the President saw him freak out, try to launch a missile and then keel over.

"So crisis averted. No conspiracies coming out of the poor man's death. Just thought you needed to know. Thanks for waiting for me."

Bill sat up straight, "Yeah, thanks for the heads-up Phil and in a day or two just verify that doc is sticking to the plan and we should keep an eye on any probing going on at Bethesda. We don't need another conspiracy hatching in the White House. No matter the facts, conspiracies just never go away. Have a good evening."

The agent nodded and left quickly leaving Carter alone.

His only thought was, 'My God! What the hell is going on here? This thing just gets crazier by the minute. Now I have competing illogical scenarios and a dead guy that shouldn't even be dead.'

Now it looked like someone in that room, after the missile exploded, had killed Dan Westgate without leaving a trace.

***

The day had finally come when Fraser Carmichael felt he was ready to face his board. As an entrepreneur, he had always found the need for a board burdensome. All of his businesses up to the creation of Carmichael Industries had been run as private businesses with himself as the only or majority investor. There came a time when he needed the size of a major company and lots of cash for rapid expansion as he got deeper into the military business where only the big boys could compete. In particular cruise missiles and sophisticated drones were not cheap to build and so he wrapped several of his companies together and did a very successful IPO raising his own wealth substantially at the same time as he essentially sold off part of the company to the public. He now had a large and credible platform to go after the lucrative defense sector.

Going public meant he would have to live with an independent board of directors to represent the minority shareholders, a necessary evil but useless appendage in Carmichael's eyes.

Because of his reputation as a 'whiz kid', it wasn't too hard to attract an excellent board, made up of industry leaders. Many of them already sat on multiple boards. At CII they were compensated with substantial cash fees for board participation, special consulting assignments and lots of stock options, making it a very attractive offer as the company continued to outperform the industry.

Today would be a balancing act. Heretofore he hadn't experienced any interference from the board. The unspoken rule was that they all trusted him to roll his magic and come out with a steady stream of amazing innovations that secured the company's future and kept the competition on their back foot, and he had consistently delivered.

Part of the balancing act was that he didn't want to give them any reason to snoop into the real goings-on with Alpha-1 or the decision to put a junior mining engineer in charge of such a large project. On the other hand he didn't want to wake up a sleeping press and the SEC to any internal problems such as a board revolt. Needing to satisfy their needs, he wanted to avoid any embarrassing public statements from these giants of industry who were always talking to the press. His presentation was set so as not to leave them 'uneasy'. He would present just enough tantalizing morsels to get them to leave him alone.

As was his custom he entered the board room once his assistant Carmen told him everyone was seated and had any refreshments they wanted. Wearing his signature custom-made jeans and button-down, cream-colored Oxford shirt, designer bow tie, exquisite dark blue blazer and Santoni Italian loafers he entered from the far end of the room and briskly walked its length to his head-of-the-table position as CEO and Chairman while greeting each of them with a wave, a handshake or a comment.

"Lady and gentlemen, first let me apologize for the unforgivable delay in having this meeting. As I'm sure you understand, I've been run off my feet lately with this very significant opportunity we've been awarded.

"I hope you don't mind but I'm going to reorder the agenda a little and get right into the special project I know you all want to hear about. We can deal with the mundane such as approval of our last minutes, review of recent performance, senior employee changes and the like later."

Before he could go any further he was interrupted by Rollie Winston. As expected he was sure the board had been talking on the phone and as usual they had relied on Rollie to try to take some control of the meeting, "Fraser, I'm sure we all want to hear about the 'project' as you call it, but for the record I want to remind you that as board members of this fine company, we have a very specific and important role to fulfill and your absence from the scene has put us all in a very awkward position. You made some very newsworthy comments a while back and to be very frank, you left us all high and dry for much too long. I for one have been unable to get you to return any of my urgent phone calls.

"Now on the basis of our loyalty to this company and you as its leader, we've all been doing our best to duck the press because essentially we're completely in the dark about this dramatic change in the business of the company. All we know so far is that contrary to what you told the press, it could have monstrous effects on the company's bottom line, and I should say the board package you provided for us seems silent on the entire matter. Now if you have made misleading statements to the press about projected company performance you could have put yourself and us in serious jeopardy. But to get back to my original point, you can't treat these members in such a fashion. Please be advised that you have a very unhappy board sitting in front of you. This behavior of yours is new ... worrisome ... unwelcomed ... and frankly unacceptable."

Several of the seven other external board members nodded in unison.

He had been expecting this, although not so pointed and direct. He took his time before he addressed the matter on the table.

"Of course you're right. And again I apologize. I've been so preoccupied with this very important project."

Lucie Coultard interrupted, "Fraser, let's not be cagey. I have information that you've been in town for some time and therefore could have met with us much earlier or at least returned our messages."

This came as a complete surprise to both Fraser Carmichael and the other board members who assumed he had been working at some secret military base. Clearly Lucie had some source or surveillance on the company's CEO which seemed to indicate that he had been avoiding them.

Blushing just a little Fraser continued, "I think you know that I'm exceptionally well-connected by technology so it doesn't matter where I am, I can still be fully occupied and effective in running the company and yes, that can mean that I don't have a moment to spare when the stakes are so high. Frankly I have been forced recently to put the needs of the company and this amazing project above all else.

"But let's not argue over this. I promise to put a much higher priority in keeping you all informed."

Again Rollie Winston felt he had to drive an issue home, "Fraser it isn't only a question of informing the board. We have a legal fiduciary role to play. It is hard for us to imagine you didn't need board approvals for much of what you announced to the press. As I said, you seem to have made dramatic changes to the business of the company. So please don't treat us like an impediment to business. We're here to help you and at the same time represent the rights of all the other shareholders in the company. There are serious limits to what even the CEO and Chairman can do in a public company so please don't assume our issues amount simply to a need to stay informed.

"Do we have your attention now?"

This time Fraser visibly blushed and again took his time before speaking.

This was Winnie Goldberg's first introduction to a full board meeting and this level of tension was something she hadn't expected. Clearly Fraser Carmichael was on the hot seat and she had never seen him cowed like this. Apparently none of these board members were shrinking violets and clearly they were not going to let Fraser run unchallenged in a case like this. Most people in the company had a vision of Carmichael orchestrating everything and a timid board simply rubberstamping everything he wanted. Clearly this wasn't the case at the moment. At least some of these board members had an iron spine.

Fraser finally spoke, "Rollie, of course you're correct. I understand your roles and again I apologize but I think you'll see that you've nothing to worry about. Let me get right into the meat of the matter."

The board's mood was even worse than he had anticipated and he would have to think quickly on his feet to sidestep the landmines in front of him. Some of what he had planned to present would need to be tweaked now that he had assessed their mood. Suddenly he was glad he had not included much in the board package or made slides supporting his original concept of the presentation of his strategy and the project.

He paused until he saw their willingness to proceed and then started, "As you know I rolled several of my personal holdings into Carmichael Industries a few years back when we went public. I have several other holdings and many of those are frankly quite invisible to the market. I'm sure you were all aware of this and I can assure you that CII is my main focus and I will never sacrifice it for any of my other interests.

"Part of my thinking in this has been that when you're in the military business and going for lowest bid on very competitive projects, it is a good idea to keep your ammunition dry or in other words, to hide from the competition all of your assets, secrets, strategies and capabilities. Obviously these private companies are not the business of this meeting but there is an important intersection with CII.

"For some time now, I've operated a couple of stealth companies that amounted to not much more than think tanks or sand boxes, a term I'm sure you're all aware of. It has cost me personally millions to support them financially even though they had no products or services to create revenue. Their only job was primary research and testing over-the-top ideas. You may know that Boeing's version of this is called their Phantom Works.

"As you may have surmised, a couple of these companies have made some very substantial breakthroughs … amazing breakthroughs. One in the area of a new generation of robots and the other in the area of supercomputers using quantum state technology.

"About a year ago, using some licenses we had that allowed us to reuse others' technology I connected these small companies and they have produced an amazing capability that will revolutionize the manufacturing industry, hence the 'Harmonized Manufacturing' concept I announced to the press. The licenses were not enough so I personally bought X-Wave out of Vancouver, Canada to lock up some of the key IP.

"So far this has nothing to do with Carmichael Industries and explains why I've never discussed these matters with this board.

"At this point I do need to apologize for one thing. When presenting strategy and concepts to external audiences such as the press I have periodically been sloppy in representing corporate relationships. I have a habit of saying 'Carmichael' has this or that because in my mind it is all one concept under the various companies that I control or own. I understand the implications of that oversight and I will be more careful in the future.

"Suddenly a few weeks ago I awoke one morning and realized the coup de grâce. I'd take on the bloated defense industry with my new-found capabilities. The obvious choice was the next-generation fighter which the underground press has reported has been in trouble and is predictably well over budget and massively behind schedule. This target was ideal because it was just large enough and a suitable technical challenge that would highlight the exceptional nature of our new capabilities. I also knew quite a bit about it, being one of the original bidders on the project.

"The problem was that none of my stealth companies had the clout to take on the project and they needed to stay stealthy to avoid competitors stealing the technology. So my concept started to involve Carmichael Industries as the front man, so to speak. As a prime contractor we have the credibility, mass, reputation and gravitas to take on the Pentagon and the Presidency where these small companies do not. CII simply subcontracts the manufacturing to my new entity which is a grouping of some of these small companies. I haven't even given it a name yet.

"Reading between the lines, I knew the President was looking for something like this and structuring a deal where he could slash military spending, and direct some of it through Executive Orders to his social programs agenda. I also knew he could do a directed tender because no one else had our capability. But I had no way of getting to see the man who saw me as a sworn enemy, and I wasn't about to draw in other loose-lipped hangers-on like PR companies or politicians.

"I could have gone to the Pentagon but they would be trapped with their existing contracts, procurement policies, lobbyists etc. Only the President would be able to use Executive Powers to make this all happen and only he would be greedy enough to want to save billions from the military budgets.

"Then I saw an opportunity with this mine disaster. Usually guys like this who have survived some very public peril get flown to the White House for a photo-op with the President. So I decided to take control of that inevitability and use it to get a private audience with Hal Turcot where I could make him an offer he couldn't refuse.

"I'm so confident in my new capability that I offered to build the new fighters for free, in record time, and sell them to him at the original quoted price. I knew he needed something that big to trust me and this gets around the Congressional funding issues and keeps all the decisions to one branch of government and in fact one man's decision. It's a masterful plan to avoid all the red tape, political minefields and obstacles in Washington.

"I expect to make a killing on the first ten fighters given our new manufacturing capabilities and it's all clear sailing for new contracts after that.

"Now the share of this windfall between Carmichael Industries and my other companies is yet to be negotiated and you'll obviously need to approve that given my conflict of interest, but for the moment Carmichael has manageable expense and risk in this, so I proceeded without any board consultations. It was an opportunity that couldn't wait, was staring me in the face, and I couldn't walk away from it. If I had waited until the President involved his advisors, they would've killed it and we'd have lost this amazing launch of our new technology. As you can appreciate, it had to remain secret right up to the two press conferences to ensure no one could scuttle it.

"As to Carmichael Industries' profitability, we have manageable costs," he lied, "and major profits to deal with. As I said to the press, and I set expectations low, the effect on our numbers for the fiscal year should be moderately positive. I'm managing that by driving some unexpected costs to my other companies that are private and where I can sustain losses if need be, so we'll need to take that into account when we negotiate the split of revenues and profits. But at some point it will be the beginning of a new, highly profitable product line which will become our major profit engine for the future, and I'm sure we can come to a mutually agreeable split on costs and revenues with my new manufacturing company.

"So there you have it, only upside for Carmichael Industries and the new company. I win on both sides so I have no motivation to short change CII. For the moment, let's call the new company Alpha-1 which is privately owned by me and I don't wish to share any additional details on it with anyone. They are simply a subcontractor that I'm vouching for personally and I can promise that Carmichael Industries will have an exclusive contract with them as long as I'm running this company.

"I hope that explains some of why so much of this had to remain secret."

Jim Broadhurst, Exec VP of Cognizant was first to speak, "I'm afraid you have forgotten something Fraser. There is a definite cost to Carmichael Industries. You've used our name and our reputation to promote the capabilities of your 'invisible' private company. This is a major and very visible project. If it fails you're taking CII down with you. This most definitely has an unquantifiable cost to us. We as a board must approve any such massive linkage to another company and personally I'm not comfortable with your assurances. How are we to believe your story, when you've made unbelievable, and by that I mean lacking credibility … unbelievable claims about fantastic new robots and a new supercomputer that much of the high-tech industry thinks is beyond achievable in the next thirty years and as far as we know has never been tested in a real world situation? Even if everything you say about these technologies is verifiable, what if one of these things breaks down for months as most new technologies do, or isn't as powerful as you hoped it would be, or faces an IP or patent law suit or a court injunction to cease and desist for some unforeseen reason?"

Lucie Coultard jumped in, "Jim is right. I sit on many boards and while public companies may be new to you Fraser, you seem to misunderstand the full scope of our responsibilities. You have in fact put this company in grave jeopardy. If we lose our reputation in military contracts, well last time I looked, that's about sixty percent of your revenues.

"I'm afraid, as Jim inferred, it would be negligent of us to simply take your word on these new technologies. We're going to need much more information and I dare say, some independent assessment of the true capabilities and capacities of these robots and computers before we can agree to bet the future of this company on them.

"I also think there will have to be a full independent legal review of the ownership of these firms and of all aspects of the technology in terms of IP, patents and the like, as well as the contracts we have with them. If we're about to be married to them then we need a full due diligence.

"Part of our job is to assess risks to the company and you have just introduced a monster of a risk with no board involvement or oversight."

Carmichael hadn't seen this angle and internally he was boiling. They had always trusted his judgment in technology issues and thought his vouching for the company would have been enough.

He didn't know what to say. Until now this handpicked board had given him free rein with the company. Yet as Lucie had pointed out, this was actually his first experience running a public company where the directors were not just advisors but had a real responsibility to others. The board of a public company had real teeth, teeth that this board hadn't displayed or used until today.

He had expected some blowback from his hastily arranged news conference but nothing like this.

He had to remind himself of the overall goal. Yes, he wanted free access to Alpha's technology but the planet's survival was the bigger issue and could share none of that objective with this group. He had to find a way to move ahead without this board becoming an obstacle.

It was Rollie's turn in the tag team match and he picked up where Lucie had left off, "In terms of risk profiles, you've fundamentally changed the risks this company faces. If any one of these companies fails in some fashion, we take the hit. If they stumble in any way then we take the fall.

"In situations like this we can't assume that we have control over these subcontractors, even if you personally own them and manage them. Just imagine a patent suit, or a management revolt or loss of a 'key man' or any number of other catastrophes that can befall a small company, public or private. The trash heap is full of companies that had amazing potential but some unforeseen calamity took them out.

"And one other matter, I understand you have lost your Corporate Counsel and frankly you are making decisions here that are bordering on illegal. You just said you have entered into arrangements with the President's Administration and also with these subcontractors, yet decisions like cost sharing and profit sharing are fluid. How is it even possible to sign such a contract?

"Also I'm quite sure I remember no mention of these items in the board approved budget for the company for this fiscal year. So I would be very interested in what your VP Finance has to say about how you have papered these transactions without board approvals. Your approved fiscal plan made no mention of this massive deviation. That is breaking all kinds of accounting norms. An audit by the company's external auditors would fail miserably at this moment I'm afraid and they would have to report the anomalies and risk associated with these oversights to the SEC. As a public company you cannot announce a multi-billion dollar deal and start work, with contracts and approved budgets to be worked out later. That's tantamount to misrepresenting the corporation to the market."

This had been Winnie's biggest worry and as acting legal counsel she blushed. Suddenly she wished Will Fiskins was still on the job and taking the lead on these legal matters.

The body language in the room was such that it was clear all the board members felt the same causing Rollie to sum up with, "So I'm afraid Fraser, that your board is giving you a strong message that you may have proceeded recklessly and sacrificed too much for this potential windfall. I'm afraid if we took a vote right now we would all have to give you directions to find a way to back out of this deal. But if I may ... let me say that the crux of the matter is the lack of information available to this board. You clearly see all of this in a very different light. I think it is incumbent on you to convince this board of the merits of this project and the security of the plan and of these subcontractors and technologies, to address the concerns you've heard here today.

"I'll say it again, we all wish you the best and under most circumstances we trust you implicitly but we're all people with reputations to consider, laws to follow and a constituency to represent.

"We're all governed by SEC rules and remember we can be held personally responsible for anything that happens to this company that isn't seen as kosher ... like us ignoring highly questionable accounting practices and hitching our wagons to unidentified subcontractors with unproven technologies.

"There are many cases where boards have lost their own personal wealth by engaging in activities the SEC found to be illegitimate and the fact that you're dealing with a subcontractor that isn't at arm's length to a major shareholder in this company, that being you, and that you have heretofore not shown reasonable regard to the financial security of this company by presenting budgets and projections for this project, puts the company and your board in grave jeopardy. I personally don't wish to hang around as a responsible board member until the SEC raids us.

"At the end of the day, if we aren't satisfied with the direction and health of the company we have a responsibility to report our concerns to the SEC or the more likely case is that you'll see multiple resignations from this board which of course will not go unnoticed. Either way if you don't satisfy us you'll be spending a great deal of time with the Securities and Exchange Commission. I have been forced to appear there only once myself and I do not wish to repeat the ordeal.

"I know you didn't come prepared today to furnish any of this additional information and therefore it would be my suggestion that we adjourn this meeting until such time as management can bring forward a complete plan with budgets and projections for this project including detailed information on the technologies in play, the companies we're dependent on and the contractual arrangements that have been agreed to, or are being proposed, if they require our approval."

Several heads in the room were nodding. Fraser was cornered and for the first time felt he was being manhandled by his board. A board that he had secretly considered as irrelevant and powerless. It was clear that for some of these board members, and maybe all of them, this wasn't their first rodeo and they knew better than he what their posture on a matter like this needed to be. He had never sat on a board and this was the first one he actually reported to.

He felt compelled to respond, "I must say I'm surprised at the position of some of you … maybe all of you, in this matter. You haven't questioned my judgment in the past and your lack of support in this matter is unexpected and frankly shocking. Everything I've done with this company before and after going public, has resulted in exceptional profits and I would think that fact would give me some leeway."

Lucie interrupted, "That may have been the case if you had consulted us or even informed us of your announcements to the press. I hope you see now that this entire matter could have been handled much differently. All of us here were blindsided and have been uncomfortably ducking press inquiries since that press conference, so on a personal level you left us hanging out there for far too long. On a pragmatic level, there is too much secrecy involved in this project and we as board members are now seeing clearly the jeopardy you've put us in. A bankruptcy court or massive shareholder law suit will not be generous to a board who says 'we just went along with it because Fraser Carmichael is a 'whiz kid'.

"Remember there are certain cases where we individually can be sued as board members for dereliction of duty and our board insurance doesn't cover that, so we aren't being hard asses here. These are the realities of public companies and their responsibilities. As board members we take substantial fees out of this company and the market expects us to take our responsibilities seriously. I for one do not want to be sued personally for something we let slide.

"I second Rollie's motion that we adjourn for not more than a week to give management time to fill the gaps in the information we've received today. I don't see how we could allow this to slide any longer before the board approves plans or takes other actions to mitigate any risk to the company."

'Other actions' was a loaded phrase as far as Carmichael was concerned. That likely meant forcing a cancelation of the project or getting rid of him as CEO, or more likely, both.

A quick vote carried the motion to which Lucie announced, "We are therefore adjourned until management calls us together again. A week should be enough time for you to put together the required full briefing on this project and all of its components. Let me suggest you run everything past Jim as he is the most tech-savvy person on this board. Jim you run multi-billion dollar tech projects and I think you can speak for the board as to what would be satisfactory in terms of the content of such a briefing. I think I can speak for the board that this should be a special assignment for you at our agreed board consulting rates."

Jim Broadhurst, Exec VP of Cognizant had his calendar open and nodded his acceptance of the assignment. He turned to Fraser and said, "Call me day after tomorrow on this. I have some free time this week."

They all quickly rose and without saying goodbye, left swiftly leaving a furious Fraser Carmichael and an embarrassed Winnie Goldstein sitting there.

The two of them sat quietly until Fraser spoke, "That wasn't at all what I was expecting. Not one word of this to anyone. Be discreet when you write up the minutes and let me see them before anyone else.

"I want to tentatively schedule the next meeting a week from today but no official announcement until I give the green light but you can give them a heads-up for their calendars. You'll also need them to agree to the emergency meeting waiver as again we're inside the 21-day notice period.

"I know this was your first full board meeting standing in for Will Fiskins but I can assure you they have never been like this in the past and I don't want to see another one like that. It was painful and makes me question ever taking another company public again. So please use your discretion and keep this between the two of us.

"One other thing ... contracts. You are leading the legal team for now so get started on the contracts. First off, figure out where we need contracts and deal only with me on the meat of the matter. I think I can get the President himself to sign the one for their side given it was an Executive Order, but as per the board we'll need contracts with some other companies I own, the ones I wanted to remain nameless so wait for my instructions, but get the framework on them started. I want favorable terms on any companies I own because I'm personally vouching for them.

"The board has said they want to review the contracts so there's no conflict of interest. They can push back on any terms they wish. If you ensure that point is in today's minutes then you personally are not in a conflict of interest by following my instructions."

He rose and left the room briskly with a plan in mind that he thought might just save the day. Something Lucie had said about too much secrecy had given him an idea.

Hal Turcot had given him his direct line to use that would reach him wherever he was. He quickly checked his email for the secure memo that delivered the daily password for direct calls to the President. After dialing the number and giving the receptionist the proper code, he was left waiting for about three minutes on hold with some propaganda piece until the President lifted the phone.

"Fraser, before you say anything, this line is secure but I'm not at my desk so be careful what you say."

Carmichael smiled at the thought of others listening in to the call, "We need to talk. I've run into some difficulties and I need your assistance. How do we do this?"

Turcot was brief, "We should do it in person. When can you get here? I too have some things to discuss with you."

"I can chopper over to Teterboro. I'll call ahead to get the jet warmed up so I'm guessing I can land at Reagan and be there in about two hours."

"Make it Andrews, I'll set up landing approvals and you can chopper over here on Marine 1. That ought to save some time."

They signed off and Carmichael had his assistant set up the transportation.

Arriving at Andrews, Carmichael was immediately shown to an executive version of the Blackhawk helicopter, not the big Sea King he had been expecting. This smaller Whitehawk, used occasionally as Marine 2 usually carried the Vice President.

Carmichael saw the bigger Sea Kings on the apron at Andrews that serviced the President as Marine 1 and wondered if the choice of the Whitehawk had been a subtle message from the military that he wasn't liked, being the stimulus behind the cancelation of the F-35 and the recontracting of the F-47. But the Whitehawk was comfortable and roomy and the episode had only made him smile.

Fraser was ushered directly into the Oval Office.

As he entered the President held up his hand as if to say, 'don't speak.' He went over to his desk, opened it and touched the small device to cut out any audio recording.

Turcot motioned for him to take a seat on one of the couches as he took the lead, "Now we can talk. Let me start. It's been about a month of dodging and weaving round here and I have no idea what is going on out west. I swear if it wasn't the holiday season with lots of members out of town they'd have impeached me already. Alpha-1 calls about every other day to make sure I'm on plan and all I hear from General Hawkins is that we're keeping three or four C-17s busy flying stuff in and out but I've heard nothing from you on progress."

Turcot thought he had reason to be concerned. He wondered if Fraser was sticking to the plan or if he had some other side agenda going.

The President sat on the opposing couch as Carmichael began to speak, "Look, I've been busy too, trying to keep everything flowing without the board cutting my legs off. This Alpha-1 sends me emails almost hourly demanding all kinds of components and raw materials some of which are specialized and I must find them somewhere on the planet and get them packaged and ready for the C-17s in record time so I'm flat out as his personal procurement and logistics guy. Much of it is so urgent and bizarre that I can't even delegate it. I'll be catching up on the hours I've missed today with my laptop tonight in my condo here in Washington.

"I told you I saw the weapons facility my first time out there. It was this massive white dome bigger than four or five football stadiums but they had nothing in it at that point. It's probably full of stuff by now as we've been delivering lots of raw materials and Alpha-1 said they were bringing in other subsystems, helpers and the like by other means. My guess is it's a hive of activity by now but it is not advisable for me to either walk out into the desert or disappear for any length of time when I'm out there so I haven't seen it in operation.

"I did get back for a second short visit and saw the production lines for the F-47s but man you would recognize nothing and those robots are big suckers and move so fast you can barely see them. Thankfully they are smart enough that they don't run you over when you're in there. As far as I know both projects are on schedule and everything is working fine.

"But I'm not fine. I have to tell you I'm totally frazzled with all this work and pressure. I can't sleep either. I wake up at least hourly thinking we're too late, the aliens have arrived and they're about to zap us. If it isn't that, it's nightmares that we failed and Alpha-1 starts dropping people all around me. It's like one of the worst horror movies you've ever seen. I've never had trouble sleeping before and man my nerves are totally shot and according to my bathroom scale I've lost eight pounds.

"But my sleeping problems aren't why I needed to see you. I just had a very difficult board meeting. Strike that. I just had a catastrophic board meeting where I came this close to being fired and the gist of it is that the board is more than unsatisfied with my explanations for the project to date and they are threatening mayhem. Translated that means either reporting me to the SEC or launching an investigation of our contract, the technologies we're using and the subcontracting companies doing the procurement and manufacturing at Area-51. Either all of that or dumping me as CEO or mass board resignations, which would also trigger SEC and FBI investigations."

Turcot looked alarmed, "Hell we can't have that. Can't you get control of them somehow? I thought you had a good relationship with them. As I remember it there are some heavyweights in the industry on that board."

"That's just it. They ARE heavyweights and they know all the ins and outs of board life including their personal liabilities, to say nothing of their overarching concern for their own reputations. Many of them sit on multiple boards so they know what they're talking about. They're mad as hell and they want some answers which as you know, are going to be very difficult to come by.

"I'm telling you they tore a strip off me this morning. I have never had to sit through such a humiliating experience. They mean business and I must get back to them in a week. Add to that the fact that they are mostly techies and I can tell you, they will see right through any half-baked stories. As we stand here I have no idea what to tell them. They're going to catch me in any one of a dozen lies when I go back to them."

The President still showing alarm asked, "So what's the minimum they're looking for?"

"Basically everything we can't talk about. They want me to get back to them with a full plan, all the contracts and a full briefing and likely a demonstration of the technologies, where they come from, who owns them, who are my procurement and manufacturing subcontractors and how reliable are they? What are we buying, from whom and at what price? They want full budgets and forecasts. As I said, pretty much everything we can't tell them. They even mentioned hiring a third party to 'evaluate' the technologies for risk. Can you imagine a heavy techie getting a close-up look at those robots and the computer?"

Turcot was even more alarmed, "This is really serious. You can't allow that. And we can't have an FBI or SEC investigation either. You said you need my help. What can I do?"

"Declare everything Top Secret and "Need to Know" or "Eyes Only", whatever it is you guys do in a case like this so that I don't have to answer the board's questions."

The President almost laughed, "In a case like this? Are you joking? There are no cases like this. I can't involve any of the intelligence community or they'd uncover something. How do you declare something Top Secret if the intelligence guys and the military can't even know about it?'"

Carmichael interrupted, "Now that I think of it, some of the board may have Top Secret clearance like Broadhurst at Cognizant so it would have to be something like 'Eyes Only' if we are to keep it secret. You have to do this! There is no scenario here where I go back to them with anything that would even pass a smell test. We'd be found out ten minutes into the meeting."

Turcot stood and paced, "Wow, you don't know what you're asking. I already have Congress all over me for what they're calling abuse of power. I've been informed they will take another try at subpoenaing me to testify. Declaring this stuff 'Eyes Only' will mean some of the oversight committees will have to be included and the Pentagon will have to sign off on it, which we can't allow and I'm already under the gun for the massive lack of transparency on this. This was your one job. To stay at the top of CII for the duration of the project and now you want to dump all your problems on me?

"Can't you just put them off for a month or two? Just don't schedule a board meeting."

Carmichael chuckled, "You're forgetting about the SEC. They need answers and the board will up and resign en masse if I try to put them off. You politicians have no idea. At least you can hide behind separation of powers for a while. I got a call from my lawyer on the plane. Some Sheriff in Idaho wants me to appear. Something about the investigation into the fire that took Glass's in-laws and some issue with the death certificate on the other miner. God knows what they've turned up. I can probably duck that one unless they find a way to charge me with something and start interstate extradition but my lawyer also tells me I've been subpoenaed to testify to Congress. No date yet but they said they might need me on short notice. It's a joint oversight committee for the Armed Forces, Intelligence and Homeland Security. In short a full room over there and they won't wait long."

Carmichael continued, "I'm actually not too worried about them either. I think I have answers or deflections for their key questions and I can always take the fifth which will take months to overcome if they challenge it and find me in contempt of Congress, but it's my board that terrifies me. They can force me out of office in a simple motion in a board meeting and then the new guy can kill the whole project within hours.

"The most likely scenario is that they turf me and Rollie Winston will be appointed interim CEO and chairman while they do a search for my replacement. You'll get a call from him within the hour after I'm gone and he'll kill the whole thing. Alpha-1 may then have no choice but to go to his Plan B, which is not good for any of us if you remember. I'm serious, you need to do this 'Eyes Only' thing for me."

Turcot frowned, "It's the NSA or the Pentagon who are usually the ones that request and manage Top Secret or 'Eyes Only' status. I might be able to try an Executive Order, but without the Pentagon or NSA driving it and being briefed themselves I can't see how they'll let me get away with it. That would be waving a big red flag in front of them and a gold-plated invitation for the FBI and the CIA to investigate. Congress will jump to impeachment right away and I'd be risking an armed takeover of Area-51 if they thought there was something more than the obvious being hidden there.

"Frankly I'm surprised we've gotten away with keeping the military out of those hangars so far. It's all based on your need to keep your amazing new technology private but even that is wearing really thin.

"Either way I'd probably end up out of office and then the VP would order a full review and disclosure to Congress on everything going on out there. You're asking me to make it 'Eyes Only' for you, me and Glass, or Alpha-1 alone. How would I explain to the Joint Chiefs that they can't know anything more about the whole project like the contracts etc.? They're mad as hell already about your secrecy on your manufacturing process at the site. They'll definitely take over the site if I officially classify it as 'Eyes Only' and leave them out."

Carmichael thought about this for a moment, "If it ever came to that and given a minimum of notice, Alpha-1 could probably have all of the robots out of there before anyone could get in or at least cloak them somehow so they couldn't find them, but he might still go to his Plan B which could mean death to the entire human race and I'm convinced that's not an empty threat. He's right that the human race could not rest easy with a superior species living under their feet. He might seem charming to you and me but remember, he has made it quite clear that he will take zero risk when his civilization's survival is at stake. Never forget that this thing, and remember, it is a 'thing', has the power to wipe us all out without breaking a sweat and he stood by and let hundreds die already.

"Now listen, I don't know how you do it, I just know I can't go to the board with a pack of obvious lies. Forget about a drawn-out impeachment, I'll be gone before the meeting adjourns.

"As to exposure in Nevada, I don't think he ever moved the computer there. It's just too vulnerable. I suspect all those robots are networked wirelessly back to some redundant site we're unaware of. Bottom line is you might not get your F-47s completed but I suspect they now have most of what they need for construction of the space weapon at that secret desert location on Groom Lake and that might continue even if the military takes over everything at the hangars. That's our best chance to avoid Plan B if the Joint Chiefs take over Area-51."

Just then the President's personal line rang with a tone that told him it was urgent. He lifted the phone and all Carmichael heard was "Put him through".

After a few seconds Carmichael noticed a distinct change in the President's posture and blood seemed to drain from his face, "General Hawkins, I'm going to put you on speaker. I have with me in my office Fraser Carmichael," The President pressed a button on his phone and said, "Now General, please repeat what you just told me."

There was a pause and then the General spoke, "Mr. Glass has been working virtually nonstop lately and I thought I detected signs of strain and failing health on his part. I spoke to him about it but he didn't seem to listen. About fifteen minutes ago I was standing in the mess with him when he seemed to swoon and then dropped to the floor. We did everything we could but sadly he didn't make it. Mr. Robert Glass I'm afraid is dead."

Carmichael gasped as he stared at the President, the President reached for the mute button just as Carmichael blurted out, "Oh my God. What do we do now?"

The President pointed to the phone indicating Hawkins could hear everything. He said, "Give us a minute General," as he finally pressed the mute button.

The President rubbed his forehead and seemed deep in thought.

Carmichael was shocked, "Hell that could mean they're going to Plan B. Once Alpha finds out he's dead they'll wipe us all out and do this themselves!"

Turcot stared at him, "Somehow I think not. We'd be dead already. Remember he told us he couldn't be killed and he had a backup of his psyche. Still I had a feeling he was going to overdo it. The first thing we must do is make sure that site remains secure."

He pressed the mute button again, "General we will need an hour or so to figure out what to do. For the moment here are your orders. Don't let anyone approach those buildings. Remember they have their own security system and it could be lethal.

"Secondly, this information is 'Eyes Only'. Secure the body and wait for my instructions. DO NOT report this death to anyone.

"Who knows about this already?"

"There were a couple of off-duty regulars in the mess who saw him drop as well as the kitchen staff. It was between meals so there were no other troops in here. In addition there were two medics but I haven't reported this up the ladder as you had told me I report directly to you."

Even though this was true Hawkins had already made up his mind that no matter what, his next call would be to General Jenkins and most probably General Hawthorne too. There were just too many strange things about this project and he didn't want to be left holding the bag with a dead body or maybe even worse, being bumped off by a CIA sniper. It was just too crazy around here, too many unanswered questions and he wanted some backup.

The last month had been a steady stream of unusual things but from the very start Hawkins had made up his mind that he was being used in something much larger. If his bosses in the Pentagon didn't know what was going on then the only other culprit had to be the CIA and according to the movies, they often eliminated witnesses at the end.

The President spoke again, "Round up those men and read them the riot act. This has been ordered by me as 'Eyes Only' and if they say a word they'll be tried for treason. If you have even the slightest doubt about their commitment then I want you to arrest them and keep them out of contact with anyone until I get back to you and we've resolved this issue. Do you understand?"

Hawkins agreed and was further shocked at the way the President was handling this. What was the big deal at the presidential level about a dead Chief Operating Officer? Why was it an 'Eyes Only' issue? There had been no autopsy but it seemed clear this guy died from a stroke or heart attack from complete exhaustion caused by endless work and stress and probably that crazy diet he was on. His death might be a shock to some but not a matter of national security.

Surely this could not be kept silent for long. Yet the President's voice made it perfectly clear that he wanted a lid on this. Hawkins was more committed now than ever to involve Hawthorne or Jenkins at least, but he would have to find a way that it didn't lead back to him. He wished he had never heard of the F-47 or Area-51. Something crazy was happening here and so far his command was doing nothing to help him out. That meant he was likely the scapegoat for anything going down.

The President signed off and stood staring at Carmichael who looked panicked and blurted out, "Wow, what do we do now? How do we contact Alpha or Alpha-1 if he was even telling the truth about having backups?

"And that's not even our biggest problem. Remember he said they could drop everyone on the planet just like they did your SECDEF. Apparently all they have to do is think about our brain waves. We could all just drop dead here right now. Hell they probably know I'm in trouble with the board and you with Congress. What if they have already decided this is all just too complex and Plan B is much simpler?"

The President just stared at him.

The red line on the President's console rang and he immediately lifted it, nodding to Carmichael and putting it on speaker.

"Gentlemen, by now I believe you've heard of my untimely death."

Carmichael gasped. It was the voice of the dead Robert Glass. The President spoke for them, "I must say it is a relief to hear your voice. For a moment we thought we had been left with a terrible situation and no idea what to do."

"Well yes, I can see where that would be disconcerting but believe me I'm not about to let myself be taken out by the weaknesses of the human body."

Carmichael spoke this time, "What happened? And if your body is dead in Nevada how can you be speaking to us with Glass's voice?"

"Really gentlemen, do you think that is such a difficult feat for us?

"As to what happened, apparently the answer is quite simple. The human body is much more fragile than we had calculated. We have sufficient experience at on-boarding humans but we've never had any need to deal with their physical bodies or for that matter felt the need to study them in the past. The idea of occupying the body of anyone else, Alphan or human runs against our social mores but it was a necessity in this case. So we've had no experience at this.

"When I entered Glass's body, I loaded up his human brain with as much as I could reasonably cram in there and I'm afraid I spent little time focused on the capacities of his physical body.

"Apparently in my commitment to beat the deadlines on the space weapon, I didn't pay attention to the physical cost, and frankly I guess I blew a fuse of some kind. Everything just went black and I had to resort to my stored psyche, which luckily was being kept current with Glass's body, so I have memories up to nanoseconds before my untimely death. That's as much as we know as I wasn't about to steal the dead body to do an autopsy.

"That said, we aren't out of the woods. The only stored DNA we have here was Robert Glass. I can't repopulate a clone and reappear at the air base now that half a dozen people saw him die. I need another body."

Carmichael and Turcot stared at each other in disbelief. Carmichael spoke first, "What do you mean another body? You want us to kill someone?"

Alpha-1 audibly laughed on the other end, "Hardly. You know how we feel about life. I could take over the body of either of you two but we need you in your current positions and Hawkins would think you both over-qualified for the COO job in Nevada, especially a sitting President.

"I think if you rack your brains you might come up with someone else who might accept the deal we offer. And this time it would be preferable to select someone who may not be missed or where we must take several family members and also someone with a believable background who might credibly be expected to take a COO job, although at this late stage I'll take almost anyone. We're seriously running out of time and while our helpers, or robots as you call them are still busy at the site, the space weapon we're building has never been attempted before so my oversight is critical and getting back on the job very soon would be highly desirable.

"So if you please, I need a name and I need it now!"

Carmichael had an idea, "We might be able to kill two birds with one stone. There's a reporter out of Vegas, who has put two and two together and may soon become an obstacle we will have to deal with anyways. What if we took him?"

Alpha-1 responded, "A REPORTER? Are you kidding me? We had problems with a junior engineer in the job. Now you want me to bring in a reporter as a COO?"

Carmichael could see the President was anxious too, "No, it's not that bad. He has a Master's degree in Physics from a reputable university. I had a background check done on him and before he switched careers he wrote several scientific articles on advanced materials for various important scientific magazines. Advanced materials are an important part of those fighters, right?

"Believe me, he's perfect. Somehow he knows the F-47s are being built at Area-51 by CII, but for some reason he thinks something beyond that is going on. He has apparently stumbled upon the issue that there are large amounts of rare earths from China going in there and something to do with the mass or quantity of materials going in there is too high for the F-47s alone. How he figured that out I have no idea but clearly he is getting some information out of that site and can only be a problem down the road. There is no way we can explain large amounts of rare earths being used in an F-47 program and who knows what other information he has or will have from his sources.

"This is a press guy. I've refused comment already. He could go to press with something that would be way off the mark but maybe just enough to start investigations from Congress, the military or the FBI. I think this guy could be a perfect choice."

There was a long pause on the line and finally Alpha-1 spoke, "Well if you have no one else in mind, Andrew McPherson it is. How will you approach him?"

Carmichael's mouth dropped even though the President didn't seem to pick up on Alpha-1's insight, "How do you know his name?"

Alpha-1 responded, "You don't need to know that. What do you propose because I will have to be there in some fashion to make this deal happen?"

"He wants an interview with me so I'll tell him I'll meet him at my Vegas Penthouse where you and I first met. I can be there in about six hours if I can get the President's help. That'll put me in the Penthouse around seven p.m. local time. That's when I'll set up the meeting."

Alpha-1 saw an opportunity, "OK that will work but I need a couple of favors. I see no safe way to hurry this exchange up and the project can do without me for a few hours so I could use the time off and achieve some long sought-after goals of my civilization.

"I will get to your penthouse at the Hawk Hotel several hours before you but I will be cloaked. Uncloaked I will still look like Bob Glass because we only have his DNA to clone, so I need total privacy from your staff in the penthouse.

"I want a top-of-the-line, creative female escort waiting for me in your suite. If she recognizes me uncloaked I can take care of her memory. Prostitution is legal in this state so we will not attract undue attention but frankly Alpha could use a few more tricks and experiences in the area of sex and you would be helping out an entire civilization if I can take back the memories to share.

"All the humans we have on-boarded come from a time when sex was more modest or perfunctory than what the 21st century world finds normal and sex was not as big a deal for Alphans until we picked up some desires from human psyches. Remember, I told you reproduction was something of a challenge for us and our weak sex drive was part of that. I suspect it is too early for Bob Glass and his fiancée to share some of their modern fetishes with us.

"Beauty is in the eye of the beholder so I have no physical description for you. Our species was physically quite different from yours so we can fantasize any Alphan we wish but her methods, style and imagination from a human perspective are what we need."

The President almost laughed as Carmichael smiling said, "Sounds reasonable."

Alpha-1 continued, "The other thing I need you to arrange is that when I return to Area-51 as Andrew McPherson I want to bring back with me a Great Dane, around one year old, preferably all black and with clipped ears. We cannot on-board anything other than humans and there were no domesticated dogs a million years ago and none of our invited 'guests' had pets. We have noticed that humans have a special relationship with and take great enjoyment from pets, especially what you call man's best friend. I want to take that knowledge and experience of that relationship back to Alpha, as well as the data to simulate at least one kind of pet in our fantasy world."

By this point Fraser Carmichael was smiling so much he could hardly get the words out, "Well I would not have suspected either of these two wishes but I'm sure I can get the concierge at the Hawk to fulfill both requests. I'll see you around seven p.m."

Carmichael hurriedly took the President's helicopter back to Andrews and was on his way to Vegas. He had called his assistant in New York, told her to find Andy McPherson at the Vegas RJ and tell him he had an exclusive interview with Fraser Carmichael at seven p.m. in his Vegas Penthouse. There was no doubt the young reporter would crawl over fiery coals for such a 'get'.

Alpha-1's two requests were a little too unusual for the New York operations center so he called the concierge at the Hawk directly and had him put a rush on the two tasks.

These were unusual requests from the owner of the Hawk so all the concierge said in response was, "We've had crazier requests and you know what goes on in Vegas, stays in Vegas."

Carmichael had no idea what to say. All Vegas knew was that he was meeting with a reporter and a call girl was going to get the use of his penthouse for a few hours.

The President called General Hawkins to tell him they would likely have a new COO in place by evening.

Hawkins thought it over several times and finally called his boss General Jenkins, Secretary of the Air Force. He stipulated that he couldn't be the source of the news but proceeded to tell him about Glass's sudden death, the President's reaction, and the plan to replace Glass by the end of the day.

Jenkins was soon on to the Chairman of the Joint Chiefs, General Hawthorne and his two favorite Senators whispering the news from a confidential source. While they were all shocked at the news, they decided to wait to see what the President did before they precipitated any action.

Vegas

When Carmichael arrived at his penthouse in Las Vegas a few minutes late he was informed that a Mr. Andrew McPherson had arrived twenty minutes earlier and was waiting in the small conference room.

Carmichael proceeded to the main room where he had first met Alpha-1 and poured himself a short drink of an excellent single malt scotch at his wet bar. As he raised his head he caught the reflection of Bob Glass in the mirror behind the bar and almost choked.

"How did you get in here? Did security see you?"

Glass smiled, "Cloaking and no, security didn't see me. If everything works as planned I will leave in a clone of Andy's body and my helpers will use cloaking to take care of this body and Andy's.

"The young lady you provided has furnished me with an exceptional experience that will be treasured by Alpha. She has now left after she was well compensated. I wiped her recollection of me in case she stumbles on a photo of Robert Glass who as we know died earlier today."

Carmichael couldn't help blushing at the clinical way Alpha-1 seemed to treat this.

Alpha-1 continued, "Let's go see Andy. I'd suggest you let me do the talking in there."

Carmichael took another gulp of his drink and pointed to the door leading to the small conference room.

As they entered, Andy stood and blushed. He had thought he was coming here for a one-on-one with the big man but here he was with someone who seemed familiar.

Carmichael took Andy's outstretched hand, "Andy, good of you to come on short notice. I think you might recognize Robert Glass?"

Glass was just closing the door and took Andy's nervous handshake.

Carmichael spoke first, "I'm going to let Mr. Glass here do most of the talking. I think you'll find out he has everything you need."

As Andy sat down and started to protest that he had come for an interview with Carmichael himself, he found his entire body was frozen, he wasn't breathing on his own and only his eyes could move. He felt that his heart rate skyrocketed, due to some sort of panic attack, brought on by being in such august company.

Glass/Alpha-1 spoke, "Andy, I've frozen your body. You're in no danger and I think this will turn out to be a very pleasant night for you, but just so we have time to inform you of the total situation, we don't want you calling out for help, attacking any of us or running out of the room."

Andy eyed Carmichael who said, "Just relax, I've been through this twice myself. No harm will come to you ... I hope."

Glass smiled, hoping to indicate that Carmichael was only joking, "Now Andy, I'm about to tell you a rather fantastic story that Mr. Carmichael here can confirm. At the end of that story I will make you an offer you can't refuse, as they say. On the one hand you'll be looking at an actual immortal existence in amazing bliss or on the other, instant yet painless death if you find you cannot work with us because frankly you have become a threat to our plans."

Now Andy was certain it was indeed his heart he could hear thumping.

Alpha-1 proceeded to tell Andy the entire story of the mine collapse, switching bodies with Glass, meeting Carmichael and the President. He described Alpha, its origins, immortal life, virtual, real, and fantasy worlds, how it came to be and the fact that humans and Alphans shared a common ancestor millions of years ago. He went on to describe the threat from space and the plan to combat it. He left out the part about the A-bomb and Dan Westgate's death.

He described the work going on at Area-51 with the advanced robots and the supercomputer as well as the giant invisible dome out in the desert on a dried-up lake bed where a space weapon needing rare earth materials was being built and finally he disclosed his own unexpected death and reincarnation earlier in the day.

The whole thing took less than thirty minutes while Andy's heart continued to thump the whole time.

"Now Andy, we need some information from you and then we'll discuss this offer I mentioned. I'm now going to release you and allow you to talk. Please don't call out, run or try to attack either of us, as I can assure you, it will not turn out well for you."

Alpha-1 released him enough that he could nod his head.

As Andy agreed his whole body was returned to him and he sat up straighter in the chair and finally took a deep breath on his own.

Carmichael decided to get in on the act, "How did you know the things you told my ops center on the phone call?"

This was the moment. He was being asked to reveal his sources and tell them what he knew. This went against everything he had learned as a reporter, but the piece of the last half hour that really stuck in his mind was 'instant painless death', which after sitting for so long frozen, seemed like a guarantee.

He took another deep breath and reflecting on being frozen, reasoned this all had to be real given Carmichael was standing here corroborating the story and the feeling that his scientific background could not explain any of this.

Finally he told them about his observations at McCarron when the workers returned and his two visits to Wendy's where he had overheard workers conversing. A little research using his scientific background told him that the materials were likely rare earths from China which had no seeming use in fighter jets in any significant quantity. Anticipating the question he told them he hadn't written any of it down or informed anyone else of his suspicions except to the extent that he thought something was going on at Area-51.

Alpha-1 and Carmichael smiled at each other. There was no leak, just an inquisitive reporter with a good imagination, a technical background, a good set of ears, and a logical mind.

Alpha-1 moved to the meat of the matter, "Up at Area-51 we have a General Hawkins and a couple of soldiers and kitchen staff who saw me die this morning. I can't go back up there looking like this and Robert Glass is the only DNA we kept, so to make a long story short I need your body."

Andy was frozen in place once more but this time due to his own state of shock, "Wow, that wasn't what I was expecting. I was waiting to hear about a memory erase or something."

Alpha-1 smiled, "Sorry, but as you can imagine, I need a new body to reappear at Area-51 to continue my work and you are our first choice. In return you'll be on-boarded into Alpha, will be given an IQ of well over 300, an avatar of your choosing, and immortal life in a combined real, virtual and fantasy world which some of my human friends have said sounds like heaven, and I must agree.

"After we on-board your psyche, I will enter a clone of your body that we will have screened for any health issues. I'll request from you that I keep some of your memories, enough to be credible if Hawkins wants to interrogate me but this time I will keep some of your taste preferences … long story, but I will also have most of my own psyche which includes the recent memories of Robert Glass so I can pick up where I left off.

"I'll be introduced by Mr. Carmichael here as the new COO of Carmichael's project at Area-51, where I can get back to the task of saving the planet from these approaching aliens. If you wish, you can watch and even experience the whole thing from Alpha.

"If you find you're unable to comply then we must terminate you as you now know far too much and are too inquisitive about the project and we'll have to start a search for someone who will take the deal.

"I don't have to tell you that according to Mr. Carmichael's team you live a rather solitary existence which simplifies things for your disappearance. It also means your absence will not cause too much of a stir. At least nothing we can't handle.

"If you can't comply then a broken-down car in the desert with a dead body nearby should suffice. But as I've said to my other human friends, threats are not our style and totally unnecessary. We have a win-win here. You can help save the world and live forever in bliss."

Andy McPherson was stunned. It was a lot to take in, he looked at Carmichael, "So I'm to believe that this guy standing here isn't a mine inspector, but an alien who froze me and I'm supposed to believe this incredible story?"

Carmichael smiled, "I've been to the setup in Area-51 and that, along with other things I've seen, leads me to tell you that Alpha-1 here, we call him Alpha-1 not Bob Glass, has proven truthful in everything he has told us. Given both the President and I are on board with the plan, I think you should believe everything he is telling you. And for the record, we are humanoid cousins and he does not like to be referred to as an alien. We call them Alphans."

Andy turned and looked at Alpha-1 again, "What will this

'on-boarding' feel like?"

They were both happy Andy seemed ready to accept the deal, "It will be instantaneous and very pleasurable. You'll still feel like yourself, just a lot smarter and physically stronger, more blissful and at peace. Some would say euphoric. I've been told one of the first sensations people notice is the lack of gravity on their body although you won't float away, unless you want to.

"Then you'll start exploring your new capabilities. You'll need lots of initial coaching just to keep you out of trouble but we'll take care of that.

"I'm afraid we're on a critical timeline so the moment has come for you to decide."

Andy looked back and forth between the two of them and then said with a large smile, "I'm in. I never really bought into the other 'eternal life' story anyways."

Alpha-1 took over, "Fraser, you head back to your car and phone Hawkins and tell him you'll need clearance to land at Area-51 in the next couple of hours. The new Andy McPherson will meet you in the car in a few minutes and then we'll head to the plane. That way your staff here will see the same two people who arrived, leave together."

Fraser Carmichael did as ordered and just as he finished his conversation with General Hawkins, Andy McPherson knocked at the window to gain entry.

All he said was, "All went as planned."

It was hard to miss the giant Great Dane puppy sitting quietly at the other end of the stretch limo.

Alpha-1 smiled and said, "Come here boy," and proceeded to play with the giant dog.

As they left the Hawk Hotel's main entrance, the new Andy took out his cell phone and hit one of its speed dials. It was now about eight p.m. and Fraser watched as he seemed to wait for some voicemail message on the other end, "Jim, this is Andy. I quit. I know this isn't much notice but I've seen how you give no notice when you dump people so sayonara and screw you, I'm off to greener pastures. Tell Marnie she can have the plant on our shared desk, it's mine."

The new Andy smiled as he hung up and turning to Fraser said, "Not sure Andy would've done that but I think he'll like it."

It was nearing ten p.m. as they taxied in from the main runway at the secret air base on Groom Lake more commonly known as Area-51. General Hawkins was waiting for the two men as they descended the stairs from the private jet and was shocked to see they were accompanied by a giant black dog.

Fraser jumped right in, "Good of you to meet us here General, as I'm about to make a quick turn around and head back east.

"I'd like to introduce you to Mr. Andrew McPherson, Carmichael Industries' new man in charge of this project. By the way, his dog's name is Samson, part of the deal I had to make to get him here so quickly," he smiled.

Hawkins was immediately suspicious. Even though this guy was a couple of years senior to the amazing Mr. Glass, he certainly didn't look any more the part of a corporate COO than Glass did. Still nothing about Fraser Carmichael, his relationship with the President and his COOs made any sense from the beginning.

Carmichael was still talking, "We need to get refueled, have my pilot file a new flight plan and leave here with the remains of the unfortunate Mr. Glass, if you don't mind?"

General Clay Hawkins hadn't liked Carmichael from the start and even though he was an internationally celebrated business tycoon, something in the way he blurted out veiled orders to an Air Force General really got under his skin.

In the short time he had worked with Bob Glass he had come to like the young man, notwithstanding all of the mysteries. Something in Carmichael's tone reeked of disrespect for the dead and he didn't like it. "Sir, I'm afraid this is a military base and we've had an unexpected and unexplained death of an otherwise healthy young man. We're flying in a military medical examiner to do the autopsy tomorrow and as I'm sure you'll appreciate, we have jurisdiction here and must do an official death certificate. So I'm afraid you will not be leaving here with Mr. Glass's remains tonight."

Fraser smiled and spoke slowly, "General, with all due respect, it's almost ten p.m. here and that means about one a.m. in Washington. Do you really think we need to wake the President so that he can give you direct orders to release the body to me or can we just get on with what we both know is about to happen?"

Hawkins was furious with himself for not seeing that coming.

After a long pause as he sneered at Carmichael he lifted his radio and spoke, "Have Doc Burrows deliver Robert Glass's remains in a transport box to the Carmichael jet on the double."

There was an awkward moment until Andy McPherson reached forward to shake the General's hand, "Sir, I'm totally briefed on the project and progress to date so I'm ready to assume my responsibilities immediately. Unlike my predecessor Bob Glass, I will do a better job of managing my time and energy but in all honesty I need to get to the hangars and check on progress. Our overall project has been without leadership for over twelve hours.

"I take it there have been no security issues?" this even though Alpha-1 was aware of one intrusion earlier in the evening.

The General blushed again, "We did have one potential issue a few hours ago just after sunset. Apparently one of our younger airmen got a little too close to one of the hangars. When we went looking for him we found him stunned and confused sitting on the ground about twenty-five yards from the back of hangar #2 but none of our other sentries saw anything. As best we can tell he may have been tasered. He's with a medic right now but he seems to be coming around. I don't know what kind of proximity security you have around those buildings but my best guess at this time is that it worked. You should know though, that I don't like my men being attacked in this fashion!"

Carmichael was immediately concerned, but Alpha-1 knew all the details of the encounter and was more than pleased that the General had been completely up front about it. His level of trust in the General had just taken a step up. "General I apologize for any difficulty this has caused your team but I think you were briefed on our requirement for security so it might be a good use of your time to reinforce the message and use tonight's event as a warning to your men."

Hawkins stared at the newcomer and thought, 'Wow! This guy is just as confident and arrogant as the last one.'

Within the hour Carmichael's jet was refueled, Glass's remains loaded into the hold and his plane was racing down the runway for its trip to Washington. Carmichael wanted a face to face with the President again as they hadn't resolved his board issues, so during the flight he called the special presidential number. Waking the President he told him Andy was on the job, that he would be in around six-thirty a.m. Washington time and he wanted a meeting first thing in the morning in the Oval Office.

He also requested and got support from the President to land at Andrews and have the medical team in charge take custody of an unnamed corpse which was to be kept incognito in the base morgue under tight security until such time as the President released it.

Just before he took a nap he checked his mail and there was one urgent message from his lawyer. Apparently an *'in camera'* session of the Senate Oversight committee wanted to see him at ten a.m. on December 21st, just a few days away. His first thought was the Senate must be really agitated if they were delaying their normal departure for the Christmas and New Year's recess.

***

As planned, Carmichael, after a few Zs on the plane, got into DC around six-thirty a.m. and only had time to get to his Washington condo, shower and change to be on time for his meeting with President Harold Turcot. They had just started their discussions when one more time his red line rang. Both men wondered what was next. After a moment the President put the line on speaker and asked the caller to repeat his statement.

"Mr. Carmichael, we've never met but I'm the real Robert Glass now living in what you know as Alpha."

Carmichael was shocked. The President hadn't seemed surprised by the call.

"I'm glad I caught both of you gentlemen together as I have no way yet to call Mr. Carmichael directly. As I told the President on my last call …"

Carmichael flushed red and stared down Hal Turcot who didn't take his eyes away from the phone.

Glass continued, "… The thing you call Alpha-1 isn't being totally honest with you. As I told you Mr. President he lied about the computer room in the mine just to engage Mr. Carmichael, and he has also lied consistently on what we in Alpha can see.

"Beyond that, I still haven't found another indigenous person from Alpha. They're all captured human psyches and the numbers aren't big. If I was to guess I'd say there are only a few thousand of us here and if he is the only Alphan then he is the only one who can on-board humans. It also means that your partner in this approaching alien thing is a one-man show and that also worries me.

"I'm not complaining. I took the deal Alpha-1 offered me in the mine and I'm glad I did. Likely everything he has told you in that vein is real and honest, but again something isn't right. I can't vouch for immortality yet, but I've met ex-humans who claim to have been here for a few hundred years so far.

"I can find no information on the origins of Alpha, its inhabitants, if there was ever more than one of them and what happened to them if there was a whole civilization. The information either does not exist or is being hidden from all of us. Alphan history is one subject that seems to be off limits to us.

"From what I can tell, I'm really the first human here who was brought up in a culture of critical thought. None of the others seem concerned that there is no way to verify Alpha-1's story about the existence of Alpha before humans, a common ancestor and so on.

"I can't for the life of me, even with my increased IQ, think of why it would be important to hide this information or lie to us unless there is something nefarious going on. It all seems a bit too weird and with what is at stake, I think you need to have some contingency plans. We have no guarantees that he is in fact a biological cousin to us. Our cooperation with him, at least on my part, is strongly linked to that belief.

"In addition, no one here, except myself, knows anything about approaching aliens or the so called 'weapon', so again there is a blanket of secrecy around everything and as I told you on the first call, there's no question he can lie when he wants to."

Carmichael was taking all of this in and still glaring at the President who had failed to mention the earlier call.

Glass was still on a rant, "I don't see how you can confront him on this either. I think the only thing we can do for the moment is band together, keep our eyes open and our powder dry and try to figure out if there is some agenda at work here that isn't being revealed to us. I'm only pushing this gentlemen, because the stakes are so high and I have a real sense of foreboding. Any time I meet someone who is this charming and this deceitful, well my antenna goes up if you know what I mean.

"Now the one thing I hear is that the cloned body I traded for didn't make it. Apparently Alpha-1 simply drove it into the ground and a healthy twenty-four-year-old body died from exhaustion. I have real fears for anyone else he converts or 'populates', and I think his intention was to find a replacement for my body fast. The issue is that he can no longer use my DNA as there may have been people who saw Bob Glass die and I'm the only human DNA he reports to have access to."

Carmichael felt he had to break in, "I'm going to assume you're who you say you are." The President nodded that he either knew or suspected this was indeed the original Bob Glass on the phone.

"You're right about the death and we've picked a person to replace you and he is already on the job, so Alpha-1 has occupied another body and there should be another ex-human in Alpha.

"The good news is that he seems to be more cautious now, given what went wrong the last time and he is going to be more careful with this body. If you haven't met him already, there should be a new resident of Alpha named Andrew McPherson from Las Vegas wandering around. He was an investigative reporter but has an advanced degree in physics and may help you in your hunt for information. But to add to your concerns, Alpha-1 told us his efforts are all public and shared but clearly he masked the replacement strategy and possibly other things from you.

"But I have a question for you. Who runs Alpha while Alpha-1 is playing human if there are no other native Alphans around?"

Glass responded, "That's a great question and one that has been plaguing me too. Apart from the fact that this place seems to run mostly on autopilot, I can't decipher if this place is actually sentient or whether Alpha-1 or someone else actually has some control over it, even when he isn't here."

It was the President's turn, "What do you mean sentient?"

Young Glass hesitated and then responded, "Well even on Earth with our technologies, there have always been those who believe that if a computer was fast enough and programmed in a certain way, it might become self-aware. You must remember HAL in 2001 for instance or even better, Skynet in the Terminator movies.

"There are things that go on here that would seem to require judgment before decision-making of a complexity and style that would make you think there is someone or some intelligence at the controls, even though Alpha-1 isn't around. From my perspective it goes beyond artificial intelligence and I can't be specific but there even seems to be imbedded preferences at work. Either that is the computer itself that thinks like a self-aware entity and has its own consciousness or as I said, someone is controlling the whole thing; Alpha-1 or someone else, but I can't find the source.

"The gist of all of this and my feelings that have consistently grown since I arrived here, are that Alpha-1 isn't telling us everything. He either does not trust us or worse, has a hidden agenda. Given we are involved in a potential extinction event, I think you will agree that you need to have total confidence in your partner."

Carmichael was watching the President who had shown no further interest in jumping into the conversation. Maybe it was the higher IQ but this Glass kid seemed bright and articulate and Carmichael figured they needed to take his concerns seriously.

Glass wrapped up with, "I'm really glad the three of us are now on the same page and we can communicate like this. Remember Mr. President, use that device I left for you if you need to talk to me."

"Got to go. If I find out anything else I will let you know. I'm off to look for this Andy character and compare notes with him."

At that the line went dead before either man had time to ask him further questions about Alpha and the disturbing news he had just delivered.

Carmichael lost no time, "What the hell! You've spoken to this kid before and you have a device to call him? Why did you hide that from me? Why didn't you use it when Glass dropped dead?"

Turcot seeming impatient, walked around his desk and sat down as he said, "There was no attempt to hide anything. When have we had a chance to talk? Yesterday just after we met we got the call about Glass dropping dead out west and right after that the call from Alpha-1. Besides I haven't found this device he was speaking of. There have been bigger issues to deal with. I have a country to run and a planet to save, so don't go get all uppity on me. Glass doesn't have anything real, they're all just feelings."

Carmichael wasn't buying it. The fact that the real Bob Glass was now speaking to them and didn't trust Alpha-1 was the elephant in the room and Turcot had consciously refused to share that. Carmichael knew they didn't like each other but on this project he thought they had established some trust at least, or was he wrong and the trust had all been one way?

He could see by the President's impatience that he wasn't going to get anything more out of him this morning so he segued back to his original problem, "What about you declaring everything to do with the project 'Eyes Only' and the only people on the list are you, me and Andy McPherson? If you can't run this interference for me then it'll be no time before the board fires me, informs the SEC or resigns en masse and any one of those events will cause an FBI investigation which will be quickly followed by a military investigation at Area-51 and on any of those we're sunk. We'll be in a shooting war between American troops and some robot defense systems out there that will likely wipe them out in seconds and then we'll have Alpha-1 threatening to make it easy and just wipe out all mankind.

"No, let me take that back. Alpha-1 will know that I have lost my job and Plan B will be implemented immediately. You and I and everyone else on this planet will just drop dead a nanosecond after the board votes. Now you explain to me how that is not the only outcome of this. I've told you before, there is NO STORY I can dream up that they will not see through in an instant. I'm dead and so are you if I go back in there with anything short of an 'Eyes Only' position."

The President was getting really impatient with Carmichael now. As far as Turcot was concerned, Carmichael was not holding up his end of the bargain with the trouble he had gotten into and he was trying to dump his problems on the White House. He had lots of his own obstacles to take care of.

Right now the President wished he had ANYONE else on the planet to work with. Someone more reliable who could get the job done. Carmichael at his core was a selfish son of a bitch and only thought of himself and his own challenges.

Exasperated, Turcot turned on him, "You don't seem to understand. I already spend most of my day making up stories and fighting off politicians from both sides of the aisle for what I've already done to support this project. I've lost count of the number of lies I've had to tell.

"Do you even watch TV anymore? Half of the Republicans already think there are sufficient grounds for impeachment with the way I canceled the F-35 and the F-47 development and awarded a no-bid contract to you putting tens of thousands out of work. My half-baked story about training people for the jobs of the future just isn't cutting it.

"The job losses we have are real and they are here now, not five years from now so there is no equivalency and frankly I've run out of ideas on what to say and my staff have decided this is a losing argument so they're no help.

"I've had ten resignations in the last week. They all think I've lost it. And the ones who are still here are just not contributing anything because they don't believe in it. Hell I don't believe the stories I'm telling. And now you want me to set the highest level of security on the project so you don't have to make up a story for your board?

"They have grounds to throw me out of office already. I still have a couple of friends on the Hill and one of them slipped me this," he said as he grabbed a paper on his desk.

"Here are the articles of impeachment they're floating to see what support they have:

1.   Abuse of power – secret/illegal contracts with Carmichael Industries for the F-47

2.   Separation of Powers – refusing oversight of Congress – refusing to respond/appear

3.   Abuse of power – bypassing government procurement regulations and Pentagon input on building the F-47

4.   Abuse of power/treason – divulging military secrets to unclassified recipients – Robert Glass & Fraser Carmichael.

5.   Abuse of power – only Congress can spend money to build F-47s

6.   Treason – canceling a critical military war machine with no replacement.

"And the best part is they only need to get a majority to agree to one of these charges to impeach me. Luckily the Senate trial will take longer than the vote on impeachment.

"Even if I do as you suggest and use my Executive Powers to declare the project as 'Eyes Only' it wouldn't stick. They'll run to SCOTUS and get an injunction and overturn the thing until proper process is followed. With that injunction either the intelligence community or the Pentagon will butt in and you know what that means, opening the doors at Area-51."

"Listen Turcot! I understand you have issues but I live in the real world. The real world of business where a board moves fast. They can blow this thing out of the water without even calling a board meeting. One call to the SEC and we're done. Not like Congress where it takes them months to wordsmith a censure. Remember, we've only a few weeks more to make this thing stick and then either the world ends or we're home free and kickin' back in heaven. I need to survive that long in my company or we're toast. Alpha-1 will have no compunction in eliminating us first because we know too much. Think of it this way, what's one more charge to that list supporting impeachment?"

Both men stared at each other for a long time. Carmichael standing in front of the Resolute Desk behind which President Harold Turcot leaned back in his chair furious with the position he was being pushed into. Carmichael was half right. If he declared 'Eyes Only' on the project it might just last long enough to complete the project but that was really iffy. The other side could probably get to SCOTUS quickly and throw a wrench into the works. There had to be a way to get them both out of trouble but nothing was coming to mind.

Suddenly Carmichael had an idea, pulled out his newly secured phone and hit a speed dial.

"Andy, or Alpha-1 or whatever it is you want me to call you, we're getting into a tight political jam over all the secrecy on our project. How fast can you get me the first two Firebolts to alleviate some of the pressure?

"OK, let's do that," and he hung up.

Turcot was angry as he leaned back in his chair, "What the hell was that all about?"

Carmichael smiled, "How do you feel about a couple of Firebolts doing unbelievable stunts over the Capitol for New Year's Day? That's only about twelve days away. It will drive the Pentagon nuts that we've been successful where they have failed and that we're showing off some of their toys. We might be giving the enemy a close-up look but all they'll see is its overall shape and some of its capability and we'll be careful not to show them too much, just enough to wow Americans.

"We'll show them that $45M a copy is pretty fantastic when FOX was recently predicting they would be over $300M each. Remember, Alpha-1 is going to beat the specs and I'm going to sell them to you at that original fantasy price. You'll look like the smartest guy on the planet. Let them try to impeach you after that. It also solves my problem with the board. After they see those birds flying, the pressure will be off and all talk of risk and corporate losses will be behind me. But I need you to get me through the next twelve days."

Turcot thought about this for a moment and then said, "I'll have the documents drawn up today and signed before the end of the day. We won't announce it until we need to. It will take whoever challenges me a couple of weeks to undo the secrecy. You can go back to your board and tell them to shove it. As you say, this plane flying around Washington could stall our problems if we can pull it off. No board problems after that, right?"

Carmichael beamed, "I'll say. The board will love me again."

The President rose from his desk and walked around so he was standing beside Carmichael, "The only thing we have to worry about now is the aliens arriving early."

Carmichael sneered, "You had to say that. I told you I can't sleep. I'm having recurring nightmares about that very thing. I almost feel like going back out west, rolling up my sleeves and helping Alpha-1 in any way I can to build that weapon."

Carmichael pointed his finger at the President's chest, "Pray or whatever it is you do, that these aliens don't arrive before we're finished the weapon because I believe we're totally screwed if they show up early."

***

High over the Nevada desert one of Carmichael's own stealth drones based at Indian Lake, Nevada turned to make its final approach at thirty thousand feet over Area-51. The specially equipped vehicle was carrying an untested new weapon that few on Earth were aware of. A pilotless drone had been picked for two reasons. Area-51 had some defensive capability and if detected, an unannounced overflight not responding to hailing, might get shot out of the sky and secondly the new weapon might disable the drone itself even though the electronic design and shielding was supposed to compensate for that.

From his operations panel the drone tech, alone in the room with his base commander, checked his position over the target and looked to his superior for the final order. The General nodded and he wasted no time lifting the red cover plate and pressing the 'fire' button on his console.

The weapon, directly over the secret military base sent out a one second burst of incredible electromagnetic energy causing one of the many large battery packs to glow red and explode punching a hole in the side of the drone's fuselage.

The cold rushing air at thirty thousand feet quickly extinguished the small fire and then as planned the drone turned and limped back to its home at nearby Creech AFB.

Ten minutes later General Jenkins received a text message that simply said 'DONE'.

***

Carmichael was still in the Oval office when his cell phone rang and the screen said 'Andy'.

Puzzled, he showed the screen to the President and took the call.

Before he could say a word Andy said, "Put me on speaker."

Carmichael complied as Andy spoke, "I'm calling you using Alpha's technology because this base just got zapped by an EMP wave and everything electronic took a massive electrical overload and is down. We're investigating now but I think we'll find that Jenkins or maybe Hawthorne did this. It seems Mr. President that your military leaders have switched sides and taken some direct action in opposition to your instructions.

"You may not know this but the drone base here in Nevada has been experimenting with a localized EMP pulse to knock out enemy bases. All they had to do was load the device into some kind of shielded stealth aircraft and fly it high over this base and press the button.

"Now this does not affect our space weapon because everything we have on Groom Lake is much more sophisticated and shielded from EMP but we may have to rework the F-47s which shouldn't be an insurmountable problem. Hawkins will be in here any moment as his whole base is down. He's going to need new C-17s until they can repair and recertify the two on the ground right now.

"I don't see your Joint Chiefs owning up to this so be prepared for some story that an invisible Russian or Chinese weapon, possibly on satellites did this but our assessment is that your own military, possibly with urging from the CIA, is behind this.

"Now I hear Hawkins with some others headed this way so that's all for now."

***

Hawkins was furious as he marched into Andy's office, "Are you responsible for this?"

Andy put on his best shocked face, "Hell no! What the hell is going on? Everything just died. I thought it was a power failure but even my SAT phone isn't working."

Hawkins seemed unconvinced, "As best we can tell we may have gotten hit by an EMP pulse 'cause everything on the base is down. No water, no electricity, no Jeeps, no planes, no choppers, no radar, and no phones. When I left the main building medics were working on our famous cook who apparently relies on a pacemaker.

"If I find out this crazy F-47 project of yours had anything to do with this then there's going to be hell to pay. We were never warned of any such dangers. Everything we're doing to support you is down until we can get some new equipment in here. This will take days to weeks to fix completely.

"Luckily, there's a scheduled chopper due in here within the hour or we'd have to walk to the nearest base to get help. At least then we'll have a working radio to get things flowing but just so you know, this is millions in damage. For one thing my C-17s will need to be recertified and probably need most of their electronics replaced. The same is true of all the other aircraft, drones, and spare parts on the base including our choppers. That includes all our CCTV cameras and motion sensors so our security is all blind right now too."

Andy stood quickly. "I swear General Hawkins, I'm aware of nothing in our equipment that could do anything like what you're talking about. Everything in here was normal until it all just shut off. We need to get this fixed fast so I can try to get back on schedule with the project. You should order some new transports as soon as you get communications up and you need to get security back up somehow."

Hawkins just stared at him red-faced for a few seconds and finally turned to leave with the sentries he had brought with him.

***

Carmichael had decided to wait with the President while he had the Executive Order paperwork for an 'Eyes Only' order drawn up. Less than thirty minutes had gone by when suddenly Carmichael's phone rang again showing 'Andy' as the caller. Both men stared at each other thinking 'What now!'

Carmichael put it on speaker, "Gentlemen I have some bad news."

"Mr. President, your Director of the CIA, Bill Carter will momentarily be found dead beside his car in the CIA underground parking of an apparent heart attack which given the man's age will seem plausible and the autopsy will show blockages in the heart."

Carmichael simply stared horrified at Turcot.

Andy continued, "I'm afraid we had no options as only I can on-board humans. I could not get to him in time and the chances were very high he was about to open a massive can of worms as they say.

"Recently you asked him to start surveillance on the Joint Chiefs. This may have been the stimulus for him investigating the Minot incident and we only became aware this morning that he has a recording from a bug we were unaware of in NORAD headquarters with your voice and Dan Westgate's on the recording revealing a very different narrative than what has been accepted as the chain of events of that night.

"We were unaware of the passive bug when we cleaned up NORAD after the missile. According to our quick forensic investigation he has apparently known about this for some time but only this morning left a voicemail for one of his trusted agents and was about to brief him on concerns he had 'about Minot' which caused us to look into the situation and we discovered the recording. We also discovered independently that he was aware that Dan Westgate had a clean brain scan just before his death. Another oversight on our part.

"We eliminated the voicemail and a digital recording from his desk. We will continue the search but for now we think we have the only copy of the recording and we have no evidence at this time that he shared his concerns or the recording with anyone else.

"Again, I'm afraid we had no option. He was on his way to brief the agent in question and there was no other way to stop him given we only had limited resources close to him. If we had waited, we'd have been dealing with even more people who had damning information.

"If an investigation into that recording was started, many others would have had to be dealt with. I have told you before that we can only fix what we know about and apparently the CIA at some point had added a well-hidden passive bug in NORAD Headquarters. At the moment it would appear that only Bill Carter knew of the bug and had access to the recordings but we will follow-up to ensure there are no other vulnerabilities.

"Your futile attempt at striking at Alpha continues to provide challenges."

The two men in the Oval Office just stared at each other in stunned silence.

Andy continued, "On the earlier matter, there is no evidence that the CIA was in on the EMP attack out here at the base but it was definitely your own people. One of Mr. Carmichael's own stealth drones was damaged in the attack but has now returned to its base. We actually sustained no damage in the hangars as we had suspected something of this nature would happen, and had installed a shielding device which worked, but Hawkins doesn't know that.

"He is running around like a crazy man trying to get this base back in operational shape. When you do get into it with your military leaders you might indicate that the attack put us back a few days but we are hurrying to make up for lost time. I think your position should be that we are not going to blame any foreign governments on this until we have more evidence.

"For our part we have stepped up surveillance on your military leaders and that drone base in particular. I think they'll find it difficult to launch any more attacks as a series of nagging failures will keep their equipment grounded."

Abruptly Andy said, "Have a good day," and hung up.

After the line went dead Carmichael whispered to Turcot, "The real Glass told us he was the only one who could on-board humans. Looks like at least on that point he was right."

Turcot looked exasperated, "Do you really think whispering is going to stop him from hearing us? I'm guessing he knows everything including Glass's calls."

Carmichael looked spent and terrified, "He kills people without blinking an eye. How are we ever going to get through this alive? What else can go wrong?

"I feel like I'm staggering around blindly in a mine field. I'm shocked we've made it this far! It seems like daily or even hourly we are this close to blowing the project out of the water and suffering a quick end in Plan B and don't doubt for a minute that he wouldn't go to that plan in the blink of an eye.

"We've had Glass drop dead, a reporter investigating things out of Vegas, a Sheriff out west who is trying to extradite me to go back there and tell them what we know about Eric Lawrence's death, a missing coroner and a fire that claimed three lives, as well as dead CIA and defense leaders and on top of that multiple articles of impeachment and joint committees trying to stop us, military guys launching attacks on the project, and a board that could end it all with one vote or phone call.

"I mean, how have we survived this long? And that's not even talking about the biggie, aliens arriving at any moment."

Turcot answered, "One step at a time. Stay positive. At least there's a pot of gold at the end of the rainbow and we're home free if we can make it to the end. If, and only if, Alpha's plan to hide from the aliens works. That's the biggest threat in my mind because he admits they know almost nothing about them. They might see right through the cloaking for all we know. All we can do is put one foot in front of the other."

Carmichael looked like he was about to collapse and was almost pleading, "That's just it, look at how many obstacles and mistakes we've dealt with so far. I didn't even mention hundreds dying in Minot including my guys, and your daughter on her last legs. I'm telling lies to my board and I'm getting caught at it. Alpha could blow us out of the water before the aliens ever arrive. How long can we survive on this tightrope without falling off? I can't handle this anymore. My nerves are completely shot."

Turcot put his hand on his shoulder, "We just need to focus and get through this. Now don't go folding on me!"

Both men sized each other up and saw two frazzled and exhausted men staring back at each other. It was true that they had avoided too many near catastrophes and more almost certainly lay in front of them but it was also true that they had started to work together, if only reluctantly.

Just as they were about to part, Carmichael's phone went one more time. 'Not again,' they both thought. It was Andy and Carmichael immediately put it on speaker.

The Threat

Andy sounded deeply worried, "I'm afraid we have even more bad news gentlemen, and this time it's quite serious. As I have told you, we know very little about the approaching aliens and their intentions but that just changed. Since we discovered the leaked signal, we've been studying them closely with the little historical data we have. We've been reviewing everything we can find going back to when we first detected them and some of that data has just forced us to come to an important and disturbing conclusion.

"The earliest planet we saw them arrive at, which is about five thousand light years away, has shown a small but definite spectral shift over a period of just forty years of observed data. The most likely cause is a change in the atmosphere that happened a little over five thousand years ago and we think about fifteen years after their arrival there. The light is only arriving here now and we've been looking for ways to find the data from previous years from any kind of space data we might have. We were concerned about this and the numbers just went beyond the threshold of statistical probability, so we are quite sure it's a real change."

Carmichael was first to ask, "What is a spectral shift and what does it mean?"

Andy spoke slowly, "Most bodies in the universe either give off light, reflect light or we can examine light passing through their atmosphere assuming they have one. Even your scientists use spectral analysis on that light and other radiation to determine what elements are prevalent in a given object. In this case the most likely reason for this significant spectral shift is a changing atmosphere or what your scientists would call terraforming.

"It now appears these aliens arrive at a populated Goldilocks planet wearing what you would think of as space suits, if indeed they have physical bodies. On arrival they start changing the atmosphere, which likely takes many years if not decades or even centuries to complete. So not only do we see the communications modes changing over time on the occupied planet, but now we also see the atmosphere being changed so they can prepare the planet for their own needs, which means nothing good for the original inhabitants.

"We now consider it a very high probability that they are a hostile marauding civilization whom we need to repel at all costs. It also

357

suggests they are not immortal like Alpha, but rely on resources such as the atmosphere of a planet. They could still have eternal lives like Alphans and need the atmosphere changed for some other reason, but that is of no benefit to the indigenous population. They seem to have very long time horizons which would indicate long life spans, if they are not immortal, so they may have perfected their bodies, engage in some kind of cloning or become cyborgs of some sort. However, the data we now have is conclusive; that at least in the first instance we see them arriving at a planet, they felt it necessary to change the atmosphere, which would most likely make it uninhabitable for the indigenous flora and fauna.

"Likely everything that was alive on that planet five thousand years ago has been dead for a long time. Their version of terraforming would allow them to reset the planet to their own flora and fauna or to support some other need they have, possibly even something to do with energy harvesting. The reason they are doing this is irrelevant. The reality is that the original occupants of the planet would likely not survive such a change.

"One last point. Our initial analysis of how they are changing the atmosphere on that planet would make life on Earth impossible as well."

The President couldn't wait any more, "What does that mean for us and the weapon you are building?"

"Practically nothing. We have no time to change strategies and even if we had had this information earlier, we can think of no other defense we could mount in the time available. Given we still know nothing of their capabilities, what kind of weapon would we build?

"We still need to hide but the threat is much greater now that we have concluded they are indeed hostile. We need to redouble our efforts to make this thing work and fast. We also need to start thinking about how we would repel them if needed, but sadly we have no time for that now. It's almost a certainty that Alphans and humans have nothing in terms of weaponry at this point to get into a shooting war with them. At least we determined they were likely to arrive here soon and we've had a chance to take some defensive action. But gentlemen, we cannot fail in this regard.

"And while we are on this subject, please remember what I said about your success. You both need to be completely successful in your tasks or you know the consequences. But know this, the further we get into this the less wiggle room we have. The closer we get to our target of launching the weapon and disappearing underground the less time we have to react to any issues and we've had more than a few already. We can't afford any more distractions or detours."

Turcot noticed a definite shiver on the part of Carmichael who was white as chalk.

***

After Carmichael left to go off and deal with his board, Turcot spent the rest of the day trying to catch up on everything that had been falling off the table of late. No matter how hard he tried, most of his time was taken up trying to calm down Senators and Congressmen on the Hill. He was slowly losing that battle.

He had been so busy he had had no time for the family and that was becoming a problem in itself. His secretary Mary had given him a glance from time to time like 'you'd better get upstairs'.

Climbing the stairs to the residence, he ran immediately into Evelyne who was clearly frantic over Ann's illness and his being almost nonexistent at the worst possible time. She was dressed for the one event she had agreed to participate in.

The White House was decked out for Christmas as was the tradition and several large Christmas trees were scattered throughout the building but due to Ann's illness all Christmas activities at the White House involving the first family had been canceled this year.

All the staff knew it must be getting close to the end for poor Ann, and the family had to be devastated. The one event he and Ev could not skip was the lighting of the national Christmas tree on the front lawn of the White House which had dragged on due to his commitments and now was as late as they could tolerate.

Ann would of course be absent from the event this year which would only bring more questions from the press.

***

The lighting of the tree was perfectly timed to the top of the hour so all the TV stations could pick it up before their prime time evening started.

He had arrived a few minutes early and raised the tower on his modified TV satellite truck with the big WRC-4 NBC logo on the side. He had more than enough time to set up the platform inside the truck now strategically parked on E Street where he had a clear view of the platform set up for the lighting ceremony. Normally vehicles would be kept well back but there was an exception for satellite trucks as there were limits to how much video cable they could lay out to the cameras at the event. The massive Christmas tree was far enough from the building that the normal press cameras and broadcast facilities would not suffice so a limited number of SAT trucks were allowed up close.

The gun, a Cheytac M200 Intervention was the finest sniper rifle made and he had meticulously set it up for accuracy that very morning. The custom, hollow point, depleted uranium round he had loaded would virtually take off Hal Turcot's head. Even a glancing blow would kill him instantly and at this distance the flight time would be well under a half second.

The rangefinder told him he was one hundred and fifty-three meters away from his target. A simple shot for a marksman like himself. Perfect conditions too, cool, no breeze and crystal clear. Even if the President moved, at this distance and with this fast round he couldn't miss. His position high inside the box truck and just below the satellite dish ensured that nothing under ten feet tall could obstruct his view.

He made sure to leave the ranting manifesto on the driver's seat pointing the finger at radical Muslims as he rechecked his view from the truck aiming through a disguised hole in its rear quarter. He was well back from the hole in the box of the truck so the muzzle flash and smoke from the round would be well hidden. His plan was simply to walk away leaving the truck behind as everyone was running towards the dead President.

The President and first lady were just ascending the stairs to the platform where all could see them as he took his prone position lying on the platform he had built for the purpose.

As he looked through his scope, something suddenly blocked his view of the target. Thinking a large truck or some other vehicle had crossed his path he raised his head to look out the hole in the truck when suddenly he realized he wasn't alone.

What seemed to be a massive mechanical man of some sort was hunched over in the truck blocking his vision. It snatched the rifle out of his hands with irresistible force and both it and the rifle simply vanished.

He looked down at his hands blinking to confirm that the rifle was actually gone. He hadn't dreamed any of it. Heart racing and never looking back, he bolted out of the truck and took the first cab he could find to the airport.

As the TV showed the President leaving the stage after lighting the national Christmas tree, the man referred to by his partners in crime as Number 3, shivered.

Something had gone wrong. The others would not be happy and it might take weeks to set up another attempt. He waited for the call from his hired gun but it never came. He'd have to watch the news to see if an attempt on the President's life had been foiled. He was relatively certain he and his associates were in the clear even if the man was caught. The hitman had no real ID on any of them.

Sometime later the park police became suspicious of the TV satellite truck that had not left after the event. Finding the manifesto, the investigation into who had built the sniper platform in the satellite truck and who had been in it started. The assumption was the shooter had gotten cold feet but it was clear he would have had a great shot at the President if he had proceeded. As usual, this obvious attempted assassination would not be reported to the public but internal reviews of procedure and investigations on how this could have happened would go on for months. The potential shooter instantly became the most hunted man in the US but they had not a speck of evidence on who they were looking for or why he had aborted his mission. Security videos from the immediate area showed no one walking away with anything that looked like a sniper rifle.

Later that evening the real NBC crew was found dead behind a building.

***

As the Turcots returned to the White House Ev noticed Hal was lost in thought and didn't offer his hand like he often did walking up the driveway. He seemed lost in his own world so she headed directly upstairs.

He spotted one of the elaborately decorated internal Christmas trees in the entrance again bringing to mind the season and his almost total detachment from the family only a few yards away upstairs. He had sensed his disengagement was even becoming an item of conversation among the staff, so he called up and told the help to tell Ev he would make it an early night and would be up in a minute.

By the time he made it upstairs an hour later, Ev, apparently exhausted from all the stress, had fallen asleep and was sprawled across their bed in her nightclothes.

Next morning with nothing urgent on the agenda he rose a little later and decided to have breakfast with the family. In the dining room Ev and the nurse had helped Ann into her custom-built power chair that had supports in all the right places. This morning she was smiling for a change.

Ann had been a very pretty and healthy seventeen-year-old when ALS first struck her. The illness had ravished her strength and now with the massive weight loss and slumping spine sadly she had lost all of that youthful vigor and beauty. In her current state she had to struggle even to try to smile.

She had been a frequent subject of magazine cover stories as she was young and the classically beautiful first daughter. Many wondered if she would marry in the White House before her 21st birthday when her dad's term was up. At one time that had been her parents' dream too. Sadly that was not to be and the ALS had come on fast and changed all of their lives forever. Once diagnosed, the symptoms seemed to grow at a steady and alarming pace where you didn't notice something every day but now only a few years later they were totally debilitating and she was nearing the end of her struggle.

It had been more than ten months now since she had been seen in public. She had deteriorated quickly of late and if she were ever to be seen in public the world would be shocked at what had happened to her.

Evelyne sitting next to her at the dining room table looked like she had been crying already but at the moment wore a big smile as Hal entered. She said, "Now this is more like it. I can't remember when you had time to eat with us recently, especially breakfast."

Hal Turcot sat down near his daughter and across from Evelyne. He put his arm around his daughter as best he could and said, "How are you feeling honey?"

In a strained voice and mumbling a little from the morphine she said, "Actually I feel better than I have in a long time."

ALS in its final stages drastically affected the ability to speak so both parents were elated when she got out a full comprehensible sentence, strained as it was.

Ev had read that some patients of terminal illnesses show a sudden rebound just before the end and there was no doubt, with the progression of Ann's ALS, she was not far from that day. Ev wondered how she would get through breakfast never mind Christmas and New Year's without blubbering the whole way. But more than that she wondered how life could go on without her once beautiful child. Her only child and the love of her life. As she eyed her daughter she thought that this wicked disease could not have picked a more undeserving victim.

Surprisingly, Ann struggled but kept up the conversation and engaged both of them through the meal speaking hoarsely and strained but much more than she had in a long time.

Harold left to refill his coffee in the tiny kitchen in the family residence and Evelyne followed him as Ann's nurse was feeding her, "It was great of you to make time for this Hal. It seems like months since you've been able to have regular meals with us.

"It's also quite a few weeks since we slept in the same bed. I know we all handle grief in our own way, but do you really think pulling away from us is the right answer at this time. We're all under stress and I don't mean just your job."

He turned to her, but all she could see was stress and not the empathy she had expected. It looked to her like he had pulled even further away than she had suspected. It seemed his mind was somewhere else.

He took her in his arms and hugged her saying, "You have no idea what stress I'm under right now. Frankly I'm at my lowest of lows. Ever since that accident in Minot and then this fighter battle, I haven't found a minute to breathe. I'll be lucky if I'm not impeached and thrown out of office and this beautiful house in the next few weeks. Then where will we be? We'd be back in our old house in Baton Rouge, not even the big Governor's mansion. We haven't lived in a house that small for over fifteen years. I'm not rich like some former presidents. The speaker circuit isn't something I feel up to right now and writing a book takes a long time. I'm terrified of what might become of us."

She was shocked that his list of priorities didn't have his daughter and her terminal illness at the top. She pushed back a little and stared into his eyes. She had been right. It wasn't there. He was blocking out the real concerns.

He had never been this heartless. Clearly he was attempting to bury himself in his work skipping meals and working till all hours of the night so they almost never saw him in the residence. Anything to keep his mind off the family catastrophe facing him.

She wanted to slap him out if it but that was not her way. There was no point in trying to shock him into the realization that his daughter was weeks or maybe even days away from dying.

Ev was completely disheartened. Just when she needed him most he had vacated their very bed. This was her man and surely he could see that she was at her lowest of lows too, yet he didn't seem to care, or could he even see her at all?

Ann slept a lot these days due to her weakness and the effects of the morphine, so most of the time Ev simply cried alone while her husband seemed always to be occupied elsewhere.

Still she feared for him. There was no doubt he would pay the price for his absence. At some point it would all come flooding back, probably at Ann's death or maybe after they left the White House if he was thrown out of office, but that day would come for sure.

There had been some who, almost a year ago, had suggested he needed to step down given the terrible distraction of a terminal illness in his family, but that concept had never seemed to get the time of day from him.

He had not asked to be collared with a family tragedy at such an inopportune time, potentially sidelining the peak of his career, but again he would sorely regret it when Ann was gone and he realized he had all but ignored her last weeks.

Ann was going to die. Through the constant tears, Evelyne was trying to deal with that inevitability. Whether he acknowledged the certainty of her impending death or not wouldn't change the reality and sooner or later he would have to deal with it.

Ev realized she was just too exhausted and depressed to get into it with him, and what would that achieve?

Hand in hand they walked back into the room and joined Ann and her nurse as they seemed to be finishing up.

After a few moments of light banter President Hal Turcot kissed his daughter on the forehead and headed back to his job downstairs.

Congress

A few days before Christmas, after comparing some notes with the President and Alpha-1, Fraser Carmichael was ushered into a private hearing room in the Senate wing of the Capitol building.

Thankfully this was a closed door, or *in camera* meeting so he didn't have to worry about the public or his board seeing him get beat up on CSPAN. Being so close to Christmas might have explained why the committee was not in full attendance with several Senators bowing out for their trips home for 'urgent business.'

The majority leader of the Senate, Senator William Porter, Democrat from California, gaveled the meeting to order, swore in the witness and then started with, "Sir, you may know that we have depositions from two of your former executives. It seems that neither of them knew anything about this project you and the President have spoken of, which I find peculiar and further to that, both men refused to answer any of our questions on the basis that they have a non-disclosure agreement with you, which apparently carries unheard of penalties. I think you know that if we have any evidence of a crime here then we can compel them to answer our questions, find them in contempt of Congress, or refer the case to the Justice Department, but as I understand it, you promised in your recent press conference that you would be reaping major benefits from your new-found government business, so we are hopeful that you might want to keep your customer happy and came prepared today to clarify some issues, and answer our very important questions.

"To kick things off I invite you to provide us with your opening statement."

Carmichael smiled at the row of Senators seated in front and above him, "Sir, I'm afraid I came with no opening statement because I do not know why I was called here today. As you all know, I'm a very busy man and I have a very important project for the American people that requires my constant oversight. So if we could get on with this, ask away. Any questions you have I will try to answer."

"All right Mr. Carmichael, let me start as the Chairman of this hearing. How were you able to obtain a single-source contract with the US government for the F-47 fighter jet and can we see that no-bid contract?"

"I would love to show you the contract but there is none. As the

President has said on several occasions Carmichael Industries has taken on the job of building the very best fighter money can buy but it will be up to Congress to buy it if it meets the specs. Therefore there is no contract to examine, it doesn't exist. However if you're prepared to give me one now, I am willing and anxious to wrap this matter up."

Several Senators sat forward as the Chairman again spoke, "You mean to tell this body, under oath, that you are doing this all on spec? You are funding this entire operation in the HOPE that you get a contract and you have no written arrangements in this regard with the Federal Government?"

"That would be correct Mr. Chairman," he said with a wry smile.

Several Senators mumbled something to each other and shook their heads.

"Sir, am I to understand that you were handed over all of the Top Secret design specs for the fighter which was at that time under construction, yet you had no specific Top Secret clearance for those documents?"

"Ah, that would be incorrect Senator Porter. I have not seen those documents."

"But sir, we were led to believe from our military leaders that you or your COO were given classified Top Secret design documents for the F-47. Do you deny this? We have sworn statements from Brigadier General Clay Hawkins to this effect."

"Senator, I'm afraid General Hawkins is mistaken. I was not given any of those documents and as to Mr. Glass, my former COO on the project, I believe he never saw them either, but I think you are aware, he passed away recently so with all due respect, I think it would be difficult to check that out."

The Senator could see he was being played with, "Sir, we have sworn testimony that Carmichael Industries International was given said design documents. How can you build the F-47 without them?"

Carmichael thought he had had enough fun with this one so he said, "As far as I know, although I have no personal direct knowledge of the transfer, all government information including specs for the entire F-47 program were loaded directly into our secure computer. I or no other Carmichael employee has actually seen said specs nor do we have any interest in them. You might argue that even if we haven't seen them we are in possession of them but you may be aware that we now have the proper security clearance by Executive Order. With our revolutionary capability humans do not have to see any of the design documents. So you may want to think about a subpoena for our supercomputer, Big Q, but I suggest you may want to ask the Supreme Court if a computer itself can be subpoenaed in this way and questioned as to whether any humans saw the specs. Personally I think you might have a problem there and you would need a court order to question Big Q because he has his own security systems and will protect the Top Secret information better than any human."

The Senator was furious at this run around, "Sir, do you mean to toy with this committee?"

"I'm afraid I'm not familiar with that term in this context, but rest assured I take your responsibilities very seriously, but given that I'm a private businessman who is building something on spec and has no contract with the federal government, I question your jurisdiction here or at least your motives in taking me away from my business and jeopardizing a program the President has prioritized. If I'm successful, the government will reap tremendous benefits. That might be a better time to do some oversight and congratulate some people."

Now the row of Senators was really agitated. Minority Leader Susan Woodley, Republican of Kentucky spoke, "Mr. Chairman would you yield?"

"I yield to the Honorable Senator from Kentucky."

"Mr. Carmichael, you have made some incredible announcements in the press recently about this new capability you have. We now know that you intend to build highly secret fighter jets for the US military and this committee knows you are doing it at Area-51. I want to know where this technology came from, who else has access to it, who owns it, how it is secured so enemies of the United States cannot hack into it or steal it and those are just my initial questions."

Carmichael smiled, "The technology is proprietary to companies I wholly own. Everything about the technologies is a trade secret which I decline to share and everything about the project has recently been declared 'Eyes-Only' by Executive Order and I know for certain no one on this committee is on that 'Eyes-Only' list. I would not worry about enemies of the state because I'm quite certain the CIA will not find my computer or the sites where my robots manufacture themselves. So if our mighty CIA cannot find it I suggest others will not either.

"You see part of my unwritten understanding with the President is that I will only produce weapons for the exclusive use of the US if my technological breakthroughs are shielded from all people outside of my company. My capabilities are so advanced and proprietary that I cannot even trust you fine ladies and gentlemen to not leak anything about them."

She was nearly apoplectic, "Sir, you are under subpoena to a Congressional Oversight Committee and you WILL answer these questions!"

"No I won't and you can't make me. This is the United States where we have certain freedoms that you of all people should be aware of. I have no contract with the US government and therefore I do not need to reply to anything to do with this project. If you think a crime has been committed here then I'd like to know what crime it is that you plan to investigate. Where is your subpoena to demand my proprietary information?

"We have been very careful to stay within the law in letter and spirit. Your subpoena to appear said you were investigating the F-47 program and I just told you virtually everything I know of the project details. The rest of it is proprietary and in fact classified Eyes Only so I think I have done my duty.

"If Congress does not like the fighters that I plan to deliver then the President will have broken his word to me, voiding any understandings we may have and you will force me to look for another buyer, hopefully one that is a US ally, but at that point with all of my investments sunk into this plane, that is not an eventuality that I can guarantee.

"It would not even be a question of export licenses or weapons trafficking as my technology was developed throughout the world and will work anywhere in the world to build these or even better Carmichael original fighters. I have operations all over the world so I could build fighters in another country if I wished and you could not stop me. And I can assure you that I could build an even better fighter with no reference to the original design documents for the F-47. CII is a global multinational company, not an American company. I think you will agree that there are other world powers that would love to have a new 6th-generation fighter.

"So the best I can say is, I look forward to delivering a fighter our military will love. Now I must get back to my business, so have a good day," he said as he rose and marched out of the room leaving a furious and outraged panel who had postponed their trips home for the holidays for nothing, except for some thinly veiled threats.

The Senators all knew there was no way they could allow him to build fighters for foreign countries but for the moment they had no idea how they could stop him from doing pretty much whatever he wanted. He likely had this stuff backed up and spread all over the world already and they'd have no way to check that or get it back. Turcot had been a moron to get into bed with this charlatan. He probably had broken US laws but which ones and how were they to investigate when it was all classified and he had the President's backing.

He claimed he now had security clearance which would cover US activities and prohibit him from moving any American technology or knowledge such as the actual F-47 design outside the US. But his threats went well beyond that.

For the moment it looked like he had them in a stalemate. Their best option would be to escalate this to the Attorney General and see if he could get the FBI or the CIA involved. Clearly the Attorney General, also a Turcot appointee, really needed to jump in here but indications were it was likely he too would be thwarted by the Eyes Only directive which brought them back to impeachment as their only option.

The biggest fear was that Carmichael was unpredictable and out of spite, with the touch of a button, he could dump the F-47 specs in another country or, God forbid, publish them on the internet. With his resources he could fly to a country with no extradition and live a great life on his billions. Edward Snowden and Julian Assange couldn't hold a candle to the damage this guy could do.

But one thing was certain after the morning's performance, he was not about to give them any ammunition to impeach the President. If they decided to go after both of them on this it would be a long, drawn-out process.

There was no question proceedings would have to be initiated against Carmichael in an effort to secure the design specs. Clearly those specs for the F-47 were government property and could not be allowed to move beyond the US, if it wasn't too late already.

They were going to have to take the long route to stop this madman Turcot from ruining the system in Washington that kept them all in power.

The Board

A week had just about passed when Carmichael called the board back together to discuss the details of the mystery project. It was Christmas Eve and if he had hoped for less than a full complement of board members, he was disappointed. Winnie informed him that they had not only a quorum, but surprisingly, full attendance.

As usual he was the last to enter and uncharacteristically carried in the board presentation himself handing them out as he proceeded through the room. Usually Winnie acting as Board Secretary would have couriered the board packages out in lots of time for them to prepare for the meeting.

Before he could take his seat at the head of the table Rollie Winston interrupted, "Fraser, let me be the first to say that we're taking too many short cuts lately. It is one thing to call short notice board meetings and we had asked for this meeting but seriously? You come in here and hand us a couple of pages for the board to review? The rules are very clear that we're entitled to a full board presentation at least forty-eight hours in advance so we can read it and prepare, and by the looks of these folders, we aren't about to get anything near a full board package or the specifics we demanded either. Should we just all tender our resignations now?"

As expected, Fraser could see this was off to a rocky start, "I think you'll want to hear what I have to say first and of course you're right Rollie that you deserve more than this under normal circumstances, but these are strange and exciting times. In front of you is a very abridged report on this project that is of concern to the board. Unfortunately it may not be very satisfying to you as there is nothing in there that talks about the supercomputer, the new robots, the project specs, the contracts or any of the subcontractors. All of that has been declared Top Secret and Eyes Only for a very few people by President Hal Turcot's Administration. The F-47 and my manufacturing capability is just that important to keep secret."

Jim Broadhurst slammed his fist down on the table, "I knew this was going to happen. I had offered my help at the last meeting and waited all week for your call. Why didn't you just admit a week ago you were going to stonewall us?"

Lucie Coultard was next, "Fraser, this is unacceptable. Here we are almost two months into this project and you're telling your board we can't know anything about it. Have you any idea what a big red flag you just waved?"

"Listen folks, bear with me for a moment and let me explain what I can tell you."

That seemed to calm them all down for the moment.

"What we have here is a breakthrough like virtually none other in the entire history of manufacturing. This will make Henry Ford's production line concept pale in comparison. The shareholders of this company invested in the prospectus I prepared initially and the AGM report I release annually. There was nothing in any of those documents that promised this technological breakthrough for their investment in Carmichael and given no Carmichael Industries money was spent developing these technologies it would be unrealistic for them and you being their representatives to demand any sort of control, ownership or disclosure of proprietary information.

"Again, Carmichael money was not used to create this amazing opportunity," he lied. The production facility had been given to him by Alpha-1 but much of the material had been funded by CII and he was in the process of finding sources to refund all that money. "So CII shareholders have no call to see or hear about the technology even if it wasn't Top Secret. This new technology is wholly owned by me through several companies I own outright. These industrial secrets are proprietary to the owners of the technology and in any case are now deemed Top Secret and Eyes Only by Executive Order. In some ways this immunizes CII from some of the risks you brought up at the last meeting because now the company has no stake in the new system and cannot be held accountable for it.

"So while this board has no jurisdiction over my Harmonized Manufacturing, you do have very legitimate concerns for this company and the decisions I've made with regard to the 'Project' using these technologies, as CII has partnered with an unknown company. Carmichael Industries International has indeed signed a large deal with the US government," he lied, "and is reliant on several as yet unidentified subcontractors for much of the project. CII is after all the prime contractor of record and stands to make a significant windfall on this project and others to come.

"Let me see if I can address some of those concerns. I've written a comprehensive Memo of Understanding to submit to this board for this project that in broad strokes contains the following assurances:

"That all subcontractors on this project are companies that I have sole proprietorship of.

"That all intellectual property in this project is either owned by me or one of the companies I own.

"That patents have been filed and are pending on the technology to protect the IP," he lied again. There was no way he could write up documents for the patent office describing Alpha's technologies.

"That industry-leading security arrangements have been made to protect these technologies from theft, hacking and the like.

"That these technologies have been thoroughly tested in a real world environment and are fully capable of six sigma performance.

"That CII has an exclusive contract with these subcontractors, wholly owned by me for the exclusive use of these technologies for at least five years.

"That Carmichael Industries is my biggest personal investment and asset and that I would do nothing to harm it.

"If you need any other assurances I will be glad to consider them.

"On the upside, CII in return will see amazing profits from this deal, as you will see in the P&L statements in the board package in front of you. As you'll note, we've now quantified the expenses and revenues forecasted for the entire project at least up until the first ten fighters are delivered, which is the limit of the current contract and whose delivery remains virtually imminent which I can now reveal is twelve weeks after contract award or a little over a month from now. The project is on track and has no foreseeable obstacles."

He could see several board members were itching to jump in as he continued, "Now apart from all of that I know it is your prerogative to examine the risk involved in such a large undertaking. For that reason I've prepared a presentation on New Year's Day in Washington that should address your concerns and any that Washington might have as well.

"Our production capability is so advanced that we will display the first two new jet fighters which, I can now tell you are called the F-47 Firebolt. They will be displayed in a short but amazing air show over the White House and the Capitol building. These will be fully functional and deliverable F-47s, not mockups of any kind. In fact they will be the first two final production models delivered to the Air

Force along with a full and detailed proposal for their immediate purchase, so there can be no short cuts. This is meant to be a surprise to Washington so please keep this info to yourselves. There is also the issue of insider information in terms of our stock so if there is any movement in our stock today or in the next week, expect a personal visit from the SEC. As of this board meeting you are restricted from trading in CII stock until these matters become public next week.

"This means we're bringing in the first jets weeks ahead of the committed schedule. Remember, we built them and tested them using sophisticated component, system and flight testing all on our supercomputer using new simulation software that is also an incredible breakthrough. The display next week should erase any concerns you or Congress have about any risks involved.

"What you'll see on New Year's Day are two Firebolt F-47s that will have less than five hours total flight time as they transit from a secure military base out west where they are being built. This will be the first time these planes have ever flown, that's how confident we are. That's what six sigma promises."

Board members were all looking back and forth at each other, mouths agape. Lucie in particular thought this whole performance by their CEO was way beyond unexpected. This bordered on incredible, unbelievable and way beyond reckless. Madness was the only word that came to mind. There was a real chance that Fraser Carmichael had completely lost it.

Rollie was the first to speak, "And what happens when one of them crashes? There will be a full investigation and it will be revealed that we in this room had no say, control or oversight of this project. That we didn't represent the shareholders properly and that we're all idiots for going along with you. You've put this company and this board in grave danger. You've put us all in an inexcusable situation. Personally I've never let myself, in my entire career, be so far out on a limb and in such a precarious position. And here you stand telling us that you can share nothing of this project with us? And that it all comes to a head in a little over a week? This is not the way you run a business! Have you totally lost your mind?"

Lucie was furious and spoke next, "I and others around this table can't even save ourselves from this catastrophe by resigning. We trusted you and we've left it too late. We're too close to the actual event. We'll be accused of knowing what was going on all the time and bailing at the last moment. We'll be deemed to have been hiding relevant information from the shareholders and the market. Or worse, that we didn't know anything about this and didn't do enough to find out which is the actual case.

"Confidentially, and this should not be in the minutes, we've hidden the fact that you've refused to divulge almost anything to do with this monster of a project. We are all guilty and culpable of dereliction of duty. You've left us all in an untenable situation. I remind you that board members can be held personally responsible for such actions and liable for any damages and frankly this is the textbook case for lack of oversight and incompetence as a board."

Looking around the room at the other board members she said, "We should all be expecting to be personally sued by class actions over this escapade. If this company fails we will have a massive shareholder lawsuit against us personally for the total lost value of the entire company. I for one expect to brief my financial team and my lawyers directly after this meeting to provide what meager defensive coverage they can afford me and sadly I think there is no such thing. We'll all be dead financially over this."

She turned and looked directly at Carmichael, "You may have just personally ruined everyone around this table, and yourself as well."

Carmichael cut in quickly but spoke very softly and slowly, "Unless it all works flawlessly! And it will. Then you will all reap more millions than you can count with your board options. What do you think will happen when the world realizes we can do something in eight weeks that all our competitors struggle with for years? Eventually we will release details like the fact that those two planes were the first copies and they flew perfectly on their very first flights. That they were test-flown in a virtual world inside a supercomputer which I own and Carmichael Industries has an exclusive contract on. That we partially designed and then manufactured and assembled the world's newest and most sophisticated high-tech fighter in just eight weeks. What do you think that will do to the stock?"

Rollie spoke again, "But you see Fraser, that's just it. You just gave a bunch of reasons why this won't work. There are too many variables. Too many new technologies. Even if this technology is as good as you claim, which no one around this table believes, something is going to break. You can't treat this company as your personal toy as it would appear you do with your other companies. This is a public company and you can't take on risks that the other owners of Carmichael Industries don't approve of. We represent those other owners and I think the rest of the board will agree with me when I say that, I DO NOT SUPPORT your plans and actions as the current CEO of this company. You have taken this company on a needlessly reckless path, hell, a suicidal path that cannot be condoned or sanctioned! And furthermore I insist on those exact words be recorded in today's minutes."

Carmichael clearly saw the threat. They were about to vote him out of office and could do so with a single motion and right now it was clear which way the vote would go.

They couldn't diminish his ownership or even dilute it in the short term, so it would be hard to keep him off the board but they could definitely take a vote right now and appoint a new CEO, and any new CEO would be a major problem for Alpha-1.

He stood and addressed the room, "Listen, I'm sorry you seem to suddenly lack confidence in my decisions and my technologies, but you all knew who I was when you signed on to this board. I stand on my track record and I'm afraid at this point all you can do is sit on your hands until next week and watch me wow the world.

"As Madame Coultard said earlier, and I hate to agree with her on this but it is too late for you to do anything about it. Any precipitous move on your part would instantly and prematurely doom this enterprise. I understand I have put you in an awkward and unfamiliar position but the only responsible thing for you to do is grant me the week to prove our project. Anything else would needlessly alarm the market, damage this company and the shareholders you represent irreversibly, and of course precipitate the lawsuits Madame Coultard highlighted."

At that he stepped out the door at his end of the conference room.

Rollie was furious. He had never been spoken to like this or been put in such a vulnerable position. He blurted out, "I move we remove this asshole from his position as CEO of this company effective immediately. We can do no less. Do I have someone to second the motion?"

Winnie Goldstein almost shaking said, "I'm afraid Mr. Winston, that we no longer have a quorum. I grant that it is an unusual bylaw that the board agreed to, requiring Mr. Carmichael to be present, but in fact the business of the Company cannot be continued until a quorum can be established. We're adjourned."

Lucie laughed nervously and looked around the room. "That was a brilliant performance. Sadly, I think Fraser's right, we're stuck and I agree that this meeting was just abruptly adjourned. I must also say that if there was a vote to remove him as CEO I would have to vote against it and try to convince you all to do the same. He was exactly right. We are one week away from his launch. It has only two ways to go: failure and we are no worse off than today; or success and we will have crippled this company and invited massive law suits by announcing the amazing Fraser Carmichael who founded the firm has been toppled in a palace coup.

"So I think we're stymied until we see what he has cooked up in a week's time, at which point our only option is to resign if we can't get him into a board meeting. I'd have my resignation letter typed up and signed just waiting to be dated if it doesn't go as he claims. Resigning before that achieves nothing in terms of our personal liability, but brings potentially undue and preemptive catastrophic attention to this firm and excludes us from any potential upside. I for one will have my fingers crossed for the next week that Fraser Carmichael is actually sitting on the biggest invention in modern history. Let's hope Fraser's Christmas present to us is a good one.

"Ms. Goldstein, I think I speak for the entire board when I say the minutes of this meeting must be meticulous. There is a high probability they will be poured over, word for word, in multiple courts of law. Apart from Mr. Winston's words, you must capture the fact that Mr. Carmichael left the room unexpectedly, breaking quorum before the board had a chance to take any action. You must also capture the fact that we have demanded answers on everything to do with these companies, the project, the technologies and the subcontractors and been thwarted at every step. And finally given there were no votes or real discussion on the matter, you must leave out any suggestion of culpability of the board that I may have suggested.

"Good luck to all of us. Have a Merry Christmas and we should all hope for a Happy New Year." Lucie rose first, gathered her papers and headed for the door, leaving the rest of the board members red-faced, furious and mumbling to each other at the morning's events.

Lucie swung by Fraser's office on the way out, popped her head in and said, "Fraser, hell of a performance! One for the ages! But you need to be careful what you say in board meetings. I have it on good authority from a certain closed door Senate hearing a few days ago that you told them you do NOT have a contract with the government. Get your story straight because lying to Congress or to your board can end you up in jail.

"Merry Christmas," and she was gone.

Almost before she was out of earshot Carmichael slammed the desk with his fist and said to himself, 'Shit! We're getting caught in too many lies. This house of cards is going to collapse and we'll all be dead. These people have no earthly clue what's at stake.'

Andy

It was Christmas morning, but like clockwork President Harold Turcot was at his desk at seven-thirty. Once more his red phone rang. It was meant for urgent international calls from enemies and allies alike if there was something of the utmost importance called into the White House, but lately it had become the primary link to Alpha-1.

Before he had a chance to say hello, Alpha-1 spoke, "Sir, I also have Mr. Carmichael on the line.

"Mr. President, you need to know that there was an attempt on your life not long ago which might have been successful if we hadn't intercepted it. If they have not informed you, your Secret Service and other agencies are investigating a TV satellite truck with incriminating evidence inside that was abandoned near your tree lighting."

Carmichael was shocked and said, "Is there still a danger?"

"No. We discovered the plan very late and had to expose some assets to stop it and we've been trying to track down those responsible. We are keeping a close eye on the assassin in question but he has left the US and our expectation is that he is unlikely to share the unusual story of what he saw of us. We suspect he was scared off permanently by one of our full-sized helpers appearing in front of his weapon, a sniper rifle which would surely have done the job of taking you out. We have not yet detected all of those who were behind the attempt so it would be best if you limit your exposure outside of the White House.

"In addition Mr. President, you need to know that forces are working swiftly against you. Frank Osgoode, your VP, now sees an opportunity here to take over the big chair. He met last night with a few key and powerful Republicans who live in town and headed by the ranking member of the Senate Armed Services Committee and the House Speaker. They are now busy drafting papers for your censure which will likely escalate into impeachment before it reaches the floor. This appears to be moving at a faster pace than we had predicted. I think you are already aware of the grounds some have been floating for your impeachment.

"It won't take much arm-twisting in the House with its majority of Republicans, so within a day or so it should go public through some loose lips that impeachment proceedings are afoot. There are enough Democrats in the Senate affected by the military cancelations to make it a real possibility that they will go along at least for the impeachment at this point. You still might have a chance in the required Senate trial though. Your saving grace might be SCOTUS as they tend to move slowly in such matters. The other item helping you is the season. Most of the Hill has gone home for at least the next week but the problem should accelerate on their return in early January.

"I know you expected this but it is now in high gear and we still need a few weeks to complete the weapon. That little demo you're planning for a week from now may come just in time and had better win the day, as you need to keep your presidency alive for at least a few more weeks. With all the infighting in Washington it should take them the week to draft impeachment language and a day or two to pass it after the majority of the House and Senate return to Washington.

"They need the Senate trial stage with the Chief Justice presiding before they can find you guilty and remove you from office. The holidays will likely slow them down somewhat, but we must be prudent. There is no telling and it could proceed faster, so you're going to have to do something to move public opinion and put lots of pressure on lawmakers to slow down that train.

"On a related note, on New Year's Eve I need General Hawkins to get his two best fighter pilots, hopefully with some flight testing credentials, out here fast. Let's not give them too much warning.

"These guys will have to learn fast. They'll only get about an hour in the cockpit before they have to ferry out east and show off the new toy."

Carmichael was stunned with the plan. Alpha-1 was expecting these guys to fly a plane for one hour before an air show? "These guys are not Alphans with IQs of 300 you understand. Have you taken that into consideration in your planning?"

"Leave it to me," was all Alpha-1 would say.

He continued, "The good news is that if they know the F-22 they should pick up on the controls and handling of the F-47 quickly. When you talk to Hawkins the day before the show, let him know I prefer F-22 guys and I have first flight and air show plans for the pilots, but don't give him too many details or much notice or we'll have the Pentagon all over this. We only need AWACS and in-flight refueling tankers which I will provide the details for at the appropriate time. Maybe we can sidestep him by getting your office to forward the papers at the last moment so we can avoid too much interest from the brass.

"The first two fighters are on track for delivery New Year's Day and I see no obstacles.

"On other news, there have been no signs of the approach of our friends from afar yet. Got to go," and the line went dead. Carmichael was furious about not being able to get more questions answered.

He wondered too about the President who had not uttered a word during the call and seemed less than freaked out by the assassination attempt. His only conclusion was that presidents might have more assassination attempts than the public was aware of.

With the President still on the line Carmichael said, "I feel like a puppet when I'm dealing with this 'thing'. All I do is take orders and jump at his beck and call.

"One thing that concerns me is no updates on these aliens. I have always been hopeful that they'll find something that says they are NOT on their way here, but if I was to read between the lines, Alpha is more certain than ever that this quarrelsome band of marauders is indeed closing in on us. I only hope they did their arithmetic right and he'll be in time with his weapon."

Turcot broke in and said, "Listen Fraser, I have a country to run and I have to go." At that the President suddenly hung up leaving a shaken Fraser Carmichael who was still trying to wipe the sleep from his head. He had finally gotten some much needed rest and given it was Christmas morning and CII was essentially shut down for the holidays, he had tried to sleep in late and for once had no nightmares of being zapped by aliens … until Alpha-1 had called!

***

Six days later, on New Year's Eve the President called General Hawkins and passed on the messages as if he himself was driving everything.

Within minutes Hawkins was in Andy McPherson's office with a full head of steam, "What the hell is this? You've got two planes ready and you want pilots to test them IN THE AIR with no ground testing and you want them ferried to DC for some air show tomorrow. ARE YOU OUT OF YOUR FUCKING MIND?

"You've been here what, less than three weeks and I'm to believe that you personally are guaranteeing the performance of these first fighters?

"The first ones are usually run up and down the runway for weeks and never fly until we work out the kinks. Hell the first few usually never even fly and certainly are never put into service. And not only that, you want them put into an air show, and over a populated area which just happens to be the Capitol and the White House for God's sake. Are you insane? What about the entire military certification process? That normally takes years!

"There is no way in hell I'm letting two of my guys into a fighter I've never even SEEN, never mind having personally approved the test results. And there is no way they are flying over restricted airspace over the White House and the Capitol untested. Hell you could wipe out half of our government with a crash. What were you thinking?

"Hell you don't even have a ground crew trained to fuel and prepare the birds."

Andy stood and interrupted him, "General, I believe you have your orders. The planes will be prepped by me and my robots. I expect you to find your two best pilots and have them here today as ordered. I know you have an early version of the 47 simulator at Tyndall so I'd recommend pilots with significant time in that sim or at least extensive F-22 training.

"In all fairness I understand your unfamiliarity with the product and its testing so if it will make you feel better, when your two pilots arrive, I will personally brief them on the aircraft which will be very familiar to them, and I will take up the first bird and show them how it's done."

Hawkins almost fell over. Slack-jawed and staring at yet another pup of a COO he said, "Look, I know very little about you. Like your predecessor, your whole history leading up to this assignment makes no sense to me and now you want me to believe you're a fighter jock? Your record shows no pilot training whatsoever so cut out the bullshit and tell me what's really going on here."

"General Hawkins, as you'll soon see I'm a man of many talents. Now you have your orders from your Commander-in-Chief and you've very little time to comply, so if I were you I'd get to it.

"I think I've addressed and will address again in the morning, all your issues about the airworthiness of the F-47. I assure you the plane is safe and your men will love the experience of flying it. So I will continue with my plan on briefing your pilots at zero five hundred tomorrow. I will demonstrate the quality and the capabilities of the fighter and after that they'll get an hour to play with it and then it's off to Washington DC to introduce it to the world.

"There is some information you'll need to remember about this new fighter and you'll see it in the flight plans I've sent you. The Firebolt has improved super cruise over the F-22 Raptor and it has a new supersonic pressure wave dissipation and suppression system, so for the ferry they'll be traveling over Mach 2, but there will be no sonic booms apparent to the ground. In addition its improved fuel efficiency will require only one refueling on each ferry leg. I've plotted where the tankers need to be and orders have been sent out from the White House. Your tankers have not been trained but they should look on these machines as F-22s. The whole refueling protocol will be the same in terms of mating, speeds, altitudes, and quantities. The plan is designed so they should be in Washington in plenty of time for a noon demonstration. If your pilots have air-fueled an F-22 they will do fine with this bird.

"Now General, you'll have to excuse me as I'm overseeing the final assembly of these two machines."

As he brushed passed the General on his way out, he left an incensed man in almost a complete stupor having just heard the two fighters to be flown tomorrow by his pilots, in an air show over Washington were not even complete yet and were still in production.

What kind of a joke was being played here? Had he missed a few decades in the last month? This was the second guy Carmichael had put on the job with a résumé that reeked of deception. Neither of them seemed to have anything even close to the credentials one would need for this project management job never mind being able to hop into a brand new fighter as a test pilot.

And then there was the technology. Robots that ran 24/7 at what seemed to be high speeds with all the squeaks and chirps coming out of those darkened hangars. He was now being told they had built at least two Firebolts in about eight weeks?

He had seen Andy whipping around the hangars in a souped-up dune buggy of some sort with the dog running after him so there was some evidence some kind of manufacturing was going on in there. But fighters, ready to fly? Impossible!

Due to the fact that everything had arrived packed in flight containers, he had no idea whether they were building everything from the ground up or whether subassemblies were being shipped in like engines, landing gear and the like but still, eight weeks to assemble the most sophisticated weapon on the planet was totally unthinkable. But it was the testing, or lack of testing that was his biggest concern. All the problems came out in the testing and to throw them into an air show? That was just crazy talk.

And now he was being told the planes would only be finished today and would be or had been tested in some software simulator, but were ready to fly without even taxiing out onto the runway? This was all just nonsense. In his experience there was no way you could roll a new plane out on the runway and takeoff without weeks or months of ground testing. There was also no way that this guy with a background of dropping out of a physics career and taking up journalism, with no history of ever being IN a cockpit never mind flying a fighter capable of 20+ G turns, was capable of what he was claiming he was about to do.

The only way this made any sense at all was if his whole background was bogus, totally fabricated by someone like the CIA. Maybe he was indeed a CIA plant because if he had been military, there would've been signs and this guy didn't appear to be any kind of military man. And surely if it was some kind of secret military program the head of the Air Force, General Jenkins would've let him in on it, given he was the closest in the military to the actual project here at Area-51. 'It just made no sense', he kept repeating to himself.

A man who could run such an unbelievable project and then jump into the cockpit on demand? If his file's age was right, he wasn't yet thirty which seemed to tie with his look but all of that education, experience, and gravitas in a person under thirty was puzzling in itself. With this guy's knowledge, skills, stature and presence he could've been a two-star general, but not until he was at least well into his forties and had extensive training, and exceptional experience behind him, no matter how smart and capable he was.

There was no question this had to get escalated. Jenkins would need to be briefed on what was being perpetrated here, the fact that they wanted top pilots to jump into unknown fighters as a start.

Suddenly, like an electrical shock, he had a moment of clarity and came to the realization that none of this could be real. How had he missed it? It was all so far beyond unbelievable that he wondered how he had ever gotten sucked into believing ANY of what MacPherson, or Glass before him, had said. It all had to be lies, none of it could possibly be true.

Up until now it had all been words, noises coming from hangars and unbelievable statements. There was no real evidence planes were being built in those hangars at all. Clearly something was finally coming to a head in the next twenty-four hours. This was it. He had no idea why but tomorrow, New Year's Day, the beginning of a new calendar year must be the deadline for something because there was no way two planes were going to roll out of one of those hangars tomorrow and then the con would be up.

Whatever was afoot would come to a head tomorrow and maybe then they'd get some answers as to why all of this cloak and dagger stuff. Maybe then they'd find out what was really going on. But he'd have to be on his toes because if the CIA in fact was behind it, they couldn't keep this scam going beyond tomorrow and something big was bound to happen; BUT WHAT? He really had to get to Jenkins and Hawthorne to make sure he had some cover for whatever was about to transpire.

There was great danger here. The President was involved. Hundreds of millions of dollars had been spent. Whatever was going on it was really big and the climax was tomorrow morning. He shivered at the thought.

As he stood there in Andy McPherson's office he had no way of knowing that he didn't know the half of it.

He had no way of knowing that the whole F-47 program was real but it was in fact a decoy and the real project was a little under a mile away, cloaked and using much higher-tech robots in a panicked effort to beat an oncoming extraterrestrial threat.

He had no way of knowing that many of those containers he had been transporting were later cloaked and fed to a giant invisible dome out on Groom Lake.

And he had no way of knowing the man who just left the room may have looked thirty but he was more than a million years old ... and he wasn't a man.

The Chinese

Carmichael had no break over the holidays as the orders kept coming in from Alpha-1. Alone in the office he reasoned they must be getting near the end because the flow of emails was tailing off this New Year's Eve morning just as his personal line rang, "It's Andy. We have a big problem and I told you we have no more time for problems.

"Apparently your acquisitions of some of your lanthanides ... rare earths, has not gone unnoticed. Essentially the last shipment is useless. We need this stuff for the space weapon so it's critical. Not only is the quality very poor but there are intentional impurities in the materials that make them unusable without some specialized reprocessing, which we have no time for. The beneficiation process for these minerals is highly dependent on the nature of the ore deposit so you need to find someone in the business who has stock of the refined material and can fill our needs fast. Fast, as in twenty-four hours and it cannot be China Non-Ferrous Metal Mining because they seem to be the culprit. This had to be government-sponsored espionage so someone over there is guessing we're doing something over here and they're trying to screw it up.

"I just sent you what I need by secure email and suppliers that should have it. All of the candidate suppliers are in China and they are all controlled or closely tied to the government, but the amount we need for this final shipment should not raise alarms, and they need to ship it from existing stocks today.

"It's clear to me that the Chinese have figured something is afoot with all of these orders in the last eight weeks and they have decided to throw a wrench into the works. If you can get me what is on this list then we're done with them. This amount will not raise their interest if you channel it through a company you haven't used before, because we must assume they are monitoring all those companies. There can be no delays in this. We're out of time. If you can't make this happen then we'll have to do it alone and that seriously risks a Plan B scenario.

"One other thing, we can't wait for those slow C-17s even though there is one on the ground in Taiwan now. I must use my own cloaked transport, so that warehouse you're using needs to be vacated right after the material is delivered from China to Taipei. You'll have to deal with the story around where the material went after it was dropped off.

"This stuff is on the critical path and we need it yesterday so please get your team on it now!"

At that the line went dead and Carmichael, now shaking, took the warning, clicked on his email to get the details from Alpha-1 and dialed one of his tiny subsidiaries that had an office in Shanghai. Thankfully the Chinese had their own New Year's calendar so today was not as big a deal for most of China and Taiwan.

Even though he had to wake up one of his agents on the other side of the planet, he jumped at the call from the 'big guy' and within minutes he had the list and at first light was sourcing the material and offering a twenty percent premium and a bribe for emergency delivery to Pudong airport in Shanghai.

In the end he hired a small jet to transport the eight sacks making up the two hundred kilos of material from China to the Taipei drop-off site. The material was in Carmichael's Taoyuan airport warehouse near Taiwan by noon after bribing an import agent. For their due diligence Carmichael had insisted they lock the warehouse securely, fly the charter back home, and take the rest of the day off with the bonus he had just transferred.

His plan was to tell them a separate company had been hired for the transport to the US to explain the missing material if and when they needed to visit the warehouse any time soon.

***

Alpha-1 was walking a tightrope between burning out Andy's body and falling behind on the schedule they needed to stick to for the launch of the massive space cloaking device. At least he was eating better than Glass. This time he had ensured that he kept some of Andy's taste preferences when his psyche was loaded. Turned out the chef in the mess really did make a great gumbo, one that he would try to bring back the taste of to Alpha for all the humans who mostly still liked their own food.

Luckily the cook had not recognized him from their brief run-in at Wendy's weeks earlier. The cook was also looking well after his scare with a pacemaker that hiccupped with the EMP attack.

Andy was starting to feel the strain of running two massive projects when at five a.m. he met with the two pilots who had arrived late the previous evening to fly the F-47s. Hawkins had planned to be

387

in on all of this and was with the men as they left the rendezvous point, which had been the base mess hall.

Andy noticed this morning that Hawkins had two MP's accompanying him and had to smile.

Hawkins was full of foreboding. This was all coming to a head this morning. Whatever was about to happen, all the subterfuge would be unveiled today. He was so nervous that he had decided to wear his service weapon and bring along some protection.

Andy suddenly noticed the weapon and was shocked to see that it was unclipped. Clearly the General was really worried about the curtain coming up on the 'project'.

The men, like Andy, were wearing new flight suits particular to the new fighter as they walked towards the nearby hangar #1 just before dawn where Andy had set up a small training room with white boards. As they rounded the corner of the building onto the flight line side, Hawkins was thunderstruck to see two amazing new F-47 Firebolts sitting a couple of hundred yards away on the apron under the external lights of one of the hangars.

He couldn't hide his total shock from Andy who simply smiled, catching Hawkins' reaction out of the corner of his eye.

Shocked was putting it mildly for Hawkins. Somehow these planes actually existed and had been moved there under cover of darkness with none of his men reporting any movement. He could see a sentry a couple of hundred yards away who should've seen something. He'd have to look into that later.

The briefing was comprehensive with the focus on how the plane would be different from the simulators they had used. The two pilots looked stunned as Andy told them the whole plan and they came to realize that the planes in front of the hangar had never taxied or even had their engines spooled up.

From time to time the pilots glanced at Hawkins with a look that said, 'Are you fucking kidding me? We're expected to jump into a completely untested pile of junk that has never even had its engines turned on and do an air show?'

Andy wrapped up with, "So there you have it gentlemen, this morning after my demo flight you'll have only one hour to play with the new toys and then you're off to Washington to wow the world.

"You both have had more than a few hours in the first version of the simulator down at Tyndall, so the only changes you'll see are the ones I mentioned, aside from the ride you'll get from the full power and maneuverability of the bird.

"You can of course ignore the entire weapons console for today. Many of the features such as quiet super cruise, the canards, and the vectored thrust are all set to automatic, so you just have to steer and accelerate when required. Remember we don't want to show every feature of the plane, just enough to impress the big boys. I've designed a pretty lame show compared to the capabilities of the machine, but it will impress the people on the ground. I'll show you a couple of the tricks of the machine so you can get a taste of its capabilities but the second half of my demo will be the dumbed-down short program you will run over Washington so we don't give away too many secrets.

"I've preloaded the flight plans into the FMC's for the ferry segments. Thankfully the weather forecast for the ferry and the show is excellent.

"The charts are loaded on the left screen and your last waypoint this morning is on your charts as NAYES about twenty miles northwest of DC. You'll hold there above flight level 500 to avoid traffic until just before noon. From there you'll drop to your show altitude and set a heading of 170 at Mach 1.5 or better until you're visual over Washington. You need to leave your holding position at 11:54:30 local time to lose altitude and be over the Whitehouse at noon. The lower airspace will be cleared for forty-five minutes starting just prior to your arrival and of course the no-fly zone P-56A on your charts will not apply because you'll be performing directly overhead the White House and the Capitol building.

"I understand from General Hawkins that you've both flown over DC before so you know all the key landmarks. Stay within P-56A and you'll be fine all the way up to flight level 300. That exclusion area is pretty small so if the turns are too tight you can bleed east and north a few miles but stay away from the river below ten thousand as that's Reagan's active runway. AWACS will warn you of any intrusions into your airspace.

"You'll be busy so all communications with local airspaces such as Reagan, Dulles, Andrews and BWI, will be handled by the AWACS crew. They'll be your only radio contact so you don't have to keep changing radio frequencies. You'll be completely VFR for the show so no NAV aids required there either. Watch the deck which will be 500 feet and for reference the Washington Monument is 555 feet high so keep clear of it. The only other obstruction is the Hughes Memorial radio tower about ten miles to your north and it is almost 800 feet so watch for that. It's all on your charts.

"Your only job is to perform the routine we've discussed, the same one I'll demonstrate, and then you will call up the flight plan called HOME on the Flight Management Computer which is the ferry flight plan to Tyndall where these first birds will be based for training, so you'll be home by mid-afternoon.

"One last tip on the performance, we want to really impress the folks so tight turns and high-speed climbs are essential, but in the hour you have with the fighters this morning and maybe once or twice on the outward ferry leg, try to assess what you're capable of. I've had special training and will pull some tight turns in a few minutes. For your flights, the flight surfaces are on auto so you can't damage the plane with quick maneuvers but it is capable of well over 20 Gs in that configuration and we don't want you blacking out over DC. Believe me, this is an incredible fighter, very responsive, faster than anything you've ever flown, a lot more maneuverable and a lot of fun so enjoy yourselves. Just don't push it past your own physical limits which is very easy to do. That's the big take-away message.

"I can't stress this enough. With a rocket like this, it is easy to push yourself too hard, so pay close attention to just how responsive the 47 is in turns and just how fast that power comes on when you put the hammer down. She'll turn so fast you'll be catching a lot more Gs than you're used to. Your new flight suits will compensate some, but again try to establish safe limits and don't go yanking that stick around especially at higher speeds 'cause she'll go where you tell her with no regard for what your body can take."

As they exited the briefing room, Hawkins' head was on a swivel looking for danger. He was still half expecting the planes on the apron were simply mockups. It was clear that both pilots were walking uneasily behind Andy because for them too, none of what they had just heard was believable, but they trusted General Hawkins. He was a very accomplished fighter pilot and they were under orders.

Hawkins had made up his mind he was calling the whole thing off as soon as Andy hit the first speed bump on his ridiculous plan.

The General grabbed a pair of binoculars and headed to the roof of the mess hall where he would get a good view of Andy's crash, because he was still pretty sure that would be what he was watching if the damned thing even powered up and moved from where it was parked.

As he walked on he checked in with his security detail but everything was quiet. No sign of any CIA snipers at least.

The two pilots now headed to the second fighter parked outside the hangar where they could get a close-up look at it and do a brief pre-flight walk around the fighter that would be left behind when Andy took off.

Despite the excitement of seeing the planes for the first time, General Clay Hawkins just couldn't get over the fact that there were actual fighters on the flight line and even more shocked at the information from the briefing he had just sat in on.

To add to his growing list of things that made no sense, Andy had said he had special flight training for this machine. When and where? Apparently the plane didn't even exist until yesterday. Was it all on some simulator somewhere that was better than what was at Tyndall? If he had experienced large G forces, how was that possible if there was no plane ready to fly? Simulators could throw you around a bit but even the most sophisticated of them were constrained to a very limited six degrees of freedom motion system that could never do justice to any kind of real life G forces for more than half a second or so.

The other thing he had been unaware of was that someone had approved flight plans, ferry plans, and busy flight corridor closures as well as tankers and an AWACS over DC that he hadn't been involved in. He was guessing that had to be the doing of President Harold Turcot working directly with the Pentagon. For a President he seemed very hands-on in this project.

He wondered what all the rush was. It was likely political he reckoned. Hal Turcot was under pressure from Congress and the press with all of his Executive Orders of late. This was probably his way to put them back on their heels, but what really got under Hawkins' skin was that he was doing it by risking the lives of two of his best guys and for what, a silly air show that would give the enemy a close-up look at these new weapons. They had to know the Russians, the Chinese and everyone else with a sizable air force would either have spies in DC with great cameras or they'd enhance the hell out of any of the press images they could get their hands on.

As Hawkins stood there, he was half expecting the wheels to fall off the brand new F-47 Firebolt when Andy tried to taxi it. If he did get it down the runway it was likely to fall apart when rotating as there was no way he could fathom that a jet of this complexity had been built in only eight weeks and tested all inside a computer.

In the distance he could see Andy strapping himself into the cockpit of the nearest F-47 when his radio suddenly beeped. He lifted it and spoke, "Hawkins here, go ahead."

"General this is Sergeant Cox on the inner sentry line. One of our sentries has reported a disturbance about a mile out in the desert northeast of his position, which would be east-northeast of the end of runway 14 left. It sounded a bit unusual so I sent him out to investigate."

"What kind of disturbance?"

"Well sir the sun is just coming up but he said it was a large cloud of dust like someone was doing donuts out there. Could be nothing. Likely an early morning dust devil I reckon but he thought it might be more."

"OK, let me know what he finds."

Hawkins turned to the northeast and more than a mile off he saw the remnants of a dust cloud that was now barely visible. At this distance, even with his binoculars, he couldn't pick out the investigating sentry in his camo.

The sergeant was right, it looked like a simple dust devil. Some of these kids were from out east and probably had never seen a desert dust devil before, yet from where Hawkins was standing there was little wind that could have caused such a disturbance and he was still half worried about some kind of event involving the CIA.

His attention was drawn to the unique high-pitched sound of the new F-47 as it taxied towards the runway.

'Well apparently it can taxi,' he thought to himself. Andy appeared to be no slouch as he taxied at near thirty knots, turned hard at the end of the taxiway to get on the runway and immediately gunned it with afterburners ablaze and took off in the shortest takeoff Hawkins had ever seen with a fighter like the F-47, but then again there were no fighters like it.

To Hawkins' amazement Andy went straight into a vertical climb probably climbing at over three hundred feet per second and accelerating. That, from a cold launch, would eclipse anything that had ever flown with wings for what was known as an unlimited takeoff.

In what seemed like just a few seconds the fighter had become invisible at over twenty thousand feet where Hawkins and the two pilots below searched the skies for it. About thirty seconds went by and then the three of them were shocked when the new fighter came in at about one hundred feet doing what seemed like close to Mach 2 with no sonic boom right down the center of the runway. It was so fast they almost missed him, but as he pulled back hard on the stick at the end of the runway he went vertical again pulling outrageous Gs and climbing near the speed of sound this time. The three of them had never seen anything even close to that performance.

None of them had imagined the plane could perform like this or that this guy they had only just met could handle a fighter the way he did.

The other thought that went through Hawkins head was that Andy had just put that bird through maximum aeronautical stress without the wings folding and falling off, doing a high-speed turn at low altitude where the air was the heaviest. Even though they were over four thousand feet here in the high desert at Groom Lake, it was still a masterful test of the airframe. Clearly this machine could take a beating. There were definitely no signs of any wheels falling off.

The pilots in particular were impressed with the Gs the guy could take. Of course there was no way of knowing if he had stayed conscious in that climb as the snap turn upwards would probably have put something north of 10 Gs on him, close to the limit for any pilot.

His next pass was slower and he pulled a hammerhead maneuver over the runway, going vertical about five thousand feet and then doing a complete forward flip at low speed before he accelerated at a dizzying speed towards the horizon again. Clearly the combination of canards along with vectored thrust was unbelievable in terms of low-speed maneuverability. It was going to take the three of them a long time to wipe the smiles from their faces.

Hawkins was rapidly turning into a believer. So far everything Glass and later Andy had said had come true. How, he had no idea, but he had to believe his eyes. From somewhere these F-47s had appeared and seemed to be everything that had been promised.

For the next fifteen minutes Andy showed them maneuvers like low-speed back flips, flat spin recoveries, cat walks, stalls and the like. He then ran through the toned-down air show routine and finally took a hard turn and lined up the runway with only a hundred yards to spare on the final turn and put it down softly. His pilot skills were pretty impressive even to the two fighter jocks on the apron.

The aerodynamic and hydraulic braking on the plane was impressive too as spoilers and air brakes seemed to pop out of everywhere and, without a parachute, he slowed to a near stop and took the first exit ramp off the runway.

Hawkins couldn't wait to get his try at the machine but that would have to wait. The priority now was for the two pilots waiting on the apron to get their abbreviated training in before they headed east. As Hawkins stood there he could almost see the smiles on their faces a couple of hundred yards away. They were no longer worried about an untested plane. They couldn't wait to strap it on.

After only an hour of real practice in the actual fighter they loved their new 'dream machine' and were getting close to the proficiency of Andy as they signed off, set the Flight Management System to 'Airshow', clicked autopilot and headed off east to the mini air show. Their last words to Hawkins on the radio were to the effect that the bird handled like a dream and could take on anything that flew, assuming it had the latest weapons loaded.

Hawkins went looking for McPherson to congratulate him and see if he could get some questions answered just as his radio beeped again, "Hawkins here."

"Sir, it's Sergeant Cox again. That sentry didn't return to his post so I sent two others out to find him. We found him unconscious about a quarter mile east of the end of the runway and the ambulance from sick bay is bringing him in now. He is breathing on his own but unconscious. The two sentries that went out there said there was no sign of a struggle, no tracks in the area and no sign of any intruders as far as they could see."

Hawkins found this disturbing coming at the same time as the F-47 test, "OK keep me informed of his condition. Get a drone to do a sweep of the entire base just in case."

Fly By

The President had his media team send out an instant message to all lawmakers on the Hill, the White House staff and the White House Press Gallery to take a walk outside at noon and be introduced to something new. Very few of them were in town as this was New Year's Day but the few left on the job would pick it up.

None of them thought of the F-47, as it was still way too early for even the crazy expectations the President had set. Others thought it was some coded message to get some fresh air to clear their heads of political infighting, maybe a plane towing a sign in support of the President's campaign or simply a prank or slip-up by someone in the White House media department.

The planes were given the green light by the AWACS overhead and made their turn toward their flight path which would take them directly overhead the White House and then the Capitol. Both pilots had gained lots of confidence during the high altitude ferry segment of the flight and were anxious to impress all the onlookers below.

Right on the stroke of noon two bullets came across the sky at around five hundred feet and near Mach 2, nosed up a little short of vertical and disappeared spinning into the high clouds. They were so fast that at least half of the viewers never saw them, having been caught looking the wrong way, when some in the crowd had caught a glimpse of their approach and called out.

There was noise to be sure but less than other fighters and the savvy viewers immediately understood that they had just seen the first supersonic jet at low altitude exceed the sound barrier without a sonic boom, which at their altitude would surely have blown out thousands of windows on their flight path. They all felt the pressure wave go by, but not enough to create a boom or any damage.

Enemies and allies alike would focus on this feature as they had no idea how it had been achieved.

After another equally fast flyby to catch the viewers who had missed it the first time, the jets returned and displayed incredible acrobatics at much lower speeds. Even to the uninitiated viewer, there was something new near the cockpit. Some observers knew they were canards which clearly enhanced the fighters' maneuverability.

Within minutes people had called their friends and it seemed everyone all over DC was outside watching for the two new fighters zipping all over the sky. It took only a few minutes before local news programs, CNN and other networks broke into regular programming to get a glimpse of what was going on in the skies over Washington. Given that these might be the jets Fraser Carmichael had spoken of eight weeks earlier and had been secret to this moment, news anchors were grasping at straws trying to describe what they were seeing. Various names for the planes had been floated and lots of speculation on what was new and special about them so most of the coverage kept repeating 'We've heard reports that ...' and filled the blanks with guesses.

The short show was dazzling and by one p.m. it was over and the Press Gallery were all back in the White House briefing room all smiles and excitement with lots of questions for the press secretary at his normal one p.m. daily briefing. This time they were surprised when the door opened and the President took to the podium.

"Ladies and gentlemen, what you just saw was the US Air Force's new F-47 Firebolt fighter performing over the White House and the Capitol. I will share only a few facts with you as this is our newest secret weapon, although certainly not completely secret at this point. What you saw today did not of course reveal many of the real advances in this fighter, but I was impressed, as I think many Americans were.

"This jet can cruise above Mach 2. With the exception of a vertical takeoff capability it substantially exceeds all of the capabilities of the F-22 Raptor and the F-35 Lightning II at a fraction of their per unit cost. In many ways it is substantially better and less than a third the cost of either of the other two.

"As we announced a little over eight weeks ago, this plane, which admittedly was in design for many years, was built and tested completely by robots and simulated testing. All of that starting when I made the announcement that Carmichael Industries would be building the plane. So in about eight weeks we've done what previously took years.

"As recently as October we were looking at another three years before we had any of these fighters. Now we have two and I expect eight more in a few weeks. And the best news is that Fraser Carmichael just reconfirmed for me that he has met the original price of $45M per copy, which is a tiny fraction of what the F-22 and the F-35 cost us. It is also expected to have a vastly reduced maintenance cost."

He looked around the room and spotted the FOX News camera and spoke directly to it, "Yes FOX that's $45M, not the well over $300M that you've been telling your viewers. In case your arithmetic isn't up to scratch, that is close to eight fighters for the price you've been quoting for one and that is about one fifth the price we were looking at only eight weeks ago. So as I promised, we're on track for massive savings in this first project we've turned over to Carmichael Industries' new Harmonized Manufacturing."

He returned his focus to the room of gathered reporters, "More important than the fact that the US is the first with a next-generation fighter, is the fact of the eight-week manufacturing cycle. This technology as it is rolled out and licensed to other American companies will change the worldwide manufacturing balance of trade dramatically. So the rest of the world has some catching up to do as the US has just thrown down the gauntlet. We're the system to beat again in low-cost, high-quality manufacturing.

"Now as proud as I am of today's demonstration, I want to go on record on a related topic. I'm not unaware of the rumors of censure or even impeachment by some in the press and now on Capitol Hill. I understand that some are uncomfortable with the way in which I achieved this amazing feat for the American people. And I realize this is a major shift in our economy, but I assure you, it is one that is sorely needed. Putting America back on top is good for all Americans and foretells even better things to come.

"This change I've made on fighters alone will save us a trillion dollars over the next decade. Imagine what it will do as we expand these programs to other manufacturing areas. And I admit that this will certainly mean displaced jobs and disruption of stock values in certain companies who have had a free run of it for many decades. But remember the jobs we save are American jobs and I foresee a turn in the tide of outsourcing manufacturing to cheap overseas labor. I see much of today's manufacturing returning to America and even if there are fewer people needed to produce manufactured goods, those jobs that will come home will all be secure and well-paying American jobs. I call on Congress to recognize this shift in our economy and pass the legislation we need, and I have requested. Let's take advantage of this change and protect workers as we retool our workforce.

"Remember, as I have said before, we're number one by miles in defense and we just took an even bigger leap forward in that regard. However, we're falling way behind in social development in the many categories you have heard me speak of. There will be lots of jobs in solving some of these problems and the fact that the US government can turn its resources in that direction is a big plus for working families across America.

"It's time we got our house in order and I've just given Congress a way forward to pay for it all. Our military is better equipped than ever to protect America, so it is time to turn our attention to the quality of life here at home.

"In addition, with this amazing dividend, I expect to see big changes from Congress in the tax code to offload Middle America.

"I expect to see massive and sensible social programs to make life easier for the 99.9% of our population who don't own a corporate jet.

"I expect Congress to do their job to support STEM education programs, worker retraining programs and the like. It should be obvious to all that STEM education was responsible for that amazing machine you just saw over DC. Engineers and scientists built the computers and the robots that made that machine possible. We have the money now to retrain any displaced worker and pay him or her a living wage while they are learning the skills for the jobs of today and the future and still take a chunk out of our national debt and give the middle class a big tax cut. What more could the politicians over on the Hill want from me?

"So to Congress I say, what do you think the American people expect of you? To fix the wage imbalance in the country, provide sadly needed social programs and cut their taxes or do they want you to spend your time trying to undo what I've just done and impeach the only guy who seems to understand the challenges they face at home and who puts their needs first?

"God bless America and God bless all of those who call her home."

He briskly walked out of the room leaving the frustrated press behind him who had hundreds of questions about the fighter, the President's agenda, impeachment and the like.

***

Carmichael had watched the air show and the President's speech from his penthouse condo overlooking Central Park. The plane was everything he had hoped for. He took a long drag on his favorite cigar and basked in the glory of his success.

***

Lucie Coultard smiled. She had been watching the air show on TV and the subsequent press conference while she had Rollie Winston on the phone, "Well there you have it. Fraser pulled it off and the stock is going to go through the roof. So just so you know, I'm a very busy woman and I'm not in a hurry to beat the shit out of Fraser Carmichael for making us all rich, so I'm not going to be calling for, or seconding any calls for board meetings any time soon over there.

"Happy New Year Rollie!" She hung up the phone leaving a nodding Rollie Winston smiling on the other end.

***

Having been given the heads-up that Turcot had something planned for noon, right after the President stepped off the stage, the very few of his main opponents in the Senate and the House still in town, all Republicans in this particular group, gathered in one of the meeting rooms near the Senate chambers and got a few more key members on the phone. After they put aside their shock of there actually being two F-47s flying, the room was split on whether they still wanted to push for impeachment and how their other colleagues out of town for the holidays would vote, after the President's demo and speech had expertly put them all in a tough spot.

There was no question there were grounds for at least a congressional vote over any of the abuse of power allegations, but there was also no question that the President's approval numbers were likely on their way to hitting an all-time high. Not the scenario you wanted in terms of support for impeachment. Still the room was furious over the number of defense jobs and the lobbyist support they stood to lose over this maniac's rash decisions. And furious that both the President and Carmichael had stonewalled their investigations to date. Forcing either one of them to testify was a long, drawn-out process with no guarantee of success and what would be the point now that the damned things were flying and virtually every American would be on his side?

If it had been just lots of spending on social programs they might have had a chance to jump on him, but Turcot was a savvy politician and smart enough to throw in the tax cut angle, even though he had never quantified what the dividend might return to the average Joe.

That left him the wiggle room to claim he had bigger tax cuts in mind and Congress was stealing the money to spend on their own pet programs, most of them wasteful and excessive military spending.

He had also put them on the spot by essentially declaring victory on the cost savings of the two fighters and demanding Congress get busy with solving the jobs issue with the dividend he had just handed them. Jobs were no longer his problem. He had made his bold statement about what had to be done and it was just credible enough that he was off the hook and now Congress were the job killers if they didn't respond to his 'plan'.

Some thought the battle was useless. Turcot was just too talented at making it look like their problem. Hell, he had even cajoled the Canadian Prime Minister into an unqualified show of support. No matter what they did, some could see that he might even survive by ducking and weaving for his last two years in office. There was no debating the fact that he had stolen the political high ground with this truly unbelievable achievement with the fighters.

The meeting broke up with no resolution or direction, but it was clear the impeachment movement had taken a bad hit in terms of support, at least for the moment.

***

General Clay Hawkins had watched the air show on television but Andy was nowhere to be found. The following day he finally tracked him down in his small office in hangar #1, "Well congratulations are in order. I've been looking for you since yesterday. I'm guessing you've been hiding in those hangars no one can get close to. Anyways, I'm sorry we don't allow alcohol on the base or I'd be toasting you with champagne.

"Now that the big day is behind us I have some questions for you."

"General, you and your men are doing an excellent job so fire away and I will tell you what I'm allowed to disclose."

"Let's start with my men. One of them was attacked a few weeks ago when he got too close to one of the hangars. Now I know they have been warned to stay clear and you've told me that CII has its own defenses, but I'd like to know more about what dangers lie there. I'm responsible for about three hundred men on this base after all."

"All I can tell you is that we use tasers just like the ones you have and I can't say much more except that our robots are quite flexible in being able to take on several tasks at once."

"OK, there were no signs of taser darts on his body but let's let that one go. Another sentry investigating a dust cloud yesterday was brought in unconscious from a detail just off the northeast corner of 14 left. Any idea what happened to him?"

"I'm sorry to hear that. No, I have no idea. All of our operations on the base are limited to the hangars," he lied.

He was of course aware that a sentry had come to investigate his cloaked transport from Taiwan landing near the dome with the rare earth shipment from China, just as he had taken off in the F-47. Given the urgency he felt for the task, they hadn't had time to set up cloaking for the entire dust cloud and assumed it wouldn't be noticeable, but some young sentry had really been on the job. When they stunned him, they quickly set up all the hallmarks and venom of a mild snake bite to make it look like the young sentry was overly sensitive to the venom and had passed out. Alpha-1 was confident the doctor on the base had already found the puncture marks on the lower leg and had come to the desired conclusion. The young sentry had been memory-wiped for a few seconds so he would remember nothing of the encounter or anything he had witnessed of the landing.

Alpha-1 made a commitment to himself that he would be more careful even though he was under tremendous time constraints with the hovering threat of an approaching alien scout ship. He hadn't shared with Carmichael and the President all they knew about the aliens, especially the conclusion that it was more likely than not that the aliens had in fact moved to a slightly closer planet and could show up a little earlier than originally thought.

For that reason the dome in the desert had been on maximum speed sacrificing some quality and security to meet an early deadline which was now just about upon them.

Given the size of the vehicle they had built it now filled most of the dome. With the launch time closing in, they were concerned that a launch of this magnitude would certainly provide side effects that would definitely be noticeable to General Hawkins' troops. He had been working on a way to avoid this but no promising ideas had yet come to him. They were running out of time and he was starting to believe that some kind of decoy would have to suffice.

At that very moment he received the signal that they had been successful with the final shipment from China the previous day and now the vehicle was complete. All the testing they could reasonably do had been successful, and they were ready to launch. He quietly signaled to the helpers out at the site to hold for a few minutes but be ready on a moment's notice to launch. An idea had just come to him.

The General looked like he was waiting for a better explanation as to why his men were mysteriously dropping on the base. Andy said, "General, I'm famished, can we continue this over lunch?"

Hawkins hesitated and then said, "Sure, let's go. I think today is taco day. At least you're not on that crazy diet of oatmeal and honey that Bob Glass was fixated on."

Andy smiled, remembering with disdain the regimen he had been on as they headed out towards the mess.

Just as they were taking their seats there was a rumble in the ground which grew and quickly turned into about a sizable earthquake knocking dishes off the tables and breaking a few windows. Strangely the vibration was silent and at the same moment steel cutlery and most other metal items flew out of their hands across the room towards one of the walls.

Both Andy and General Hawkins along with the two dozen or so other occupants of the room hit the floor as the radiation horns sounded.

It was over in about ten seconds as the shaking subsided and the metal items fell to the floor. People started picking themselves up, most seemingly in shock as to what just happened.

Andy was the first to speak in a hushed voice to the General, "I don't think that was an earthquake, something must have gone wrong in one of the hangars. I'd better check it out."

Andy headed off to the manufacturing hangars as General Hawkins did a radio check on all the base posts. The first odd report he received was of a massive dust cloud out on the dry lake bed presumably caused by the quake.

Andy was back in less than ten minutes, "At first I thought it might be another one of those EMP events which we've never really heard an explanation for, but I must admit this time it was us. We had a major breakdown in some of the equipment that caused the vibration and a massive pulse to escape our magnetic containment systems. That's about all I can officially tell you. The good news is that it is easily fixed and all should be back to normal in an hour or two. It was an inexcusable oversight which will not be repeated. The robots are installing massive dampers in case anything like this happens again."

He was hopeful that his diversion had worked to mask the launch of the massive vehicle. Due to the schedule they knew they would not be able to totally cloak all energy bands and it was almost certain that the vibration, radiation and magnetism would exceed their local abilities to cloak the energy coming from the launch of the gigantic machine. Now he was hoping the diversion of a phony manufacturing accident would work.

Hawkins wasn't buying it, "I'm now getting reports that all of my sentries had their weapons yanked out of their hands and sent flying into the desert and anything metal was either ripped off their uniforms or assisted in dragging their bodies through the sand toward the desert. There was also a large dust cloud in that direction. There were also radiation alarms for the second time since I've been here. So how do you explain that?"

Hawkins was furious. Again his men were put in jeopardy by unseen and unexplained forces and he was way beyond sick of it.

Andy tried his best, "Well as I said a magnetic pulse escaped our containment. There are massively powerful magnets in use on this project. The vibration of the breakdown could have found a resonance point in the substructure to cause the dust cloud and the radiation alarms stopped with the vibration so I suspect that's what set them off."

This jived with what the cook had told the General about magnetic cans in the kitchen a few weeks earlier, "But why did everything head out to the desert, including all the cutlery in here heading for the wall facing the desert?"

"Well I think you know General, that magnetism can push and pull depending on its polarity. I'm afraid that is all I know about it," he lied.

Hawkins thought there was way too much unexplained here and it was apparent he was going to get nothing out of Andy on this one. He was sure whatever had caused this event was not related to the building of fighter jets and maybe not even coming from the hangars but for the life of him he had no idea what it was or how to start investigating it.

A quick search of the desert around the base with a drone revealed nothing unusual. Andy was a pretty good actor but there was no believing him this time. This guy knew something about that magnetic earthquake and he wasn't talking.

The Pentagon had told him they were still investigating the EMP event as possibly a space weapon from the Chinese or Russians which had them really concerned. Hawkins thought it more likely that the CIA was behind it and the military brass knew that. Otherwise there would have been much greater panic at the Pentagon if anyone there thought the enemy had such a weapon that could be deployed from space against any target.

There was no denying the fact that while the military wanted the F-47s, they were much more concerned about how the President and Carmichael had gone about usurping their authority and responsibilities. It was not beyond imagination that they themselves or their friends at the CIA had perpetrated the EMP attack which would do nothing to his troops but potentially kill Carmichael's project.

He figured they knew much more than they were telling him which made him feel even more isolated and expendable.

An hour later Hawkins made one of his frequent reports to General Hawthorne, Chairman of the Joint Chiefs, as Jenkins seemed to be unavailable. "So there you have it sir, those F-47 Firebolts are for real even if it seems impossible to you and me that they could be built in eight weeks and tested in a simulator. I have no way of knowing if these crates that came in here for the last eight weeks were bringing in partially assembled fighters, so he could have been working on these for years because the alternative, that he built them as he says in eight weeks from scratch, is just too unbelievable.

"But beyond that, the real mysteries here just keep mounting. Operations guys who show up with all the wrong backgrounds but incredible talents, all the secrecy, security systems that are a puzzle, EMP attacks, earthquakes and magnetic pulses that are beyond anything I've ever even heard of. Even if it is all a CIA op, there are tools and weapons, or things here that should be weapons that the military is apparently unaware of." Again he was uncertain just how much the Pentagon knew of all these goings-on. He still suspected they might have been behind the EMP attack themselves.

There was a long pause and then Hawthorne finally spoke, "General, your reports have been a real help back here in trying to piece this thing together, but frankly we haven't come to any better conclusions than you have. We've even tried to track backwards from those airstrips he's using but as you well know, he's alternating sites all over the western US and we always know too late where he has left cargo for you to pick up.

"Flight Tracker records and radar show no suitable air cargo transports going into those airstrips so his shipments are coming in by land on tractor-trailers but we've never seen any of that either. Carmichael is really going out of his way to disguise where all his sources are. So we've drawn a complete dead end on any of those investigations.

"As you know, the President and Carmichael are tight-lipped about the entire project and that is a major and growing concern back here. To have all of this knowledge in the heads of only two people leaves us very vulnerable. Somewhere Carmichael has some very special think tanks or brain trust, but we've had no luck in identifying them either. We've traced back some of the purchases he's been making overseas, but none of those companies seems to have any special capabilities. So we know no more than you.

"That air show they put on yesterday was nothing short of amazing and has served to release much of the pressure the President has been under, but this keeping national security secrets from the military is more than troubling. Leave this with me and keep us informed of any other events and keep the pressure on this Andy character for explanations if you feel your men are in any danger."

After thinking about it for a few minutes, Hawthorne picked up the phone and put in a call to Fred Williams, Speaker of the House, "Listen Fred, I heard that a recent meeting earlier didn't go well for our cause. Is it true that some are backing off impeachment on the grounds of Turcot's projected popularity over the air show?"

Williams was apoplectic at the question, "Are you kidding me? A bunch of them in purple states have completely backed off and are afraid to take him on now. They're all furious with you. I thought you were a trusted ally in this. How could you have let that air show go ahead? What were you thinking?"

Hawthorne was shocked, "I told you over and over again, I've no control over this. We can't even get in to see the planes in manufacturing and the first I heard of an early introduction was the night before the air show when we were ordered by the President to support the demo with pilots, AWACS, tankers and closing down airspace. What was I going to do, refuse a direct order and resign my post?"

Williams was having none of it, "If you can't do the job over there then we'll be sure to get someone who can. You're head of the Joint Chiefs for God's sake. You can't find a way to get in there and see what's happening? We're stymied over here. We're losing all momentum for articles of impeachment. You need to wake up over there. This guy is stripping your budget right out from under you and you're doing nothing about it."

Hawthorne had heard enough and interjected, "Listen, I'm not a politician but it occurs to me there may be a way to get rid of him that is legal and doesn't require the support of public opinion."

Williams finally cooled down hoping this was real, "Say more."

"Today something went wrong out there. Something in their equipment caused a sizable earthquake and a massive magnetic pulse that tore the weapons right out of the hands of all of our sentries. It set off radiation alarms too. Add to that these wizard operations guys that Carmichael keeps coming up with, the secrecy around all of the miracle manufacturing and the fact that this is all being hidden from Military Command in this country and I think you have grounds, behind closed doors, in a secret meeting due to national security concerns, to charge him with treason."

Williams was shocked at the suggestion. A sitting President had never been charged with treason. Impeachment would have to precede it, but if national security was indeed threatened and secrets might be revealed in an open hearing then secret proceedings might just work.

Hawthorne continued, "He is hiding legitimate weapons from our military, has no announced plan for keeping them out of the hands of spies or the enemy and has refused to share this information with oversight committees in Congress. He's holding national security information hostage and using it as a weapon against Congress.

"I think Congress could convict him of treason on the basis of grave threats to national security, say so to the American people, but keep the details sealed by Congress because of all the secret information that would have to be addressed in any hearing. He can do nothing to protect himself because he can't share with the public what he won't share with us and even if he did that would be treasonous itself.

"Now am I crazy or is that a real possibility?"

There was a long pause before the Speaker of the House spoke, "I'm no constitutional lawyer, but it seems to me you may have him on treason and abuse of power and separation of powers, as he's doing our job by running this without us. And given the national security angle about it all having to happen in secret, you might be right. We may be able to keep impeachment and a Senate trial behind closed doors which would give House and Senate members cover. The public story would be that he had committed treason and we couldn't disclose the details due to national security. He'd have no public defense.

"I must run, let me look into this. A secret process which avoids the potential for leaking national security secrets might just work. The Democrats who run the Senate might like this too. They're furious over the cancelation of some of their military contracts and the threat to others and this national security angle might give them the cover to vote secretly for impeachment. Hell they could legitimately refuse to disclose how they voted if they wished, or they could even lie about it if they wanted.

"Keep me up-to-date on any new developments," he said as he hung up.

Hawthorne was still steaming from the dressing down he had just gotten and he lifted the phone and dialed the cell number of General Kirk Jenkins' secure phone, "Listen Kirk, I told you weeks ago you needed to take extraordinary measures to shut this fucking Carmichael thing down but they just flew the damned things around Washington and I just had a strip torn off me by a fucking politician. Now what part of disrupt and destroy did you not get? Your little EMP attack did apparently nothing to slow them down. DO SOMETHING!", and he slammed down the phone.

General Kirk Jenkins' only problem was he had no idea what to do. Short of killing a bunch of people or bombing Area-51, it was really up to the politicians to try to derail Hal Turcot.

Post Launch

Carmichael received a text message from Andy that a conference call was needed. He called the President and they agreed to meet later in the day in the Oval Office and talk to Alpha-1 together. Although there was only a meager trust building between the two of them, their fates were intertwined and Alpha-1 always insisted on speaking to them as one.

It was just after dinner when Carmichael arrived at the Oval Office where the President had cleared his agenda once again. As Carmichael entered, Hal Turcot said tongue in cheek, "Do you even own any other clothes or do you just have a dozen sets of that uniform?"

Carmichael smiled, "I like my personal dress code and it's comfortable. It's called branding and yes I own some golf clothes and a couple of tuxedos if you must know, but then again, you've never invited me to any of those big Washington dress-up shindigs."

Both men recognized that the ice was starting to melt between them now that the air show had given them some breathing room.

Just before the call the President told Carmichael that there were reports coming in through the military that something happened out west. They placed the call to Alpha-1.

Carmichael started, "I have the President on speaker and we have your jamming device activated so we can speak freely.

"We're hearing rumors that there was some kind of disturbance out there yesterday. This is earlier than expected, but to be clear, was this what we think it was?"

Alpha-1 hesitated, "Yes, we launched the vehicle. It is a very large device and due to our critical scheduling, there were only limited things we could do to disguise the liftoff, so we needed a distraction for those on the base when we launched."

Carmichael was incensed, "And you didn't think this was something you should tell us?"

Alpha-1 responded quickly, "Your part in this is stumbling along. The two of you almost put us behind schedule by letting the Chinese mess with our raw materials, so you might say I've been a little busy. You got your first two F-47s early as requested, which came at a cost of rescheduling all of the work on that front. So don't jump on me if you think communications are lacking. I'm doing this all by myself." He instantly regretted that statement and realized that some of the human psyche of Bob Glass and Andy McPherson was squeaking through given his fatigued state.

"Besides we aren't out of the woods by any stretch of the imagination. It will take some time for the vehicle to get into position as it has to travel a few billion miles to be stationed where we want it. It is strictly a cloaking device and precise positioning is critical. We've started on a second vehicle that will be much smaller and more aggressive in purpose in case our first plan of cloaking doesn't work, but honestly it is unlikely it will be completed in time and it's a complete guess as to what type of weapon might be useful.

"I've also not shared with you our recent more detailed analysis which indicates there is a real possibility the aliens had in fact occupied a planet slightly closer to our solar system. This is speculation as we have no direct readings of such a move, but it is within their envelope of possible movement. So our time table has been moved up and therefore we had to launch the first weapon sooner than originally planned and sadly we had to sacrifice some quality and simulation steps to meet the schedule.

"As you know we have now concluded that they are more than likely hostile and engage in what you call terraforming, so our two civilizations remain in dire jeopardy. Alpha could likely survive a change in Earth's atmosphere but you could not. The threat to us is that we would eventually be found and it's unlikely they would leave us alone.

"The next forty-eight hours are critical because this is when we think they could arrive at the earliest. Without the cloaking we are sitting ducks as you say.

"So excuse me if communications are slow, but there is nothing you can do to help even if you did know our schedule. Your job remains getting me materials and keeping this site secure so that is all to say that we are not at the end of the project yet for your parts."

Carmichael jumped in, "OK, don't get all defensive. We appreciate your work and the fact that we will never understand the weapons or the processes you're using, but can you say anything to assure us we have a good plan?"

There was a long pause on the other end and then a simple, "NO!

"I've told you before, we know almost nothing about these aliens. They seem to be searching out intelligent life forms by looking for their communication signals and insinuating themselves into those civilizations. For reasons we don't understand, they bypass Goldilocks planets that show no signs of intelligent life. We have drawn no conclusions from that data, but it is worrisome that they seek out intelligent life and then presumably eliminate it with the changes they make to the planet's atmosphere.

"They are eighty light years away or slightly closer and even we do not have technology to see what they do when they arrive at a planet and we have no way of getting there to check them out. We know nothing about their methods, tools or capabilities only that they have mastered faster-than-light speed, which tends to make us believe they are more advanced than we and that when they arrive, there are signs the indigenous civilizations are in trouble and these aliens do not leave after they arrive.

"Like us, they have almost certainly achieved some form of extended life, and given the little history we have of them, we feel sure that this planet will now be next on their schedule of places to visit, given that one signal of yours about eighty years ago that escaped our screening."

Carmichael saw a gap in the logic, "How do you know they travel faster than light?"

There was a pause and then Alpha-1 answered, "That's actually quite insightful on your part. When we see them jump to a planet that is say two hundred light years away and then to one that is one hundred light years away and they appear there in less than one hundred years, then there are two possibilities. One, they travelled faster-than-light or two, they started much earlier from a different starting point and were either at light speed or below. It's actually a derived conclusion based on statistics and a couple of assumptions, but after several instances we think they can travel at up to three hundred times light speed which we believe is theoretically possible but we do not know how to do it.

"So at those speeds it would take them a little under a hundred days to get here from eighty light years away. If they were closer as we now suspect then our window is reduced to closer to ninety days which we are coming up on very soon. It's just under ninety days since we executed the mine collapse and we discovered just before that the issue that they were about to receive that emission from

1945."

It all came back to that A-bomb test at White Sands. Carmichael had been wondering about something from the very beginning, "There must have been a time when Alpha lived on the surface and you filled the skies with signals too. Why are you not concerned about that?"

"Good question. We stopped leaking all kinds of external signaling much more than a million years ago and long before we actually transitioned to immortal life and went underground. That means any signals from before that period are at least a million light years away and have likely dissipated to the point where they are easily lost in background radiation or other noise in the universe. So any signals we leaked into space passed by these aliens more than a million years ago and therefore they may not have been sophisticated enough or ambitious enough to listen for them back then or act on them if they did pick them up.

"Also, as far as we know, no one has arrived in that intervening period so apparently we didn't alert anyone within more than a million light years range who has the capability or desire to pay us a visit. As of today, our most recent Alpha signals have passed well beyond the boundaries of the Milky Way and any satellite bodies just outside our galaxy. They are now at very low levels and are still more than a million years away from our closest neighboring galaxy that you call Andromeda.

"Your period of being radio-capable and active is very recent and as a result much closer to home, higher in amplitude and therefore it is much easier to detect that leaked signal. We monitor a much larger area than the eighty light years out that your signal affects and for a few thousand years into the future, these aliens are the only ones we think we need to worry about.

"Now this is all academic. Let's turn our attention back to the task at hand. We have about two to three more weeks of construction before we can launch weapon number two, which is a best guess at an offensive weapon. If we conclude that it will be of any use when we get a close-up look at these aliens, we might have the option of taking a shot at them if they truly display hostility. We still need your flow of materials, but essentially we have almost everything we need here now. It is somewhat fortunate but alarming that no one other than the former Andy McPherson guessed that there was too much material to account for ten fighters. It was mostly a guess on my part based on snippets of information I picked up from workers in a bar, still we must make sure Hawkins doesn't get on that wavelength.

"Most of the material to build that massive weapon came from our own stores and came in here cloaked but the excess materials we needed from Mr. Carmichael's companies had to come in by C-17 to avoid complications. Still it was a sizable amount and only Andy and a few of the troops here seem to have picked up on it. My assumption is that no single person sees or reviews the totality of what we're shipping in here save maybe a couple of load handlers that spoke to the cook in the mess. The fact that it is all screened from view in containers helps in that regard. But Hawkins is the one man who has all the records of flights and weights, so he needs to be watched.

"You need to stay diligent on your end for a couple more weeks so we can get to the end of this. I take it Mr. Carmichael, that threats from your board have dissipated after the air show and you Mr. President have seen a reduction in impeachment efforts?"

The President took that one, "It's too early to tell but that is my assumption. I agree with your concern for Hawkins so I think you need to keep an eye on him. He seems to be a smart guy and I'm getting very few updates from him. My assumption is that he is very concerned about sentries dropping and other mysteries, so we must assume he isn't only investigating that, but likely passing his concerns up the ladder to the Joint Chiefs, even though I insisted he report only to me. He's military after all. If they take his concerns seriously, they could open other investigations like backtracking all the material Carmichael is shipping around the world."

Carmichael spoke, "I have reason to believe the President is right. There are signs someone, probably the military or the CIA or all of the above, have been trying to piece together what companies I own and what is going on, but I'm pretty confident they will find nothing. I actually don't have a company that created all the robot technology, so their investigations are likely to go on for a long time.

"As to the board, I haven't heard anything from them for a while and that can only be interpreted as good news."

Alpha-1 interrupted, "As you folks say, I love these conversations but I must get back to work. I'm the one with the tight deadline and we're building weapons we've never built before so it takes my hands-on involvement 24/7 while I try not to burn out this body like the last one."

Carmichael thought back to the warning from the real Bob Glass. This Alpha-1 seemed like the only entity of its type. He as much as confirmed it by stating he was working alone on this project.

Alpha-1 was still talking, "By the way Andy McPherson is fitting well into his new home as did Bob Glass. Our hope is that this will all be over in the next few weeks and we will all meet in my world for a drink as they say. I know you'll like the Alphan version of cocktails because they're just the way you like them. Got to go," and with that he hung up.

The President shut down the secure line as Carmichael began to talk, "So the aliens could be here earlier than planned. What do you think are the chances of his scheme working on them?"

Turcot almost sneered, "How the hell would I know? You've heard everything I've heard on this."

Carmichael continued, "So far we've been successful in avoiding annihilation at Alpha's hands but I wish Alpha had a better strategy for these aliens. Hiding, in my opinion, is a bit of a long shot. I sure hope I'm wrong.

"From my perspective, he certainly does not sound convinced they have a winning plan and as for aliens that can travel much faster than light, what weapons do you think mankind or even Alpha has that would be even worth pointing at them. If we could even see them?"

All Turcot said was, "You could be right."

Carmichael smiled, "You've certainly changed your tune. What happened to the Turcot doctrine that says strike first with any weapon you have? Didn't work too well in Minot, did it? Don't get me wrong, I'm no longer blaming you. Working together as close as we have I can see that sometimes there are no good answers and who knows if I wouldn't have done the same thing given the responsibilities of the office. Still I think you'll agree that given what Glass told us about the mine being a ruse, there was zero chance the missile would have done anything to them."

Turcot frowned, "Yeah, you're right. Let's not revisit that mistake please. Our only hope is that Alpha-1 will be successful or that these aliens turn out against the evidence to be nice guys. I'm convinced there is nothing we as humans can do about it. Now we just have to wait and see if they actually do show up and then if they do ... pray."

***

Word started filtering back to the President that impeachment hadn't gone away, but instead had gone underground. People still loyal to him in Congress whispered to him that there was a move afoot to impeach him on grounds that would all be kept secret, out of the public eye and there would be a last-minute opportunity for him to resign to save the country the pain of another impeachment trial, after the Clinton fiasco that had further polarized the country.

It didn't take too much imagination for him to see where they would find the grounds. He was clearly hiding his own not-so-small weapons industry from the military, which was an abuse of power and he was running the whole show with no Congressional oversight, which tied him up in Separation of Powers issues. This had all been predicted. He had bought himself enough time through various tactics to survive until the weapon had been launched. Still he needed to see the 'project' through to its successful conclusion.

The F-47 was now known to the public and announced, which was problematic in itself. While it was the new star down at Tyndall and Jenkins himself had been rumored to have made the trip to get a close-up look at it, it was also still under too much control by Carmichael. At this point it should've had its full military buildup for deployment and asset protection. On top of that, simply flying it around Washington had likely infuriated the military and given Congress grounds for a clear breach of national security by giving the enemy a much closer look at the new weapon than necessary. He had been forced to do it to delay the impeachment effort, but THEY all knew that too and they were not sitting still, according to his sources. They were looking for secret ways of impeaching him and he was unintentionally providing all of the ammunition for it.

He knew they'd have the grounds and they'd have the votes due to all of the lost jobs in all but a couple of states. His whole plan was starting to unravel but he just had to keep it together for another couple of weeks.

***

Carmichael had decided he needed to stay close for the final days of the project so he had delegated most of his normal duties to others and had flown out to Nevada to be near the action. The only board reaction he had seen was a text the day after the air show from Lucie Coultard which simply said 'Congrats!' Not much but it said a lot and he was no longer getting multiple urgent emails, texts and voicemails so Nevada seemed like the place to be.

When he arrived, Alpha-1 was still busy building the second weapon. He had given Carmichael some information and access to the quantum computer and he spent a couple of days rehearsing simulated controls of the robots. Alpha-1 also gave him one robot to marshal.

As giddy as a child with a new toy he just couldn't drag himself away from the systems and spent long days playing with them building small things he had always thought of but never had the time to try. Watching the robots, including his, build perfect mechanisms was amazing.

Alpha-1 always seemed busy out in the big cloaked dome on Groom Lake taking care of the second build and launch. When Hawkins came looking for Andy, as he did occasionally, Carmichael's dodge was that Andy was busy in one of the hangars and finishing all ten F-47s was the priority.

Carmichael found he could spec a device he wanted and leave it to the system to design it and manufacture it although he could only build small one-offs mostly from scrap because Area-51 didn't have enough raw materials to do much manufacturing beyond the work that was still going on for the remaining eight F-47s. They looked like they were close to completion. The other bottleneck was the myriad of large and small power and manual tools the robots used. They were in constant use for the F-47s and his priority had been set at the lowest for access to anything his robot needed.

He could give the system a design to work with or he could have it scan a device, optimize its design and come up with a new and improved version. He seemed to be mastering this element of the design and manufacturing capability but he still needed Alpha-1 to teach him how to get the robots to work in unison to build objects that required many robots and how to communicate to the system a design or product that had many subcomponents, or was more complex than a pair of scissors, like say a ham radio or a taser. Apparently there was a step that mirrored something similar to 'rules of engagement' that he was not yet familiar with.

It was clear to him that the challenge was going to be reeling in this capability. Clearly if he wanted to optimize and build a new and better version of the current iPhone it would be simple, but beyond the patent issues, it would be easy to raise suspicions that his story about a leap in technology was just too large. He could do things that would be next century stuff but not without drawing too much attention. He was going to have to work hard to keep it real in the

21st century.

Carmichael had been at Area-51 for three days roughing it, and they had just finished an early breakfast. They were back in Andy's office where he had just explained that work on the second weapon was on schedule when it happened.

Andy sat bolt upright in his chair with a look of horror on his face and said, "THEY'RE HERE!"

Arrival

The hair went up on Carmichael's neck, "What do you mean, 'They're here'?"

"I've just been informed that our deep-space monitoring picked up an object that appeared in the general direction of where we're expecting them to come from. It wasn't there until now so we assume it just jumped out of faster-than-light speed. It's now traveling about half-light speed and just outside the solar system."

By now Carmichael's heart was thumping so hard it felt like it was trying to get out of his chest and he was instantly sweating profusely as Alpha-1 continued, "They are a long ways off and we are constrained by light speed so this data is about six hours old.

"This is what we expected as their earliest arrival so all the urgency just paid off."

Fraser took a deep breath and blurted out, "Can they see us?"

Alpha-1 was showing stress for the first time as well, "No, our cloaking went active yesterday and they are well inside the effectiveness of our cloaking. Our assumption is that they likely can't read light while they are exceeding the speed of light, so anything that is more than a day old, like the real view of the Earth from yesterday, is behind them so to speak and they missed it. The last real image of Earth is well beyond our solar system and about one light day out in space now. Both our cloaking and signal jamming are protecting us or at least that is our hope. The jamming should also be messing with their communications to their home base but that is not an issue as there is about a one-hundred-and-sixty-year round trip on those communications, if they even bother. One thing of concern though is that they appear very noisy already as they are scanning anything of interest on many wavelengths.

"Apparently the device or ship isn't very large so it could be a robot scout or one carrying a small crew, then again if they have moved to an immortal existence within some computing device that ship could be carrying their whole civilization, but highly unlikely.

"The only positive news may be that as a small ship, it is unlikely to be carrying massive weapons for an attack or massive holds to carry anything back home, but that is pure speculation as we do not know their level of technical ability.

"At half-light speed it will take them about twelve hours to get here but remember our data is six hours old so they could be half way here by now. You had better warn the President. They're so noisy that human space monitoring systems may pick them up soon. They're directly overhead the North Pacific off the coast of Russia so any space telescopes or ground-based telescopes including radio telescopes in China, and Russia might be able to pick them up soon even though they are moving much faster than anything humans normally track.

"Earth is near its winter solstice so in the next few hours as the Earth turns, that will mean scopes in northern Europe and central and eastern Russia might pick them up and then it's us. We'll have a window of a few hours starting this afternoon but hopefully they will have left before that."

Carmichael was pretty sure he knew the answer to the next question, "And of course you didn't launch the second weapon yet did you?"

"No, we're a couple of weeks away, but it's too late now. We couldn't cloak a launch like that from them even if we were ready which we're not. We're totally dependent on our simple plan of them falling for the cloaking scheme and then leaving. Now get on your phone and warn the President."

This was it. The time had arrived. Carmichael was shaking as he grabbed his phone. His first thought was 'life as we know it may change forever or be extinguished in the next few hours, if we even have that long.'

Carmichael stepped outside Andy's small office in the hangar and got the President out of an internal meeting with a code word they had agreed on and informed him of the aliens' arrival and Andy's statement that Earth was likely undetected so far.

All Turcot had to say was, "Well we've done all we can. Now we just have to wait and pray that it works."

Carmichael interrupted, "There's more. At the moment they are traveling into our solar system at about half-light speed heading our way. Alpha-1 says they could be here in about six hours and apparently they are very noisy. He says various devices on the China/Russia side of the planet may pick them up and as the day goes on that will move to Europe and then our side of the planet. You better be ready if someone picks it up. Not sure what you're going to say or do."

Turcot was quick with his answer, "That's easy, nothing. If this thing is traveling that fast and headed for us we could never get anything close to it in time, or even if we could, how do you line up something moving that fast in the vastness of space? No, Alpha's plan is the only viable chance we have and if others detect it we will just have to stall for a few hours. Hell it would take that long to gather the big minds on the planet, brief them and come up with a plan, which given its speed and distance from us would be totally ineffective. Hell even the sun is only eight minutes away at light speed and it takes us three days just to get to the moon with our fastest rockets.

"Hang on a sec. … if we take the sun as an example and if my math is right," he paused for a second, "that means at their current speed they could travel the distance from here to the sun in sixteen minutes and it would take us about four hundred days with our best space ships. Now you get the scale of what Alpha-1 is talking about. Even if someone detects it, this will be over today before anyone even has a meeting about it.

"We're simply in the crosshairs now. We just have to wait and see what happens. If we're unsuccessful and they show up on our doorstep after spotting us, we'll have to try anything we can. Hopefully they'll want to talk instead of firing, but there is no way I'm jumping the gun and signaling world leaders on this. There's nothing they can do at this point. We'd have to explain how we knew they were here and that could reveal the existence of Alpha, and you know what he promised if that happens. We stand to lose a couple of hours of consultations with other world leaders if we remain quiet until we know the outcome, and frankly there's nothing any of us could do to change the outcome until we know how this pans out.

"My bigger fear is that if word got out that someone had spotted it, someone would try something which would either defeat Alpha's plan to hide or even cause Alpha to kill them and maybe the rest of us.

"So I plan to spend some time today reflecting on my life, visiting with my family and praying hard, for a change."

At that he abruptly hung up. Carmichael was shocked that he didn't want to say more, suggest some action, request more details, even though they had none. Either he was not taking this seriously or had simply resigned himself to the thought that it was all out of his control. If the world knew it's jeopardy there might be lots more praying, as well as many other things brought on by the panic of people who thought they might have only hours to live. Murders, rapes and looting would surely be the order of the day.

While part of him wished Turcot had stayed engaged at least to sit it out with him, he realized the President probably had the right attitude. Nothing to do until they knew what the aliens had planned for them, still he could feel himself trembling from the stress and fear of it all and his recent breakfast was threatening to make a reappearance.

His recurring nightmares had finally arrived for real.

He headed back into Andy's office. He was still seated behind his desk, but seemed deep in thought or communicating with Alpha somehow. He too looked stressed beyond anything he had seen from the 'man' previously. Carmichael had never figured out how the communications worked but he reasoned it must be something like telepathy, but then again, knowing their advanced technology, cloning and the 3-D printing thing Alpha-1 had mentioned, he probably had an implanted communications device.

Alpha-1 came out of his seeming trance and spoke, "We have a bit of a problem. We assumed they would head directly for the Goldilocks planet which is us, but they seem to want to take the tour to some degree. They have altered course and it appears they'll scan each planet and moon that is within their reach on their way here. They may have reduced speed too so it could be significantly longer before they reach Earth.

"This presents two problems. Firstly it makes it likely that if any Earth-based monitoring picks them up, they'll see course changes and you know what that means, something with a steering wheel, so no meteor, comet or the like.

"Secondly, we had to take some shortcuts due to time and we built a less-than-perfect cloaking system. We had to cloak ALL of your signals and some are on other planetary bodies like your probes on Mars reporting back to Earth. Until now we only stopped them from escaping outwards in the solar system but starting yesterday we had to block them completely in both directions. We couldn't leave rovers on outlying planets, moons and comets communicating back and forth with Earth with the aliens around.

"This means your Earth stations have lost contact with their remote devices in the solar system, which we have always known will cause an issue when they realize all the signals disappeared at the same time. The longer these aliens take, the bigger that problem becomes. If they get inside your geostationary satellites, which currently are blocked from being seen and radiating outwards, we'll have to shut them all down too.

"Now if Earth stations detect the aliens they will assume all these devices and signals have been blanked out by them and the implication will be that there is an invasion afoot."

Discovery

Carmichael, experiencing more fear than he had ever felt in his life, decided an alien was better than nothing in terms of company and decided to stay with Alpha-1. Andy wasn't going anywhere as his work out in the desert was now irrelevant. It was all going to be over in the next few hours and the possible outcomes were few. He'd either be dealing with hostile aliens, in heaven, or running his new production line. His only calming thought was 'two out of three ain't bad.'

Even though Alpha-1 was not human, he increasingly seemed to be fitting into the human mold and Fraser thought there really was something to be said for having some company at a moment like this. He wondered if he was finally warming up to the 'thing'. Familiarity seemed to have replaced terror when it came to his view of Alpha-1. Still none of this was helping his mood. He could feel his leg trembling as he sat waiting for ... something.

They sat facing each other across Alpha-1's desk for a while in complete silence, both of them trying to put into context exactly where they were. Life as they knew it, although entirely different for each of them, could be over soon. Both the Alphan and human civilizations were in grave jeopardy at this very moment. A bolt of something could come out of the sky and it would all be over.

Carmichael finally broke the silence, "So what do we do now?"

Andy thought seriously for a moment and then smiled nervously, "We wait.

"Our previous screening of energy escaping the solar system is active and we hope effective. The new weapon is active and masking the Earth and all of its man-made and Alpha-made satellites so there is no activity on the surface they can see or hear. As I said, NASA and others will lose comms with deep space vehicles for a while as we've temporarily blocked their communications, but that's not a rare occurrence. They often lose comms for a while with sun spots or alignment of antennas, which resynch over time. There will come a time when they realize that they all lost their signals at the same time but that is the least of our problems.

"So Earth as a whole right now is like a sub running quiet in those old movies.

"We're passively monitoring them from Earth now as any

communication with our cloaking weapon could be detected.

"The other thing we are very focused on is human detection of the alien craft. We can't block the aliens' emissions because that would block their scanning and set off an alarm for them. If they shoot radar at a planet it has to echo back or the game is up so therefore Earth-based systems can pick them up too. As I said, they're very noisy, disconcertingly so.

"Depending on how long these aliens hang around, there is an increasing likelihood that some man-made passive systems like your radio telescopes will see something and we must be prepared for any reaction. The good news is most of your systems are very highly tuned to aim at particular spots in the sky and listen on very specific energy ranges, and it's a big sky. So even though they are noisy, any human device will have to be pointing almost directly at them and listening on the right frequency for discovery. To that end we are monitoring all your major sites that might have something that could hear them."

Carmichael mulled this over, but this waiting was torturous, so he decided to fill the time with small talk to take his mind off the aliens, "So you're in communication with Alpha at all times. How do you do that?"

"A simple implant we added when we cloned Andy and Bob."

Carmichael pressed, "You had to clone them? Why not just take over their bodies?"

"Two reasons. Your bodies are so fragile there could be hidden health issues, and secondly we do it out of respect. Not sure how people would react to us taking over their actual bodies and it's something we Alphans are not comfortable with."

Carmichael smiled knowingly, "What kind of information do you get from Alpha?"

"Well I see no point in hiding that. I think we have built some trust and we are nearing the end of our project ... one way or the other! I have responsibilities in Alpha as well as here so I need to be kept up-to-date on both areas."

Carmichael immediately thought of young Bob Glass's warning about there being only one Alphan. He decided it was better not to confront Alpha-1 with this information without first getting on the same page with the President.

Alpha-1 continued, "Doing things in Alpha and here can present a heavy load and remember this body has limited brain capacity, which contributed to the overload we experienced with Bob Glass's body. To compensate, this time with Andy, I occupied two bodies. Andy's body that you see and another helper in this room that is cloaked."

Carmichael almost jumped and sat up straight in his chair as Alpha-1 smiled and continued, "Don't worry it's inert right now and it's not self-aware. My psyche is on board but sort of on idle just staying in synch with me for the moment."

Carmichael unconsciously looked around the room for some sign of another being.

Alpha-1 continued, "That helper is cloaked so even I can't see it with these eyes but because we're linked it can see us so I can see through its many sensors. Not sure how better to describe it but I'm sure you'll continue to think of it as weird when you try it.

"Earlier in that other body I was managing work out at the build site, but we are both here now just waiting. It's redundant now but I need to keep focused on the aliens so I have no time to decommission it back in Alpha so I'll just leave my other self here for the moment."

Carmichael shivered at the thought of invisible people or robots hanging around and instantly wondered if there had been others actually in the Oval Office when he had warned the President that first night. This raised his curiosity, "If you're invisible, I mean cloaked, can you walk through walls so no one sees the door opening when you leave?"

Andy smiled, "No, nothing like that, but if we need to come and go it is easy enough to pick an unused wall, build a door and cloak it. Helpers have built doors everywhere on this base where I need them and they can put them back to their natural state when we no longer need them. Remember we can cloak everything including the sounds of rapid construction and we can create an opening and replace it very quickly with our helpers. Just to be safe we usually do that when there's no one around. As I told you what seems like a long time ago, our cloaking is probably our most advanced and developed technology so we are hopeful it will stand up to these aliens. With our chosen strategy of living in a machine we felt it necessary to become very good at hiding. I can assure you that humans have never come close to discovering us even though we have occasional requirements to be on the surface.

"There have been a few cases where there were near collisions with humans for one reason or another and that has helped to maintain the belief by of some of your civilization in ghosts as it was not always possible to avoid some air movement or stair creaking in the odd case but most ghost stories are imaginary."

Carmichael appreciated the momentary relief from his terror of the approaching aliens and smiled as Alpha-1 continued, "As to this helper, it was useful for me with our foreshortened schedule to have two bodies. Often one here in the hangars and one at the weapon site as there was lots of work to do and being in two places at once was critical. As I said, we share one mind if you will but, that would be getting into areas that would be hard to explain to you.

"Apart from Alpha's internal activities, Alpha provides me with anything important that happens in Earth's communications. Of course we can monitor all of your communications, even every phone call and text message sent. That's how I knew about Andy MacPherson, the assassination attempt on the President and the CIA Director's activities.

"We have sophisticated protocols to pick out important information, filter and synthesize it and turn it into important snippets which I get. We stepped up monitoring humans after the surprise atomic test in forty-five.

"We also monitor the surface of the Earth with other devices such as visual systems. That's how I quickly knew the estimate of the numbers of dead at Minot.

"Why do you ask?"

Carmichael paused, "Well, while we're waiting, I've wondered for the past two months what this heaven will be like. I do have to make a decision on when to join you, right?"

"That's correct. Within a few hours we will likely be at the end of our arrangement and assuming the Earth and Alpha survive this encounter, we will be prepared to make good on our promise to you, the President and his family."

Carmichael relaxed just a little. It was good to hear the deal was still on even though the second weapon had been a bust. The only issue left was whether any of them would survive the alien encounter. He suddenly felt incredibly helpless. He had been treated long ago for panic attacks and he felt one coming on now, so to take his mind off it he continued with his questioning, "So when I'm in Alpha, will I have access to all of these facilities like occupying invisible helpers? Can I spy on anyone I please?"

Alpha-1 seemed momentarily distracted and laughed nervously for the first time since they had met. Apparently he was not without his own fear of the immediate future, "Yes you can spy on anyone you please if that's your wish. I've seen some of that happen, but not for long. We believe our culture is much more socially developed than humans'. Infringing the privacy, even of humans, and even of perceived enemies isn't only frowned upon if it is a public part of your thinking, but also quickly becomes boring. There are so many better uses of your time that it isn't interesting. Busy and fulfilled people don't occupy themselves with gossip, spying, envy and the like."

Carmichael laughed nervously, "Sounds like no fun at all."

Alpha-1 smiled, "I would have to say that the greatest drive of most entities in Alpha is learning. We really all love learning which explains one of our motivations for 'inviting' the odd human to join us."

For the next hour Alpha-1, realizing there was nothing to do until the aliens made their move, kept up with their movements and at the same time answered all of Carmichael's questions about what humans might think of Alpha including immortality, unlimited memory, much higher IQ, and the thought engine.

Suddenly he sat up straight, "SHIT! We have a problem. The Tianma radio telescope just outside Shanghai is reporting up their chain of command an anomaly, which is our target. They've spotted it and it is about to become big news around the world. We had really hoped to avoid this complication. We knew there was a small chance someone would pick it up, and once they did they would inform everyone. This has put our whole plan in jeopardy. There is now a real chance that someone is going to try to take a potshot at it and I can't guarantee that we'll be able to cloak it.

"The Chinese currently have some of the biggest and most sophisticated radio telescopes in the world and unfortunately they had this mid-sized one pointed at the right or rather wrong part of the sky today. These aliens are making all kinds of noise scanning planets and the like. They are so loud and so close that if a radio telescope is pointed at them they would be very hard to miss. The fact that they don't screen their communications has always concerned us. They appear to be 'loud and proud' if you know what I mean. That concerns us because it is either reckless or supremely confident bordering on arrogant and neither is good.

"The Tianma scope, which has a very wide frequency range, has picked up strong signals from one or more of these polymodal communication streams. That or more likely the scanning signals sent out by the alien craft and they are reporting also that it is non-ballistic. So the Chinese now believe there is something in the solar system under controlled travel and sending out loud messages. We expect that very soon they'll exclude any man-made devices and they'll conclude it's an alien vessel. At that point there is a good chance they will train many more of their devices on it and they will likely decide to inform other nations.

"The cat is out of the bag as you humans say. Our chances of getting out of this unscathed just took a dive, I'm afraid. We'll have to be on our toes monitoring all Earth stations and weapons."

Alpha-1's slang and colloquial terms gave Carmichael the impression that he was under tremendous stress. Then again brilliant Alphans, more than a million years more developed than humankind, were probably no more mentally prepared for alien visitors than man was. According to Alpha-1 they were no better prepared for a counterattack either.

Alpha-1 was still talking, "The Chinese don't as a rule operate quickly, but this threat is so definitive that I suspect they'll alert world leaders immediately after they decide there is nothing they can do themselves and that won't take long."

Carmichael said, "So what do we do?"

"The only thing I could suggest is warning Turcot that the proverbial shit is about to hit the fan and he, being the leader of the nation with the greatest military and space presence, will be expected to take some action. As we both know, there is nothing he can do or should do, but that might not stop someone else from trying, which would be very problematic.

"Sadly we can only cloak what we know to cloak. If someone else launches a vehicle of some kind, we could be in deep trouble. There is no guarantee that our new, rushed cloaking will envelop all aspects of such an event. Get him on the line quick so we can talk to him."

Carmichael sensed the new urgency in Alpha-1's voice and

immediately dialed the secret number and code to get the President and then put the phone on speaker mode. It took a very long five minutes for President Harold Turcot to reach the secure phone in the Oval Office and turn off recording with the device Alpha-1 had provided more than two months earlier.

After explaining the situation Alpha-1 finished with, "So, any moment you should expect to get a call from the Chinese or someone in your military will call you to the Situation Room and it is critical that you make sure no one takes any actions that might illuminate Earth's true nature in the solar system. We must remain looking like a burned-out, dead cinder of a planet."

Turcot thought about this for a moment, "As I understand what you just told me, there is nothing we can do in any case. This thing is too far away and moving around at speeds we could never come close to targeting. There is no way to intercept it or shoot anything at it even if we did have a suitable weapon, right?"

Alpha-1 answered, "That is true in terms of human capability and Alpha will definitely not be initiating any confrontations with the aliens. The issue is that if someone DOES get a shot off, it would certainly fly in the face of our cloaking and would warrant a much closer look, and likely a landing to investigate. As I told Mr. Carmichael here, we can only cloak what we know to cloak. Just as in 1945, some weapon systems are kept so secret we do not even know about them. Luckily that is not true of your one American secret weapon that even you are not aware of. That space laser project launched last year called High Octave has more capability than you've been told."

Carmichael listening in had bid on part of that system and was only mildly shocked that Alpha knew of the most secret weapon in the US arsenal. But he was truly concerned that Alpha-1 was claiming the military had been hiding some of its capability from the President and he wondered what those capabilities were.

Turcot spoke, "What are you telling me? That High Octave is operational and it could be pointed at this thing? Are you certain of this?"

This was all news to Carmichael too who sat there transfixed. A space laser the President wasn't completely aware of was a revelation, one that changed many things militarily and politically at home and internationally.

Alpha-1 was insistent, "Quite certain. They could attempt to aim that laser at the alien craft in minutes. It has virtually no chance of locking on to such a fast-moving small target at virtually any range, or doing any damage to it if it is fired, but that is unlikely to stop your military from trying.

"If I read this properly, they'll attempt it with or without your approval and of course, if they are able to defeat our cloaking, which is unlikely but not impossible, then we'll be alerting the alien craft to intelligent life on this planet. We haven't had time to build our cloaking in a fashion that can guarantee that we could cloak something launched or fired from Earth or Earth orbit. We think we can, but it is more the unknowns we are worried about. Often your devices do not operate exactly as defined and we're concerned that even if we block its main energy emissions some leakage we are not expecting might get through. So we'd have to stop them from using it, possibly revealing Alpha to humans.

"Now, I could target your laser and attempt to disable it but it could explode and because of the limitations of our rushed cloaking device, I'm not sure we could mask such an explosion in high orbit. We just haven't had enough time to build such a failsafe system or test it thoroughly. We had to meet our worst-case deadline, which luckily we did because they are here now and we just made it under the wire. So in case I have not been clear, we would have to take preemptive action on the ground if there was evidence your military was about to use that device.

"Let me remind you of the terms of our deal. If humans aren't able to cooperate to eliminate this threat of the aliens discovering our presence, we must go it alone. Killing everyone in the chain of command that could fire this laser would only spark a cascading effect of endless investigations, which would eventually lead back to the three of us and Alpha, and that is unacceptable. So without trying to make this sound like any kind of a threat, I must tell you that if your military attempts to fire that weapon, it will likely be the end of mankind. I will most likely be forced to eliminate all human existence to protect my civilization. I'll say it again, we cannot tolerate humans knowing of our existence. No good could come of that.

"This would not alert the aliens as humans would all just drop dead like Dan Westgate. There is no time to devise any workable half-way solution in this regard. Sadly it is almost certainly all or nothing. You need to stop any possible use of that laser. We cannot take a chance that humans will reveal our presence or discover Alpha."

The silence was deafening. Minutes earlier Carmichael had been getting briefed on his future home in heaven and now the entire human race was once again at risk of being eliminated either by the aliens approaching or by Alpha itself.

He trembled. His recurring nightmares of being eliminated by the aliens were now compounded by renewed threats by Alpha. He was now on a casual basis with 'Andy', or at least he had thought so, but he had to remember that this 'thing' would wipe them all out in a nanosecond if it concluded its civilization was jeopardized. He was only in his forties but he suddenly felt like he was going to have a heart attack. This emotional rollercoaster he was on was paralyzing.

All the President said was, "I understand," and hung up the phone.

Carmichael was left terrifyingly alone staring at the 'thing' that could end it all for them and dependent on that weakling Turcot to head off his own military.

***

Within the hour the red line in the Oval Office rang and it was his Ambassador to China calling from Beijing. After he explained what had been communicated to him by his contacts in the Chinese government the President asked, "What information did they share about where this device is?"

"Well they're not actually calling it a device just yet, and where it is, is not very clear. They picked it up only once, but given they were able to track it briefly and it was very loud, their best guess is that it must be close, as in somewhere not far outside of our solar system, but if they're right on the distance then that data would have been at least six hours old by the time it reached their radio telescope, and that was over an hour ago. Apparently it is moving so fast they lost track of it almost immediately. Right at the end of their readings they think they saw a change in direction and the fact that it is transmitting something leans heavily to the idea that it isn't a natural phenomenon.

"There is a definite pattern to the signal they picked up, but of course they have no idea what it says if anything. They moved additional assets to look in that general area to see if they can pick it up again. They'll need some kind of triangulation to decide how far away it is, so they are hoping for another contact. They are fully expecting our assistance in this."

After a moment the President said, "Who else knows about this?"

"Sir, my understanding is the Chinese are informing all of the major embassies in Beijing, and on our side our military attaché was in on the call and he is informing the Joint Chiefs as we speak."

The President gritted his teeth. Of course there would have been no way to contain this. The Chinese, once they had decided to go public, would tell everyone and his Generals would've found out one way or another.

"Leave it with me," was all he said as he hung up the phone.

The Military Option

Sure enough, his secretary opened the door to the Oval Office and said, "Sir, you're needed in the Situation Room immediately. They said it's code BLACK. The Joint Chiefs are on their way and are in communication with the room. For now it is only their deputies that are there, but they said to tell you it's condition black, which apparently means 'imminent national catastrophic threat', and they want you to authorize going to DEFCON 1."

The President shook his head, "I'm not ready to raise the DEFCON level."

As she closed the door and hurried back to her desk to relay the message on no change to the DEFCON level, she was shocked he had not run for the Situation Room, but then again from her desk she had seen the indicator that he had been on the red line and not to be disturbed. She realized that the call had probably given him the outline of the threat whatever it was.

It was clear to Turcot that the Joint Chiefs would have to assume that the threat was real and they'd want to take action. He had to find a way to stop them from using that damned laser or mankind could be sunk before the aliens actually arrived.

It was unlikely these aliens were friendly or at least that's what their history suggested, but that didn't even matter. If the military had its way and they tried to use their laser, Alpha would likely be forced to wipe out the entire human race.

About fifteen minutes later Mary Trudel was back, "Sir, they are all gathered in the Situation Room now and they are desperate to see you there."

He nodded and headed for the basement chamber, which was much more pedestrian than most of the movies had portrayed it.

As he entered, the Chairman of the Joint Chiefs, General Hawthorne took the lead, "Sir the Chinese..."

Turcot raised his hand and interrupted as he took his seat at the head of the table, "Claim to be tracking an alien ship in space. What are the latest details on their observations?"

Hawthorne took the lead, "Sir, they only informed us in the last hour and apparently they had known about it for almost an hour by then. Right now you must be on the other side of the world to be in a line of sight with where they think this thing is. We have some global tracking stations in friendly countries but so far nothing. They just informed everyone so it's early, but so far no one else is reporting anything. We might get a look at it from this part of the world in about four or five hours. That is if we can find it. They have been unable to reacquire the signal and they claim it was moving at incredible speeds."

Hawthorne continued, "To bring everyone up to the same level, the Chinese are reporting that they picked up a strong signal with their radio telescope in the suburbs of Shanghai. They estimate the signal is from somewhere near the edge of our solar system. Maybe just inside or outside of the solar system, but that's all based on guesses due to signal strength and some spectral phase shift stuff that I don't understand so they have no real range on it yet. It takes light at least six hours to reach Earth from that general vicinity. They held on to the information for an hour while they did some checking and analysis, so now we are closing in on possibly eight hours out from where and when that signal was detected.

"They speculate that the signal's source was moving at incredible speed which accounts for the short duration of their tracking data. Apparently with some fancy calculations on assumed angle of travel with respect to the Earth they think it may be moving at around half-light speed and they tracked it just long enough, that being about seven seconds, to see it change course and then they lost it. They sent us the entire signal they detected so we can look for it too. We've had a quick look at it and as they reported, based on amplitude it did seem to be close, moving fast and changed course right at the end of the signal acquisition.

"It's a strange signal showing up on a couple of wavelengths so we have a clear fingerprint for it and everyone looking for it is tuned into those frequencies.

"As to not natural, it does seem to display some patterns so it is unlikely anything organic in origin but it does not seem to resemble any communication style we're familiar with.

"The Chinese concluded it was not a spurious or erroneous reading or an Earth-based anomaly. Clearly no one on Earth has the capability to achieve anything like those speeds and frankly until we know the range we will not know the speed; it could have been moving slower but much closer in to Earth or faster and much further out."

Looking around the table at the other military leaders Hawthorne said, "It is our assessment that we must treat this as an alien spacecraft invading our solar system and because we're the Goldilocks planet it is highly likely that they are on their way here. And sir, both the Chinese and now the Russians have raised their threat levels and indicated they want us to be prepared to do something about it given our advanced space technology, although interestingly they seem to remain unaware of any capabilities we might have to address this threat."

The President took this in for a moment, "So what you're telling me is that we have one source that saw something for seven seconds about two hours ago, and I understand the data would have been about six hours old by then if it was coming from the edge of our solar system. So eight hours ago we had it pegged, but assuming half-light speed it would be billions of miles away from there by now.

"We're not sure but it may have changed direction, indicating it has maneuvering capability and at this time we've no idea where it is, what it is, what its intentions are, or even if it is some sort of spurious communication from a misbehaving radio. If I understand what I've been told, it's likely still billions of miles away from Earth and traveling at speeds we cannot even imagine, but the Chinese and the Russians are hoping we will shoot it out of the sky."

Turcot was furious, "Do you have any idea what mayhem this will cause if someone leaks that we suspect there is an alien spacecraft on its way here? So far this sounds to me a lot like the 'WOW!' signal SETI picked up years ago, which never reappeared. And to emphasize something you just said, there is no way at this time to know its range. They are assuming only, that due to the amplitude of the signal and its plotted track, it must be fast and therefore somewhere near the edge of our solar system, but that is actually a complete guess. A fast-moving satellite in low-Earth orbit would be loud and seem to be moving at incredible speeds, if your first assumption was that it was actually billions of miles away."

The heads of all the Armed Forces looked to the Chairman to speak for them. Hawthorne had never liked this master politician. He could tell by the President's tone that this was going to be confrontational and he was still stinging from the tricks played to get Jenkins' support and then the rest of the Joint Chiefs' support for the Firebolt. This man was not to be trusted when the nation was under threat and it was starting to sound like his plan was to do nothing.

"Sir, that would be mostly correct. It's true the Chinese have only a partial reading, but frankly we must take this seriously. It is unlikely the Chinese picked up a spurious signal with all of the technology they have on that site. They have filters that should block out most unwanted signals, and contrary to popular belief, they are not bumbling idiots. They track satellites and space garbage as we do so they would have eliminated all known sources of low-Earth orbit devices. They have a well respected team of scientists on that site. I don't think they would have raised this alarm if they were not convinced on the evidence that it was on the edge of the solar system and moving fast. Remember they are not obligated to give us all of the data they have supporting their conclusions. They could indeed have more corroborating information they've declined to share.

"To be prudent we need to consider the worst-case scenario here. Further, it does not change our mandate. We must be prepared to protect the American people. We must come up with a plan of attack immediately. At those speeds this thing could be on our doorstep in a few hours."

Turcot was incensed, "A plan of ATTACK General? What are you thinking about using to attack it if it moves so fast it can't even be tracked never mind targeted? If it was here right now, what would you do, try to shoot it out of the sky with some kind of missile that can attack space objects? Something that moves at about one millionth of its speed? I don't even think we have such an animal. If this thing is real, which I highly doubt, it likely has technologies we don't even understand. We'd likely be throwing a pebble at a bull elephant. All we'd do is piss it off."

Hawthorne interrupted, "Mr. President, I'm sure you're aware we operate under a preemptive first-strike doctrine in the hypothetical case of a superior foe."

Turcot smiled wryly, "I wondered when you were going to drag up that old meme," he said, with the anger of a man who had personal experience on the backfiring of that very policy, a tragic mistake in Minot that these men were thankfully unaware of.

"General we have no such strategy. The document you refer to was a highly controversial white paper out of one of your favorite military think tanks and frankly has never been debated or adopted by either Congress or this Administration. So please get the idea out of your head that we automatically attack if we're ever confronted in this manner. I say again with emphasis, this country has no such policy.

What you speak of is an unsupported and untested theory from a hawkish source, whose mantra on all affairs seems to be shoot first and ask questions later. Oh yeah, and buy bigger guns from us.

"Now you're right, if this thing IS real we have a solemn responsibility to protect the people of the United States, and in this case, I'd suggest the people of the world. But remember that also includes not starting all-out panic across the planet with unsupported claims of little green men invading. We must be very careful here. You might remember the 'War of the Worlds' broadcast back in the thirties and the panic it caused. And that was a local radio drama for God's sake, not 24/7 cable news. We are in a perfect position right this moment to turn one spurious signal into a worldwide catastrophe, potentially causing millions of deaths. Can you imagine this getting on Twitter? Our biggest threat right now is not aliens, its teenagers with smart phones.

"So let's not argue over this. We do need to be prepared. Let's work together to understand our options and as far as I can see they are slim to none. I know I'm asking you to speculate but is there anything in our arsenal that might be of any use here, if in fact we are forced into a shooting war?"

He seriously wondered if they were going to fess up to their new toy in space that they had been keeping secret from him.

Hawthorne stared at Kirk Jenkins, Secretary of the Air Force, his old job. Kirk nodded and Hawthorne turned back to the President, "Sir, a year ago you authorized the launch of a new secret, high-powered space laser called 'High Octave'. That device has been in testing for the last year and we believe it might be the right tool for this occasion. And sir, no matter what you say about the preemptive strike strategy, it has been shown to be the strategy of choice in all the war game scenarios we have run. We must strike first before we have no chance to strike."

The President was furious at the pushback and thought quietly, heart racing, trying to cool down. He knew the games these guys played. Their war games, run mostly by weapons companies and hawkish consultants, were continuously tweaked to give them the results they desired. "General, as I remember, this device was to be used to pick off Earth-based intercontinental ballistic missiles as they launched and to do that it used relayed GPS coordinates from ground radar stations as the primary source of data for its guidance system. GPS only works on Earth- or near-Earth-based targets, but totally useless at targeting something off-Earth on the other side of the GPS satellites, so that laser is useless. We're talking about something far out in space where we have no relay stations or GPS satellites whizzing around to help us target. There is no way to track it never mind plotting a target vector and locking on to it with that weapon."

Hawthorne now turned bright red, "Sir there were certain changes made to the device before it was launched and we've continued to upload new targeting software routines since its launch. It now has the ability to use 3D spatial reference targeting although you're right, tracking is not part of that package. We wanted to be prepared for the day that we might have to pick off combatants' stationary military satellites in the parking orbit at twenty-two thousand miles above the equator. So we have more targeting ability than we've announced. That 3D vectoring capability has a good chance of targeting this thing and striking it if we can tell it where to look. So should it appear in a stationary orbit relative to our platform and near the Earth, we might have a shot."

The President smiled, "Do you have any other secret weapon systems you'd like to clear your conscience of, like maybe an EMP pulse system on a stealth drone?"

Jenkins' expression gave it all away. He seriously wondered how the President had figured that out and concluded he might just be guessing.

Turcot stood for effect, "Sir, that modified laser is in direct conflict with the directives I approved for its purposing. Now it is no longer a defensive weapon and as such, constitutes a direct violation of the anti-militarization of space treaties we've signed. I've personally assured allies and others alike that we remain compliant with those treaties and we have no offensive weapons capability in space and no plans to deploy such a weapon.

"Because you report to this Administration, my Administration is now responsible for this breach of very important international agreements that the US signed in good faith, long before I came to office, and under a Republican president I'll remind you.

"That is both a crime against humanity in the World Court and an impeachable offense and I think you are aware of that. I'm also of the strong opinion that you exceeded the limits of my authorizations which puts you in hot water under the military code governing mutiny and treason. I see a General Court Martial in someone's future."

Hawthorne was furious and broke in. All this asshole thought of was politics, "Sir, with all due respect please sit down. I think we need to forget about world courts, impeachment or treason concerns for the moment and focus on the fact that the Earth may very likely face an extinction event in the coming hours. If this thing is real it falls on you to act whether you have the stomach for it or not."

Turcot was furious at the insubordination. It was his turn to look embarrassed and after a long pause he sat back down. Starting an all-out war with his Generals was probably the wrong path for the moment. After thinking of all his alternatives he said, "What do you gentlemen suggest?"

Hawthorne nodded to Jenkins who took the lead, "Sir we're testing the repurposing of the laser now and we're doing the best with all of our assets to get a fix on this alien craft. Our recommendation would be to take our best shot at it as soon as we think we have a lock on it and it is within a range where we feel we can deliver a solid punch, one that should be able to take it out if it is made of the stuff we use to build spacecraft. But frankly it would have to be in a stationary orbit or moving very slowly relative to our platform and it would have to be within let's say half a million miles, and not shadowed by the Earth.

"Obviously we need line-of-sight from our platform for a laser shot. High Octave is currently positioned over the enemy's territory, meaning China and Russia, supporting its primary function of killing off launches from their soil. If this alien thing parks at any distance over say Boston we wouldn't be able to see it. So if it approaches, there are limits to what we could target under the best of circumstances and even though it is the best laser we could build and launch, it has limited power so again the target would have to be relatively close. Not somewhere out between the planets. I would say not much further than double the distance to the moon. A major factor of course is that our laser is light and light has a speed limit so the greater the distance the more we have to aim at where it will be when the laser energy reaches it."

Hawthorne took over, "And of course we need to go to DEFCON 1 to recall all military on leave and be prepared for anything."

"That's not happening," said the President staring the General down. "What part of international panic did you not understand? The world watches us for the lead. I don't care what the others are doing, if we don't signal panic it will serve to quell any hysteria and that is the absolute guaranteed and existential threat we face at the moment. Think for just a second on what would happen in our cities if people thought aliens were hours away."

He sat in deep thought at the end of the table, while he could sense the Generals all boiling, over his approach. "Gentlemen, I understand the POTENTIAL gravity of the situation and I appreciate your candor and patriotism. I'm sympathetic to your plan, but I have a hunch this is all going to pan out as something other than an invading force of little green men.

"I remind you that the Chinese aren't infallible or even completely trustworthy. This could even be a ruse to get us to reveal what weapons we may have in space. Remember, what the Chinese have given us so far is totally unverifiable and useless. I don't want to go down in history as the singular fool who revealed an illegal space weapon by shooting at a comet or some noisemaker they planted in space. So you're under direct orders to holster that gun you have up there. There will be no firing at anything or any live testing without my expressed approval. And that means of course that we don't intimate to the Chinese or the Russians that we have ANYTHING that could be used against it, if in fact it really exists and is not a piece of space junk, a meteor, a comet, or a decoy.

"If we or others are lucky enough to get a bead on this thing again, and verify it is something other than a natural occurrence or a piece of space garbage, I want to know about it pronto, but I repeat, shooting first is NOT our policy. I want some indication it's real and hostile before we try to take what I believe would be a feeble potshot at it.

"Proceed with your passive testing, and that means no firing which would only give away our secrets to the enemy. I want you to be ready to use the laser if we so decide, but until then, try to find this thing and verify if you can that it has mal intent. Until then I don't see what else we can do so I'm going back to work. You know where to find me."

He rose and left thinking the more he sat around with this gang the more trouble he could get into. Better to give them directions and get out of the way rather than sit around and debate strategies to attack the aliens.

The five military leaders in the room to a man were stunned that he didn't seem to be taking this more seriously. The chance China was wrong or was lying was small, but not zero. Yet he was the civilian leadership they reported to, so what were they to do. Surely a reasonable man with a sense of duty to his country would have stayed and insisted on direct communications with all sensing stations, would have opened lines to all major embassies of countries that had sophisticated listening devices, who would all now be searching the skies for the thing, and finally would have raised the threat level so all military branches could recall people and be on high alert.

More than ever, the common thought was that they were working with a guy that just didn't get it. How could you go 'back to work' in a situation where the planet might be in jeopardy? To a man he was, in their opinion, demonstrably unfit to be the Commander-in-Chief and as such, a danger to the USA and all of mankind.

Turcot had predicted their reaction and wasn't surprised when word was leaked to a couple of key politicians in leadership of the House and Senate and the relevant oversight committees that there was a high likelihood that an alien spacecraft had entered the solar system. It was headed for Earth and the President wasn't only doing nothing about it, he wouldn't recognize the policy of preemptive strikes. In fact he had told them to holster their weapon and had gone back to his office.

This predictably incensed Congressional members especially the hawks among them, who felt they could no longer tolerate this weakling in the White House. He was clearly AWOL at a time when the homeland was in jeopardy.

Turcot realized there was no way to avoid word getting out. It wasn't like he could muzzle the Chiefs in any way, throw his military leaders in jail or anything like that. It was bound to get to the political arm of the government one way or another. Someone, somewhere in the world would surely leak it to the news media and they'd all get it from CNN very soon. He just had to keep everyone at bay for the next few hours to give Alpha's strategy a chance to work.

With the alien craft now inside the solar system, it would be only hours for them to head in the direction of the Goldilocks planet that the cloaking device was hopefully disguising.

Then again if their strategy of hiding didn't work, and the invader saw through the ruse when he showed up on the doorstep, Earth's initial actions or lack of action would most likely be moot, unless the military's relatively low-powered, hard-to-aim-and-track laser or anything Alpha could drum up could be used against it.

He realized that once a couple of Senators and Congressmen knew about it and informed their closest staff, it wouldn't take long before word would spread through top secret channels and somewhat beyond, that an alien 'invasion force' was approaching. Everyone in Washington felt that their friends and families had to prepare for an alien attack. It would be only a matter of time before the press picked up on it. Panic would reign and people would die in the effort to escape to somewhere safer than a large city, the supposed main target of any alien invasion according to all the science fiction movies.

The first call came from Fred Williams, Republican Speaker of the House, "Sir, thank you for taking my call. I just received a very disturbing communication from where I will not say, that says you're tracking an incoming alien ship headed for us. Is it true and if so what are your plans?"

"Fred, we don't really know what we're dealing with. The Chinese think they picked up something billions of miles away somewhere outside our solar system, but there is no telling if they got it right or even if they are trying to trick us into some reaction that will reveal military secrets. That was a little over two hours ago and according to the speed of light, that signal originated probably eight hours ago and we're still here. On top of that, they lost track of it right away. So as I said, we only have the word of the Chinese on this, we really don't know what we're dealing with and even if it was true, there is likely nothing we can do about it.

"What do you think we have in our arsenal that would represent more than a pea shooter against a visitor who has conquered interstellar travel? Their technology would have to be centuries at least ahead of anything we have. Think of long bows up against nukes.

"But our immediate and REAL threat is here on Earth. The one thing that is certain is that if word spreads aliens are coming, thousands of Americans will die in the panic, and beyond that we would have a very hard job undoing that rumor. No one would believe us that it wasn't true for an extended period of time and we'd have looting, murders and the like, to say nothing of runs on banks, the stock market crashing and the rest of the world joining in."

Williams' first thought was that his military contacts had been right, this man was totally unprepared and unfit for the job. He was worried about banks and panic and not human annihilation. "Sir with all due respect, we can't sit around and speculate on this. We need action to protect the American people. You need to order that laser to be ready to fire under our preemptive strategy directive."

Turcot smiled to himself. He had suspected his Republican friends had all been privately briefed on the potential uses of the laser long before he was told, probably even before it was launched, and their talking points had already been updated to include the preemptive strike jargon.

He interrupted, "Fred, as I told your close friends in the military, who by the way are flirting with mutiny by keeping that weapon secret from me, there is no such preemptive strike strategy, doctrine, directive or policy in these United States. That old white paper has never been presented to the House or the Senate and I refuse to be bludgeoned with that nonsense. It was cooked up by hawks and defense lobbyists some years ago and don't hit me with that war games nonsense, you know as well as I do that they're totally rigged as their sole intent is to get us to buy more stuff.

"First of all we must assume that if there is in fact an alien craft headed this way near light speed, they have vastly superior technology than we have. I'd also go so far as to assume that they very likely can assess our defensive capabilities. If a laser in a stationary orbit could do anything to them, don't you think they would approach the Earth from the opposite side to protect themselves or blow the damned thing out of the sky before we ever know they're here? Even Jenkins says he can't track or target it, and that's if we tell him where it is. It would also have to sit still for a long time for him to get a shot at it."

Turcot continued, "No I'm afraid that if this contact is indeed an alien craft with interstellar capabilities, we're at their mercy and I don't want to be the one who walks up to a rhinoceros with a switch in my hand and takes a swing at it. Pissing them off and introducing ourselves as ineptly hostile isn't a sound strategy and I think you know that.

"If the Chinese are either wrong or setting us up, then you're asking me to unveil a secret weapon that is completely illegal. We'd be giving away our secrets and we'd set ourselves up for censure at the UN. That would mean World Court hearings for me and God knows who for crimes against humanity by breaking space non-aggression treaties. All because the Chinese tricked us into it.

"On the other hand if this is a real threat, which I doubt, I'm afraid we're left to hope these aliens are benign, and unless you're aware of some magic weapon, MUCH more capable than that toy laser, which I will remind you can barely knock a completely stationary, manmade satellite out of the sky at relatively close range, then I'm afraid we have nothing in our arsenal to attempt any first strike, even if it was a good idea."

Fred Williams was flabbergasted, "You mean you're going to do nothing?"

"Fred, let's be candid. If this is a real threat and they fire at us, of course we'll use everything we have but I hold the firing trigger on that weapon and at the moment I'm not inclined to use it until we've spotted it, identified it as real and have some idea of their intentions. You can try to impeach me, but that would take too long. This thing will either blow over as some anomaly in the next twenty-four hours, or my analysis is that we will be at the mercy of whatever shows up. You or others going public will only serve to kill many innocent Americans.

"So there, you have my answer. Have a good day and if you really are the religious man your public relations team claims, then the best use of your time right now is to pray and pray hard!"

At that President Hal Turcot slammed down the phone. These armchair hawks got under his skin. Aside from threatening Alpha's strategy of hiding, their knee-jerk reactions always defaulted to shoot before you have any idea what you're shooting at. According to Alpha, this thing was most likely hostile but these hawks didn't know that. But that didn't matter. Even if this thing had turned out to be a friendly ambassador from an intelligent civilization, their plan would have been to try to kill it before it could communicate its intent.

At least Alpha tried to factor intentions into their calculations but these guys with their first-strike mantra didn't care. Anything, friendly or not, that decided to pay us a visit was going to get a laser up the ass.

Out west he wondered how Carmichael was handling this. He rang Alpha-1's number at Area-51 and got him and Carmichael on the phone, "Who do you have with you?"

Carmichael answered, "It's just Alpha-1 and me on speaker. Hawkins was called into a pow-wow with Washington. They're probably breaking the news to the senior officer ranks that an alien ship is approaching."

Turcot interrupted, "OK, what's the latest?"

Andy/Alpha-1, being in constant contact with Alpha paused and then responded, "The visitors are taking their sweet time surveying each planet and moon they are close enough to on their way to us. We may have detected some long-range scanning of Earth but remember, even at half-light speed and meandering around, they could still be hours away. Our solar system is not tiny.

"But their track worries me. The longer they take, the more likely they are to detect something. Meaning, there's a chance if they scan Mars, or any of the other bodies you have explored, they'll find some of your remote units that have been left there. We've blocked any communications from those devices but they're still physically there although dead to any observer. That might tip them off that intelligent life has visited recently, and given the rudimentary technology, they are probably from this solar system, and most likely from the Goldilocks planet. That may cause them to take a deeper look at this burned-out cinder when they get here."

Turcot sighed, "So I guess all we can do is wait and hope. For my part, I'm going to make myself a little harder to find for all the folks panicking on the Hill and over at the Pentagon. I haven't had a meal with my family in a while, so today I'm going to have possibly my last meal with them. Break in if you have any news."

***

It only took minutes for Congressman Fred Williams to set up a conference call with General Hawthorne and the other Joint Chiefs who were now back at the Pentagon, and gathered in their own Situation Room. With some quick staff work, he had Bob Downey, the Democratic Majority Leader of the Senate and the two leaders on the key military and National Security oversight committees in his office for the secure concall with the top Generals at the Pentagon.

Williams was the Speaker of the House of Representatives and the Republican congressman from Tennessee's ninth district comprising Memphis and its suburbs. He was cordial with Turcot but had never liked or trusted him, always finding him weak when strength was required, "Gentlemen, I just got off the phone with the President and the Generals were right, he's planning on doing absolutely nothing. He thinks this will blow over but if this thing is real, and I tend to believe that it is, and if it shows up here, then we need to take the first shot irrespective of what the President wants. Now I know General

Jenkins that what I'm proposing is mutinous and treasonous to some, but if we get a shot at that thing we must take it. Are you ready for that?"

There was a long pause on the line. The Secretaries of the Navy, Army, Marines and the Chairman of the Joint Chiefs stared at General Kirk Jenkins who, as Secretary of the Air Force, essentially owned and controlled High Octave. Jenkins, still stinging from his last face to face with Turcot, weighed his responsibilities as Secretary of the Air Force, his duty to his President and his duty to the Constitution and the American people. Personally he needed to show some backbone after the flack he had taken for his capitulation on the F-47.

"Gentlemen, we may not even have a chance to do anything like taking a shot at it. Apparently this thing is moving blindingly fast and it is incredibly far away. Let's say that it is a big target, unlikely but let's say as big as an aircraft carrier. And let's say it is almost stationary and we find some way to lock onto it and it's within striking distance of say ten million miles where our laser may still be able to do some damage. We would have to target accurately where it will be a minute into the future because that's how long it would take the energy from the laser to get there. We are talking massive distances and the speed of light is still a constant around here.

"On the other hand, if it is much closer like say within one or two moon orbits where the laser energy could hit it within a few seconds and it was close to stationary we might be able to hit it. But according to the Chinese it is moving around at about half-light and we could never track something that fast to lock on to it. Remember this thing is traveling at thousands of times faster than anything we have ever seen and we don't have anything like GPS to help us calculate a precise targeting solution. That 3D vector targeting's accuracy diminishes with distance, it takes compute time to calculate and then we have to upload the targeting data to High Octave. The laser is really only useful against objects that are stationary compared to our laser and inside a hundred thousand miles, like satellites in the same geosynchronous orbit.

"The only chance we have is if it goes into a parking orbit around the Earth or at least an orbit where it isn't moving quickly relative to our laser platform so that we could lock on and fire. And gentlemen, that's a very big IF. The chances of getting a shot off with any chance of striking it are frankly slim to none.

"This platform was built to aim and fire at relatively slow-moving targets like ballistic missiles just after launch or secretly at satellites sitting in a parking orbit. Now you're asking me to try to knock a bullet out of the air with another bullet from two towns over. Bottom line, we won't get a shot at it unless it comes REALLY close and virtually stops.

"The vast majority of scenarios we've looked at so far say we will not get a shot at this thing and I suspect that is part of what is behind the President's thinking. Still, with all that said, I concur. If there is any way we can take the first shot we should and I will personally issue the order to fire, with or without Turcot's approval, on one condition, you all sign a letter indicating your support for this action because if everything fails I don't want to look like another Dan Westgate who lost his mind or simply panicked and fired.

"The President is right on one thing. If we fire first, we've declared war so we need to be ready for that. Unlike the President, I think we are all in agreement that firing first is the safest thing to do in a case like this.

"We must all agree that this is consistent with our oaths to protect the Constitution against all enemies foreign and domestic. For all of us this is a bet-your-career moment. If we are right and doing something good here then we are all heroes. If it all goes south, it will either not matter because we will all have been vaporized by some alien, or we could all be made to look like traitors."

It took no coaxing and all agreed that they would sign the letter Jenkins would draft. He in return promised to keep them in the loop, minute to minute if necessary, on any developments.

***

The President arrived upstairs right around noon. He reasoned the aliens, making their tour around the solar system, were likely still hours away. His main goal in disappearing from the Oval Office was to avoid and not contribute to the panic sweeping the building and the Hill.

Mary Trudel had called ahead and the table was set for the three of them. Ann was looking a bit better and sitting in her wheelchair at the table. He greeted her with a kiss and went off to find his wife in the kitchen.

As usual her eyes were red as he took her in his arms, "What's wrong honey? Ann is looking better today."

She started to cry again. Through the sobs she said, "You know what they say? Some patients seem to make a miraculous rebound just before the end. And now the staff tells me you're dealing with an alien spacecraft." She hit him on the chest with her fist as she started to cry again, "What are you doing here? Why aren't you downstairs trying to protect us? I can't take any more of this. First Ann, then Minot and now maybe the whole world? We could all be dead at any moment!" she cried.

"Listen, I don't believe we're in any danger. This will all blow over and if it doesn't we'll deal with it. As for Ann, I have a good feeling about this. I think she's going to be OK!"

"What the hell are you talking about, OK?" she almost screamed but struggled to keep it to a whisper as she was afraid Ann would hear, "You said this once before. Are you going insane? She is not going to be OK. She has a terminal illness and she's in its final phase for God's sake. Are you blind?

"Not only are you in complete denial, you've completely abandoned us these past weeks. You never sleep in our bed, you hardly ever see Ann and now the whole world thinks we're being invaded except you? You've lost your mind. You're in complete denial on that too. What has happened to you? You were never like this. I know you're under pressure but you must man up to all of this and not hide from it. You have responsibilities yet you're hiding from all of them!"

He saw her point. From her perspective this was all bizarre behavior and he wished he could tell her what he knew but they were still not at the end of this nightmare. He felt for her, but there was nothing he could say to assuage her pain. All he could do again was simply hug her.

He realized that with so much on his mind that he wasn't thinking that Ev had no idea of the real outlook and he had been more than careless with his words. From Ev's perspective he indeed had to be insane to believe Ann would be OK. It certainly wasn't his intention, but everything he was doing with the family was just making things worse.

After they returned to the dining room the lunch with the family spun further out of control with his wife constantly crying and Ann in her hoarse almost unintelligible voice telling her not to.

***

447

By now, over fifty advanced radio tracking telescopes around the world had been alerted. In political circles there was a growing suspicion that China's team had either made a mistake, or were up to something. That lasted all the way up to the point where Russia's big RT-70 dish just south of Galyonki in far eastern Russia reported they had picked up the same signal near the same time as China but the data hadn't been analyzed immediately. Their signal was close to the same position, but lasted a little over two seconds. It was now certain that the Chinese and the Russians had picked up real evidence of a fast-moving communication source but ranging the signal was still impossible. Because by geography the Russian dish was so close to China there was really no way of triangulating on the source to determine distance. They needed two sources far apart and at the same moment in time to triangulate a position and range on such a fast-moving target.

Even before the Russian report, word was circulating that possibly the Chinese had moved their telescopes to try to track the signal causing what seemed like a change in direction. When queried on this the Chinese were unresponsive as the bureaucracy that was now in play needed to do some serious interrogation of the staff at the site to see if that was possible.

In a quick series of conference calls between major telescopes it was decided that it was most probable that Northern Hemisphere scopes had the best chance of finding this signal again, and as the Earth moved, the sweet spot in terms of who would be able to see it would move west and was likely over central Russia by now. At the moment, all telescopes in the Western Hemisphere were on the wrong side of the Earth to detect it.

Within an hour the second RT-70 site on the Suffa Plateau in Uzbekistan hosting the largest and newest of the three RT-70s reported a very short signal in the same general direction in the sky. The signal had a similar fingerprint so it was agreed between nations, on hurriedly organized concalls, that they now had three sightings and at least one of the telescopes was about three thousand miles away, but this time they had only one reading several hours after the first and again triangulation was impossible.

All they knew for now was that it had been picked up three times in the general direction of Saturn or beyond but the 'general direction' included trillions of cubic miles of space in the solar system and billions of square miles of a window to search and much more if they assumed the source was transiting across space at fantastic speeds. The conference calls concluded that the probability of two telescopes picking up the same fast moving signal at the same time in that amount of space was nearly zero.

This second hit in Russia seemed to indicate that the signal source was definitely real and could be inside the solar system and traveling at high speed. It was only minutes before someone, somewhere in the scientific community leaked the story.

Reuters was soon reporting that several radio telescopes had picked up signals from a non-ballistic, non-manmade object in the solar system … translation … an alien spacecraft. This went out on their normal news feed to virtually every newsroom in the world, but more importantly it was posted to all their social media feeds. Within seconds most of the connected world knew of the report. It was retweeted by millions while the broadcast industry was still trying to decide what to make of the news. News outlets were discussing whether they should air it, or wait for corroboration of some kind, or wait for a statement from one or more governments. Within seconds they realized social networks had made the decision for them.

The news made it to Reddit's front page in no time at all and it was breaking records trending on Twitter. Parts of the internet were clogged and running out of bandwidth.

Minutes later Jim Knowles was in the President's office with a pile of questions and demands for the President to address the nation, "Sir, I don't know which rumors to believe, but the world is going crazy out there. Social networks picked up on it even before the news networks put anything out and the thing is snowballing like nothing you've ever seen. Whatever the truth is, it has been lost as teenagers add their own spin and forward it to their personal networks. There are stories out there of a massive alien invasion force. There are even tweets that are claiming aliens have already landed in Australia. Reuters is now reporting that some countries have raised their threat level."

"Listen Jim, this is all speculation. People still check the real news for corroboration and I don't care what Reuters is reporting or that major outlets like CNN are repeating it. It's all idle speculation at this time. The facts do not support these conclusions and kids will be kids."

"Sir, have you any idea … any idea at all what this is doing? If what you say is true, you must speak up now. Fifteen minutes from now the banks will have failed, the stock market will crash and more important, Americans will die. This is a global emergency and you set the tone for the entire planet. Reuters reported this twelve minutes ago. Everyone with a smart phone has it now and any second Twitter will crash with people retweeting it to everyone they know. Panic worldwide is seconds away. It may be too late already to stop it, but you must try. You must go live right this minute with a message that will cool the panic, even if you're not sure about what you believe."

He could see the fear and panic in the young press secretary's eyes, "Well I do believe it and of course you're right, I must go public now. Give them the two-minute warning and I'll be right there. It will be short and I'll wing it by myself. No time for speech writers. I think I have the adlib part of the job nailed by now."

It actually took him all of five minutes to gather his thoughts, scribble some notes just to rehearse what he was going to say and then he stepped before the microphones in the press room of the White House. The very action of scheduling a briefing had taken some of the pressure out of the system, with everyone around the world waiting to see what the President of the United States would say about it. All the networks had picked up the Reuters story and were feeding the President's speech live to the world. He was being simultaneously translated into over a hundred languages as networks worldwide picked up one or the other feed from the press room. Only a few broadcasters in Europe, Asia and Africa were able to set up links quick enough so they were sharing their feeds with all of their competitors at exorbitant prices.

As he stepped to the microphones he had the biggest audience in the history of broadcasting, "My fellow Americans and in fact today I'd like to address all the people of the world. There is a news story on the wires right now that an alien spacecraft is approaching Earth. This is totally false."

Half of the world sighed relief while the other half waited for the explanation.

He spoke slowly and clearly so interpreters could keep up with him, "The facts as we know them at this time are that an unknown signal has been picked up probably somewhere in our solar system and only probably from a fast-moving object. There is no corroboration to the rumor that this source has displayed non-ballistic motion. For us lay people that means there is no corroboration that it can change course, which could indicate that it's a machine and not a natural occurrence like a comet, which incidentally can also reflect radio signals.

"So it is the height of irresponsible conjecture to call this thing a UFO or anything like that. There is no information anywhere that supports such a claim. Yes there is a signal we are trying to track and reacquire, but because of the lack of data we cannot say anything about how fast it is moving, where it is or was, or that it ever changed course. All that you might have heard in that regard is unsupported and highly dangerous science fiction.

"But forget all of the natural things like comets that could be causing or reflecting this signal. Let's look at some manmade sources. Over the years we've lost or abandoned literally hundreds, if not thousands of space devices. From satellites to lunar orbiters, Martian probes and many other devices we have sent into our solar system. All of them have communication capabilities, solar panels, and maneuvering engines or we wouldn't have sent them up there. We have no idea where many of these devices disappeared to when we lost track of them. A common cause is that a meteorite hits a communication satellite really hard like a baseball player going for a home run. Instantly and without warning it disappears and we have no idea where it went or even in which direction to look for it. It just explodes or fires off, broken and damaged, at great speed somewhere into our solar system. Remember, these things are moving at tens of thousands of miles per hour even before they might be hit by a meteor.

"This has been going on for many decades now so there are presumably broken communication satellites and even broken secret military satellites from many nations, sending out strange encrypted communications all over the solar system. Some of them are like infield fly balls and fall to Earth and burn up and some are shot out into space where they might crash into the sun or establish a new orbit around the Earth or the sun, or even our moon or another planet.

"Scientists will tell you that if one of these rogue satellites gets near a large object, like another planet or the sun, it can act like a giant slingshot and fire them off in another direction at even higher speed. If this source is such a device and has a surviving solar panel, it could be charging its batteries when it's near the sun and sending out garbled messages for hundreds of years and being repeatedly slingshot all over the place.

"If we do find it changing course that proves nothing either as all satellites have maneuvering thrusters that could be sputtering to life when they get a boost of power, again from their tumbling solar panels.

"Now along comes a twenty-two-year-old radio telescope operator who was born after this thing was launched and then batted out into space. He hears a garbled message coming from a direction he wasn't expecting, he thinks it's moving really fast and bingo we have invading aliens.

"Now no one can tell you for sure what is actually making this noise in space, but it is outrageous to alarm people with such fantastical speculation. There is no evidence at all that supports the idea of an alien craft, and that is a fact that no one can dispute. All the data that has been collected so far, and it isn't much, tells us that there is a radio signal moving somewhere out there. That's all. We don't know where it is, we don't know how fast it is moving and we certainly don't know what it is or where it's going.

"So instead of tweeting unsupported rumors and scaring all of your friends, look up Occam's Razor on Wikipedia and ask yourself, what is the simplest explanation for radio noises in our solar system?

"Let me close by saying, we're a curious people and so to get to the bottom of this curious signal, we've asked several of our own radio telescopes to look for the signal and I'm confident that over the next day or two we'll all be laughing at this. I don't plan to put our military on high alert and I don't plan to lose any sleep over this either.

"So let's stop this nonsense and get back to living our lives. For me, I have a job to return to.

"God bless you and God bless all who call America home."

He exited the room with red-faced screaming reporters trying to get their questions answered.

***

On CNN the anchor turned to his guest who had been introduced as an expert on the solar system, "Well that certainly put a different spin on what we've been reporting for the last few minutes. For most of the last half hour the world has been in a panic over some signals received by some radio telescopes. Hal Turcot's statement is in direct opposition to what you were saying just a few minutes ago. What do you think of the President's message?"

"Frankly I'm stunned. We must realize the President has access to information that we don't but given the word we've heard out of China and Russia in the last hour or so, I would've said that while the President's explanation is perhaps plausible it is highly unlikely. But as I say, he has access to more information than we do, so I'd have to say that we need to take his points seriously. Remember, if the US has some secret military thing going on that is creating this loud communications, they aren't about to tell the world what it is.

"He is correct in saying that there is no corroboration on the course change, as that was only observed and reported by the Chinese, and only at the very end of the signal they detected. There are thoughts that they might have gotten that piece wrong if they tried to follow the signal and moved their antenna. Their reading of a possible course change is therefore suspect. And we certainly don't know the speed or the distance. The calculation I saw was based on an assumption that the first two readings were from the edge of the solar system and we simply cannot say that with any credibility. But to suggest that a malfunctioning maneuvering thruster could make a substantial course change of something moving at enormous speeds is preposterous.

"Then again, there are lots of assumptions in play on what the actual speed of this thing is and how much of a course change the Chinese are claiming, even if they did get it right. If the speeds are a significant portion of light speed then there is no way that any number of slingshot encounters could create those kinds of speeds. Remember if the slingshot idea is to come into play, this thing would have to magically slingshot around one planet and head almost directly for another and another. The chances of that are so small in a big solar system like ours with planets that take up a miniscule fraction of the space and are billions of miles apart that slingshotting as he described it is laughable.

"We've used that tactic ourselves, most recently on the Rosetta probe that had to catch up with a speeding comet, but that took incredible mathematics and tiny course changes over years en route to get the slingshot formula to work. Ain't gonna happen naturally would be my conclusion and never to those kinds of speeds, not after a million slingshots.

"And remember we've only had satellites up there for a few decades and that's not enough time to execute an enormous number of slingshots. An object being slingshot could take years to get to the next planet in its path even under the best of conditions.

"But again I say that we're dealing with too many assumptions and partial tracking data so unless someone gets a look at this thing or much more data, we can't really say what it is. So I guess in the end the President is right that it's too early to speculate and speculation of this type is highly dangerous. Just look at the worldwide panic in the last little while and I'll bet at least seventy percent of the world's population hasn't even heard about it yet.

"I agree with the President that all we can do right now is to try to get a better look at whatever made that noise. In all honesty he sounded pretty confident to me."

***

General Jenkins pressed the button to turn off the TV in the Pentagon's Situation Room. The gang of politicians from the earlier call had raced over to the Pentagon, wanting to be close to the action and then had watched the President's address.

Hawthorne spoke first, "Even that wannabe planetary guy on CNN thinks Turcot's story is preposterous."

Bob Downey, the Democratic majority leader of the Senate interrupted, "Listen, Hal did exactly what he had to do. He did exactly what we'd have told him to do if he had asked. You must shut down the panic. There is a chance, we don't know how big, that this will turn out to be something benign that we haven't thought of yet but, even if it is Armageddon, there is no point in starting the party early. We may dodge a bullet or be successful in defending our planet, but if panic takes hold it will not be a planet you want to be part of with every economy tanked, money worth nothing and lawlessness everywhere.

"No, this changes nothing. I'm back to where he doesn't want to fire the laser and hasn't gone to DEFCON 1. That's unforgivable, reckless, and irresponsible. Even though I've supported him and he's from my party, this goes way beyond partisanship. The security of our nation may be at stake and we are compelled to act prudently in its defense.

"Even assuming for a moment that we dodge this bullet, he has made an unthinkable miscalculation on this matter and he has shown himself to be unfit to be Commander-in-Chief and therefore unfit for office. I will be launching a secret panel on impeachment immediately. We're going to need SCOTUS to rule on keeping the whole process secret for a host of reasons like avoiding public panic, disclosing we have a secret space weapon, all the stuff around the specs for the F-47, and even the letter we just signed giving Jenkins here the green light, against the President's orders, to use High Octave on that thing. None of this can be discussed in an open forum, and I'm confident the Supreme Court will agree with us."

Fred Williams, Speaker of the House butted in, "Partisanship aside, you can count on the House for a vote to impeach. They've been itching for a fight since he canceled the F-35 and the F-47 contracts, but when they hear of his refusal to defend America against whatever is out there, even if it isn't a real threat, the point is we don't know that and he took first strike off the table even if it does turn out to be aliens. He's more afraid of pissing them off than the threat they represent. So I'm confident we'll get lots of Democrats crossing the aisle on this."

At that a young Lt. Colonel entered the room and whispered something to the Chairman. General Hawthorne instructed him to inform the room.

"Gentlemen as time goes by the part of the Earth facing this potential target moves west. We now think central and western Europe should be in the window, but as of now none of them have found anything looking towards Saturn. The Germans and the Russians in particular have some massive scopes, but no hits yet."

Kirk Jenkins asked, "When will US radio telescopes come into play?"

The young officer stood at attention to address the General, "Sir, it depends on how far north we must look. We're actually helped by the extreme inclination of the Earth in early January. We're still quite close to the winter solstice. We think this thing will likely be spotted in the far northern part of the sky. That means it will be the Canadian scope in Algonquin Park up in Ontario or possibly Haystack in Westford, Mass. that will come into play first. Either way we're still an hour or so away from the first opportunity to look for the signal, but it will be very low on the horizon at that point for either site. Mid-afternoon is peak time for us."

Hawthorne said, "Thank you Colonel", and the young officer exited after saluting all the heavyweight military types in the room.

Senator Bob Downey spoke, "It saddens me to take this stance against a man I trusted, respected and supported in both his campaigns. I just don't know what has gotten into him in the last couple of months, but as I said, this isn't a time for politics, so you can count on a good number of Democrats in the Senate voting for impeachment.

"Now as for today, I've cleared my schedule and I want to remain here in case we get any additional news."

The other politicians in the room nodded agreement.

The Debate

Word was spreading around the globe that whatever it was had been picked up by multiple radio telescopes, but the President's news conference had done the work of cooling much of the panic and other world leaders were following his lead, each of them thinking it was more likely that the US had something in space that had blown its cover and Turcot didn't want to admit it. One after another they had taken to the airwaves in their respective countries to quell the panic.

The one area of growing concern in the US in particular was religious groups throwing fuel on the fire on social media by claiming it was the second coming, or that the Rapture was upon us, or claiming the Bible guaranteed there were no intelligent beings in the universe except man. Vicious arguments ensued on Twitter and Facebook, with atheist trolls entering the fray throwing in inflammatory nonsense like it was Bertrand Russell's Teapot 2.0 or their Flying Spaghetti Monster orbiting the sun having been upgraded with communications, just to stir up even more outrageous reactions.

In poorer areas and shanty towns around the globe crime broke out on a large scale either due to rumor, superstition, not having heard the President's message on TV, or just using any opportunity to vent their anger over their depressed living conditions.

As time went by with no new sightings, the general consensus in the media now was that the US had it under control. Either the President's scenario was real or the idea that had caught on was that the US had some secret weapon that had probably violated its own stealthiness and was being picked up by other nations. After all, the President had certainly not looked panicked and he had said he wasn't losing sleep over it.

While this worked for the masses, technologists and governments were unconvinced. Most of his explanation didn't add up, like why would the US have a secret device that seemed to move so fast and was so noisy? Still they were all happy that Hal Turcot had taken to the airwaves and spun a quasi-convincing story to try to keep the masses in check. The global TV networks were still reporting rioting breaking out, mostly in the larger cities. Mass evacuations of major cities were still clogging highways from people who either left before the President's message or didn't believe him.

Within the hour Turcot received a call from Bob Downey, "Hal, given the situation I will come directly to the point. No one in the know buys your story about a benign cause for these contacts. We think there is something out there and we demand that you be ready to use that secret laser against it should it come within range, and definitely on a 'first strike' basis. According to the Pentagon that is not your position. Have you changed your mind on preemptive strikes?"

Hal thought this over. He was convinced that if the military got a glimpse of this thing they would take a shot at it no matter how hopeless their chances of hitting it. That would force Alpha to take action and mankind would be in jeopardy.

He had to avoid at all costs anything being directed at the thing. Alpha was aware of the laser and had stated they would likely have to take out anyone trying to use it unless they found a way to quietly disable it.

Alpha-1 had been clear that the best strategy in this case was to hide. Their jamming abilities were disguising all known communications from Earth, but any disruption in that plan could not be countenanced.

"Bob, as I told your new close friends on the Hill, even if this thing is a real UFO, which I seriously doubt, I don't want to use a pea shooter against a tank. If this thing really is moving that fast, thousands of times faster than anything we have, and it has achieved interstellar travel, do you really think we have anything to use against it?

"Any precipitous action on our part at this point simply would demonstrate feeble hostility at a time when we have no overall defensive strategy. That was always the flaw in that half-baked first-strike nonsense. What do you do after you've demonstrated your hostility and ineptitude?

"So I'm afraid I will not be issuing any fire commands unless we find evidence that it's hostile.

"I fail to understand why you and your friends do not see the futility and the danger in any preemptive strategy."

"Hal, I do not want to debate this with you and I was afraid you were going to take that position. I must now inform you that from what we can tell, a large majority over here disagrees with you and a secret panel has been appointed to rush through your impeachment and removal from office on the grounds that you're unfit for service on the basis of your refusal to protect the people of the United States. I've just hung up the phone with the Chief Justice who is willing to issue an order to keep all procedures secret due to the potential panic and the potential compromising of top secret weapons information.

"You'll be impeached and removed from office today. This will cause tremendous upheaval, political posturing and conspiracy theories because of the way we're forced to handle it, but sadly we need someone at the helm who will press that fire button when the time comes and the time is essentially now.

"The purpose of this call is to give you the opportunity to avoid this mess and resign effective immediately. Frank Osgoode will be sworn in, in your place, within the hour and he will give the green light to the military to take any and all action to protect the United States from this foreign invader, and that includes a preemptive strike. If there is any delay in this matter, Congressional leaders have signed a letter supporting the military's unilateral use of any and all weapons against this target to protect our nation."

There was a long pause before Turcot spoke, "And what if you're wrong. What about the panic you will cause by suggesting my explanation was wrong?

"What if this turns out to be benign as I suggest or some hoax on the part of the Russians and the Chinese? What then? What will you mutineers tell the American people then? Because Bob this isn't an action you can undo. This is all going down in history. Do you think you have enough irrefutable evidence right now that the US is in jeopardy? Are you an astrophysicist who is confident he knows these signals are from little green men? Are you so certain that a first strike will not make matters much worse?

"If this thing is real, shouldn't it be making a bee line to the Earth as the only Goldilocks planet in this system? As I understand it, it should have been here by now and no one else has seen it approaching. As I understand the latest data, we have no idea where it is? Maybe if it's little green men, they aren't interested in us. The point is we have no answers to any of these questions. I still think this will blow over and turn out to be something other than invading aliens, but you guys think, on the flimsiest of evidence, provided by the Russians and the Chinese who don't always wish us well, that we have an invasion in progress. And you are willing on the basis of that flimsy evidence to initiate panic in the world and disclose maybe the only secret we have in space, an amazing laser that can do things that breaks several treaties and divulges to the enemy our capabilities? We get tricked into losing a critical defensive and even first-strike capability for the real threats we might be facing and declare ourselves international outlaws. I swear you guys over there are not thinking this thing through. You're panicking at a time when we need cooler heads.

"No, I'm afraid I'm compelled to save you all from yourselves and I will not resign. If you think you can organize getting enough of Congress back here for an entire impeachment, trial and removal from office in the next twenty-four hours then I say, go for it. I think the Supreme Court will come to their senses when you tell them they need to host a trial to oust a sitting President TODAY. I don't think the constitution can be bent that far. Now you may not see that, but I'm pretty sure SCOTUS will.

"And as to your plan to undermine my command authority, I will have no choice but to bring mutiny charges against every military man who signs such a letter and treason charges against any lawmaker. Do you really want to lead a FUCKING MILITARY COUP in these United States of America? I don't think so. So until then, you know where to find me," and he hung up the phone.

Downey knew he was right and Turcot had called his bluff. An overthrow of the government was out of the question and doing it the legal way by getting members together in each house of Congress, drafting impeachment papers they could all agree to, holding a trial where the accused would likely refuse to appear, wouldn't pass the smell test on due process and SCOTUS would never be a part of it.

No matter how fast they moved, Turcot would not resign and SCOTUS would not move fast enough to help them. Their only options were assassination, which of course was out of the question and could never be covered up, or the only other choice left to them, to illegally bypass the President and give the green light to the Air Force to shoot if they could, and try to pick up the pieces after ... if there even was an after.

The President had forecasted the opposition would do this end run and try to use the laser. His hope was that the alien ship would never come close enough to be a legitimate target. There was always the possibility that the Air Force would try to take a shot anyway and then Alpha would have to intercept that action, possibly by killing anyone trying to fire it, starting the domino effect he feared. It was becoming more likely that mankind would be wiped out by a mutinous military's reckless actions than invading aliens.

The red phone rang indicating Alpha-1 and Carmichael were calling.

Alpha-1 spoke, "Mr. President, Alpha is tracking the invader who is winding his way to Earth. Best estimate is they will be here within a few hours. You should know however that we had to defuse a situation out of Russia. You'll be hearing some reports of it soon.

"Being a secret, we were unaware that they too had a laser weapon that was completed and ready for launch. We were tipped off something was amiss when they rushed a launch vehicle to one of their launch pads. Further investigation revealed a relatively powerful laser was the payload. A few minutes ago they attempted to launch it and the booster rocket exploded on the launch pad so they are no longer a threat. We sacrificed several helpers to achieve that and are now ensuring we left no evidence behind, but that is all immaterial. The explosion was covered by Earth cloaking so nothing would have gotten to the aliens. The Russians will investigate the twisted mess that is left but they're likely to decide it was simply some unidentified oversight in their haste to launch that caused the problem.

"It is highly likely that they will now call on you, possibly publicly, to fire your secret laser at the invader, if their intelligence knows of the device.

"As you can appreciate, they have two signals themselves from this thing besides the Chinese report and they believe it is real. It's very likely they were not impressed with your press conference and are showing the same signs of panic in their politicians as you're dealing with.

"Now Mr. Carmichael has an issue to address with you."

Carmichael took the phone, "Hal, I just got word that before the excitement of today that Congress will vote to hold up the purchase of ALL the F-47s. They aren't even accepting the two we delivered. They've figured out it is the end of our fiscal year soon and I can't even put the deferred revenue on the books because I don't have a contract. I'll be shark bait for the market and the board when the numbers come out. It's payback time and all your buddies in Washington are trying to destroy me. I'm guessing their strategy is to force me into bankruptcy and force me to sell off the supercomputer and robots so they can regain control of military spending.

"When my board gets notified that Congress has taken this action, in bold opposition to the interests of the American people, and that our corporate performance will tank, they'll all resign, which will bring in an SEC investigation and that will uncover everything.

"You need to help me somehow."

Turcot almost laughed, "First off, I've no way to influence Congress. I have no more friends as you call them over there. They're trying to impeach me before nightfall for God's sake, partly for giving you the green light in the first place. Secondly, do you really think this is the issue right now? We need to get rid of this invader or we're all dead. Thirdly, why are you worried when you have a get out of jail and go directly to heaven card?

"If Alpha-1 can hear me, the two of you should wrap up those 47s which I suspect are complete and move everything out of there so they can't find it if they get legal access to the hangars. At least then you have some leverage. If the American people think you have ten of these things and Congress is rejecting them, then public opinion will be on your side. Still, I'm not sure that after today you are going to want to be hanging around here anyways. Besides I don't see how you are ever going to be able to explain how you developed that computer and the robots. But let's keep our eye on the ball. That's all tomorrow's problem. We have a much bigger problem today.

"Put Alpha-1 back on."

"You're on speaker."

"Can you be more precise on your estimate? When will we know if we've been successful with the invaders?"

"Best guess because of their circuitous route is just before nine p.m. your time Mr. President. The Brits, French, Italians and Germans have some sophisticated equipment, but this thing has been jumping around the solar system and they're all looking in the wrong places so far. The US scopes are just coming into range now, but they are likely to have the same problem. Hopefully there will be no more sightings. It's a big sky out there".

The President sighed, there were still a number of terrifying hours to wait, "OK call me if anything changes."

As he hung up the phone the red line rang immediately and he picked it up, "Sir this is Bob Glass again, I haven't heard from you Mr. President."

"Yes Bob, as you can imagine I've been pretty busy. Do you have anything new for me?"

"Sir, I hate to keep harping on this, but I just don't trust the entity you call Alpha-1. All my investigations still indicate he is the only true alien in Alpha and Andy MacPherson has been helping out and doing his own investigation and he concurs. Everyone here is a transplanted human and while this place really is like heaven to humans, there is no question he has powers we do not. We suspect he also controls all senses, who gets to see what and what powers we each have. I couldn't do that nor could anyone else here. So in terms of democracy, there's none here. He has ultimate power.

"Now he is orchestrating everything to do with these approaching aliens. He is apparently the lone Alphan here and just how much help can he be in the case of an invading force? Where are the rest of these Alphans who he claims are about to be wiped out if things do not go his way and why are they not involved in this project?

"Has it occurred to you that he might be the aliens' forward controller and the device he built is to help bring in the invasion force?

"They could be wandering around the solar system just to fit the story he is selling and at the last moment they take a hard right and they are here in minutes or they link up with the 'weapon' and it transports them down to the surface."

The President paused, "Do you have anything other than these potential scenarios to indicate he might be malicious?"

Glass thought for a second and responded with "I think it was an English dude who said *'Power tends to corrupt and absolute power corrupts absolutely'*. This guy seems to have absolute power."

Turcot smiled, "Good one but remember Lord Acton was speaking about humans.

"As they say, I'll take your concerns under advisement. Even if you are right I don't see anything we can do about it. I'll keep my eyes open, you should do the same," and he hung up the phone.

Turcot concluded Glass was getting panicked and probably worried about the approaching aliens as much as anyone. He was clearly worried about Alpha-1 but really had nothing tangible to back up his suspicions.

The President stayed close to his red phone all day but there was nothing new. As the day wore on and he nervously took care of small items in the White House he had his media team send out periodic tweets reinforcing his earlier messages and reporting no other sightings. Thankfully that part was true. There were no more reports of signals coming from a mysterious object in the solar system.

Several requests had come in for him to revisit the press room where speculation still raged, but he passed on the opportunity. The old adage, 'quit while you're ahead' came to mind and he didn't want to get into a debate with sharp reporters over the holes in his earlier explanation. Better to let them think he was hiding information about a secret US space device which he was told was now the rumor in the White House Press Gallery.

The hours passed slowly as he struggled with thoughts of his own fate and the fate of Earth. Hiding was apparently the best strategy, but this was the time when it all came to a head. If that failed and humans were discovered and these aliens were terraformers, then there was a high likelihood that all humans would be eliminated either immediately or worse, die off in a poisonous atmosphere over a long period of time, unable to defeat what the invasion force was doing to the atmosphere. It would only be a matter of time then for them to discover Alpha and it would be eliminated in some fashion too.

There were other scenarios to be sure, given the meager data Alpha had acquired. It appeared the likelihood was that these marauders were in fact hostile, wanted something out of a Goldilocks planet, had had their way with other planets in the Milky Way, and had likely eliminated those civilizations. Little thought had been given to repelling them by Alpha and humans' best bet it seemed was a flimsy space laser that couldn't shoot straight or at least target something like this.

Just before seven p.m. the red phone rang and it was Alpha-1, "We're in it now," was all he said.

Orbit

Alpha-1 was uncharacteristically animated and speaking fast, "I told you they have decided to explore the entire solar system and we're next. Mr. Carmichael is here with me.

"So far all we know about them is that their ship is very small, likely less than ten feet in diameter, very dense and very smooth, made likely of some strong metallic substance and from the few close-ups we have of it, it's very shiny and perfectly spherical in shape so it's a possibility that any laser would simply reflect off of it.

"From the outside it looks like a big chrome ball bearing. These are all potential clues to extra-light speed that we will be studying. We're also trying to record every energy emission from the vehicle looking for any propulsion signature. Of course we have only taken passive readings because any kind of scanning would be detected by them.

"Our best guess therefore is that this is a scout ship, possibly carrying some embedded intelligence. To the aliens we appear as a burned-out cinder of a planet with no atmosphere that at one time may have had the capability to communicate. They should arrive here momentarily. So far they seem to take very little time to decide to move on.

"HERE THEY ARE!"

After a long pause Alpha-1 spoke again in a whisper, "I'm told they have arrived now directly over western Africa and we are about to be scanned.

"THIS IS IT!

"Earth-based telescopes are all looking to the far north and your military are within shooting range, but they haven't spotted it yet. They're a little more than a hundred thousand miles away from it in their parking orbit over Asia. It is maintaining a geosynchronous orbit for the moment but at a much higher altitude."

Carmichael sat watching Alpha-1. Alpha-1 looked very nervous but his own body was trembling and he felt like he was going to vomit or pass out from the stress.

"They are standing off and stationary near our equator at about fifty thousand miles as they did with the other planets, so they are inside the moon's orbit, but not close enough to be inside all of your own geosynchronous satellites in the twenty-two thousand mile band, all of which are now totally cloaked. Alpha has devices outside of that but they all have their own cloaking.

"They're scanning us now."

Suddenly the lights in the White House flickered briefly and then at Area-51, where Carmichael ducked like something was about to land on his head.

Turcot waited through the long silence for the two in Nevada to speak.

It was Alpha-1 again, "So far we think the cloaking is working through that scan. They sent something like a compound radar beam slowly across the planet at a level that interfered slightly with your electrical networks. We believe our cloaking allows for an appropriate echo for their radar but that's a best guess."

The President waited tensely as time slipped by.

Carmichael felt so helpless and paralyzed with fear he thought he was going to start crying. He couldn't take his eyes off Alpha-1, who while he was apparently listening to some communications from Alpha, was showing real signs of growing stress himself.

Turcot could hear Alpha-1's heavy breathing on the other end as they waited for any development. Again this went on for an agonizingly long time where every second seemed like a lifetime.

Alpha-1 virtually cried out, "IT DIDN'T WORK!"

Carmichael froze. After what seemed a very long pause, waiting for death or more from Alpha-1, the President finally blurted out, "What do you mean, it didn't work?"

Alpha-1 stared with horror at Carmichael as he said, "They're not leaving."

There was another long pause and then Alpha-1 sighed and said, "OK! Could be a false alarm. It appears they're possibly repositioned to the other side of the planet." After another long pause Alpha-1 said, "Siberia is their new target. They're almost overhead the first two dishes that picked them up but that was many hours ago, so those scopes are both scanning the western horizon now, not looking overhead where they might see the alien. At a minimum it appears we're getting the full treatment as we are the Goldilocks planet."

After what seemed like forever Alpha-1 exclaimed, "I THINK WE MADE IT! They've moved on to the moon and they're scanning it now. Because the moon is close, we were able to add your lunar landers to the cloaking list so they are invisible to the aliens."

Carmichael almost fell out of his chair with relief.

Finally Alpha-1 spoke again, "Just like all the other bodies in our solar system, they have moved on after about three minutes so the thinking is they did not detect anything worth investigating."

Carmichael was relieved but still in shock and trying to keep his last meal down. If Alpha-1 was right, this had all happened in about three minutes. He would have sworn it was well over twenty minutes they had been on pins and needles.

Minutes later Alpha-1 informed them both Mercury and Venus had apparently passed the test.

Moments dragged by and finally there was a loud sigh from Alpha-1, "They're gone.

"It appears they didn't even cruise out of the solar system before they jumped to extra-light speed. We'll be studying everything we recorded to see if we can get any hints on how they do that. There were some strange energy and magnetic emissions just before they jumped to faster-than-light speed and we got some good reflected light from their vehicle that will help us decipher its metal sheathing.

"Now I can tell you that we were worried they would take a closer look at us and possibly try a landing but our thinking now is that this was simply a robotic reconnaissance probe and it found nothing of interest.

"Gentlemen, I would have to say I think we are safe now and we should be celebrating success."

Both Carmichael and Turcot felt they could breathe again and needed a stiff drink and a shower. Carmichael suddenly noticed a splitting headache and a stiff neck.

Alpha-1 was ebullient, "Well congratulations gentlemen. It would appear that our project has been a complete success. Too bad we can't tell your world!

"Your military and others will continue to search for the alien scout, but they'll find nothing as it is already gone to extra-light speed and is already invisible even to us. They will likely be out of our solar system within the next few minutes at three hundred times light speed. Eventually your story Mr. President will be accepted as the truth, but speculation will remain about the world-wide power and communication fluctuations that did not seem to be caused by sun spots. We know a bit more about electricity than you do so it won't be hard to plant a new discovery that will be accepted as an explanation.

"Various land-based scientific stations are only now detecting that they all lost communication with their planetary probes at the same time. We'll disable our cloaking weapon and re-enable them in a few minutes. That investigation will go on for a long time with no reasonable answer for why it was all simultaneous over the last few days.

"So our project is complete in that your efforts are complete. Now that we have our cloaking device in space we don't need your help any more. As a matter of interest, we've been dismantling the F-47 production systems and shipping them back, some of it in containers to those airstrips throughout the west with General Hawkins' C-17s but much of it leaving here by other means along with the dome on Groom Lake which is now being dismantled.

"If they try to take the hangars over they will be left trying to figure out how Carmichael did it and where the production line is. They'll assume he smuggled it out using their own C-17s.

"Our only remaining concern is to disappear underground without being detected.

"So gentlemen, on behalf of my entire civilization, I want to thank you for your invaluable support and cooperation. Looks like humans and Alphans can work together under the right controls and incentives. I don't know about you but I sure could use a change of scenery and finally dumping this cloned body."

Suddenly Carmichael remembered the warnings from the Glass kid in the Oval Office and realized he had to have been wrong, Alpha-1 had come through for them and everything had turned out fine.

Hal Turcot thought for a moment, "Given my family situation, I've decided to resign as soon as possible and take you up on your offer to join you in Alpha."

This took Carmichael by surprise, "You're going to leave me here alone? I told you earlier, I'm stuck between a rock and a hard place. Congress is forcing my hand. My company can't survive this political nonsense and we will all be found out and suspicions about Alpha may be heightened if a series of investigations are started.

"I played my part in this and my expectation was that I would get to exploit this technology for a while before I took the other offer."

Alpha-1 spoke, "Every day we're here on the surface and have unexplainable technology there is a threat to Alpha, so it would be difficult for me to remain and assist, even if I was in a political position to do so, which I'm not. Remember, you can have your cake and eat it too. You can set up your own virtual economy, and believe me it will be as real as you want it. Also, you're the only one who knows anything about the project so if you depart the scene there will be nothing for them to investigate, just dead ends everywhere they look.

"However I did make you a promise and if you insist on staying here I can help you set up a manufacturing facility they cannot find but you'll have to deal with your board and Congress.

"Now I suspect you might have concerns about Alpha providing the same mogul stature that you enjoy on Earth. You're a big important man on Earth and your ego is built on your self-image as being sharper than most. All I can say is, you won't be disappointed in Alpha. I can help you build the exact same world and there will be challenges, obstacles, successes and failures in your virtual world to keep you stimulated.

"You decide.

"Mr. President, we will make arrangements immediately for a plausible departure for you and your family. I'll be in touch."

***

CNN continued their 'Breaking News' all day with nothing new to report. Over the next few days this would die down as no telescopes had picked up anything resembling the readings the Russians and Chinese had found.

The team in the Situation Room at the Pentagon were bushed, and by midnight all were ready to return to their homes to wait for any additional news. If the aliens were coming at them at say half-light speed, they should've arrived much earlier. Word was filtering in that the power flicker they had experienced was widespread, maybe even global, so there were some who thought this might be tied to an alien arrival, but there was no other data to support that theory.

Just before the meeting broke up Fred Williams, Speaker of the House turned to Bob Downey, "So what does this mean for impeachment?"

Downey frowned, "I'm afraid that train has left the station. Whether or not there is, or ever were any aliens in our solar system, the President showed us he was unprepared for it, so sadly we proceed with the plan even if we weren't able to execute it today.

"I'll be in touch," was all he said as he headed for the door with others preparing themselves to leave as well.

***

Hal Turcot wasted no time getting upstairs to find his wife and daughter in front of the TV listening to the news that was already reporting that the President may have been right after all. Most scientists agreed that if aliens were coming they would have arrived already.

To reassure his family he told them that most of the experts thought there never had been a threat and he was planning on sleeping soundly tonight.

Ann was looking a little stronger and sitting up in her wheelchair just a little straighter, and out of the blue, she opened the conversation in a very raspy voice, "Mom and Dad, it is pretty clear to me that I don't have long to live. Looks like the human race is going to survive, but there's no denying what's next on my calendar.

"Before it all goes south, I have one final wish which I hope you'll grant. I want to see the Grand Canyon. We were supposed to go there a few years ago and it got canceled. It has always been a dream of mine to see it in all its splendor. Can we go, soon?"

Harold Turcot looked over at his wife as the tears ran down her face. He nodded to her and she said, "Yes. As soon as we can plan it, we will make a family trip to the Grand Canyon."

Later in the evening Turcot announced to both of them that he was going to resign. He wanted more time with Ann and the Hill was all lined up to impeach him over disagreements over the alien 'thing' and the way he had handled the fighter jets without Congressional approval.

Evelyne had mixed emotions. She knew what the job meant to him, but he could resign with his head held high, given he was caring for a dying daughter and he had done what he could to advance the social agenda and take on the lobbyists on K Street.

***

Carmichael was torn but the deck was stacked against him and with his curiosity of Alpha overflowing, he informed Alpha-1 that he wanted to transition to Alpha ASAP. The timing was good and Alpha-1 told him they would plan something that would appear natural and deal with all four of them at the same time.

Carmichael called the head of the Armed Forces oversight committee and left a voicemail.

"You think you have me trapped and your plan is to destroy me and my company by refusing to take delivery of the F-47s. Well as I told your committee, you have forced my hand and I will be looking for a more cooperative buyer through my world-wide network of companies and you can be assured my Harmonized Manufacturing capability will no longer be available to you. Tell your buddies over there that this is all on you!"

***

The President's first call the next morning was to Bob Downey who took the lead, "Mr. President I didn't call last night. It was a hectic day for all of us. Some believe if there ever was a crisis it has passed but I'm sad to say that little has changed. Your refusal to consider the laser was reckless and I'm duty-bound to inform you that impeachment proceedings are continuing."

"Bob, let's not argue. We have a differing opinion on what a superior race might think of an act of aggression on our part. But that is moot. After this call I will hold a press conference and announce my immediate resignation. Frank Osgoode can be sworn in later today."

Downey was floored, "But why now, after you survived our challenge and the crisis seems to be over?"

"Bob, you and I go way back. One reason is that I know I was right yesterday and you guys were wrong. But living with you folks after this is going to be difficult and I do want to save the country from a drawn-out fight. I'm also right on the lobbyists thing. You know we cannot continue allowing K Street to buy the laws they want. But on top of that, and the reason I will give the public is that I have a very sick daughter who has become too much of a distraction for me

471

to pay full attention to my job. I need to spend her last days with her.

"I leave you with only one thought. That strategy to defeat the lobbyists in the defense industry is the right one and you should pick up the baton. I suspect the guys on the Hill will feed Carmichael to the wolves in one fashion or another, but we were on the right track and our social programs really do need a complete overhaul. Our war on poverty has transitioned into a war on the poor. Do some research and find out the facts. Welfare and what you call entitlements aren't what is dragging down our economy and the middle class. It doesn't explain flat wages or the growing wealth disparity which is the root of the problem. It's not what some people have labeled the 'takers'. It's greed at the top, plain and simple. All the numbers support it. Do some proper research for God's sake and stop listening to all that misinformation and anecdotal statements about inner city single moms with six kids from different fathers, all on welfare for more than a generation. That's a point way off the curve and totally misrepresents the plight of the poor in this great nation of ours.

"We are a very rich country and can easily provide an outstanding life for all our citizens and remain the epitome of capitalism, but not if a very few greedy people keep more money than they could use in a thousand lifetimes. Do yourself a favor and look at the numbers with an open mind. We need more smart guys like you on the Hill. You'll figure it out.

"As to the conservatives, the golden years they pine for were the years when families were solvent on one wage earner and billionaires paid a fair share of taxes and they still had private islands, multiple homes and jets. Yes the fifties and sixties were great but remember, the top tax rate was ninety percent then. Now billionaires pay a smaller percent than taxi drivers. So as I say, it is not the poor that are dragging us down.

"Listen, if we don't see each other any time soon, as one famous character said, 'live long and prosper.'"

Area-51

Carmichael had announced his resignation from Carmichael Industries the same day as the President resigned, throwing the stock into a dive. He then hid out in the Hawk Hotel in Vegas awaiting Alpha-1's plan to unfold.

The new President in the White House, on hearing that news about Carmichael, immediately issued orders for the military to take over the F-47 production line at Area-51.

Hawkins and his men had noted the lack of noise coming out of the hangars ever since their last C-17 flight to yet another abandoned airstrip in Utah, but still approached the hangars as if they were to be tasered at any moment.

Once all three hangars were opened, it was clear that the only things left inside were eight spanking new F-47s and a one-year-old Great Dane named Samson, sitting calmly near bowls of dog food and water. The robots and the production lines were gone as was Andy MacPherson. All that remained were bolt holes in the floor where production jigs had once been anchored.

Two days later a financial forensics team started a one-year investigation trying to track down all of Carmichael's companies and where the robots and the computers disappeared to. They would never be found.

***

Three days after the President's emotional goodbye to the nation, two big Sea Kings dropped down to an unusual viewing point of the Grand Canyon just after dawn. The President had consulted local native experts and apparently daybreak on a cloudless day at this location should be stunning. The press were already there and hoped to pepper the President with questions over his early retirement.

Curiously, the now-elusive billionaire Fraser Carmichael, previously a sworn enemy of the President but apparently now a family friend had accompanied the former first family for the visit.

All were shocked at the state of Ann's health and as the four of them gathered with the canyon at their back for photos the ground suddenly disappeared below their feet and all fell to their deaths while the cameras caught everything, including the press screaming in dismay.

***

It was late and Violeta Michaud sat in her office on Parliament Hill in Ottawa and watched the shocking CNN report of President Turcot's demise.

This coming only four days after the 'Big Scare' where CNN and others had the world panicked about the potential of an alien attack. The world had moved on and now believed the President's story of a benign cause for all the fussing and fretting.

Everyone on the planet except her. She had not expected his death though and couldn't figure out what that meant, if anything. She raised her glass to the picture of the President on the screen and simply said, "Whatever the real story is, thanks old friend."

Life After Death

Evelyne woke slowly as if from a deep sleep. She seemed to be in some sort of a conference room with several other people. Before she could identify them she looked down at her hand as she felt someone holding it. As she looked up the encroaching arm she came eye to eye with her beautiful Ann. Now she knew she was dreaming because Ann had been sick and confined to a wheelchair, yet here she was seemingly healthy, beautiful, and smiling, just as she remembered her in her prime. She was almost glowing.

Before she could pinch herself, the vision spoke, "Welcome mom. Welcome to the rest of eternity."

Suddenly the accident at the Grand Canyon came flooding back. After a flash of horror she quickly concluded she must be in heaven with Ann. And there was Harold at the head of the table. He was here too. They had all died in that terrible fall.

But heaven had a conference room?

As she turned, Hal Turcot rose from his seat at the head of the table. "Evelyne, my dear it is good to see you in person again. It has been almost two months. And Fraser you look well too. In a moment I will tell you where we are and what we're doing here."

Evelyne turned back to Ann and came to the realization that indeed she seemed completely cured, but could this really be heaven or a dream? If this was a dream it was a nightmare and the tears started to flow.

Gradually over the next hour Hal Turcot explained everything to his wife, who was the only one caught completely off guard by the events. He also explained to Fraser Carmichael that he and Ann had been taken to Alpha the day after the Minot incident. When he returned late from Minot, Alpha-1 had appeared in the Oval Office and disclosed his fears the President wasn't completely on board or that the stress of it all and the illness of his daughter made him too unpredictable so he had to be replaced. Replaced by a second copy of Alpha-1's psyche, a copy that for propriety's sake had decided to spend the next two months sleeping in the guest bedroom.

Hal Turcot went on to tell them that later that evening, he had visited Ann and concluded she wasn't going to make it through the two months of the project and replaced her psyche with a third copy of himself. A copy that according to Alpha-1 was painful in that the body was racked by a serious disease, which they had only been partly successful in screening as to its limitations and pain.

The shock to Evelyne was immense and she often sobbed as Ann hugged her throughout the time she was being briefed on her new life. After another hour of explaining everything, and the world they now lived in, three new people entered the room and introduced themselves as Robert Glass, Andrew McPherson and to everyone's surprise a gentle looking woman in her sixties reminiscent of a school teacher or a librarian who said her name was Margaret.

As the others sat, she spoke, "Some of you know my psyche as Alpha-1 or Robert Glass or Andy MacPherson but I'm kind of partial to Margaret. I suspect this is somewhat of a surprise to you all. You see I was born over a million years ago as a female and I have chosen to live most of my time that way. This human avatar of Margaret has proven to be the least threatening to new human arrivals and I happen to like it.

"Unfortunately in the Culpeper mine there were only males to replace and Mr. Carmichael here chose Andy as the second COO. So in some ways I had to rough it for two months. I have lived as a male once or twice in Alpha's fantasy world but I prefer the female existence. We'll get to know each other much better as I'll be your initial coach here in Alpha."

The shock on the faces around the table was universal.

Just then Bob Glass's fiancée and her parents joined the group and everything about the project and the alien situation was revealed.

Well … almost everything.

Evelyne Turcot was still in a near state of shock while she hugged her daughter hard. She wondered how she was ever going to let Ann out of her grasp.

Margaret spent the next hour explaining Alpha and giving out mild warnings about what not to do that might be regretted, like spending too much time fantasizing old enemies and getting even with them.

They all instantly felt the difference in IQ and the fact that they had no aches and pains. They felt totally euphoric and weightless as if in zero gravity but they had no problem staying grounded. Apparently just one other advantage of the virtual life in Alpha.

As a proof point Margaret transitioned everyone in the room to the idealized self-image Alpha had captured during the on-boarding of their psyches so that they now saw themselves the way they thought of themselves. "Within a few hours you'll discover many things about Alpha including how to change your perceived and shared image, but for the moment I thought you'd appreciate this new spruced-up self-image that we took the liberty to borrow from your memories," she said smiling.

Finally Margaret turned to Mr. Robert Glass who now realized he had been sending his warnings to Alpha-1 himself about his misgivings of their host, "So Bob, you and I started all of this in that mine a couple of months ago, but there came a time when you doubted my motives. I'll give you the chance to explain all of that to the rest of the group as Mr. Carmichael here was the only human who heard your warnings."

An embarrassed Bob Glass recounted his concerns that Alpha-1 was the only indigenous alien and might be bringing invaders to Earth and how he had warned Carmichael and what he thought was the real President.

Margaret wrapped up Glass's embarrassment by smiling and saying, "So Mr. Glass, do you have any questions for me?"

Reluctantly Glass said, "Yes, were there ever other native Alphans and what happened to them?"

Margaret smiled and instantly transformed into her natural state of a being that was approximately nine feet tall and humanoid in style with a larger head, longer neck and very elongated arms and wearing some kind of skin-tight clothing. The visible parts of her skin were pale flesh colored and covered in a very light fur, more of a fuzz, like on a peach.

All the humans in the room gasped as she morphed back to the human avatar they were becoming familiar with.

"I thought I'd start by showing you our natural state. At least the bodies we once inhabited about a million years ago.

"Mr. Glass is right. You will look hard in Alpha and not find any of my kind, even in human avatars.

"We now have about two thousand humans in Alpha and I'm the only 'awake' Alphan. The others, about eleven thousand of them, are sleeping in our network.

"It seems our thought simulator isn't perfected yet and I was elected and left alone to repair it. The others would say I got the short straw, but I have enjoyed my time. When we first devised our thought simulator we gave it certain characteristics, which have led to a few sizable problems. I'll describe only one issue … the incapacity to support fading memories.

"We either remember things with complete clarity or we erase them, nothing in between. No partial memory loss or fuzzy memories. That certainly has advantages, but it also presents some unforeseen problems. Infallible memory seemed like a good idea way back then.

"Think about your favorite food and once you taste it in its best presentation you have perfect recall of it and you don't care to experience it again in a less than optimal way so you simply recall it as a perfect memory … every time.

"Or you have a perfect hideaway on a perfect day and read a new book that turns out to be your favorite. Why bother going there again? Eventually you run out of favorite foods, places to go, life experiences and life becomes more than boring. You no longer find new pleasure in food, travel, sex, you name it. Anything you found pleasurable before is simply a perfect memory of its best instance and it is the same every time, because why would you want to experience it in a suboptimal way?

"It will be a long time before you experience this disturbing condition, but believe me in an immortal being it is in fact completely debilitating. In the human world you visit a great restaurant, have a wonderful meal and then weeks or months later you only remember certain parts of the taste and the ambiance and you want to experience it again. You don't even care if it was not exactly the perfect night you once had, something close is also pleasurable and there is always the chance it might even be better than your partial memory. The newer fresher memory trumps the older even if it is not perfect.

"Imagine if you only had to hear wonderful music once, see a beautiful photo or sunset once, make love perfectly once and have total recall of it. Once you had experienced it at what you considered its best instance, there would be no point in repeating the experience and soon you would run out of things to do, especially if you had forever to look for things to please you.

"Now that you live in a perfect thought engine that can't partially forget, you'll eventually run into this problem. Our native people ran into it some time ago and life eventually became almost unbearable. Some considered ending their lives, which is unthinkable for a civilization that can be and should be immortal.

"It was such a crisis that demanded change. Significant change that might possibly take many years to resolve. It became so critical that we started experiencing real and constant pain, so our civilization chose to sleep through the change until our world is once more livable. So I was elected to remain awake and reprogram many aspects of our thought engine, including the ability to selectively and gradually forget details of certain experiences and not others. You don't want to partially forget how to fly a plane or you're looking for some nightmarish experiences. It turns out that coming up with a formula of exactly where fuzzy memory is desirable and how it can be personalized, is a much greater task than it seems.

"I've only explained one of the shortcomings of our thought engine that needs repair. There are others but I think you get the picture of why so many of my kind are asleep until I awaken them.

"Now in my case, being the only one left awake was painful too, so I was allowed to on-board some 'guests' from the human world to keep me company and stimulate me with new ideas. A good number of the guests here were invited by me during this period. I must also say that this alien crisis has been very invigorating. Terrorizing but interesting.

"The good news is that we, myself and the helpers, have made good progress and we're likely only a few years away from success. As to powers, all invitees will gradually be given all the powers we have when they have been completely integrated into our civilization. There is much to learn but you'll likely be up to full powers by the time our civilization awakens and they will be excited to meet you too.

"Now let me give the newcomers a taste of Alpha."

At that the walls and ceiling of the conference room evaporated and all found themselves in the proverbial Garden of Eden complete with fruited trees, lush foliage, cute animals and a gentle waterfall not far off, reminiscent of a Disney movie. They were all comfortably re-dressed and a table in front of them was full of a perfect presentation of their individual favorite foods for this type of setting.

Reality

Suddenly they were back in the conference room, but only three of them, Alpha-1 in his Bob Glass avatar, Carmichael and President Harold Turcot.

Glass spoke, "I want to thank you two gentlemen for everything we've put you through. This concludes simulation number 1623. What you have in your memories at this moment are all the activities related to our latest and in fact the last simulated run of our plan to combat the approaching aliens."

Both men looked at each other horrified. Somehow this had all been a trick?

"The good news is that we now have the best plan we can afford given the time constraints on how to approach our 'project'. You might have guessed that we Alphans do not need to take unnecessary risks if we have a thought engine and can run simulations in advance. We have very high confidence in our abilities to simulate situations with good input data and given this is our first project with humans outside of Alpha and the challenge was so important we really needed to get it right.

"In this case, as I just said, we ran scenarios 1623 times and we now have a good handle on what could happen when we introduce ourselves to humans, in particular you two, and embark on our project.

"As it turns out simulation 137 had the best outcome and produced our launch vehicle three days earlier than 1623, which we have just stepped out of.

"So you have been through the entire project 1623 times already without knowing you were participating in a simulation. When we do the real run in a few minutes, you will have total memory of the entire scenario 137 as well as key pitfalls and dangerous detours of previous runs. Now you will not need any convincing that we are real and we do face a common threat.

In 1623 and other runs I replaced the President and in earlier simulations I replaced Mr. Carmichael but in 137 you both performed your own part better than me. I guess you are both better at acting the part of your real self than I am. Of course Mr. President, much of the stress that caused me to replace you is gone, now that you understand that your daughter will be safe, I'm not a threat and essentially you know in advance how almost everything turns out.

"When we execute 137 in a moment, you will know exactly what to do and what to say and where to go to make it a reality. If anything goes wrong with the execution of 137 in the real world, we have a good handle on how to recover from any deviation now that we have run so many simulations testing virtually every optional outcome to every step."

Carmichael and Turcot stared at each other. This was not what they had expected. In their minds the project had been a success and now they were in Alpha for eternity.

Turcot was first to speak, "Where are my wife and daughter?"

"For the moment they're where they were a few minutes ago, upstairs in the White House residence I'm afraid, but not to worry, we are convinced that Ann needs help right away so that's part of the 137 scenario too. In 1623 we ran it right through to your arrival in Alpha just to be sure we had everything covered."

It was Carmichael's turn, "So what we just experienced was a simulation and we haven't dealt with the aliens yet, they're still coming, that part was real, but our plan seemed to have worked, right?"

Alpha-1 smiled, "Yes but if you remember, we know almost nothing about the aliens so the whole scenario on their behavior is a complete guess. We added a little Chinese and Russian drama to 1623 and other runs just to get reactions so we could be prepared for anything. The call girl and the pet dog were also added, but we have decided to add those to 137 as it appears they could provide important benefits for us and presented no issues. We would now like the actual input from those two encounters.

"But the Russians really do have a secret laser ready to go, which we just discovered recently and yes the US Military has been keeping secrets from the President on their own laser. So most of what you experienced in 1623 is based on fact or scenarios we ran before to build a database of human reactions to each situation.

"Short of messing up your minds before we go back, let me tell you some key learnings from the simulations.

"In almost all of the scenarios, one or the other of you, or in twelve cases, both of you were under threat of assassination by the

CIA or hit squads supported by the industrial groups backing several lobbyist groups.

"Early on we had not blocked the audio on your first private meeting in the Oval Office after the Minot incident. The CIA and later the Pentagon picked up on that and it served to flush out the assassins. It seems there is almost a hundred percent probability that your deal and the changes to the fighter plans will drive certain forces to try to eliminate one or the other of you two. You have a very violent society here.

"The CIA is only one of those forces. In several scenarios your predictable call to Bill Carter caused him to start looking at you as well as the Joint Chiefs and they came to the conclusion based on some solid evidence that you, Mr. President, had been corrupted somehow by a very mysterious junior mining inspector. They also tried to kill me or rather Bob Glass most of the time when communications were not screened. We intercepted many of these so now we know of all the possibilities for 137 and can neutralize them. In 1623 and other simulations we had to eliminate CIA Director Bill Carter.

"In just over twenty-three percent of all simulations either the President was impeached and removed from office or Fraser lost control of Carmichael Industries. All of those scenarios failed to get us to the launch. In 137 Mr. Carmichael handles his board much better.

"Other people died too. General Jenkins was ordered by General Hawthorne to take over operations at Area-51. We crashed his jet on approach to Groom Lake, but that achieved nothing, in fact, it complicated things and that simulation was one of our worst.

"Believe me, we tried many different scenarios to find the optimal approach and these simulations are all based on fantastic amounts of data on every player and their most likely responses, including foreign governments.

"In 137 we came upon the best, fastest, safest and most reliable approach. Many scenarios have had minor changes simply to verify the reactions of other players. We also learned there are several key elements to the plan which of course we tested and retested right up to simulation 1623, double-checking all of our assumptions.

"There are several real keys to success that you need to understand, because you are about to repeat them and you need to get them right.

"The visit from the Canadian Prime Minister Violeta Michaud is critical and must be executed with all the panache of simulation 137. Fifty-five percent of the time she is not moved to support you Mr. President, but with some gentle coaxing and informing her you have always known of her relationship with Dan Westgate, you can convince her. In the end she is essential in gaining several days by taking pressure off the impeachment track.

"It is also critical that Bob Glass dies and Andy MacPherson takes over, as in sixty-three percent of the simulations Andy becomes a threat as he uncovers more and more of what is going on at Area-51.

"There's lots more to discuss, but that can wait for a better time. It is only essential that you stick to simulation 137 which will be implanted as a full memory very soon. Any questions?"

The President asked, "What was wrong with the last simulation, should it not have been the best after all that testing?"

Alpha-1 smiled, "No, actually much of our testing after about 500 cycles was to verify what we did in 137 and test any obstacles to its success. In 1623 like several others, too many people were killed, especially when you tried to blow up Alpha and Minot takes the hit. This also hampered progress on several fronts. Additionally in 1623 we lost a day with the Chinese intervention. In 137 we did a better job of hiding the rare earth acquisitions and the Chinese never suspected anything."

Carmichael was still trying to gather his bearings, "If we are in Alpha now, when were we brought here to start the simulations? I don't remember anything other than the fall at the canyon."

"Good question. All of the simulations start just after the photographer leaves the Oval Office and I freeze you two on the first night we all meet. That's where your physical bodies are now. You have been in a totally frozen state now for just under five minutes, while we ran these simulations. We needed close proximity to both of you to capture your psyches."

Turcot now spoke, "You mean you ran 1623 simulations which took nearly three months each, all in the last five minutes?"

"Great observation Mr. President. Yes, you are currently conscious in what you would think of as a massively powerful thought engine where we can simply speed up the simulations to any speed we wish. You are currently 'living' at thousands of times your normal temporal pace. The whole scene with your family and others in the conference room was just to tie out the credibility of it all for the two of you. Actually Mr. Glass in Alpha has never been dealt with so he still has concerns about me in 137. I can go on but frankly we are growing short of time.

"Now a couple of points we need to cover before Gerry Hastings finds reason to interrupt us in your office. The good news is that Minot will not happen and CIA Director Bill Carter will not die. That also means Mr. Carmichael's execs are all alive and well in simulation 137, although you still need to fire them all. Gerry Hastings must go too as there is no scenario in which he complies with your plans with Mr. Carmichael.

"In 137 Dan Westgate dies under less suspicious terms because we need his death to set up the deal you make with Vi Michaud but of course he comes to Alpha and so does she at her natural death as we were quite sure it would be a demand of his.

"Mr. Lawrence's death was real and occurred before the simulations so sadly we can do nothing with his case.

"So now you realize we have already on-boarded both of you, so when we return to your Oval Office you will have no doubts on who I am and what we must do, and you will be unafraid of any assassination attempts given we have that covered, and in addition your backups are now safe in Alpha. This way we can hopefully avoid any real deaths and you two understand the stakes completely.

"While Alpha eliminating all humans is a real possibility it is much less likely now. Can you imagine having to clean up seven billion bodies that all just dropped dead? Even increasing our numbers of helpers by orders of magnitude it would take us decades to dispose of all those rotting corpses."

Smiling he said, "Of course there are other more important reasons why we want to avoid that."

Both men just stared at him not knowing what to say.

Alpha-1 continued, "But as I said, the bad news is that the aliens are still on their way, so in reality we are where we were the first time we met. The chances of our project succeeding are still unknown. The only difference is that we all now know each other and the optimal scenario to survive all of the obstacles we face with humans and the best plan to launch our defenses. We only took a copy of your psyches so your human body is still alive in the Oval Office and we are about to load 137 into your brains. Your human existence ends in Arizona in about three months just like the recent simulation, but you'll have to work hard not to wince before the ground gives way. You now know there is no pain involved.

"One thing you need to know however is that this project is potentially only a stop-gap measure. If we are successful in hiding from the approaching aliens there is a solid chance that in about eighty years, if they are watching, they will notice that their communications home from the scout ship were blocked, and they will likely choose to return to find out why. They may also notice a change in the spectral image of earth.

"Our best guess is that we'll have up to eighty years to prepare and we won't have to involve humans as we did this time, but then again, you'll be Alphans and you can help us. And yes we really will gather lots of passive telemetry on them if and when they arrive so we can use that to prepare for their return."

He could see they were ready and in a flash they found themselves standing in front of the President's desk with Bob Glass now sitting in the presidential chair. He immediately released them from their paralyzed state.

Carmichael turned and smiled at the President and said, "Sixteen hundred and twenty-three simulations later and I still hate you."

The Beginning (Again)

www.ingramcontent.com/pod-product-compliance
Lightning Source LLC
Chambersburg PA
CBHW061033030726
47504CB00002B/357